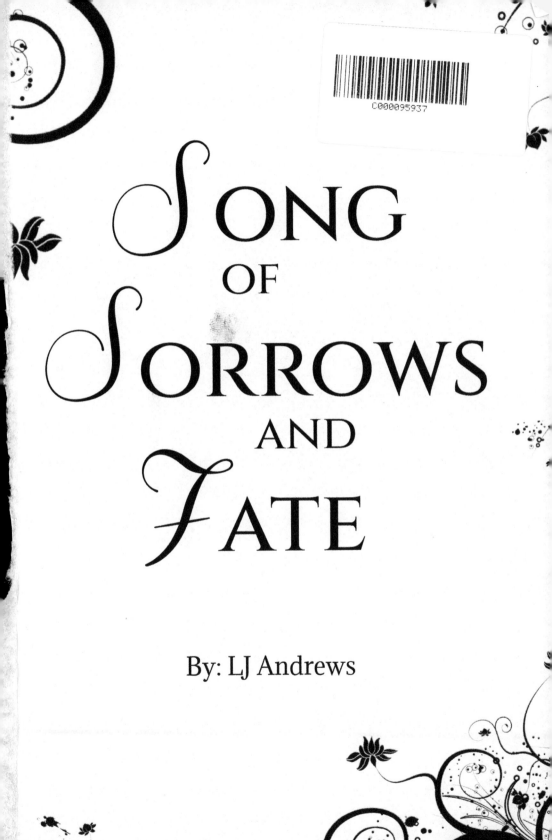

Song

OF

Sorrows

AND

Fate

By: LJ Andrews

C000095937

CHARACTER LIST
NORTHERN KINGDOM

Night Folk Clan

- King Valen Ferus: The Night Prince
- Queen Elise Ferus
- Livia Ferus: daughter of Elise and Valen
- Herja Ferus
- Hagen Strom: consort of Herja, brother to Queen Malin of the East
- Gunnar Strom: Herja and Hagen's eldest son, husband of Eryka (Fae Isles)
- Laila Strom: Herja and Hagen's eldest daughter
- Dain and Metta Lund-Strom: adopted children of Herja and Hagen
- Sol Ferus: The Sun Prince
- Torsten Bror: consort to Sol Ferus
- Aleksi Bror-Ferus: son of Sol and Torsten
- Halvar Atra: First Knight
- Kari Atra, warrior
- Daughters of Kari and Halvar: Hel, Idunn, Linnea
- Aesir Atra: son of Halvar and Kari, warrior youth

- Arvad and Lilianna Ferus: parents of Sol, Herja, and Valen
- Stieg Jakobson: warrior and friend to Elise and Valen
- Frey and Axel Viluff: brothers and warriors
- Mattis and Siverie Virke: Regents, friends of Elise and Valen
- Elder Klok: former Ruskig refugee
- Kjell Bror: Torsten's father
- Dagar Atra: Halvar's father

Deceased

- Zyben and Annika Lysander: Former Timoran King and Queen
- Calder and Runa Lysander: Former Timoran King and Queen
- Casper Lykke: Guild of Shade, half sea fae
- Lief and Mara Lysander: Elise's parents
- Mavie Asulf: former serf and friend of Elise
- Jarl Magnus: Captain of Timoran Army
- Brant Austr: brother of Kari, former Raven guard.
- Ulf: former warrior to King Ari, traitor

CHARACTER LIST
EASTERN KINGDOM

- Kase Eriksson: King, The Nightrender
- Malin Strom (Eriksson): Queen, The Memory Thief
- Jonas and Sander Eriksson: Twins of Kase and Malin
- Guild of Kryv (Nightrender's Guild)
- Gunnar Strom: Hypnotik Alver
- Raum Helvig: Profetik Alver
- Tova Unfrid: Mediski Alver
- Ash: Rifter Alver, brother to Hanna
- Hanna: Anomoli Alver, sister to Ash
- Isak Tryk-Krog: Hypnotik Alver, Husband of Fiske
- Fiske Krog: Profetik Alver, Husband of Isak
- Lynx Flett: Hypnotik Alver
- Niklas and Junius Tjuv: Alvers, Falkyn Guild Leads, Smugglers
- Jakoby Hob: thief, shady friend of Malin, partner of Inge
- Inge Vill: seamstress, partner of Hob
- Frigg Hob: daughter of Jakoby and Inge
- Bard Strom: Rifter Alver, brother of Malin and Hagen
- Dagny Grym: former cheer girl, wife of Luca Grym

- Luca Grym: former royal of the Black Palace, Hypnotik Alver, husband of Dagny
- Von Grym: son of Dagny and Luca

Deceased:

- Jens Strom: adopted father of Malin, Hagen, and Bard, Master of Ceremonies
- Vali Harvard: Profetik Alver, former Kryv
- Einar Pihl: former Falkyn, traitor
- Sigurd Bakke: steelman, ally to Malin
- Ivar and Britta Grym: former Lord and Lady Magnate
- Niall Grym: Heir Magnate, brother to Luca Grym
- Sig and Jonas Eld: Malin's biological parents
- Sander and Anje Eriksson: Kase's biological parents

CHARACTER LIST
SOUTHERN KINGDOM

Fae Isles

- Ari Sekundär: former Night Folk ambassador, King
- Saga (Revna) Sekundär: raven shifter, Queen
- Krasmira Sekundär: daughter of Ari and Saga
- Eryka: seer from the Court of Stars, wife of Gunnar Strom
- Lord Gorm: Blood Lord
- Cuyler: Heir of the Court of Blood
- Magus: Serpent Lord
- Yarrow: former Lady of the Court of Serpents, mother to Magus
- Shelba: Eldest daughter of Yarrow and Hawthorne
- Dunker: a troll in the royal household
- Rune: blood fae warrior
- Bo: royal tracker
- Ulv: Court of Serpents guardian
- Davorin Avsky: battle lord for House Ode, former consort of Saga

Deceased:

- King Bracken: High King of Court of Hearts
- Queen Astrid: High Queen of Court of Hearts, mother to Bracken
- Princess Signe: princess of Court of Hearts
- Hodag: troll, friend of Ari and Saga
- Lord Hawthorne: Lord of Court of Serpents
- Bjorn: uncle to Cuyler and brother-in-law to Lord Gorm
- Sofia Toft: Huldrafolk, former guard for Bracken
- Riot Ode: High King of Fate, brother to Saga
- Anneli Ode: High Queen, wife of Riot
- Iris and Celeste: Ladies of the Court of Stars, mothers to Eryka
- Lady Ernaline: Gorm's late wife, Cuyler's mother
- Petter and Jytte Sekundär, and three daughters: Ari's family that was slaughtered when he was a boy. His father was the royal cartographer to both House Ode and House Ferus responsible for designing the broken world, and his mother was a smith who created the heirloom blade.

CHARACTER LIST
WESTERN KINGDOM

Raven Row

- Calista Ode: the storyteller, daughter of Riot and Anneli
- The Phantom: unknown fate worker connected to Calista
- The Norns: rune seer sisters who speak in riddles
- Olaf: aleman in Raven Row
- The Mad King: King of the West no one has seen.

Deceased:

- Stefan/Captain Annon: Riot Ode's captain, adopted brother to Calista Ode

SERIES RECAP

There is a well-known myth throughout the four kingdoms that revolves around four gifts of fate and the queens who will claim them: choice, devotion, honor, and cunning.

In the Northern Kingdom, Elise broke the Night Prince's curse with the help of a fate storyteller, Calista. However, according to Calista, storytellers have come before her to bring about the tricky agenda of the Norns, and one of these storytellers was the enchantress, Greta, who cursed Valen and his family.

Fate also played a role in the Eastern Kingdom and Alver clans in the retrieval and acceptance of Malin's ring, known as the queen's ring. When someone wears the ring, the Nightrender is able to shadow walk to wherever they are, it gives the fated queen power over true desires, and eventually gave Malin the power to literally steal the memory of the Nightrender's death from fate.

Niklas once explained the history of the ring, including the civil war between an old family of memory workers. These wars destroyed the throne of the East, and eventually led to the search from the Black Palace for the heir through a vicious masquerade.

In *Dance of Kings and Thieves,* it was discovered that Malin's parents were from both bloodlines, making Malin the true queen and the one to finally bring the ring back to power in the battle of the Black Palace.

During this battle, the kingdoms had their first interaction with sea fae from an underwater realm called the Ever Kingdom. When Thorvald, the Ever King, injured Eryka, Valen killed the sea king, making new enemies with new fae.

After the battle of the Black Palace, Ari was bound to Saga, a raven shifter, for one hundred years, but Fate wasn't finished. By binding the two of them together, Saga's curse of a cold heart was ended. The curse was placed over her by her brother, the first fate king, Riot Ode.

All of it was done to protect Saga from her cruel former consort, Davorin, Riot's battle lord; he was subsequently cursed to become a dark presence throughout the kingdoms that would only gain strength as new paths of fate and heart bonds between fated queens unraveled.

Ari and Saga's fated union ended Davorin's exile, and he returned to claim Saga and take over every kingdom.

Ari was placed into a fae sleep to heal from Davorin's dark glamour, and during his sleep he was led through different moments of the past by a mysterious fate worker he knew as Wraith. During this fae sleep, Ari saw the truth of the kingdoms' history.

Meanwhile, Saga and Calista began a new path of fate that they soon discover was set in motion by Riot Ode in the first kingdom. They learned that centuries before, Ari's mother and father were part of the separation of the four kingdoms. Petter Sekundär designed the broken world, and Jytte Sekundär crafted a blade with the power to destroy Davorin's dark glamour.

With Calista's help, every kingdom rose together to face Davorin. During the battle of the fae isles, Calista discovered how similar her fate magic—seidr—was to King Riot's. Soon, they discovered not only was he Stefan, Calista's brother, but also Riot's Rave warrior captain, a man placed by the first fate king to protect Calista through the centuries. At her brother's death during the battle, Calista discovered she was the daughter of Riot Ode (Saga's niece), making her a royal.

When the plan to end Davorin failed, he disappeared beneath the sea, and the four kingdoms fell into a tense peace for nearly ten years.

But Calista's secret whispers from a phantom in the dark have now grown more urgent, and she discovers a letter from her fallen brother. The letter warns her to find "the first bond" . . . only then can their story end.

The story continues ten years after the battle of the fae isles with four kingdoms in peace, but sharing a common enemy they know still exists, and a fate worker who has fled from her destiny.

But destiny has finally caught up.

To the Wicked Darlings. Your love of this series has kept it going, and your GIFs keep me going.

Hus Rose

Norn's House

Calista's Tenement

Raven Row

Raven Row

Western Kingdom

CHAPTER 1
THE PHANTOM

Do you know what it's like, Little Rose?

A glow of red broke through the dust and grime of tall, gabled windows. With the rough tip of my center finger, I strummed a taut string on a golden lyre in the corner of the hall. The room was too spacious and too suffocating all at once, a place where ghosts danced to haunting tunes of a dream that seemed as if it would never be.

A dream where she'd want me the same and scour the earth to find me.

Do you know what it's like? I closed my eyes against the pain in my skull. Frustration and despair collided like a knife dug through the soft tissues behind my eyes. Blades against my face were a sensation I'd never forget. That cruel swipe of his sword helped twist me into . . . this creature in the shadows.

That was all I was now. A creature. A phantom of darkness. A memory nearly forgotten.

Do you know? I gripped the lyre by the edge and flung it across the empty corridor, chasing away the ghosts and their wretched songs.

"No!" My voice echoed against the walls. Dust fluttered off tattered drapes in a cloud when I ripped them open, eyes on the moon. "No. You don't know *anything*."

1

Crimson painted the moon, a sign of fate twisting our world again. A sign we should've long ago been prepared to face, side by side. Now, she would fade again. That was how I'd been taught it worked. Leave a tale unfinished, and it would fade, along with anyone in it.

Already, the heat of the song between our two hearts began to flicker, as though a flame struggled in the fury of the wind.

I couldn't . . . not again. I couldn't watch it again.

I thought the wait would've ended, I thought she'd never resist the consuming draw. The pull to her crushed me day by day. For her? I was nothing, hardly a whisper in the dark.

I was wrong about it all. She refused to see through her own fears.

The shadowed horizon in the distant seas seemed to loom closer, a constant reminder foreign shores had survived wars and battles. Long ago, it should've been our turn to face our fate, but we remained locked in nothingness.

Yet, something was coming. A panic, a tension, grew relentless in my chest. It had become a constant weight and burden that these quiet lands would not remain.

With the bloody moon overhead, his darkness was here, returned to cause havoc and pain. Gods, was it too late? Had we waited too long to find the bond lost so long ago? By my sides, my hands tightened into fists.

He was coming, but I had not endured everything to watch him take her away.

"I won't!" I pointed a finger at the shadows in the corner. They never responded. With an arrogant smirk, I pulled away from the corner and returned to the window. "I won't watch it. I won't."

Perhaps she'd resist when I destroyed her false sense of solace. I didn't care. Not anymore. She wouldn't have a choice. Waiting. Wanting. Watching. I was finished with it all. I could not take another moment of the darkness flowing like a slow drip through my blood. It was time for freedom.

Let me be your darkness, but let me be yours. Anywhere she went, I now planned to go. Damn the Norns. Damn fate. I would not go another turn, not another damn moment waiting, wanting, and watching.

Do you know what it's like, Little Rose?

There was no time to wait. Not anymore. The truth was in the sky —we were about to watch our world burn.

CHAPTER 2
THE FIRST KNIGHT

South Fjord—Kingdom of Etta

THE HAIR ON THE BACK OF MY NECK LIFTED, BUT I MADE NO MENTION OF IT, merely sat a bit straighter on my horse. I'd fought long enough not to be reckless and brush it away, but I wasn't about to sound an alarm for shadows.

Folk tunes from young voices added a touch of levity to the fjord's empty shores. I glanced over my shoulder, grinning.

Aesir tried to sing a higher tune alongside Princess Laila. The gods hadn't blessed my boy with musical talent like Herja's daughter, and his maturing voice cracked in a disastrous sort of screech, like a dying pheasant.

Mattis had joined on the patrol and kicked at my boy's boot, laughing, while Stieg mocked him, to see the tips of my son's ears turn pink.

"Horrid," Laila said, ruffling Aesir's pale hair. An official archer in the Ettan army like her mother, Laila was one of the few who could taunt my boy without him lashing out. Kari thought it was due to Aesir's glassy eyes whenever he looked upon the princess.

Boyish dreams. He'd only turned thirteen, and Laila was already

4

set to vow with Njord, a young warrior with a talent for flinging knives.

The son of an aleman and a princess would be vowed before the frosts. This was the Etta I'd always wanted, one where we were people first, and titles came second. Except when it came to bleeding Ari. Bastard was a damn king again, and after all these turns, he still took great pleasure in reminding me.

I carried his latest missive in the inner folds of my tunic. We'd stopped the patrol for post retrieval at the docks near the old quarries. Mattis and Stieg had a laugh at my expense when they saw the seal of the royals in the fae isles.

Saga had promised she'd have one made. I'd always thought we'd be the grandest of friends, but there she was, siding with her damn husband and allowing him to make horridly regal seals.

A clock toll ago, I'd been plotting to woo the aggravating Southern king in grand tales of my heroics to bring Ari down a notch or two, but the prickle of unease on my neck had chased away all bright thoughts.

Now, I was left with sharper attention and a heaviness in my gut.

I laughed a great deal, but I'd been born into the household of a First Knight. Respect for instincts and the blade had been whittled into the marrow of my bones from my earliest moments.

As we rode, I kept checking the tricky burn towers arranged every hundred paces along the shoreline. The other kingdoms had the same. Took us the better part of four turns to get the warning flare right. Niklas about keeled over from the countless revisions to his potent elixir, but we'd tested the signal until we knew it was sound.

With the kingdoms separated as they were, we needed to devise a way to get word swiftly to one another if that battle lord bastard ever returned.

Once lit, the torches on the tower burned in blue flames. Through Niklas's elixirs set to trigger at the burn, the flame traveled along our towers, the seas, then would light the towers in the East with red flames, and the South with green. The West would burn black on a single torch nearest Calista's tenement building.

The Mad King of the West had never responded to our outreach after the battles of the isles. Truth be told, we didn't think much of the royals in Calista's tattered kingdom, other than her.

If the king of the broken West wanted to live apart, we'd see our feral little storyteller was warned separate from him.

My fingers twitched. I was being ridiculous. Stillness was the only sound of the shore. There were no ships on the horizon. No threats. I was overreacting because of my boy and the other young faces in the watch tonight.

Half a dozen sons and daughters of nobles and warriors were strapped with short blades and daggers. Their bony limbs barely able to hold the blade for longer than a dozen swings. The eldest hadn't reached fifteen, but other than my own son, the youngest was the one who had me most concerned.

Prince Aleksi kept pace on his black gelding alongside Aesir and Laila.

The boy wasn't yet twelve, but was built like he had a turn on Aesir. Alek was a forest fae abandoned by the Southern clans at his first breaths, found during the battles of the East, but he looked as Night Folk as the rest of us. Dark hair shaved on the sides like most of the young ones his age. Sun toasted brown skin like our clan, but his strange bronze eyes were the only hint that he might have different fae blood.

The prince had practically crawled to my feet, pleading to take him on the patrols. After I'd heartily pointed out to Sol how much his son valued my approval, I'd agreed, on the condition the prince was joined by his fathers.

One of whom caught my gaze, and frowned at once.

Damn Torsten. We'd spent too many bleeding turns in close proximity; he knew what each flinch of my face meant.

I turned forward again. As expected, five breaths later, a pearl stallion rode to my side.

"What is it?" Tor grumbled. The man was still a bear who grunted and groused, even with his consort, even with fatherhood, even with peace all this time.

I swatted at him. "Nothing, you fiend. Get back, this is my patrol to lead. You're here to watch your sapling, nothing more."

"Hal," he said. "We're Shade. I know when something troubles you."

The Guild of Shade never truly died, I supposed. We did not spend our days chasing the Blood Wraith, but there was a rooted sense of kinship among those of us who had. Stieg and Junius included.

I let out a sigh. "Sometimes I wish you'd learn to be oblivious."

"Think of all the times you'd have lost your head if I had," Tor said.

"I take offense, Torsten. I have impeccable instincts, and I'll have you take note, those who've tried to kill me thus far have utterly failed."

He rolled his eyes and looked down the shoreline. "Your hand has not left the hilt of your blade for half a clock toll."

Damn his observant eyes. Despite calling attention to the grip on my seax, I didn't remove it. There was a heat in the air. One that settled like heavy stones in my belly.

"Just the rumblings of the gut, Tor," I told him. "Puts me on edge. No doubt we'll be descending on dock squabbles, nothing more."

I tilted my head toward the faint light of the dock houses where shippers, merchants, and fishermen slept before early hour journeys to the coves, or late-night arrivals from sea hauls.

"I've felt it, Hal. The feeling something is changing." Torsten scanned the gentle sea before facing me. "Sol too. He even wrote to Cal about it a few nights ago."

My brows raised. The Sun Prince had practically taken the woman on as a second sister, but to mention any hint of disquiet meant Sol had reached a breaking point.

Calista knew as well as the rest of us that unfinished games were still in play, hungry for more blood, but Sol rarely took it upon himself to remind her. Not when she'd struggled to find her fate words these last months.

Calista had a fierce need to protect us all, even if she'd never admit it. She'd want to write a tale for Sol, and he knew it. If he wrote her, knowing she would feel unease at being unable to aid *his* unease, then trouble was in the blood.

I focused on the shore. Nothing but night and pebbled sand was around us. One house near the approaching docks was alight with a few flickering lanterns. The rest were dark and sleeping.

"Keep sharp," I told Tor, "that's all I have for you."

He wasn't a man of many words. Didn't need to be. With a curt nod, Tor subtly began tightening the protections around the youngest among us.

The young ones didn't even notice, but Laila took note. Trained to have a brilliant eye, the princess naturally followed her uncle and took an outer flank. Mattis and Stieg kept their grins as the warrior youth chattered on about nothing, but both men had fought in our early wars. They knew the subtle signals when tensions were high. Both shifted hands to their blades, ready to strike should it be needed.

I caught Sol's narrowed expression. We'd been friends since childhood; he knew me as well as Tor. With tight lips, he flicked the snap off his sword sheath.

On the border of the dock houses, I held up a fist, halting the patrol. Jests and taunts and songs silenced at once.

On the end of one dock, an iron approach bell tinged as the wind tossed the rope and clapper against the sides.

The sea guard wasn't at his post. I drew my sword, scanning the shadows for movement. Nothing. The trouble was, *nothing* was perhaps the most unnerving of all.

"Shields," I called out.

Grunts and groaning leathers rolled through the patrol unit in a wave. Wooden shields were positioned on the outer sides, creating a kind of wall around our unit, and in the center, all the young ones were quiet, their short blades in hand.

I took the lead.

"Daj . . ." Aesir began, but cut off his own words, remembering where we were.

I looked over my shoulder, giving the boy a smile and nod.

Once as a young fae, I went to hunt with the king and his sons. I returned to a dead mother and brother, and my kingdom under attack. I'd always wished I had one final smile, one final word, to cling to before they were torn into the Otherworld.

I never left my wife and four children without a last look. Titles be damned, for a breath, I was his father first.

Sol clapped a hand on Aesir's shoulder. A mute assurance my boy wasn't alone, for my son's ease or mine, I didn't know. Didn't matter, for it brought a bit of peace to my racing pulse knowing the Sun Prince would shield Aesir like he'd shield his own son.

I smiled. "Hold steady and think of those tales to tell the girls at the dawn."

His three younger sisters adored the boy, and Aesir always made himself nauseatingly heroic. He gave me a faulty smile. Kari's smile. Truth be told, the only thing Night Folk on the boy were his dark eyes and tapered fae ears. The rest was pale and Timoran.

I pounded a fist to my chest. Aesir did the same.

With a nudge to my horse, I left the protection of the shields.

"*Vidar,*" I called out, scanning the docks for the watch guard. The heated sensation on my neck crept over my scalp.

Stieg and Laila moved into their positions on either flank. Without looking at the princess, I pointed to the higher knolls.

Laila whistled sharply, and her fellow archers broke our formation, ready to rain destruction over any threat. Another gesture, and Stieg whistled much the same, drawing out the men who followed his order toward the water's edge.

I swung a leg over my horse. Another blade in hand, I stepped onto the docks. "Vidar?" Again, my call was left unanswered.

Something was wrong here. I rolled one blade, pointing the tip down.

The docks were empty, eerily silent. Halfway down one of the planks, a wave slapped harder than others and spilled water over the laths. My heart went still. Water, dark as ink, coated the wooden boards.

I held up another arm and flicked my fingers in a deliberate gesture. Movement followed. Warriors formed a line of defense at my back, shielding the docks on all sides. Laila gave a hushed command above us in the hills, and the taut stretch of bowstrings filled the night.

"Vidar, in the name of your king, you will answer, or we will take blades against you."

Glass crashed in the dock house to my left. Made of smooth stones, it was a larger house where the dockers could drink warm ale and eat a meager meal under a roof to escape the cold winds.

Sword outstretched, I blew out a long breath, then kicked the door in.

It happened in an instant. A broad body rushed at me in a frenzied, but sloppy, attack.

My blade caught the belly of the man. He cried a wretched sound, almost more animal than human, and scrambled back into the shadows. The moment he disappeared, a knife flung at me. Much the same as the body attack, it was weak and poorly aimed. With a simple dodge of my head, it rammed into the opposite wall.

"Circle the young ones!" Tor's voice rose over the cries.

I rolled my sword in my grip and struck. The edge of my blade cut into a chair when the bastard lifted it overhead. The bloody sheen of the moon soaked his features. Or what was left of them.

"Vidar?"

The Timoran watch guard's blue eyes were wild and unfocused. Veins of black coated the whites. His mouth was scabbed in dried blood, and his teeth were dark with rusted stains. His leathery skin was battered in bite marks and blade lashes, and deep gouges were carved into his brow and cheeks.

He had enough wounds that he shouldn't be standing.

"Vidar, it's Halvar. What—gods—" I dodged again when Vidar made a furious rush for me. Bleeding hells, he wanted to tear me to pieces.

Stieg shoved into the house. At his back, dark figures stumbled about, hissing and swinging blades, lost in their minds. Vidar lunged for the warrior, but Stieg had the watch guard pinned to the ground, his dagger rammed through his shoulder in the next breath.

I used the back of my hand to wipe my mouth. Vidar writhed on the ground, spitting and lashing, desperate to be free of us.

"He's lost his mind."

Stieg wasn't listening. His eyes were wide with horror as he looked over my shoulder. With time to focus, a ripe tang of blood curdled in my nose. My insides weren't squeamish around blood. I'd seen enough torture and gore to stand steady through it all, but this . . . this drew me to place a fist in front of my lips to squelch the vomit.

Innards, limbs, bone, all of it painted the walls. Bodies of dockers were soaked in gore. Piss and bile had dried on days-dead corpses.

They'd been shredded in ways almost identical to the bloodlust of Valen when he was lost to a curse, in the days before we discovered that torturing him could keep him safe from others. Days where I'd watch my friend, my brother, shred folk with his axes.

This was too similar.

"He did this." Stieg looked back to Vidar. "He devoured them."

Vidar was a mindless beast. The same as the Blood Wraith. Calista was the only one capable of cursing in such away, and she wouldn't do this.

"This was Valen."

Stieg grunted when Vidar tried to kick his ribs. "What?"

"Not now, but this was what he was like, untamed and cursed."

"All gods." Stieg had witnessed Valen succumb to a curse in the East, but it wasn't the same. Elise had power over her husband, some strange connection that kept him less monstrous.

The battle lord was behind the hatred of our kingdom. He was the reason curses were given at all. This was a sign, a warning. A mockery at our turns of pain and suffering.

Anguish gathered in my gut. We knew, we bleeding knew peace would not last forever. The moment that damn moon turned red, the whole of the kingdom went on edge.

I lifted my blade over Vidar's chest. The poor sod thrashed and hissed like a caged wolf. I stabbed the point through his heart, holding it steady until his body twitched and went still, at long last.

"*Farväl en älskade.*" I yanked my blade free, storming out of the dock house and into a battle on the shore.

Archers flung arrows into a crowd of feral folk. Blades cut them down. All were Timoran, their pale features visible under the blood.

Our former enemies were turned against us once again. Dammit. They didn't deserve this. They deserved peace as much as Night Folk.

"Sol, Tor!" I roared. A man lunged at me. My sword rammed through his throat. He spluttered on his own blood and fell when I wrenched the blade free. "Sol!"

The Sun Prince was on his horse. Both hands on the hilt of his blade, he stabbed it through the top of a skull. Once the cursed bastard was dead, the prince faced me.

"Burn it." I swung at another dock man whose eyes had gone the blood red of the Blood Wraith. "Burn it all."

Sol whistled. Tor was fifteen paces off, but turned his horse back. Together, they slid from their charges and strode toward the huddle of cursed dockers. Misty black coiled over Sol's palms as blue fire ignited on Tor's.

Hand in hand, their fury tangled into an explosive flame. Sol pressed his hands onto the sand, guiding the blight. Blue flames collided with the cursed souls. It devoured them whole, leaving behind nothing but ash.

A swift, bloody attack that ended in flames.

Silence swallowed the shoreline. A rank wind laden in hot refuse and blood burned into our leathers and fatigues.

After a few moments, a cry of anguish came from my men. Gods, no. Someone had been injured, or . . . someone had fallen.

My pulse throbbed in my neck. Not a warrior, a friend, a youth— numbness found my fingertips as I shoved through the crowd, pleading it wasn't Aesir. Pleading it wasn't Alek, or, gods, pleading it wasn't *anyone*.

A cursed docker was sprawled out three paces away. Two arrows stuck out of his chest, two more in his face. Laila leaned over the rock ledge, a frozen look of stun on her gentle features.

Relief rushed out of my chest when I caught sight of my boy's light hair, sweaty and on end, but attached to his moving body. His breathing body.

"Aesir." I pulled him against my chest.

The boy trembled. His blade was gripped firmly in one hand, and his other wouldn't release the tunic of the man on the sand.

"I-I-I tried to get them off, Daj. They kept biting him and . . . I tried."

I froze, a bit of horrid stun stiffened my grip on my boy. As though turned to bleeding stone, I couldn't tear my gaze off the bloody face, the body twisted and mangled in the sand, the gashes in his tunic, the silver chain on his neck that his damn wife had only gifted him this last Jul.

I dug my fingers through Aesir's hair and breathed him in, "You make me so damn proud, boy."

"I couldn't save him," he said. The tremble in his voice gave up how desperate he was trying to keep steady. "He saved . . . he saved us, but I couldn't save him."

"There was no saving him," I murmured, more as a reminder to my own sensibilities that there was nothing we could have done. There *couldn't* be anything we could've done, or I'd swim in the guilt of this blood until the Otherworld called.

"Once their teeth are in, there is no saving anyone," I whispered. "He chose right. He chose to defend you and the other young ones. We'll . . ." I clenched my eyes against the sting. "We'll send him to the gods with honor."

Aesir let his forehead burrow into my chest and his narrow shoulders shuddered. I shielded him, doubtless he wouldn't want his fellow young warriors to see. They'd all learn soon enough, tears were as plentiful as blood during battle.

Sol, Tor, Stieg, and three more warriors mutely lifted Mattis's body off the sand.

They carried our regent, *our friend*, to the Sun Prince's horse. It was a sign of honor, of respect, for a royal to walk a fallen Ettan defender back to his family.

Every Ettan warrior slammed a fist over their chests. All I saw was Siverie. Elise. Valen. I saw the way Mattis had defended my favorite Timoran *Kvinna* from the beginning. He'd been her friend and confidant when he was a mere carpenter in Mellanstrad.

He'd loved Siverie through betrayal and war. He was a good man. A good friend.

He'd saved my son.

13

Away from the unit, I lowered to one knee. I kissed my fingertips, traced Mattis's name in the sand, then closed my eyes. A silent prayer rolled over my thoughts, a plea to the gods to write Mattis Virke into the sagas of the brave. I prayed House Atra would never cease speaking of his sacrifice. I prayed the gods would welcome him into the great hall with cheers and the sweetest of ale.

I flattened my palm over his name. "Farewell, my friend. Save me a place and we will share bawdy tales again one day."

Back at Aesir's side, I kissed the top of my boy's head, uncaring if any of the youth saw.

"What's your word?" Torsten was stalwart and stoic when he returned to my side.

I kept my hand on my son's shoulder, watching Mattis's body fade into the night on the Sun Prince's horse.

"Send the signal. He's returned."

CHAPTER 3
THE MEMORY THIEF

Felstad Ruins—Klockglas Region

"I'm just sayin' they coulda taken me."

I chuckled as Jonas gave a rather aggressive swipe of his knife against the wood he was whittling. The eldest of our twins, Jonas had the proclivity to pout when his father and Raum left him out of Kryv business.

"It's dull work today, son."

He blew out his lips with another swipe of his knife. "That's what you say when it's the *best* work."

I grinned and closed my eyes, letting the sun heat my cheeks. I'd embraced shadows when I fell in love with the Nightrender, but as of late, I preferred daylight vastly over the night.

A new crimson moon had put every region on edge. Kase had hardly shown his true eyes in days; they were always shadowed, always blackened with fear as he doubled down on the protections of our kingdom.

In truth, the Kryv were adding more spiked gates on this side of Klockglas, not the normal feckless schemes in which they allowed Jonas and Sander to join.

15

Raum, Isak, and Fiske enjoyed teaching the two princes how to use whalebone picks on locks, or how to read a man's eyes to tell if they were lying. The rest of the Kryv took it upon themselves to teach my sons to thieve.

Thieving princes. Perhaps in other lands it might be a thing of disgrace. In the East, most folk had a touch of thief in their blood. It'd be a disgrace if they didn't make use of their tricky hands. Jonas and Sander only snatched the purses of the Kryv or Falkyns, mostly to prove they could.

They were usually caught and dubbed the failures of the games. Each time they tried harder, grew slier, and attracted more mischief.

While they were raised to be crafty, still we kept Jonas and Sander shielded in a way. Like on days where their father joined his guild to argue over how best to prevent war and death, sights we never wanted our sons to witness.

Sights I wasn't so certain we could keep from them much longer.

"Maj. Made this for you." Jonas stood in front of me. Tall for nine, lanky like me, but a face like his father. His tousled brown hair was always on end, and his verdant eyes were always alight with some trouble he planned to make.

Jonas smiled and held out a small wooden trinket.

"Jonas, owls are my favorite." I took the piece and admired the rough cuts around feathers and a tufted face. "It's beautiful, my love. Thank you."

Despite his protests, I clasped his face in my palms and gave him a wet kiss on his cheek.

"Decent, I suppose. Beak's a little off." Frigg popped her shoulder across the lawns and held up a handful of wooden beads she'd been carving for a week. "Try making a small shape, Prince Jonas. That's where knife work gets hard."

Jonas let his eyes shade over, the same as Kase's could do, although their mesmer was different. Where Kase worked in the fear of others, our boys worked in creating it. They worked in nightmares.

"Why'd I wanna make stupid beads? Do you see me wearin' a dress, Friggy?"

"They can be for hair too!"

"Oh." Jonas snorted and mocked tossing back his short hair. "Like a bleeding *girl*."

I swatted the back of his head as Frigg narrowed her eyes in a way that made her look wholly like her father. Hob and Inge took the stronghold at Felstad after the battle of the Black Palace. Their daughter wasn't much older than the princes, and like Hob and me, they couldn't seem to do anything but aggravate each other.

I stood, letting them argue, and strode across the lawns to where Sander read near the creek's edge, back against the stone tower of one of the many warning flame torches.

With a sigh I sat beside my second son. He shared most of Jonas's same features, from the green of his eyes to the constant mess of his auburn hair. Sander was a thinker. Most took Jonas for the boisterous troublemaker, but if they knew the truth, they'd know most of the schemes were born in this boy's brain.

"What book today?"

He lifted his head, noticing me for the first time, and proudly held up the leather book.

"*Blood Herbs: Spell Cast Codex*." I arched my brows. "Have you, all at once, become a spell caster?"

Sander grinned softly. "Uncle Nik gave it to me. Teaches you all the herbs and berries and leaves and such. There's a nutshell that can cause the tongue to tie up in nonsense words. No matter how you try, you can't say anything right for at least a clock toll." He snorted and his smile widened. "I'm gonna do it to Jo sometime."

"You're not poisoning your brother." I reclined on my hands.

"Maj," he whined. "I'm not poisoning him. But you gotta admit it'd be funny to hear him go on about nothing and not be able to help it."

I wasn't going to survive my sons.

"That," Sander went on, voice softer. "Or I'll use something to kill that sea creature and the shadow man."

"Kill what?" A groove shaped between my brows. "What sea creature, what shadow?"

Sander eyed the creek warily. "I don't . . . I don't know if I should say. You'll think I'm losing my mind and—"

"Sander." I gripped his arm. "What are you talking about?"

For the first time, I noticed the shadows buried in his young eyes. Not from mesmer, from true fear. "I saw something in the water and she brought . . . a man with her."

My blood froze. Instinct took hold, and I dragged Sander behind me as I peered into the creek.

"Not today. But . . . yesterday. I didn't want to say since I thought it might've been my mesmer playin' tricks with me."

I wheeled on him. "Tell me what you saw."

Sander's chin quivered. "Why do you look so afraid, Maj?"

Dammit. Kase and I grew in a world that held little kindness. I praised the gods our children did not know the same world. But the downside of it all was they did not know how to react to dangers and tended to panic if a look of fright crossed our faces.

I smoothed his hair and forced a smile. "You've done nothing wrong, but tell me what you saw."

"A monster in the shadows," he whispered. "Not as frightening as the ones I've made in dreams, but the shadow man came with the sea creature. I think it was a girl, but sorta like a fish with needles as teeth."

"What . . . what did they do?"

"Laughed at me." Sander licked his lips and clung to the book until his knuckles turned white. "Said I was a dead earth fae. Told it I'm not a fae. Said I was an Alver, and it only laughed harder."

Three hells. There were many creatures in our wood. Cats with jagged teeth. Wolvyn with black claws. Snakes with four eyes. All dangerous, but there were no sea creatures that spoke. Not that I knew.

"May I see?" I held out my palm. Sander didn't hesitate, and pressed his forehead against my skin.

Smoke and shadows came at once. With the ring on my finger, pulling memories was swift. Once, it took a great deal of my mesmer, now it was as though a story played out in my mind. A dream of sorts.

Ribbons of misty shadows coiled around my son as he searched for his brother near the lakes Valen had helped shape behind the Black Palace. Sander cursed in the memory, words that would make Kase seek out Ash and Raum for teaching the boys that sort of language.

Another time, I might laugh, but I was bleeding panicked.

Sander paused in the memory and kneeled beside the lake. True enough, beneath the surface, bulbous eyes stared back at him.

"What are you?" Sander asked. His eyes darkened with his mesmer.

"Prepared to die, earth fae?" her voice was wet and soft.

"I'm not a fae. I'm an Alver. Get gone, or I'll give you all the nightmares you don't want."

She laughed, a strangled kind of sound, and rose from the water, revealing a jagged grin with those sharp, pointed teeth, and fins where her legs ought to have been. "Perhaps you'd like to swim with me. Or perhaps . . . with him?"

In the memory, the strange sea fae pointed over Sander's shoulder. My blood turned to ice as I watched my son spin around and face a dark, looming shadow.

"Daj?" Sander whispered.

From the darkness appeared a face, pale as stone, a sneer cruel as a rabid wolf. The creature said nothing, and in the next moments, the clearing was doused in a dark shadow.

By the gods—Davorin.

He'd stepped onto our land. How had he avoided Niklas's wards? I wanted to scream for Sander to run, but he was in my arms, he was here. Clearly, he'd managed to flee.

"Maj, you're squishing me." Sander's distant voice carved through the memory. I ignored him and clung to my boy as I observed, helplessly watching the sleek, horridly appealing features of our enemy peer at my son.

"Hello," Davorin said, voice like a chill in the frosts. "Would you like to use your power on me, body worker?"

"Alver," Sander shouted. His eyes turned black as pitch.

Davorin chuckled. "What a delightful boy you are. Like your father. Like your mother. Have you been told tales of them? Have you been told fate chose them?" His voice took on a bitter tone, sharp as new steel.

Sander ignored the bastard and reached for a stone hidden in the reeds. "Get gone or you'll find out yourself. My daj has better shadows than you, and my maj'll rip your brains to bits."

I held my breath. To taunt such a man should surely bring his rage. Instead, the memory of the ghostly spectral, like a mist of Davorin, laughed. As though my son were an utter delight.

"I'm sure you think so. Tell them I look forward to meeting again, won't you boy?" Davorin slid back toward the dark billows of his glamour. "Tell them to watch their shores. They might get a bit dodgy."

In the memory, Sander threw the rock in his hand with all his might at the darkness. All that was left was the distant echo of Davorin's laughter.

I let out a short gasp when the memory faded. Sander wrapped his arms around me, squeezing. Gods, he was trembling.

"You were so brilliant," I whispered against his hair. "But why did you not tell me?"

When I pulled him back, his mouth was tight. "I thought I might've made it up since I was reading so much, but . . . I looked it up, Maj. I think that thing was a *merfolk*. Don't know who the shadow man was, though. Maybe a haunt. Fiske thinks there's haunts in Jagged Grove."

I didn't care what the fish creature was. She could be a goddess of the deep, and if she returned to threaten my son, I'd pluck out those bulging eyes and wear them around my damn neck.

What I cared about was the sight of Davorin. He'd slipped past the wards, and I didn't understand how. A spectral? A projection? He hadn't looked whole.

"We're going to speak with Daj, all right?" I kissed his forehead, smiling as though this was another day. It wasn't.

Every kingdom needed to know what had happened here. Why were we to watch our shores? Sea fae? It was possible, the sea folk hadn't shown their faces since the Ever King had been slaughtered and Valen pulled a wall from the seafloor just beyond the Howl Sea.

But hadn't King Thorvald's brother made some threat about ten turns? We were months into the eleventh turn since our battle of the Black Palace. Late, perhaps, but if they were preparing to return to make good on their threats, if Davorin was behind it, war was near.

A shout snapped my eyes toward Jonas and Frigg. Hob sprinted out of Felstad. Lanky as always, but his beard was a great deal longer, and his eyes were filled with a strange fear.

"Mal!" Hob yanked his daughter behind his back, Jonas next, and pointed behind us.

All. Gods. The warning tower beside the creek spluttered and hissed, then a tall, red flame, rich as blood, flared at the top. Distant screams rose through the trees from the shore. No mistake, all the towers had ignited.

In the next breath, billows of dark shadows wrapped around Felstad. I gripped Sander's hand and reached out my other until the long, callused fingers of the Nightrender grabbed hold and Kase stepped through. Kryv, warriors, and Falkyns followed.

Kase had his arms around me in the next breath, crushing both me and Sander against him. He looked about frantically until Jonas sprinted across the lawn and Kase had both his sons clasped tightly.

"Sander saw Davorin," I whispered against Kase's ear. "Yesterday. Like a ghost of him."

Kase's eyes went wide. "You're certain?"

"I saw it."

Jaw tight, Kase looked to the flame, then to his sons.

"The warning," I asked, a tremble of hesitation in my voice. "Which direction?"

Kase's fingers dug into my spine. "From the North."

"That's Livie and . . . and . . . Alek! That's Uncle Hagen and . . . Auntie Herja," Jonas wailed. "Daj, we gotta go help 'em. We gotta go. Shadow walk, and—"

Kase silenced him by scooping him up. Too long to be held like a tiny boy, but Jonas crushed his father's neck and wrapped his legs around his waist, true tears on his cheeks as the boy cried for his friends and family in Etta.

Kase rubbed Jonas's back and strode toward Felstad. "They'll be safe, boy. They'll be safe."

He kept assuring the princes their playmates and cousins were unharmed, but when his blackened eyes met mine, I knew the truth —he feared he was dead wrong.

CHAPTER 4
THE RAVEN QUEEN

The Borough—Court of Hearts

THE BOROUGH WAS IN CHAOS.

"Get my daughter out of here, *now!*" Ari's sharp voice echoed down the corridor. He was near the great hall, but his voice was fierce enough it carried to the back chambers near the cooking rooms.

I hurried to help Mira with the cloak. Tears glistened on her cheeks. I took a pause to wipe them away with my thumbs.

"It'll be all right, my girl," I said. It was a promise, yet one I wasn't certain I could keep. Not when I didn't bleeding know what the hells was happening beyond our walls.

Mira lifted her eyes, holding mine for a few breaths, but soon they widened. "Maj! Maj, behind you."

I wheeled around and screamed, shielding Mira with my body. The back doorway to the cooking room was flung open. In the frame billowed shadows, like a satin cloak, and in the center was Davorin.

The Davorin who'd stood arrogant in the Court of Stars before we'd backed him into the sea. His hair was glossy and thick again.

His pale face sharp and youthful. His eyes glimmered in malice as he looked at me.

"Hello, little raven."

In half a breath I had a dagger unsheathed from my belt, blade outstretched. "Come near me, and I carve out your heart."

"I do love this new strength you think you have," he said, laughing. "It will be a joy to rid you of it soon enough." Davorin tilted his head. "Hmm. What a lovely little girl."

My heart bruised my chest, but stronger than fear was rage. Horrid, desperate rage for even the mere glance at my daughter. To imagine Davorin close to Mira sickened me. It brought a wildness to my mind I couldn't tame.

I rushed for the door in the same moment the main hall doors clanged open.

"Shit!" Ari's rough curse struck me from behind. "Seal the bleeding gates, get this bastard's head in my hands now! Saga, stop."

Davorin's grin widened at the sight of Ari. "I look forward to our reunion, Golden King. How sweet it will be. Enjoy memories of me."

Ari cursed, barked orders at the blood fae and forest fae at his back; he sprinted for us, snagging Mira out of the doorway. I screamed my anger and threw the blade when I was close enough. By the time the point made it through the door, Davorin's likeness was gone.

The shadows. Those horrid, unfeeling eyes. He was just . . . gone.

I doubled over, screaming my anger, my fear.

Ari's hand snatched me away from the door. He filled the space, the heirloom blade in place. "Where the hells is he!"

"It was an illusion," Magus said, touching the wood around the door. "A spell cast of some kind. You can see remnants. He's not here, My King. I don't know if he truly was."

Ari raged and stabbed the damp soil with his blade.

Dressed in a loose tunic, hair tousled, I could see the fear and disquiet clearly. Mira whimpered, and I wrapped her tightly in my arms, holding her trembling body close. Ari let out a long breath and softened his eyes.

Still, there was a madness in his expression. One he'd never lost since the day Davorin slid into the sea.

The sight of the brilliant, emerald flames had snapped something in my husband. Full of words and jests, tender and brilliant, now he was the brutal warrior he kept beneath it all. Blood and vengeance lived in those eyes. As though he craved it.

Now, to see more tricks of Davorin after the flame, I was certain one more game, and Ari would snap into a man made of nothing but violence.

Tonight revealed a truth we'd all known could come to pass. A dreary piece of our tale we'd chosen to keep buried while we lived and loved.

It had shattered upon the first sight of that green fire.

His long Night Folk legs had him across the cooking room and next to me in six strides. His palm cupped the back of Mira's head. She squeezed her arms tighter around my neck.

"Mira," he whispered. "We're going to the burrows now, like we always talked about."

"*No.*" She sobbed. Born a natural fretter like her mother, Mira sensed trouble before the towers burst in the warning. She'd already been sleeping between the two of us from a slew of nightmares.

Now her dreams of shadows and losing her maj and daj were coming to pass.

"My girl," I whispered. "We've talked of this. We've told you what happens if the green fire came."

"No, Maj, no! You saw him, he'll . . . snatch me up!"

"Listen to me, Starlight," Ari said. Starlight, a name he'd always called her, a name that belonged to the two of them, since Ari always said she was born beneath the stars, and they brightened with delight at her birth. "No one will touch you. But I need you safe, Maj needs you safe, understand?"

Mira tightened her hold. Ari gave me a despondent sort of look for a few breaths, then hardened his expression.

I winced as Mira screamed when Ari, patience lost, peeled her away from my body. "Daj, no, *no!*"

25

Tears blurred my eyes. I reached for her hands and pressed kisses to her knuckles. "I love you. We'll see you soon. I-I love you."

My own sobs took hold. I failed wondrously at trying to calm my own child.

"Daj, don't leave me. *Please*, don't leave me." She reached for Ari now that Lord Magus and Lord Gorm had come to collect the princess with both Serpent warriors and blood fae watchers.

Ari kneeled, brushed her dark, messy hair out of her face, and kissed her forehead. His voice cracked when he spoke. "I love you. You brighten my heart, so I need you safe, and you will be safe in the burrows. No one can reach you there, not the man in the shadows, no one. We will see you soon. Be brave and we'll go visit the vales, just you and I, very soon."

He kissed her head once more, then forced himself to turn away. Mira's cries were closed off from us when the doors to the great hall slammed. Ari's hands shaped into fists at his sides. Silence suffocated us.

The flames came from the North. No mistake, his heart was broken in more than one way. True, he was no longer the ambassador for Etta, hadn't been for turns, but his people were the ones to light the flame. His family was under attack. An attack that could only be from the man who'd nearly killed his wife. Who wanted the power we shared between us.

A man he blamed himself for not killing over ten turns ago.

I jumped in surprise when his fist slammed, knuckles-first, onto the long table, crashing goblets and silver plates together. I went to him and wrapped my arms around his shoulders, biting back tears when he sank against me. His safe, strong embrace trembled around my waist, tight enough I thought he might snap a rib.

"There were no sightings," he said, close to gasping. "We searched along the coast. Every court has seen nothing, then he is suddenly simply here. He slipped past me like a damn ghost."

"It wasn't real. You heard Magus." I closed my eyes, stroking the back of Ari's neck. "If Davorin shows himself in true form, then he will not live long."

Ari dropped his forehead to my shoulder. "I cannot lose you, I cannot lose Mira. He wants you, and he will try to take her."

"And he will die trying." I trapped his face in my hands. "What have we always said, Ari? We knew this would come. We knew it. But we face it together, and his life is ours whenever he shows."

Ari's eyes were wet. His jaw pulsed in tension. "He won't touch you again. I swore to you, he will never touch you again."

He kissed me furiously. Ari's hold was crushing and beautiful, like he was trying to squeeze me into his ribcage to keep me shielded through whatever was coming our way. Tongues and teeth, he kissed me for the thousands of moments we might face in blood and blade and battle.

"I love you," he said between kisses. "You're my sweetest menace."

"You are my beautiful bastard."

I kissed him until the door reopened to the hall and Gorm interjected himself without a second thought. "The princess is well-guarded and goes to the burrows until we know more."

I wiped my eyes and hugged Ari's waist. "Thank you, Gorm. Any word from Cuyler?"

Gorm did not show emotion well, but there was a flicker of worry in his eyes at the mention of his son. "No, but they will see the warning. It cannot be missed, I made certain it was strategically placed. If Cuyler fights as he was taught, no harm will befall the fate princess."

Ari lifted my knuckles to his mouth, holding it there longer than normal, his eyes saying a dozen unspoken words. The true fear we had to admit—Davorin might have sights for me, our daughter might be at grave risk since he would want to torment us in the deepest ways, but I was not all he wanted.

He wanted the entire House Ode in his grasp, or bloodied and dead.

He wanted Calista.

CHAPTER 5
THE STORYTELLER

Raven Row—Western Kingdom

I WAS NOT MYSELF, BUT I HID IT WELL. MY BODY WOKE THIS MORNING A traitor. My bleeding spine felt ancient and weary. Like I'd find more joy remaining in bed instead of facing one more damn day where words never came. Where the heat in my heart from seidr was ashen and dry as a scorched field.

Today, though, I was not alone in my disquiet.

The dock swayed with the ebb and flow of the tide. I'd learned long ago to breathe through my mouth this close to the dirty water of the shores of Raven Row. I folded my Sun Prince's letter for the tenth time, trying to see between every line, deconstructing every word.

Rare for Lumpy to admit he was discomposed, especially to me. We'd always been honest with each other, so I supposed I shouldn't have been surprised he'd confessed his wretched dreams. Still, there was a tone that was the ever-protective Sun Prince.

He'd filled the shoes of brother in my life after Stefan died.

For ten turns, Sol, Tor, and little Aleksi visited more than any of my royals. Even more than my Raven Queen aunt. It was a feat, since

Ari disguised his own reservations whenever I returned home to the Row alone by insisting Mira had to visit me.

Ten turns ago, in one night, a royal family of worriers had been dropped in my lap.

I loved them for it. Loved them all, even the stoic glares of my Shadow King. He fretted, but in a different way. Whenever I announced I was returning to the West, a bit of black mist coated his eyes, and I knew.

But Lump and I had a different kind of connection. Bonded through suffering, he knew more than anyone the burdens breaking my spine day by day, but he didn't know how my body seemed to be weakening with each sunrise.

I hated lying to Lump, hated keeping truths from him. Trouble was the deeper I dug into fears, the more unease unraveled inside me until I could hardly catch a breath. But if he knew, he'd sail across the Fate's Ocean, drag me—swearing and kicking—all the way into a longship, and drag me back to the North.

Besides, how did I go about telling him the fears growing more potent in my bones with each bloody moon? *Oh, by the way, my over-protective brother figure, I think our world is about to collapse. Give your precious little son an extra-long kiss now before it's all over.*

Gods. I shuddered at the thought.

I swiped at my lashes. When did I become such a spluttering, teary mess?

When Stefan died, that's bleeding when. Stefan, my brother, the man who'd been disguised for gods-knew how long. Annon Vektäre was his true name. The captain of my dead father.

His mere existence was part of my countless unanswered questions. My endless simmer of unease and fear. If my father's captain was concealed from me, what else was hidden in plain sight? What was the purpose of it? How did I avoid it?

There was the truth—I wanted to avoid the pull toward some other dreadful, cruel path of fate.

Now that I'd opened my whole damn heart to my royals, I had a great deal to lose. With the death of my brother, I knew exactly what that loss felt like. I'd rather step into the Otherworld myself before experiencing such suffocating pain again.

I read the last words of Sol's missive again, the burn of tears in my eyes.

I don't know what to think, little bird. Since this damn moon showed in the sky, the dreams never leave. Night after night I see it: Tor dying in my arms. It's dark, and I'm dressed for battle, and the dream always ends the same—at his final breath. I don't know what to do. I can't face this world without him, Cal . . .

The horizon was swallowing the sun, and in its place, a crimson moon was beginning to rise.

It appeared nearly two weeks earlier. Soon enough, Ettan ships arrived at the shore. Sol and Tor and Aleksi remained in the dregs of Raven Row until they were convinced the Shadow Bastard hadn't come to snatch me up.

Shadow Bastard. That name didn't fit. Ten turns and I still hadn't settled on a name for Davorin, my father's battle lord. The tormentor and abuser of my Raven Queen. The man who wanted to personally wipe out my bloodline for eternity.

I brushed a thumb over Sol's letter. He felt this fear deeply. Truth be told, I hated dreams like this. I had them of my own, and there was a deep foreboding that followed each one, like they weren't simple dreams.

I wouldn't let my Sun Prince lose the life he'd suffered for, the life he'd fought to win.

"It's not going to happen, Lump," I whispered to the sea breeze. "It's not. I swear to you."

I'd find the words to protect him. To fail when it came to Sol Ferus wouldn't be an option for me.

The trouble was, I hadn't been able to write a damn tale in months. Quill to parchment, and nothing came. The only hint my seidr still existed was the hum in my veins, and the dreams that set me on fire every night. Those same kind of dreams that plagued Sol, only mine made little sense.

They weren't of the future. They were of past things. Bloody things, where throats were slit and suffering was had. There was something shifting inside me, like my heart—my soul—antici-pated something life-altering, something frightfully wondrous and new.

With all that wonderment came the fear, heady enough I found contentment staying close to my ratty tenement. I was rarely willing to leave it for long, as though one wrong move would land me back in the cruel games of the Norns.

The tricky games of fate I'd been avoiding all my life. Games that would end in pain and death, and I wasn't willing to risk another damn life.

"Cal, storm's coming." Cuyler nudged my arm and lowered to a crouch beside me.

Cuyler was the heir to the Court of Blood in the Southern Isles but had devoted the last ten turns of his existence to protecting Riot Ode's lost heir. He was kind and entertaining. Not in a stupid way where folk laughed because of idiocy, Cuyler was genuinely enjoyable.

He'd give his life for me. But that didn't sit right, so I often told him he could only die for me if he beat me to it. I told him I'd be leaping in front of arrows for him much the same.

He dragged his knife along the grains of damp sand. "Ready to go home?"

Home. To an empty tenement. The patience and endurance of Cuyler and his men was admirable. Whenever I returned to Raven Row after visiting other kingdoms, they lived in tight quarters in rotted tenements well beneath the glamor and spacious cottages in the Court of Blood.

They never complained. At least not to my face.

In truth, my small tenement had felt less and less like home and more a place of empty reminders of laughter that once filled the walls when Stef and I would play face cards until the early morning, or when we'd read strange fairy tales of the sea folk in the lands below the surf.

Those stopped being enjoyable when I met some of those damn sea folk.

Their ships were horrid and they were hardly polite.

"Ready?" Cuyler pressed again. He stood and held out a hand.

"No," I said as I stood. I didn't bother wiping the mud off my trousers, more would always come. "I don't feel like going home quite yet."

"Where do you want to go?"

I hugged my middle. "I want to see my brother. I have a fate tale to write, and he's going to tell me how to get the words back."

CHAPTER 6
THE STORYTELLER

IF EVERY KINGDOM WERE PART OF A LIVING SOUL, ETTA WOULD BE THE HEART that kept us vibrant, Klockglas in the East would be the brain that kept us scheming, and the fae isles of the South would be the blood that kept us living.

Raven Row would be the shit.

Roads made of mud, goat droppings, and a touch of vomit crisscrossed through tattered tenements and haggard taverns and hostels. A haze always hugged the buildings in a low mist as though the stench from unwashed skin and refuse was too putrid to rise to the clouds, so it remained.

I hardly noticed anymore. It wasn't filth, it was home.

With a long draw of breath, I filled my lungs of the heavy essence of the Row. Behind me, dozens of boots squelched in the mud, blades scraped in leather sheathes, and murmurs of the thick stink drew a grin to the corner of my mouth.

I adjusted the wide brim hat over my wild braids and flicked my gaze to the blood heir. "Cuy, you don't need to follow me. I know how much you resent me when I make you trudge through the Row."

Cuyler's full lips spread, flashing his white teeth. "I'm delighted to trudge, Cal."

Lord Gorm would smack the back of his son's skull if the blood lord ever heard his heir address me so casually. Hells, I appreciated it.

All my life, I'd been a street urchin. A fate worker who merely wanted to survive the snatchers who occasionally came to the Western shores to buy up witches. Now, I had a crown plopped atop my head, and the thought of anyone bowing, dressing, or adorning me in finery caused my stomach to roll in disquiet.

I understood my Shadow King's aversion to titles completely.

"Storm's coming." Cuyler repeated, gesturing overhead. Dark billows of ruthless clouds shadowed the already dim streets. "Still want to go?"

"A little rain never hurt the Row." Truth be told, rain caused some of the more pleasant scents to emerge once the grime was washed away.

I led the procession of blood fae down the road, occasionally drawing a few hazy glances from drunkards spilling out of Olaf's game hall. Over the turns, Lord Gorm—possibly Ari—had casually sent no less than two units of blood fae watchers. At least forty guards meant to be at my personal disposal.

They'd merely become another spectacle in a kingdom filled with the lowliest of folk. Pleasant folk, but lowly. Raven Row, the whole of the West, was docile. Almost made up of wanderers. There wasn't much aspiration in the people who walked these streets, at least nothing behind the next drop of ale or how much kopar coin they could win at the game tables.

A few were helpful. Sometimes.

Dock men had always provided Stefan with skiffs if we wanted to sail out to cleaner coves on the far edges of the kingdom.

The old seamstress who mended and patched old tunics better than any royal tailor I'd ever encountered, did it for a few fate prophecies or a bit of sweet bread if I could scrounge any up from the stingy bakers nearest to *Hus Rose*, the crumbling palace.

The old hags who thought they were goddesses by calling themselves the Norns were irritating, but they'd delivered a few missives for me here and there.

No. Never mind. They weren't helpful. Their damn prophecies

were what got me into this bleeding mess. They were supposed to help my Raven Queen find a way to wake Ari ten turns ago, and somehow I got pulled into a battle where my bleeding world unraveled.

Better to blame Forbi and her sisters than accept this was truly what fate had in mind.

Cuyler gave a few commands to his men, spreading them out across the city like a spilled inkwell. Most corners were always guarded by blood fae watchers.

If the Mad King and whatever eerie defenses he kept behind his overgrown gates had a care that foreign forces had entered his grimy realm, he never said. He never said anything. A few glimpses of candlelight in the windows, an occasional tune from a lyre or fife, were the only signs anyone occupied Hus Rose at all.

Low, iron gates with spikes on top surrounded the burial grounds. Markers with stacked river stones and pebbles from the sea were the last remnants of the souls sent to the Otherworld.

I paused at the entrance, hugging my middle. The rising blood moon added a touch of wicked eeriness to the overgrown land. One of the few places in the Row where gangly trees grew in a pathetic kind of grove.

When I was a tiny girl, I remembered the leaves being lush, the colors of the grass being rich and verdant, not brittle and yellowed. Folk were once more boisterous and brighter, with a touch of hope in their eyes.

Since the battle of the fae isles ten turns ago, it was as though Raven Row began dying a slow death.

"I'll wait out here." Cuyler tapped my elbow. He gave me a sympathetic smile before going to stand beside a wooden pillar carved in faded runes. "Take as long as you want."

I dipped my chin, grateful for the solitude, and made my way to the back of the grounds. Overhead, branches stretched like bony fingers, reaching for me, ready to snatch me away. I swallowed and kept my focus ahead on the most recent altar of gray stones.

In the South, my Golden King erected a totem for my fallen parents, but also for Captain Annon.

On the first visit back to Raven Row, all my royals and thieves joined and helped create this small plot of land where Stefan, the brother of the storyteller, a damn fine player at the game halls, could be remembered as he was when we walked these shores together.

"I'm still a little angry at you," I whispered, brushing my fingertips over the smooth stones. "But we've got work to do, so I'm going to let it go. For now."

I sat back on my knees and looked over my shoulder before continuing, voice low. "I can't write a story, Stef. Words dry up, or they don't come at all. But I . . . I need you to help me find that voice you were so certain I'd find.

"Not for me. It's for Lump. You owe him, you know, since he looked out for me in those cells. Lost as he was, he fought those Raven bastards more than once when they tried to slap me around." I blinked through the burn of tears. "He's looking out for me now that you're gone."

I followed a vein of crystals in one of the stones with my finger, gathering my thoughts. "I need your help because dreams . . . dreams like he's having, they're not the good kind." My stomach flipped. "I'd know since I have wicked dreams much the same. Dreams of the past, but not my past. Other fate workers."

Since the battle in the Southern Isles, my mind would drift through moments of the past, as though I were looking through the eyes of another; I would dream of moments where storytellers helped bring us to this moment.

After discovering my father's broken court, it was simple to assume seidr spread throughout the shattered kingdoms.

I was grateful to those past storytellers, grateful for their words. They spoke to me, helped me strengthen my own tales.

When I was a captive in the North, I'd even found an old tale, like it had called to me, and twisted the story of a cursed beast to find a kind-hearted royal. Some whisper in the shadows of those grimy Ravenspire cells told me simple alterations to a handful of fated curses would begin a tale of hope and kind worlds.

"A whisper told me I could do it," I told the stones. "In the cells with Lump, whispers told me I could change some words and write a new tale for my Cursed King and Kind Heart. Now, I'm dreaming of the storyteller who cursed the North. The one the Ice King slit to pieces. It's so real, Stef."

More unnerving was finding the written tales of the past story-tellers amidst my dead father's scrolls of heart songs.

Ari told me Valen's curse, the same words I'd seen and twisted in the North, had been placed with a stack of other tales. Tales that drew the Nightrender toward a smuggler vowed with a lie taster. Tales where a memory thief found a glass ring. A tale of a raven finding the man who warmed her heart.

Why, then, was I dreaming of those tales?

Time runs short. Like the wind heard my thoughts, a new whisper carried over the burial grounds, lifting the hair on the back of my neck.

I whipped around, searching for the voice. Nothing but shadows and ghosts greeted me.

The familiar sensation of the presence of another spurred me to move swifter. From my jacket pocket, I removed a battered goose quill and a small vial of ink. In the other pocket was a tattered bit of parchment.

"I'm ready, Stef. Tell my daj I need his voice one more time. Just once more, to protect Lump and his family."

To protect all my royals and thieves. Pressure gathered in my chest. I couldn't lose any of them. I wouldn't.

"I don't know what's coming," I whispered to the night, "but it feels like it's only a matter of time before it all falls apart again."

I closed my eyes, waiting. I could see the desire of my heart—Sol, Tor, Alek, living long lives for a thousand turns—but the burn never came to my blood.

A distant melody hummed through my heart, a sound like satin. But it was like reaching through a block of thick ice; I couldn't break through to claim it.

Take my song. It was always yours. Time runs short.

My heart went still in my chest. I tracked the trees again. "Daj?"

My father's power was my inheritance to use until I was ready . . . for my own voice to take hold. It was what Stefan—Annon—had said in the final moments, when he'd told me I was ready to find my own strength.

Whatever power I had was failing me, and I needed my father's seidr. Anything that was left in this soil, I needed it now.

I blew out a long breath and wrote a single word: *safe*.

My shoulders slumped. The fire in my blood when words of seidr flowed was empty, and all I could conjure was my own silent plea to the Norns that all my royals would be safe. I did not want to speak to any more burial rocks.

With care, I folded the parchment up and returned the quill and small ink vial to my pockets.

I sighed and leaned against one side of Stefan's marker. "I wish I could ask you what it's like in the hall of the gods. Did my daj meet you like he promised?"

He'd assured us all as he died, to greet his king in the great hall was his only desire. To fall for House Ode.

"Could've given up a few more secrets," I said, voice rough. "If you care to know."

The plot of land was silent. It was always silent.

"Stef," I whispered. "Something is changing here, inside me. I'm . . . fading. It's like I'm pulled somewhere else day after day." I tilted my head to the red moon. "Death at crimson night. Here you thought you were the only one who'd get the honor of dying some fated death."

I stepped back from the burial mound. "Truth is, Stef, I think it's come again. But this time, it's come for me."

CHAPTER 7
THE STORYTELLER

I LEFT THE BURIAL GROUND MORE DESPONDENT THAN BEFORE. WORDS wouldn't come, and I didn't understand why. There was a heaviness in the air. A sense that the time for quiet unknowns was at an end.

That damn battle lord sod, he'd been gone all this time and was still breaking me to pieces bit by bit. My seidr had left me. I hadn't wanted it to begin with, and now it had the gall to dry up.

I needed to protect my royals. I needed to see to it Sol remained happy and alive before it was too late.

From the pocket of my trousers, I slowly withdrew the folded parchment I always kept with me. Hot, scorching pain split through my chest whenever I read the words of the missive. A missive that had been mysteriously placed upon my pillow the night the blood moon returned. Ten turns after the battle lord disappeared.

It had appeared the same as those dark roses I'd always found outside my door, or on my pillow.

I used one knuckle to swipe away another tear, reading the final line of his note haunted me:

Now is the time to restore that bond, lost so many turns ago. You are ready as he said you would be.

39

A lost bond. For a time, I'd fought mightily to convince myself the bond spoken of by my father, by Annon, by everyone, spoke of me and Saga. Aunt and niece restored as the last surviving members of House Ode.

In truth, I hadn't believed that for turns.

There was a truth I didn't want to face, one I buried beneath fear, heavy enough it might snap my spine if I let it—I wasn't alone here.

I simply hadn't determined if my ghostly spectral was friend or foe. All I knew was it wanted me. A bond, a feeling somewhere deep inside, wanted me to find secrets in the darkness that had become my existence.

"Will it help him?" I asked the wind. "Will it help Sol if I give in to the shadows?"

The wind didn't answer.

How could it? I'd been stacking walls against any glimmer of fate, any hint of my Whisper that had guided my words for so long, since I'd watched Davorin slither away into the sea.

Now it felt as though I stood on a damn precipice, peering over two different ledges. One would lead me forward, a bold move that might keep my bleeding royals safe if I but dug into the call to something frightening, something dark inside me. The other was muddled in fear and inaction. A choice where I remained stagnate and let my existence continue to fade.

A feeling, sharp and harsh, took hold deep in my gut. I crunched the parchment in my hand, eyes closed. "I want to find what was lost. This bond of fate that is missing, show it to me if it will protect them. If it saves them."

I didn't know if the words meant anything, or if I simply looked a little mad standing by the gates of a burial ground, speaking to the darkness. In another heartbeat, hot blood rushed through my veins; it raced my pulse.

The wind carried a whisper, low and deep, and wrapped around me in a cold gust. *Finally, the wait is at an end.*

I shuddered. The air was musky and damp, almost heavy, but nothing had visibly changed. I hugged my middle as foreboding settled over my shoulders, bending my spine with the fear I might've caused something dreadful with my damn plea.

"Cal, you all right?" Cuyler crossed into the burial ground and came to my side.

I forced a smile. "Fine. Stefan was closed-lipped as usual."

Cuyler smiled, but it was tight. He knew I mourned my brother, but like the others, he honored Annon as a fallen hero.

While they honored him each turn with ale and war tales, I cried myself to sleep.

"We ought to head back." His pale eyes locked on the sky once more.

Emotions were thick in my throat, but I took time to study Cuyler. Almost commit him to memory.

As the heir of the blood court in the South, he had characteristics of the blood fae folk. Some were frightening with fangs or yellow eyes. Cuyler had neither. He was uniquely handsome. Dusky, golden hair braided off his face, and wavy down to his shoulders. Skin that looked like twilight. Gray hued, with a touch of bronze to color his cheeks. His eyes were pale as frosts with small pupils that never dilated, only constricted when his moods changed.

"What's on my face?" Cuyler watched me with a furrowed stare.

Gods, I'd been gawking like a brainless sod. "Nothing." I chuckled, praying to the skies that my face didn't give up the heat in my cheeks. "I'm out of sorts tonight."

He dipped his chin and rested a palm on the small of my back. "Let us get the lady home."

"I'm not out of sorts enough not to stab you for addressing me so abhorrently."

His laugh was deep and rolling, a sound I'd come to cherish. It meant life was easy; worries could rest for a moment.

A grin cut over my face; the levity distracted me enough my toe caught on a jutting root. I let out a shriek, spilling forward, but Cuyler caught me around the waist. This close, our noses nearly touched. I could see the small bristles of whiskers on his chin, the splatter of faint bronze freckles over his straight nose.

His small pupils tightened. "Um, all right, Cal?"

No, I bleeding wasn't. His touch spurred something inside me. Phantoms danced in my skull, shadows of moments of some unknown memory. Moments of holding a rough hand with childish fingers. Of trying to keep up with lanky legs. Of laughing when a boyish voice cracked in pitchy squeaks from a changing tone.

Moments where I was safe, and my heart burned with . . . something.

Not moments of Cuyler, but his touch left me alight with the yearning to experience it again.

I swallowed. "I'm . . . fine. I'm just clumsy, Cuy. You ought to know by now."

"True."

Gods, his voice was a smooth rasp, dripping in a dark kind of desire.

Or was it someone else's voice spinning in my mind? Bleeding hells, madness was taking hold. That was the only explanation. Ghosts and memories were transforming my guard, my friend, into something else. Like my heart was wildly seeking that touch, that presence I'd once had.

I was a bleeding fool, and my Raven Queen would mock me for days if she knew I was thinking these thoughts, if she knew heat was blooming in the lowest parts of my belly.

I'd warned her that whenever fated royals rolled into bed, wars began.

Here I was with a sky that looked like blood, some ghostly memories of a love I didn't know, and all I could think of was some faceless man's hands on my body. Cuyler would be utterly horrified if he knew the torment his innocent touch had unleashed.

Gods, I'd never even *kissed* a man. Certainly never touched a man. *Find your bond.*

No sooner than I allowed the thought to scrape through my brain, a shrill, anguished scream rose over Raven Row.

CHAPTER 8
THE STORYTELLER

CUYLER WASTED NO TIME AND UNSHEATHED A DAGGER. HE FLICKED HIS EYES to my boot, a silent command that I needed to do the same. The knife from a small ankle sheath was in my grip in another breath.

We abandoned the burial grounds and cut through the sickly wood back to the main road of the Row. The faint hint of woodsmoke grew, though I saw no fires nearby, no stoves.

"Calista." Cuyler took hold of my arm and aimed me toward my tenement.

A shock, the kind that stopped the heart, rammed into my chest. Blood fae watchers muttered curses and surrounded me on either side. The people of the Row were silent. Almost as though they'd known this would happen all along.

Near the shoreline, perhaps fifty paces from my crooked, debauchery-ruined building, a stone torch spluttered with a flame, black as a starless sky.

"No." My knees went weak. *My family*. They were under attack. Thoughts tumbled in my skull. Their faces slid into my consciousness, one after the other. Ari and Saga, they would be frantic. Little Mira. Was she properly hidden in those troll burrows her father had spent turns designing?

43

The twin terrors of the East. They always wanted to be at their father's side. Would they use their unmatched skill with those damn whalebone picks I'd gifted them and chase after the Shadow King and Queen? Would they fall?

My Kind Heart. My Cursed King. Tears blurred my eyes. They'd all fought so damn desperately for love, for peace. What would happen to them now? My final thoughts settled on my Sun Prince. His missive, still in my pocket, burned like hot coals.

He'd sensed danger. No. I wouldn't let this be when his nightmares came to pass. He wasn't going to lose Torsten. He wouldn't lose his son.

Heat scorched through my veins, from rage or fear, it didn't matter. I wanted blood. I wanted bones. I wanted death for anyone who dared lift blades against my damn royals. Every surface of my skin ached in heat.

"Act, or take the blade to our throats yourself."

I knew that voice. "Olaf?"

The old aleman pinched a brown pipe between his teeth and scrubbed a dirty cloth in a drinking horn. He was slender and bony like the weakling trees in the burial grounds, but his beard struck his belly and was beaded in bone beads the Rave warriors of my past once used.

I didn't think he cared much for drying the horn, more he used it to keep his hands busy while he sneered at me. The bastard valued Stefan, and had always been kind. Now he looked utterly murderous.

"The end has come to us. Shall we greet the gods, little one, or do you prove whose blood runs in your veins?"

"How do you know?" My voice was shrill, desperate, but I didn't understand. I'd learned the truth of my bloodline ten turns ago, but I'd never told anyone in Raven Row. I didn't want trouble from the Mad King, or any foolish bastards who thought I had some royal treasury hidden in my tenement.

Olaf pointed at the bloody moon. "All tales must come to an end; ours comes now."

At his word, the air grew icy and harsh. Gooseflesh prickled on my arms. Across the horizon, inky ribbons of dark skated across the sea. Violent tides tossed about like a stagnate wave, but through the shadows appeared the shape of different ships and vessels. Sharp bows, jagged hulls. Endless, tattered sails of blood red.

On the sea, I could see the ships I'd once been forced upon before. Dark clouds gathered in an angry storm, concealing the vessels from sight until I wondered if I'd imagined it all, until through the darkness I saw his eyes. A silhouette in the storm, but the massive spectral emerging to the surface was undeniable—Davorin was returning. He'd taken refuge in the sea, no mistake, amongst those damn sea fae, and now emerged stronger than before, new armies at his back.

Bleeding gods.

"Cuyler, do you see that?"

"See what?" Cuyler was gawking at the flame.

How the hells could he not see a damn sea army approaching?

A swift gust of wind pummeled against me. I closed my eyes, bracing, but another burst knocked me backward. What the hells was happening?

I tried to cry out for Cuyler, but my voice was swallowed in the storm. I tried to open my eyes, but dust and pebbles and bits of dried leaves beat at my skin. The whole of my Raven Row seemed to be turning against me. I could hardly stand in the torrent, how the hells was I supposed to fight an army?

The people of Raven Row knew how to lift bottles of ale, not blades. They'd be slaughtered. But there was little choice left. I would stand here, I'd fight for vengeance. For the pain of the North, the corruption of the East, for the secrets of the South. I'd fight for Stefan and the life he lost.

The wind worsened. I screamed, but sound was robbed away. The abuse lessened with each step I took away from the sea, as though the storm was beating me deeper into Raven Row. I needed to stop this. I needed to flee whatever power was taking hold here.

Sing. A low, rumbling whisper filled my head.

Sing? On the shore of the fae isles when Davorin was reaching his grimy fingers for my throat, I'd nearly burst to bloody pieces when

45

my seidr erupted, not in mere words, but in a melody with a tune, a voice, behind my power that no one seemed to hear but me.

It was happening again. The same power built as though a flame were trapped, yearning to burst skyward.

I let the tune shape in my head, in my heart, until the song roved over me like warm honey. Two simple words I somehow knew would flow beautifully with the sad melody. *Be still.*

I flung my arms out to the sides and the heat from my blood scattered across the shoreline. A phantom tune echoed after it, like a voice carried on the boom of thunder. A blast of power whipped my pale hair around my face until I thought I might have lash marks over my cheeks.

When it eased, I glanced at the water. Peaceful, calm seas were all that greeted me. No army. No ghostly shadows of Davorin, but the Row was quiet. Eerily so.

My mouth parted at the sight. The people who'd been racing for their shacks at the sight of the black flame not moments before, were . . . still. As though they were sleeping on their feet, not frozen in place, merely unmoving.

"Cuyler?" I scrambled back to my feet and inspected my friend. His eyes were closed. His blades had fallen from his grip, and like the others, he was still.

What was happening?

Wind gathered again. It beat against me without mercy. I cried out when sand and water stung my eyes, and gust after relentless gust forced me back from the water's edge.

"Cuyler!" I cried his name.

He was unmoving, as though asleep on his feet, the same as everyone. What had I done?

Wood splintered when the ground shook again. I screamed as rotted beams peeled off a nearby trade shack, nearly striking my head. More wind. More chaos. The buildings seemed to groan and creak, swaying side to side.

By the gods, something was devouring Raven Row. I fought to remain by Cuyler and his men. I couldn't leave them so exposed and vulnerable.

Then sing with me, Little Rose.

"Who are you!" I screamed.

The whisper didn't respond.

"Godsdammit!" I reeled away, shielding my face, when a slat from a nearby rooftop broke free and the rusted nails still in the board nearly impaled my eye. The wind shoved me back, deeper into the Row.

When I couldn't catch a breath against the flurry, I was forced to turn. I was forced to run.

My feet skidded over the mud. Blood raced in my skull. I didn't look back, my gaze kept forward, desperate to find refuge long enough to hide, to think, to plan. To bleeding save the folk of my home from an attack I didn't know how to stop.

Darkness coated Raven Row in thick waves. Blood pounded in my head. I couldn't see a damn thing. Only a spinning maelstrom of dust and faint whispers.

I quickened my pace, desperate to find anyone. In the distance, dull light broke through the night devouring the roads and rooftops. Iron gates flung open at the end of the road, as though beckoning me inside. Darkness lived beyond, soaking spindly trees and thatched rooftops in cold night. There wasn't another choice; I took the leap.

The knife slid out of my grip as I lunged through the gates of Hus Rose, the lands of the Mad King.

Face down in the long grass, I trembled and fought to draw in a deep enough breath. Groans and creaks came at my back. I whipped around in the same moment the heavy iron gates clanged shut.

I scrambled to my feet and curled my fingers around the bars of the gates, rattling them. A rush of panic took hold of my throat when they didn't budge. Godsdammit, they were locked. I kicked at the gates once more, then an unnerving realization struck. With a slow turn, I looked back at Raven Row. The whole bleeding place had fallen into an empty, ghostly calm.

Where was the damn storm that had been raging through the grime moments ago? Where were the cracked windows, the debris, the sprays of wild sea?

A haunting hum flowed like velvet over the grounds. A somber voice that frightened me and softened the fear in my blood in the same breath. Like a damn hook to my chest, it tugged me forward with that first step. Buried deep in the back of my mind, heady trepidation grew. Warnings to keep back, to find a way out, flared like an instinct. But I could not halt my stride. I couldn't turn back, too consumed by the mystery and unknowns.

My heart kept me walking deeper into the grounds, while my mind pleaded with me to flee.

Shadows spiraled around cracked stone pillars, a few crumbling statues, as though stone sentinels once stood watch here. Mist and tangled ivy swirled over cobblestone pathways like moving water. The grounds were different than the grime, soot, and reek of Raven Row. This was as though I'd stepped into a new world.

A dream.

I didn't blink, didn't breathe, and with every step the voice strengthened. I dipped my head beneath a few low-hanging branches onto a covered pathway. Tangled boughs shaped the archway overhead, and along the edges were black tallow candles lighting the way.

"Hello?"

A whistle of wind responded. I wasn't a fool. To seek out the haunting spectral meant my world would change when I came to the other side. I'd told this to my bleeding queens more than once. Follow the nudge of fate, it was bound to upend their worlds. Did they listen? Not a damn one.

I'd always told myself I'd never be the reckless one. I'd never blindly go where my path unfolded. Like a constant thorn in the sides of the Norns, I planned to resist. To refuse.

Perhaps I owed my queens a bit of grace. In this moment, the desire to taunt fate with my refusals waned, and I yearned to follow the call forward. Warm as fire in the frosts, soothing as berry teas on the throat, I craved to discover whatever awaited me at the end of this path. I closed my eyes, pausing for a moment, simply reveling in the calm.

Some sort of tricky power must've soaked the soil of Hus Rose, for I could not recall the last time my pulse was so . . . peaceful. Like returning home to kind words and gentle, loving arms.

The longer I walked, the more the mist thinned and revealed a sprawling world of unseen darkness. Rune totems were broken. Trees were bare. Across the gray soil, dried leaves covered brittle stems of dying flowers.

Beauty once lived here. Through the somberness, I could see a world that might've been.

My fingertips were numb from the lingering gusts of wind by the time the pathway opened at the base of a wide staircase. My insides overturned. Hus Rose was deceptively large. From this angle of the grounds, the palace was like a dark beast. Black stone made up the walls, and across every arched window, dark drapes shielded the inner walls from the outside.

Iron sconces held torches as the only light, and I froze in place when two arched doors creaked, then swept over the landing at the top of the staircase.

Cast in a touch of gold from the torches, a figure emerged. Tall and imposing, the silhouette was masculine with strong shoulders. I licked my lips when the shadow paused before his full form became clear. A fleeting concern that Davorin had found me kept me quiet for a few breaths. But he didn't feel like Davorin.

He felt . . . familiar.

"Who are you?"

No words, merely a deep, raspy laugh answered. A sound I absorbed to my bones, to the damn marrow. Such a simple thing, but it pulled me a step closer.

The way he stood, he was still concealed enough I couldn't make him out fully. Truth be told, it was as though he strategically hid his features out of sight.

"Will you show yourself?"

"Show myself, she says." He laughed again, his long legs paced in the darkness, the eerie moon casting a bloody outline of his body. "Why should I when you have run from me all this time?"

Run from him? He was on the grounds of Hus Rose. I had to be speaking to the Mad King.

"Do you know what it's like?" His voice was gritty, unkind, yet flowed over my skin like a forgotten memory, as though my blood could not help but heat under the rough, burdened tone.

The sound burned through my veins like a rush of new blood, awakening some dormant light that radiated to my damn soul. I knew this voice. A voice that voice aided me in writing the steps to wake my Golden King from a fae sleep. A feat I couldn't do alone.

Like a fool willingly walking toward slaughter, I took a step closer. "Whisper?"

"Do you know what it's like?" he asked again, low and distant, like he hadn't meant to speak.

This couldn't be a dream. It was too tangible. Even his scent was real, a tantalizing combination of woodsmoke and mist.

In my cell at Castle Ravenspire, I'd always pretended the voice of the whispers in the dark belonged to another being, someone who might understand the burden of using seidr. A friend in the madness.

But I'd long ago convinced myself the words were mine alone; the way I'd convinced myself the spectral in Ari's dream hadn't existed, not really.

Until now.

CHAPTER 9
THE STORYTELLER

"ARE YOU THE KING?" MY VOICE CROAKED. "SOMETHING IS HAPPENING TO the Row, and I think . . . I think a dark fae is returning. I've faced him before, and he's a fiend, a creature. He'll take the whole of the kingdom."

"What happens is an unavoidable consequence of wasted time."

"No." I didn't care if this fool was the king, I was going to throttle him. "People I care for are out there, trapped and facing this alone, you—"

"There is no going back. It is too late. You've crossed a bridge, now watch it burn."

My heart stilled. "No. You cannot keep me here. Our people need help."

"Yes." He let the word drag over his tongue. "We helped them."

"What?"

"We have been given time." He swung his hand in the shadows. "A final *flicker* of hope and a moment of pause to see if a bond has been neglected for too long."

Find the first bond. I swallowed past a knot. "They're . . . time is standing still?"

"Time goes on," he said. "The people have gone still. For now. Will you accept the bond you have tried to forget?"

"I-I-I don't know what you're talking about."

He chuckled darkly. "When did lies come from your tongue?"

The first bond. A tale of golden light tethering two voices, two children, as they shattered a world. This couldn't . . . it couldn't be.

I tilted my head. The Mad King stood before me, yet . . . he was more. He meant something more, and I felt as though I'd suffocate if I didn't find out why. Another step placed me on the stairs. He kept to the shadows, but one hand flexed at his side. Perhaps my nearness caused him as much disquiet as he caused in me.

"Do you use seidr?" I asked. He said nothing. "Look, show yourself."

A long pause settled, then, "Will you run, Little Rose?"

Little Rose. The name was a memory, a past title my heart wanted to love, but my mind wanted to bury beneath fear.

I rolled back my shoulders. "I won't run."

Gods, I wanted to flee more than anything.

He hummed in derision. "Every story must end. Ours is fading, and it will not end in our favor."

"Our story?"

Shadows shifted and he stepped out of his hidden corner. My insides tightened in anticipation. Tanned skin and dark eyes peeled through the haze. Dressed all in black, he was tall and breathtaking in a haunting way. His jaw was made of sharp edges, and a black mask that coated one side of his face from view.

So familiar, yet so different.

Without a word, he descended the staircase. Two paces from me, his dark eyes swallowed me whole. They weren't soft eyes. A color like stone stained with rain, but buried in the dark shade was something like desperation.

Every muscle in his strong body seemed to tremble as he held out a gloved hand.

I dropped my chin, ashamed of the fear he'd surely see.

"*Look* at me," he snapped. I jolted and held his unwavering stare. "You've passed over a point from which you cannot return. I won't let you go, not now. Our world is about to burn, and I will not watch it take you."

Fear lanced through me. After surviving the North, I vowed I'd never be trapped again. Panic wanted to build, but my pulse slowed when the soft leather of his glove cupped one side of my face, almost tenderly.

Where I wanted to run moments before, all at once my body fell into a strange sort of trance, so calm, so at ease. It took conscious thought to keep from leaning into him.

"Don't run from the truth, Little Rose," he whispered.

A boy's voice fluttered through my head. *Sing with me, Little Rose. You have the words.*

Words from visions of the dream walk of my Golden King. No. This was wrong, dangerous. I conjured the Wraith from Ari's dreams as a figment, a phantom guide on behalf of myself since I could not be there with him. He wasn't real. Those memories were mine alone. I sang the songs as the child of Riot Ode, there hadn't . . . there hadn't been a boy.

I looked to the masked stranger again. Beneath the dark shade in his eyes was a look of the lost, the forgotten, the tormented. There was a plea buried beneath the shadows. As though silently begging for me to take hold, to not turn away again.

My fingers trembled as I reached for his hand on my face. The moment my palm touched the smooth leather of his gloves, memories seemed to burst like a new bloom in my mind.

Running through blood rose shrubs, giggling. Hiding beneath covered tables in Daj's study. Feeding goats in the stables. Falling asleep on the warm grass on the back lawns to the soft hum of a voice. A boy's voice. Days, memories, moments, whatever the hells they were, bloomed through my mind, bright and clear.

"Silas." His name was not a question, but a statement of familiarity. I knew him.

The dark mask on my phantom's face shifted when his mouth curled into a sneer. He yanked me against his chest. He dipped his face close. "Never forget again."

I couldn't draw in a deep enough breath when his arm encircled my waist. How could something feel so safe and so dangerous in the same moment? "Don't forget what?"

"That you belong to me."

CHAPTER 10
THE PHANTOM

W<small>ITHOUT ANOTHER WORD</small>, I <small>SLIPPED MY FINGERS THROUGH HERS IN AN</small> unforgiving grip, and pulled us up the stairs toward the palace. Untouched for countless turns, to feel the weight of another in my palm was foreign and unsettling.

Here. She was finally *here*. A thousand untamed thoughts tumbled in a maelstrom through my mind, but all led back to that single truth—my voice, my rose, was alive and breathing.

Every few paces up the steps, I'd turn over my shoulder, all to ensure I hadn't conjured her through dreary illusions and cruel dreams again.

"I . . . there are people I care for out there. They'll be safe?"

"You gave the words," I said, curious if she'd recall how our voices once entwined. "I sealed the fate song. *Be still*. A swift thought. Though, I do not know how long we will have before it fades."

"That was your voice." She didn't ask it as a question. It was more a realization.

Calista's face contorted into a painful wince. She slowed her steps, resisting slightly, as though seeking an opportunity to flee. It wasn't a secret to me that she feared losing her own autonomy to choose her fate.

In truth, the sense of destiny was heady. But she still had the power. She could run. She could deny me. It could all be over. The thought of it made me taste bile in my throat. For lifetimes I'd imagined her smile, her touch. I'd imagined the way she'd draw close, as lost in me as I'd become in her.

It seemed reality was not like lonely dreams.

Calista's arm was stretched fully. True, her hand was clasped in mine, but she made certain to keep as great a distance between us as possible. Her breaths were sharp. The kind of breaths she made when she was afraid and didn't want it to show.

I'd heard those breaths. Memorized them. Ached to ease them. Now, they came at the sight of me.

Darkness gripped me somewhere deep inside, a tangle of anger and despair. This wasn't how it was meant to be. To her, I was not supposed to be the monster in the dark.

Could she not sense the lengths I would go for her? The lengths I had gone?

At the top of the staircase, her gaze met mine, fierce like a thrashing sea. She tugged back on my hand. I spun around, prepared to toss her over my damn shoulder if it meant she stayed close a little longer, but met the touch of her ink-stained fingers instead. Dainty fingers. Slender, callused. I wanted to touch them, wanted to study each divot, every spiral of the skin on the tips.

My blood went cold when she gently traced the ridge of the black satin mask. On instinct, I drew back.

Forget what you see on the surface. See me.

"It's really you," she whispered. "What did he do to you? Was it true what happened in my Golden King's dream?"

Gods-awful pity burned in her eyes. She saw the poison of this mask, this unfeeling memory of all that was lost to me that night. It was all she saw.

"Will you let me see?" Her thumb tucked under the lip of the mask,

I snatched hold of her wrist. "*Don't.*"

"Sorry." She shrunk away, a wilting bud against the frosts, and followed me in silence through the palace doors.

Jagged angles made the entryway uninviting and formidable, but Calista lifted her gaze, gawking as I dragged her inside. Beasts with gaping maws reared over the edges from the corners, a sort of collision of the dark wolf, Fenrir, and the sea serpent, Jormungandr. I opened the door and led her inside.

When a gust of wind slammed the door behind us, Calista leaned closer. Another foreign sensation that set the skin on my arms ablaze and gathered puzzling fog inside my skull. Reality had long since been clear, but her touch, her scent of sharp ink, of birch parchment, and the faint, sweet petals of roses blurred my senses even more.

Almost as soon as she'd stepped into me, she took note of how close we'd come and positioned her body a pace away.

I left her in the circular entryway and struck a matchstick, lighting a tallow candle.

A curve teased the corner of her mouth as she took in the domed ceiling, the pale walls, as she traced the drawings scattered across them. Some were faded after turns, but the shapes were still obvious and childish from the hand of a boy who'd been left to cruel solitude.

I'd long ago ceased marking the walls to pass the time. Still, a knot of apprehension built in my chest as she strode along one of the walls and touched the leaves of blood roses and the faces buried in the brambles. The children wrapped in the vines and petals were laughing. Her shoulder flinched, as though she wanted to look over it to where I stood at her back, but thought better of it.

Clearing her throat, she moved on and touched wings on ravens in flight. She paused at the shadows coiled around a man's face, his eyes were hateful and dark, his lips were contorted into a sneer. The night was devouring him.

"It looks like him," she whispered. "Still haven't thought of his name yet. He deserves to be called something you think of when you take a piss, you know?"

So long speaking with ghosts that didn't always reply, it took me a moment to realize she'd pointed her question at me. "Sráč."

One of her brows arched. "What?"

"Sráč. That's what I call him."

Her full bottom lip slid between her teeth. "That's old language."

"I am old."

Bleeding gods, for the slightest moment, her eyes brightened more than they feared. "It means *shit*."

Her face twisted in a strange expression. I considered she might retch, until a frightening sound scraped from the back of her throat. Light, dry as though she could do for a bit of water, and intoxicating.

She laughed.

Here. In my sights. A laugh that hadn't been mine for centuries. It was beautiful and grating all in one breath. When I was too still for too long, the light in her eyes faded with her smile.

She turned back to the drawings on the wall. "It'll do for now. But mark me, there is a better name out there."

Across the flat panels she took in bits and pieces of the drawings of our fallen world. Trees and the stables where we'd run free. Forest burrows where trolls had always gathered. Stones and pebbles. Flying insects with long, slender bodies and furred legs.

Calista paused when she got to the man with bright eyes, a few scars on his sun-weathered face, and a beard braided in rune beads.

She clutched her chest when she flattened her palm over the smoking herb roll between his teeth.

"Annon," she whispered and looked at me as though needing an explanation.

What did she want me to say? Captain Annon had been my last connection to life. He'd delivered my roses. He'd done all he could to guide Calista Ode toward her path. He'd been the last breathing soul to step foot behind the gates, all to see to it I hadn't descended so far down into the shadows that I couldn't escape.

"Why do you have his likeness here?"

Odd question. "It is obvious."

Tears glistened in her eyes. "It isn't. So explain it to me."

"I missed him."

Her lips parted. The scrutiny was unnerving. A thousand prickling things seemed to traipse up my arms, my face, down the front of my tunic. For the first time since gaining her touch once more, I yearned—craved—to fade away into the unseen corners.

"Come." I took hold of her wrist again and pulled her up a curved staircase to the upper levels. "I'll show you to your room."

"My room?"

I didn't think I needed to repeat myself.

"Wait." She tugged against me. "Silas, what room?"

"Yours, as I said." I balked and took the stairs two at a time. "I do not recall you being so dense, Little Rose."

A huff followed. She tried to shirk off my grip. I was stronger.

"I'm not dense, you bleeding sod. You've said no more than ten words to me, and—"

"Then you haven't been listening," I interjected. "I have spoken many words to you, for many turns."

"In the shadows. Like a coward."

A sharp bite of anger throttled me from behind. In the next moment I had her back pinned to the wall, her heaving chest against mine.

"A coward?" My teeth ground together. "Which of us has denied the call to their fated path over and over again? Which of us chooses to unsee the signs of truth?"

This close, I couldn't keep back, and dragged my nose alongside her throat. The soft fabric over the hard shell of my mask slid across her skin. She stiffened and closed her eyes, chin lifted.

"You've ignored the call, Little Rose. Forgotten truths. You'll soon remember it all now that you are here. I'll keep you safe from whatever is to come. He won't find you." I did my best to give her a reassuring smile, but no doubt it was more a sneer than anything.

I tugged on her hand again, taking us up the stairs. The palace was a labyrinth of levels and chambers, and strategically warded against the sráč. I'd tended to each eave, each corridor, for the whole of this dreary existence.

Songs of protection, of misdirection, lived in this palace.

She'd be safe here. The Norns might have plans to destroy our world, but they would not touch her again. I'd already survived enough heartbreak when it came to this bleeding woman. I wouldn't do it again.

"You can't keep me prisoner," she whispered. "There are people I love out there. Who love me. I won't hide away in here."

In her eyes was a collision of unease, frustration, and a slow burning flame under it all. The power from which she hid, her strength, her words. A pull she wanted to avoid. I didn't understand it. In the past, she'd taken hold of her fate without questioning. As though she trusted the whisper more than she did in this moment.

Why did she resist me now? How could she ignore this *raging* fire in the soul?

"There's no use resisting, Little Rose, our bloody games have come to an end at last. There's no going back."

"You cannot force me to do anything." Her mouth set in a firm line.

This was all wrong. The king promised me our bond was fierce and powerful. If it was so, how could she shove it aside and degrade it in such a way? What the hells was the point of all this anguish?

One hand trembled as I curled a fist at my side. With my other hand, I opened one of the numerous chamber doors. "Yours."

I shoved against Calista's shoulder, urging her inside.

"Wait, no." She grabbed onto the wooden frame. "You take me, and there are kings and queens who will bring war to your gates."

"They are already in war. No backward glances. This—" I jabbed a finger toward my face, "is what you see now."

It shouldn't have ached so fiercely, but when she flinched, it was a knife to the chest. "You can't trap me. You can't, Silas. *Please.* I beg of you."

She needed to sleep. Then she'd be more clearheaded. I began to close the door, but she slammed her boot between the door and the jamb.

"No! There is something coming. I saw it in the water. He's returning."

I froze. "You're certain you saw *him*?"

Calista nodded. "In the storm, I saw his face. I saw . . . ships with his armies."

Slowly, I reached out a palm and rested it on her cheek. She didn't stiffen, even seemed to find a touch of comfort. "Then you are no longer safe outside these walls."

I closed the door swiftly, locking the knob.

"Silas!" She kicked the wood, rattled the latch. "You bastard, let me go. Let me go. I cannot stay here. I will never choose a captor. You cannot force my hand, you cannot . . ."

Her words cracked and died. The slide of her body down the door and soft, breathy sobs charred another piece of my heart.

It was for her good. I peeled off the mask when the pressure of it caused the scarred skin to ache and burn. One palm on her door, I hummed, low and steady. Power was scarce in the darkness, but I hoped to have enough to bring a bit of rest to her burdens.

My song had always been hers, should she only take it.

It took a moment before the sobs ceased and a gentle thud came from behind the door. Perhaps I could not twist the tales of fate without her, but I could still bring her to a calm. A talent I'd always had, one I'd take gladly. The more her resistance had grown, the more I'd needed to reach her in the calm moments of her mind, and I'd done it through dreams.

Another gift I carried, and the ingenuity behind the Golden King's dream walk. I didn't want to dream walk when I could touch her, speak to her, but I would if that was all she'd allow. I'd give her the rest she needed, and cling to the hope when she woke, she'd see reason.

My pace was swift through the labyrinth of rooms and chambers on the upper level until I slipped into the largest of them all. I slammed the door behind me and rushed to the window.

Red moonlight lit the fortress shores. Already the shift was beginning. Tenements stood straighter. Rotting laths were peeling back to reveal stone beneath it. She didn't know what her simple act of walking through the gates had done.

The sea was undisturbed, but on the horizon grew a swell of angry clouds.

Fate was unraveling at the edges, and if Calista Ode did not accept me, if she rejected all we'd been striving to become, then we would not see a new sunrise in a brighter world.

All I wanted was freedom for the both of us, a world with no more night, no more shadows in my mind. But I could not have any of it. For she did not want me in that world.

Only in the darkness of her dreams.

CHAPTER 11
THE STORYTELLER

AN ACHE RAGED BEHIND MY EYES. WITH THE HEEL OF MY HAND, I RUBBED IT away and took in the dim room.

Black satin shades covered windows in a sickeningly large room. I'd spent turns in the palaces of every kingdom, but I had never spent a night in such an ornate chamber. Wooden beams climbed to the rafters and marked every corner of a fur wrapped bed fit for at least four men. Overstuffed down pillows took up half the surface of it.

With a groan, I stood from the floor, rubbing the back of my head. What happened? Hells, I couldn't recall when I'd slept so soundly.

I dragged my fingers over a polished chest of drawers, pausing when I touched the golden handle of a hairbrush. Pieces of golden hair were still tangled in the soft bristles.

I knew this brush. I spun about, wincing as the blood rushed back to the slow ache, and took a second glance at the furnishings. A corner seat near the covered window. The bed, a wardrobe in the corner where . . . where a calming voice had once soothed me.

My pulse quickened. With the toe of my boot, I kicked back a pelt used for a rug. My palm covered my mouth. A few flecks of blood splattered the floorboards. On instinct, my hand went to my throat.

The barest of scars was in my skin. A scar that had only appeared after my return from captivity in the North. I couldn't recall what caused it and brushed it away as some clumsy mistake in my Ravenspire cell.

Until I'd witnessed that brutal night in Ari's dreams.

A mother that held a knife to her child's neck. The way she fought against the darkness overtaking her, as her love and desire to save her child kept the blade from digging in too deep.

The wardrobe was painted in . . . roses. I'd always loved those roses, and often sang, tracing them with my fingers as Maj brushed her hair. My hold on the handle of the hairbrush tightened. A spark of white, burning pain clung to my heart when I hugged it to my chest.

This room once belonged to Riot and Anneli Ode.

Or at least it was made as a replica. Hadn't my parents ruled in the fae isles? Then again, hadn't they shattered the kingdom into bits and pieces?

Ari's dreams never gave up what became of those empty Western seas. My father never said, only made plans with his . . . ward.

The king's ward. The boy.

I remembered the shadows all around me. The opened gates at Hus Rose. I remembered *him*. A man in a mask with smoky storms in the burden of his gaze.

Silas.

And the bastard had locked me in like a common thief. In three strides I reached the door, cursing him under my breath, prepared to kick and claw at the latch until it opened, but on the first forceful shove, the door gave and spilled me into the corridor.

I coughed, face down on a woven runner. Dust and mildew burned my nose as I hurried back to standing.

Knife. Knife. Where was my bleeding knife? I padded my chest and sheaths, recalling I'd dropped any blades before I'd stepped foot in Hus Rose. To live in Raven Row meant one was resourceful when supplies weren't readily available. I turned the hairbrush in my grip, handle out. Might not kill, but it would do damage when shoved into an eye socket.

The new blood moon brought dull light, but it couldn't break through, not in here. Like the bed chamber, dark, musty shades covered windows and an occasional glass mirror. Eerie candlelight painted the walls in dancing shadows.

Somewhere down the hallway a door slammed. "Hello?"

More slams, more groans. I held my breath and peered into the room with the racket. My shoulders slumped in relief. A window had unlatched, and the pane kept striking the latch again and again as the wind tossed it about.

I let out a shuddering chuckle and combed my fingers through my messy braids. I was a damn fool. What if it'd been a sword-wielding madman, and I'd come armed with a hairbrush?

My solitude was interrupted by a sweet, melodic strum of whimsical strings. I'd fought descending into the throes of fate, convinced death greeted me at the end of the tale, but in this moment I didn't resist. I knew that song. I knew who played it. And the bleeding sod wasn't getting off easy for locking me behind damn doors.

Certainly not while he was playing the spritely song he'd always played to get me spinning and giggling as a girl.

The more he pushed, the more I wanted to fight back. Call it a need to have a touch of control over my own destiny after living a life where everyone wanted to snatch it away. No mistake, I yearned for answers to the endless string of questions, but the day my brother died a death he knew was fated to happen, I vowed my destiny would be my own.

The sweet tune led me through corridor after corridor. Turns and twists, like a bleeding labyrinth. The room might've appeared like the one from my childhood, but this part of the palace was unfamiliar. Dark and dangerous—a wolf's lair.

It seemed the deeper I went, the darker it became. Fewer sconces on the walls, heavier drapes on any outer windows, as though blotting out the sun and moonlight had always been the intention.

A small staircase led to an upper landing with a single, arched door. The melody bled from inside. I gripped my hairbrush battle blade and softly padded inside the room. All hells. Clay statues were toppled and cracked. Shredded satin was tossed across stained woven rugs. Rawhide drums, toppled harps and lutes, and scattered pan pipes, dirtied the floor. But in one corner was a long bench, padded in coarse furs. It was placed beside a tall window, drapes pulled aside, and seated atop the furs was Silas.

His face was turned away from me, broad shoulders hunched, and propped in his lap was a tall tagelharpa, a stringed instrument with a horse-hair bow that brought the strings to life with wistful, evocative melodies.

I hadn't seen one played in . . . in truth, I wasn't certain I'd ever seen one in the four kingdoms since—my teeth clenched—since before the brutal end of House Ode.

The hairbrush made a slow descent to my side.

Silas hadn't noticed his solitude had been disturbed. His head moved with each gentle glide of the bow stick. He was my father's ward, no mistake. The boy who'd studied seidr under the tutelage of the fate king was drawn to all music after he'd found his voice.

Saga told me that my daj had been much the same.

My cheek twitched in a reluctant smile. Mornings waking to the sound of lyres or small fife tunes floating through my open window broke through my mind. As though the music unlocked the shadowed memories and brought unexpected light.

All you do is blow your breath in it, Little Rose. Give it a go.

I bit the inside of my cheek, hiding a laugh when I recalled the irritated huff and larger hands snatching the fife out of mine, with a snarly, *You're gods-awful at this and you bleeding slobbered all over the end.*

I winced and pressed the heel of my palm to my skull. Somehow this piece of my life had been hidden. Why, I didn't yet know, but planned to find out.

The draw to Silas was undeniable. Almost unbearable now that I'd crossed the threshold of the palace grounds. What had kept me from doing it all this time? More than fear. Much like the other kingdoms, any curiosity of the Mad King faded swiftly if ever thoughts of him slid into my brain.

Until now. In this moment, the occupant of Hus Rose consumed my every thought. My every breath. It was as if my heart beat coiled with his, needing his nearness.

He was the fate I'd avoided. Deep inside an ember sparked to life. A piece that had always been there, yet locked in shadows. Moments as this, I detested the tricks of the Norns. If after one interaction this draw toward my phantom had reeled me back to him, why was I parted from him at all?

I supposed fear was potent enough to keep me tethered in my dangerous notions that hiding from my fate was better for everyone. Now, I feared I'd waited too long to face it.

Two paces from Silas, I lifted my hand to reach for him. He startled when the tips of my fingers dragged along his shoulder, but he didn't cease his playing. He didn't look at me.

Heat from his skin, his dark tunic, radiated up my arm. It blazed from the inside out, and I wanted more. I wanted to be nearer.

Gently, I roved my hand along the curve of his shoulder, to the side of his neck. His fingers came to a still on the tagelharpa. My hand climbed, lost in the warmth of his skin, the rough stubble on his jaw.

With a sigh, he tilted his head into my palm as I touched his face, the curve of his ear. I wasn't bold, I'd never really craved anyone. Had I wondered about the moans and sighs coming from other tenement rooms? Often. Had Stefan stumbled into our flat more than once with his hair disheveled and bite marks on his neck? Constantly.

I'd balked at the near maddening desire that always lived in the eyes of my royals. The sort of passion and need that drove them to violence to protect their lover was confusing at times.

This burning was new and foreign and frightening. Part of me wanted to dig my claws into Silas's skin so he might never be rid of me. Another piece wanted his larger, stronger body to cover mine; I wanted him to devour me. Then, the final piece wanted to run, scream, and sever whatever this connection was before it could take hold any more.

I dragged my fingernails up the shaved side of his head, touching each tattooed rune mark, then wrapped the longer strands of his hair around my knuckles.

I forgot myself, forgot the need to be wary, and let my brow drop to the back of his head. "Why did you stay hidden from me?"

"It was not by choice." He stiffened. "You are my thoughts that rise with the sun, and my fears that come with the night."

"Your fears?"

"Fear that I will wake and you will once more be gone."

"I don't understand." My hands dropped to his shoulders and I shook my head, still pressed against his. "If you missed Stef—Annon—then, he knew of you."

"It was not as though he wanted to keep secrets. We did not . . . interact. We . . . couldn't."

"Why?" Silas looked away and frustration gathered like a stone in my chest. "Gods, what harm would come from telling me the truth?"

"Why did none of the fated crowns know their truths, Little Rose?"

I considered the question, and despised the answer. "So they would find their true destiny through sheer grit and stubbornness."

A low chuckle rolled from his throat. "I suppose. They had to find their paths. It was part of the story. They had to fight, struggle, they had to cleave to their new power for it to grow as strong as it was always meant to be, or it would be easily taken again."

"So, that's what this is? My fight. I hate to be the bearer of bad news, but I don't have the time." I opened my arm, gesturing to the window. "Don't tell me this moon means nothing. I saw him."

"Yes."

"Then we cannot stay holed away in here." I straightened my shoulders. Thoughts of Sol, Tor, and little Alek ran in my head. Thoughts of Cuyler and his men. Even the odd resentment of Olaf. No more running. "There are those who must be warned of what I saw."

"I cannot watch you take the risk."

My lips parted. "Cannot? Or will not?"

Silas sighed. Gently, he set the instrument aside and turned around on the bench. Hells, he was . . . haunted and beautiful. The way shadows painted contours in the world as the sun sets, secrets lived in the curves of his face, behind the mask he wore, in the shades of his dark eyes.

"These walls are safe," he said briskly. "This is where you'll stay."

Silas rose from the bench, and without a backward glance, he left the room.

Stunned, I opened and closed my mouth more than once before freeing a frustrated shriek that echoed through the corridors.

This was worse than being a captive at Castle Ravenspire, since I wanted to slaughter those guards, but with him I still wanted to reach out and pull him close every time my damn captor showed his masked face.

In his presence, my heart would sing.

In his absence, I thought only of how to get free of him.

CHAPTER 12
THE PHANTOM

WHERE HAD IT GONE WRONG? I'D KEPT MY PROMISES, DONE WHAT WAS asked, and I'd waited. I'd done it, all while the heat of a heart's song burned brighter and brighter.

In her, it had rotted.

Her small words would not hold the darkness on the horizon forever. Not when she did not know her true strength, not when the time to claim the full breadth of her power had passed. I'd been too docile, too subtle, and it had dulled her draw back to the beginning.

I should've been insistent the moment Annon earned his reward and went to dine with the king.

I should've carved out a place in her dreams until she could not resist returning to the first path of fate. The pain in her heart at Annon's loss ached through mine like molten blood.

She'd needed time. She'd needed her folk. I'd waited all this time, and thought I could wait a little longer for the cracks in her bruised heart to heal. In all my misplaced optimism, I'd anticipated for the desire to find me, the damn yearning for the bond, to bleed as fiercely through her as it did me.

My teeth clenched. I slammed a palm against a back door and shoved into the dreary gardens behind the battered palace.

What a reckless fool I'd been. She'd drifted for *turns* after his death, almost hells-bent on avoiding this place, as though the call to return was a plague waiting to claim her. I burned, body and blood, for her. Yet my voice caused nothing but fear and apprehension.

"It's all *wrong*."

Mists wrapped around dark, mangled trees that returned no reply to my cries. No one ever answered.

Garden paths were lined in rune totems carved with sagas and poems and warnings of a past long forgotten. I ducked my head, crossing under a stone arch onto a moss-coated walkway in a shadowed part of the sprawling gardens. In the distance, golden flames sliced through the mist in layers of brilliant red from where torches perched on sconces.

One place shut out the darkness, shut out the endless screams in my head from endless deaths. Tree limbs parted, and the stone and sod mausoleum came into focus. A small mound with deadened grass on the top and river stones shaping the foundation. In one side I'd fashioned a crooked door from old birchwood to keep the sanctuary hidden from the shadows of this damn prison.

I paused at the arched doorway. Roughly carved runes decorated the face. Runes of power and joy, of strength and cunning. They'd long ago started to fade, the same as my hope. With a grunt of frustration, I shoved inside.

One step across the threshold and my shoulders slumped; a wave of relief filled me. Here, it was quiet. Here, I could breathe.

Old shelves were topped with scrolls of parchment. Most had scratchy symbols drawn incorrectly in childish writing. I read one, a practice scroll on how to shape runes and symbols when fate's tales were written.

Three lines were crossed out. Off to the side were a few corrections and a note of encouragement:

Feel it more, Silas. Trust your heart. The song will come.

The tug of a smile built in the corner of my mouth. We'd tried for nearly three turns for seidr to give me words. Until it was obvious my song flowed with the words of another. Still, it hadn't stopped the fate king from teaching me to write, to read, to find peace in music.

You've a gift boy, hone it. Not everything must be about seidr. What makes you sing inside?

I paused at the box of dried blood rose petals. Dark as mahogany and dry as parchment. What made my heart sing? It was her. Even in childhood, when I'd been mocked by other Rave youth for befriending a silly little girl, she'd been the warmest flame.

Calista Ode was my first friend. She took a place in my heart when our souls collided that wretched day. If I'd been wise, I would've sealed up the pain of it all. I would've had a heart of stone. Instead, I left my heart as delicate glass, easily splintered and shattered.

The torch in my hand cast a haunting glow over portraits and paintings from a world long forgotten. Scrolls of old heart songs I'd kept, of inkwells and quills used by the queen to write her prophecies. Never as potent as her daughter, but Queen Anneli had a gift of seeing short distances into a path of fate.

I paused at a dust-coated tapestry with the tale of the fate king's heart song with his queen. Blue and burgundy threads were woven in vines of ivy and rivers and all the beauty of the first kingdom. A lost world. Forgotten through the lifetimes. Threads of gold spun the tale of how a son of seidr found his love match.

A beautiful tale, but even theirs was not the same as this.

This bond is new and strange. Never have I seen seidr use two souls as one. You must cling to it, Silas. Help her find the way back. Such a bond will live until the Otherworld calls.

I lowered to my knees and shook my head. "You were wrong, King.

I am never wrong.

"Ah, but you were." I adjusted the mask over the aching scars on my face. "She took one look at me and made it clear she does not want me."

Stop feeling sorry for yourself.

Bastard. I rolled my eyes. "I will do as I vowed and keep her safe. But there is no happy ending to this tale."

Then you are not trying hard enough.

I let out a sigh and removed the mask to let my skin breathe.

"I have tried," I whispered to the phantoms all around me. "I have tried time and time again. I have nothing more to give, other than seeing to it she does not fall."

"Who are you speaking to?"

My blood went cold. I scrambled for the mask, but froze in a bit of horror when Calista's slender fingers curled around it and lifted it off the ground.

I clapped my palm over the scars and hurried to my feet. My back pressed into the corner of the mausoleum, the shadows like a warm robe.

She tilted her head, glancing first at the half mask, then to me in the darkness. "Who were you talking to, Silas?"

"Ghosts."

I expected her to turn back, to flee from the madness I carried. Perhaps, I expected her to laugh. Calista did none of it, merely nodded her head. "I've done that a time or two. What is this place?"

I didn't answer. She'd already began rummaging about and would figure it out soon enough.

She scanned the shelves, read through some parchment. "Wait, are these fate songs?"

"They are."

Calista rustled through more of the parchment. "These look like some that were found in the Court of Stars during the battle. Why do you have them?"

"They are bits of comfort from a lost world. Memories I do not wish to forget."

She paused, licking her lips. "The parchments found in the fae isles spoke of my royals. Curses and memory thieves. Things of that kind."

"The fated paths," I muttered.

"Yes." Calista returned the parchment to its place. "Why were they there when they were the tales of future storytellers?"

I glanced over my shoulder. "I do not know how to answer that when you do not want to know the truth."

"What if I do?"

73

I closed my eyes. "Then, I would tell you those tales came from the same song of seidr."

"How is that possible. They are all different tales, from different fate workers."

I didn't answer. She was not ready to know the horrible truths of our lives.

In my silence, Calista studied the tapestry, then pulled it aside. A little gasp slid from her throat. "All gods."

She traced the names etched into the stone I'd crafted and built into the earthy walls.

"My parents? Are they . . . is this where they rest?"

"I do not have their bones," I admitted. "But they deserved a place."

"You made this?" She smiled, tracing her mother's name. "You cared for them. Didn't you?"

A strange burn built in my skull, sharp and aggravating. It caused me to blink more than once. "They were my home. Without the queen's help, I would've had long, matted hair to my feet, and clothes with patches. Perhaps no clothes at all. I certainly wouldn't know it was considerate to wash under the arms."

"I'm sure she took pride in doing so, since no amount of washing can tame this hair." Calista coiled one of her rolled braids around her finger.

Her hair was wild. It always had been, like her spirit. Older gentry boys had often tugged on her braids or tried knotting them, thinking the little princess was alone.

They never got far before I stepped in their path and sent them to their mothers with bloody noses or chipped teeth.

"And my daj?" she pressed. "These are written lessons you had with him, when he taught you of your power, right? I . . . I recognize his writing."

The skull-ache deepened. My voice was too rough. "The king did not need to burden his household with an orphan. But he did. When his trusted men told him my gift was dangerous, too odd, he stood for me. He prepared me for what was to come."

Calista's eyes glistened. I had little experience around others, let alone experience in reading expressions, but if I had to guess, I'd say she wanted to know more about what was to come. She wanted to know, but held her tongue.

To know would mean stepping forward into something from which she'd fled all this time. A path of fate, one where the ending was unknown.

Calista paused at a scroll with a drawing of what appeared to be a horse. The legs were thin lines and it's nose was too large for its head. I kept my hand over my face, watching.

She studied the horrid drawing for a pause, then whispered, "I remember this. Gammal had only died. He was my favorite horse."

"He was a stupid creature."

"Only because he . . . he always bit your shoulder." She faced my dark corner, pink lips parted. "He always bit your shoulder. Right? That's true?"

"I have the damn scar to prove it."

Calista dragged her bottom lip between her teeth, but when she blinked, a tear dropped onto her cheek. "Why have you been hidden from me? Why did you become my Whisper instead of . . . my Silas?"

My Silas.

Tension gripped the back of my throat. A familiar, creeping panic built. It spread like a poisonous bloom through my chest, into my head, until my thoughts could not stay focused.

"Do you know what it's like?" I clenched my eyes and pressed my fists against the sides of my skull. "She doesn't know. She doesn't *want* to know."

I didn't recall lowering to a crouch, but at the touch of her hand on my wrist, I opened my eyes. Calista was kneeling in front of me.

"Silas, speak to me." Her thumb ran over the bones of my wrist. "I am here now. What is it I don't want to know?"

I flattened my palm against my ruined cheek again, shielding the carnage away, and slid my back along the wall until I was standing.

Calista followed. "What don't I want to know?"

"That you have a place on a fated path." *That you have a place with me.*

Her lips turned down in a frown. "I promised myself long ago that I would make my own fate. It is wrong to force someone to act against their will, Silas." She licked her lips and stepped closer. "You must let me go."

"How do you know if I let you go, that you will not be stepping exactly where the Norns want you?"

Her cheeks flushed. "At least it will be my choice. I have people out there who need me. The folk of Raven Row, blood fae who have guarded me. I have friends and family in distant kingdoms and . . . I must try to protect them."

I knew all this. The royals of restored kingdoms, I both envied them and respected them for what they had done for her.

"You are safe here," I said. My thumb traced her bottom lip. Pleasure surged through me when she didn't pull away. "I will protect you now that you are back with me."

"And what of the others?"

"It is too late."

"No." She pulled her head away from my touch. "No. That isn't good enough. I'm not letting them fall simply because I took too long in your eyes to find you."

It was much more than all that. She could stand beside me until the world ended. If she did not accept me and the soul bond between us, our song would never take flight again.

"I will hate you," she said and lifted her chin in a bit of a challenge. "No matter what memories I have of you, take my freedom from me, and I will hate you. I will not forgive you for it."

Anger swept through my veins, hot and furious. "You would hate me? After . . . after *everything*?"

"I don't know everything but . . ." Her chin trembled in the slightest. "Yes, I would. Too many times I have had freedom taken from me. I won't do it again."

Calista let out a shriek of surprise when I lunged. My body pressed against her, pinning her back to the wall of the mausoleum. Each draw of air came sharp and heavy. Each brush of my chest against hers sparked anger and passion, and I could not stop. "You know *nothing* of bondage. Nothing."

"Let me go, Silas." She didn't falter, didn't waver under my nearness. Calista placed her palm on the hand I'd used to cover the scars. "Let me go to my people."

Her people. I was not numbered among them.

Jaw tight, I stepped back. "Go then. I will not stop you. Fight a battle you cannot win. Go be with your fools who are missing you."

Calista regarded me with a touch of suspicion. Gaze on me, she crept toward the entrance. In the doorway, she paused. "You could come with me. You could fight."

I stepped back into the shadows, silent and unbending. Calista's eyes flickered. Not disappointment. How could she be disappointed when she did not wish to be here with me anyway?

When she disappeared into the mists of the tangled garden, I waited for ten breaths before slamming my fist into the side of the tomb. "She doesn't know what it's like!"

You're going to simply leave her there?

"Of course not," I snapped at the darkness. "I'm not a damn fool."

I quickened my pace and abandoned the solitude of the mausoleum and sprinted for one of the numerous side entrances on the palace. The lower corridors were musty and covered in weaver webs. Twists and sharp, angled corridors branched off in a maze of rooms and warded chambers, but I'd memorized every crevice.

I shouldered through a door into a small room where I'd spent endless hours tanning hides from rabbits or small rodents that crept through the gates. On a peg near an open hearth, I snatched a black cloak. The hood was oversized, enough I could tuck it around my marred cheek and still see.

Motion was instinct. A need to protect her, a need to keep watch over her, but by the time I reached the gate, I came to an abrupt halt.

Bleeding gods, I could . . . I could leave. There was no agonizing pull to remain behind the iron bars. In one way, she'd set me free.

And I was terrified.

The world was vast, too vast. My skin lifted in sharp chills. Gods, all I wanted to do was return to my chamber, lock the door, and draw the damn shade. But she was out there. The tale was at the end, and none of us truly knew what that meant. There was greater danger than there had ever been, and I couldn't let her face it alone.

Shattered as I was to know she recoiled from me rather than embraced me, she was mine to protect, mine to guide. Mine.

I ducked my head, and for the first time in centuries, stepped into the world.

CHAPTER 13
THE STORYTELLER

RAVEN ROW LOOKED . . . DIFFERENT. BUILDINGS WERE STRAIGHTER, MORE cobbles lined the muddy roads. There were wider stretches of sturdier walls, and forests that once were dry and sickly were lush and full beyond the main roads.

Illusions? A trick of the mind?

How bleeding long had I been behind the damn walls of Hus Rose? I shook the questions away and took note of my folk staggering free of their trance.

But the sea had changed. Murky water lapped against the shore, like dark oil glistened over the surface. Storms near the horizon rolled in angry clouds.

I let out a gasp, squinting to be certain I was seeing the truth this time. Bleeding hells. Once more, dozens and dozens of strange, jagged, cruel-looking ships were splitting the surface of the waves, then sailing toward the Row.

The snap of sails. The spray of mist from the coming maelstrom. All of it was real on my skin. This was no vision. This was a damn attack from bleeding sea fae.

"At the shores!" I screamed to the disoriented folk of the Row. "Sea fae! Protect yourselves!"

I'd never forget diving under the dark water when that dead bastard of a king summoned me with that strange little gold disc of his. The sensation of the sea crushing me, yet never fully robbing me of my breath was horrifying. If my Golden King had not been at my side, I might've succumbed to death from nerves alone.

There was power in the seas, and we'd sent Davorin straight to it when the coward turned himself into a slimy eel.

"Cuyler!" I skidded around the bend in time to watch my friend stumble out of the trance I'd leveled against him. "You all right?"

He coughed and gripped my arm. Damp hair stuck to his forehead, his clothes were soaked from the storm that had beat around him, his breaths were heavy, but he gave me a brisk nod. "What happened?"

"I think I put everyone to sleep," I said. "Don't ask me how, there isn't time. Look."

With a slight nudge to his shoulder, I spun him around to face the shore. Cuyler's eyes widened. "Dammit. Are those sea folk?"

"Yes. From the looks of it, a great many of them." We were likely going to die trying to defend this miserly town and those wonderful, lust-filled royals I wished I could see once more. But as I told my Whisper—I would choose to face that fate on my own.

"If this is that battle creature, kill me should he take me, Cuyler. Don't let him use me against my royals," I shouted over the wind.

"Stop talking about it, Cal," he snapped back. "We fight until we can't. Understand?"

I accepted a short blade off a sheath from his back. He took a broadsword from his waist.

"One last comment you won't like," I said. Cuyler groaned in frustration. I tried to keep my voice steady and went on. "I'm glad I won't go to the Otherworld alone."

His icy pale eyes locked on mine. Cuyler's brow furrowed, but he gave me a soft smile. "Fight to your final breath, Cal."

"Fight to the end," I muttered. A saying offered by my Shadow King often, but it meant more. Oddly enough, it felt like a notion burrowed deep in my bones.

Fight to the end of this tale.

I shuddered. "Whisper?"

No one but dazed people wandered the Row. A few dockers and tavern workers stared at the approaching battle with a touch of longing or desperation. They did not know how to fight. No mistake, everyone knew this was the day our wretched little kingdom would fall.

No sign of Silas.

I scanned the streets, caught sight of Olaf, and waved my sword. "Get people to shelter! Hide as best you can and—"

"That's enough chatter," Olaf shouted back. "We stand here as we always have, awaiting the call."

What the hells? "You old fool, they will not attack with warm embraces. At the least, grab a damn knife."

"Is that your command?"

"To grab a knife?" I spun around. "Do as you please, you fool. I suggest sharp things."

Do the same, Little Rose.

"Silas?" I muttered.

"Who is Silas?" Cuyler followed my gaze, tracking buildings. "Calista? Who is Silas?"

I didn't answer, simply searched the windows, the alcoves, and alleyways for his form. I'd left him behind his gates, but there was a fierce rush of relief to think he might've followed. Odd when I ought to be angry at the sod for trying to trap me in that battered palace.

"Silas, show yourself."

Cuyler glanced side to side. "I'm truly going to need you to fill me in on who you're talking to, Cal, but after we face this. Looks to be smaller vessels."

"Likely sending the grunts first," I said. Made sense. Davorin was a battle lord. He knew his strategy. He wouldn't ride with a first wave. He'd torment and destroy and weaken, then he would come and devour what was left.

"Watchers!" Cuyler's commanding voice drew me back to the shore. "Focus on the seas, boys. Guard this land with your blood if asked."

From the surf, frightening faces emerged. These weren't the

same sort of sea folk who'd sailed next to the brutal king. These creatures were made of rotting sinews and veiny eyes that looked ready to pop free of their skulls. Cheeks were sunken. Threads of flesh opened on the sides, revealing yellowed teeth.

They looked half-dead, but no matter, each was strong enough to raise a blade and sing in voices like cream and sweets. A sound I might give my whole heart to hear again and again.

They slithered from the water. The longer they sang, the more beautiful they became. They were perhaps the loveliest creatures I'd ever had the pleasure of viewing.

Until hands clapped over my ears and sound muffled.

"Cuyler, don't you hear them?" I tried to shove him away.

"Siren songs. Don't listen." I took note of the cloth shoved inside his sharply tapered ears. All the watchers were doing much the same. "Close them off, Calista. Sea singers are the male sirens of old lore."

Little Rose! Silas's voice ripped through me, harsh and panicked.

Somewhere in my heart his voice soothed the delirious need to follow the intruder's stunning song. But . . . their sound was so delightful, so intoxicating.

Desire and unfettered arousal burned through my belly, between my legs. I groaned, mortified at the rush of lust. Heat flooded my face when it was Silas I saw in my head. His intensity, his mystery, what would it taste like on my tongue?

"Push them back!"

I thought it was Cuyler who shouted the command. Cuyler. He was strong and, no doubt, as the heir of his fae court had, more than one woman he'd taken beneath his body. His broad, firm body. It felt wrong. I dreamed of Silas, but Cuyler's body was here. Did he know how delicious he smelled? Like a rainstorm and musk and leather.

I arched—truly arched—against him. In the back of my skull mortification blared to life. More so when Cuyler's frosty eyes went wide. "Cal. No, it's in your head. Shield your ears."

"I need . . ." My body throbbed in tension.

"Come with me, lovely."

I spun around. A glorious sea fae stood fifteen paces away. How frightful he'd been upon surfacing, but now . . . my mouth was wet, my body throbbing. He could bring me some relief.

I walked toward him. Somewhere in my senses, I thought Cuyler might've screamed my name. What did it matter? I needed this sea man. He was so beautiful. He held out a hand, curling long fingers, beckoning me forward.

Stop! A dark, silky voice broke through my mind.

Whisper. My Whisper. My Silas. My broody, masked, shadowed phantom.

He was here somewhere. I looked around, desperate to find him. More than my delightful sea creature, I wanted Silas to relieve this scorching ache of desire.

Don't you take another step, Little Rose. You are mine.

Damn him. Did he not know that was, in fact, exactly what I wanted? Silas might be lost in shadows, perhaps he chatted with ghosts, but I had no doubt those fingers could do miraculous things to the flesh. Did he touch with the same ferocity as his gaze? Did he use filthy words as demanding as his tamed voice? Would he take me fast and passionate, or slow and sweetly?

In my head lust flared to something deeper. Desire pulsed into something lasting.

I wasn't convinced it mattered. I thought I might take Silas any way.

Odd. The rush of primal need burned into a new sensation in my chest. Something hot and forceful. The want was there, but it was more.

"Come to me."

Ah, my sea creature. In my whirling thoughts, I'd nearly forgotten such a stimulating being was awaiting my hand.

I reached for him.

"Calista, no!" Cuyler shouted.

My friend and his blood fae watchers were fighting. Blades clashed over the horrid-looking sea folk the instant they emerged. Some fell. Others fought back. The people of Raven Row shouted words that turned to haze in my ears. Muffled, like I had already stepped into the sea.

"Come with me." The sea delight's breath was next to my ear. He held out a hand.

I wanted to take it, so desperately, but I hesitated.

"Come with me," he said, angrier than before.

No. This . . . this was wrong. I faced him, head tilted. "I don't want to leave him."

For a fleeting moment, the smooth contours of my sea creature's face twisted into something horrific, something deadened. Gods, they were walking, hideous corpses at first. This . . . this was a ruse.

"Your heart is mine!" He roared, needle-like teeth showing, and rammed his crooked fingers into my hair.

I pulled back, tufts of my hair snapping from my scalp, and yanked out a knife from my boot. "No!"

"You cannot run from—" His silky voice gurgled as though he were choking on the sea.

Bleeding gods. A hooded figure had a twine rope twisted around the sea singer's neck. His movements were swift. Precise. With a clever flick of his hands, the cloaked man twisted the sea singer's neck in a ghastly way, a vicious crack sent a rush of sick through my gut.

But when the rotted face returned and the sea singer fell forward, the trance of his beauty and intrigue faded.

I stumbled back, heart racing. All gods, I'd nearly been a bumbling sod and . . . followed him.

My gaze bounced to the man in the hood. The side of his face where he wore his mask was strategically tucked, but those furious, burning, dark eyes were my Whisper's. His shoulders heaved as he glared at me.

Part of me wanted to shrink away, but the clang of blades kept me rooted. We were under attack. "You came for me after I left."

Silas narrowed the only eye I could see. "When have I ever left your side?"

I didn't know the answer, but for the first time, more than I feared, more than I wanted to run from the games of the Norns, I wanted to know what had kept me from him.

"Do I hide you," Silas snapped. "Or do we fight to our final tale, Little Rose?"

Cuyler and his men were slashing against the slow steps of the sea singers.

Doubtless, the return of sea folk was a first glimmer Davorin would greet our shores soon enough.

I spun the knife in my hand, narrowed gaze on Silas. "He isn't taking any of us. Never again."

CHAPTER 14
THE STORYTELLER

I STUFFED MY EARS WITH CLODS OF MUD AND TOOK A DEEP BREATH WHEN THE lure of the sea singers faded.

"We won't win this if they keep coming," I shouted. We needed a damn army.

"They await your call," Silas insisted. "Tell your people what you demand of them. Do not hesitate. You have the words."

"What are you talking about? The folk here aren't warriors."

Silas gripped my arms, urging me to hold his gaze. "What do you *need* them to do? If you could have the people of this land be anything what would you have them be? We have power here, Little Rose. Accept it, use it."

If they could be anything, what would I have them be? Hells, I'd have them be an army. I'd have them protect these damn shores so those monsters in the tides couldn't leave their ghastly ships.

What would I have the folk of the Row do? This was mad. They were drunkards and simple folk, but I whirled around and raised the short blade overhead.

"People of Raven Row! We are under attack, and if you wish to see another grimy sunrise, then fight to protect our shores. Fight for our land and our people."

Olaf's leathery face turned up in a wicked kind of grin. "Finally."

The next moments stopped my heart.

The oddly sturdier buildings groaned and shifted even more. Chipped stains and crooked paneling peeled away, leaving behind gleaming paints and smooth stones. Walls with parapet barriers were erected around a hillfort with stone towers, wood and wattle cottages, and in the center was Hus Rose. Only it was not the same misshapen palace. A sprawling fortress of sharp, angled peaks with lancet windows, walls made of stone and sturdy beams had replaced the wooden shingles and crooked doors.

Hus Rose was large enough to fit countless folk, and wretchedly familiar. This was a palace from my earliest memories. This was the palace of House Ode.

Raven Row tore apart. Stone buildings and sod huts with smoke from indoor fires took the places of broken tenements and shacks. Along heavy stone walls hung blades and bows, axes and seax from thick beams. Shields marked with dark runes or ravens were arranged below the weapons, ready to snatch.

Soil rumbled underfoot. Roads widened. Like a different world had lived beneath our battered kingdom, debauched buildings melted away and Raven Row was transformed into something beautiful, something formidable.

I let out a shriek of surprise as we stumbled. A few blood fae lost their footing. Sea singers retreated, no doubt the most unsteady of us all on land. Some stumbled and found the tip of a blade, most dove into the tides.

"Take one for questioning." Brilliant Cuyler, a true warrior, had the brains to act in strategy.

Blood fae moved at once. They battled the shudder of the earth, but managed to surround one of the fumbling, horrifying sea fae, smashing his rotting face to the sand before he could dive beneath the waves.

Cuyler looked for me and held tightly to a post. I staggered back and slammed into a firm body.

Silas gripped my arms, keeping me steady. I didn't think, merely turned into him, clinging to his waist as an anchor in the turmoil. It took half a breath, but soon enough, his arms wrapped around my shoulders, keeping me pressed to his body until the quake ceased.

"Cal." Cuyler pointed through the dust. "Look."

More than the buildings, the people of the Row had fallen forward, unmoving in the road.

"No." Agony ripped through my chest. They were gone. The folk I'd known. The folk I'd mocked with Stefan when they staggered from game halls. The folk who'd irritated me, yet celebrated my return from captivity in the North with honey cakes and mead ale, as though I belonged to them all.

One shoulder moved. Next, a knee. Followed by groans as men, women, the people floundered back to their feet.

Blood fae watchers grouped closer to Cuyler, to me. Most hesitated at the sight of Silas, but still lifted their spears and knives. I wanted to tell them there was no need to protect against the people of Raven Row, but the thought died like ash in the wind.

These were no longer the people of Raven Row.

Dressed in leathers. Belts thick as my arm. Boots with hard soles that struck the knees. Loops and sheaths marked their waists, shoulders, and backs. Their rugged faces and vomit-stained tops were now dark, woolen tunics spun with silver threads on the trims.

No one seemed to pause for a single breath to consider the impossibility of transforming from drunkard to . . . warrior.

A man with a deep blue mantle tossed over his shoulders barked strategic orders. Others followed in a ripple of different commands.

"*Wall at the shore.*"

"*Archers above.*"

"*Shield formation.*"

"*Move your asses!*"

The final command came from the man in the mantle. When he faced me, beneath the smooth, sun-kissed skin, the tidy beard, and braided hair, I could just make out his true features.

"Olaf?"

The aleman looked thirty turns younger, arms thick and chiseled with divots and strength, but he hadn't rid himself of that irritating, stern expression.

He pressed a hand to his chest and bowed his chin. "The Rave fight for the first kingdom."

The Rave?

"Wasn't the Rave the army of the fate king?" Cuyler limped toward me, a little breathless.

I nodded. "Annon was Rave. I don't understand what's happening."

"They've awaited the call of their royal, Little Rose," Silas whispered against my hair. Low and seductive. His arms tightened around my waist. "You are the heir. They bow to you."

"Silas, I . . . I don't know how to command anyone."

Lines of warriors—people I'd known from my earliest memories—trudged forward in uniform steps.

"Silas?" Cuyler tilted his head. "Now that I'm thinking on it . . . I know that name."

With an irritated grunt, Silas turned us away. He practically recoiled away from anyone but me. "You do not need to be anything you are not. No one needs more than who you already are, Little Rose."

Over his shoulder, I gaped at the people taking positions, snatching shields, arming their strong, lithe bodies for a damn war.

A woman stepped into view; the corner of her mouth was tilted in a knowing smirk. Silver braids wrapped around her head in a crown. She was dressed in a simple woolen gown with satchels strapped over her shoulders and pig-skin pouches tethered to her belt.

Runes were inked across her long fingers, and bone chips draped around her neck. Old-world seer attire.

Two more women came to her side; one was half a head shorter with a touch of sea blue to her hair, another with stern braids down the center of her skull, but all three had the same eerily pale eyes, like a frost storm.

"F-F-Forbi? Oviss? Danna?"

The taller of the three women stepped forward. She paused at Silas, and nearly caused him to stumble backward when she patted the spot over his heart. He shoved her hand away and shuddered.

Turns of solitude, no doubt touch from others burdened him. Well, touch other than mine.

After a few breaths, she ignored him and cupped my cheeks. "This is the part where she rises."

Damn the hells. Where were the cracks in their faces? The wiry hairs from their moles? Where were the hunches to their spines? These women were fierce, formidable, and looked mere turns older than me.

Danna beamed and took my face next. "This is the part where captives are free."

I recoiled against Silas's side when the women strode past us and set out rune stones, chanting spell casts for protection and strength. Rave warriors spread out like a beautiful pestilence. From alleyways, rooftops, from the stone parapet walls, warriors bloomed and marked positions. As far as I could see, all along the shore, warriors stood at the ready.

Bleeding. Gods. We had an army.

"Blades ready!" Olaf roared, one fist raised near the shore. Every Rave lifted their swords the same as Olaf. At the aleman's cry, every warrior near the water's edge shouted a battle cry I'd long forgotten, one of old words. One shouted under loyalty for the father robbed from me.

Berjast enda. Until the end.

In a furious wave across the line of warriors, sword points rammed into the pebbled sand.

A slow burn, like embers catching flame, began in my fingers. The heat of it scorched and ravaged my veins, spreading like molten ore through my gut, my limbs, until it reached my chest. I burned with a new sort of power.

"Shield, Princess." Olaf looked to me.

Silas dipped his covered face alongside my cheek. "Sing with me, Little Rose."

I pressed a hand to my heart, the skin warm to the touch. I did not have my quill, nor my ink, but I had the words. I could write them. I dropped to the mud and used my finger to carve a simple lyric, a few words. Each symbol brought music to my head, the sweet, gentle voice in the shadows.

My body trembled with the flow of heated seidr in my veins. Soon enough I'd be spewing magic from my pores if I did not release it soon. I had the words written, and had no way to burn them.

Sing with me.

I closed my eyes when his voice bloomed from my heart to my mind. A thought connected with my own. I leaned over the mud-carved words—a simple command to shield, to ignite the true power of the first kingdom.

What it would unravel, I didn't know, but the rightness of it burrowed deep in my belly like churning waves.

My palms burned, they ached. I slammed both palms over the muddy symbols. Heat crackled beneath. Brilliant, burning orange ignited along the divots of my symbols, flaring for a few breaths before smoldering and taking the symbols away.

The low, somber voice heightened in my mind, my heart. As though his sound seeped into my skin, there was something about the tune that ignited a strength I'd never truly embraced. My voice joined in, and I felt as though I'd fallen back into a basin of warm water. Sound muffled but for the song in my heart.

It lasted for a mere moment, but when the song ended, something dreadful happened within me.

When I looked back at my Whisper, heat from my blood pooled in my belly, dripping even lower until I clenched my thighs tightly. Gods, no. Absolutely, unequivocally, no. What had I told my Raven Queen? The bleeding instant one of those lust-crazed royals leapt into bed, damn wars began.

I would rather go the rest of my life without risking the necks of everyone I loved simply because my masked phantom all at once looked like a morsel, one I wanted to taste over every surface of my tongue.

The words, the connection, something had awakened a fire in my body, and I could not control it.

If the pulse to his jaw, the rapid rise and fall of his chest, were any clue—he felt the same. I reeled through every reason touching him would be a disastrous decision until the shock of need and desire faded.

"Calista." Cuyler's voice broke my delirious pull toward Silas. My friend stepped in front of me, a touch of fear on his face. "Are you all right? You . . . you . . . you glowed."

"I'm fine." I peered over his shoulder, searching for Silas, but instead caught sight of the shore. "What the hells? Look!"

Threaded between every Rave blade was a brilliant string of golden light, connecting each blade to the next beside it. Warriors didn't move, but kept hold on their hilts as the light reached one edge of the small Western shoreline to the next.

A blast of golden light split into beams across the sea and tossed great walls of violent waves against the dark streak of the open Chasm of Seas. Monstrous walls of water shot toward the sky, creating another barrier against the ships.

With the water and the light barrier between the Rave swords, the sea folk wouldn't be able to reach us.

At least, not for now.

Silas had drifted to the side and loomed in the darkness of an alleyway ten paces away. His tension, his need to flee and cover from the sunlight and countless faces was palpable. Still, he remained. Fists clenched, but he stayed.

For me. He didn't need to speak it. He'd bid me farewell, allowed me to leave when he didn't want it, and still followed me into a fight that, doubtless, terrified him to the bone.

I made a move to go to him, all at once empty without his nearness, but paused when Cuyler placed a hand on my shoulder.

"Calista, you did this on the shore in the fae isles. The glow."

"I think . . . it's part of my seidr. A deeper part." It was my song. *Our* song.

I lifted my gaze to my Whisper when he crossed the space in stiff steps. On instinct, I gripped his arm, pulling him closer.

Silas lowered his voice, so only I could hear. "Accept the truth and you will do all of it without writing. Accept the truth and the words will come from your heart."

"How can—"

I didn't finish before Olaf shoved his way through the lines of warriors. "We've been given more time. Fight with us."

I blinked. "I . . . I just bleeding did, you big oaf. Didn't expect damn Rave to show up, mind you, but—"

"There is a final piece, Princess. The captain believed you were ready to return to the beginning? Are you?"

What he was truly asking was if I stood ready to face my fate after all this time.

"She has no choice." Silas's deep, damn-near seductive voice brought the answer.

Somewhere inside, I knew he wasn't wrong. Whatever I'd done, crossing into Hus Rose, commanding hidden Rave warriors, I'd unlocked something in this place. A power I could not deny.

Cuyler lifted his blade until recognition dawned. "The fate king's ward, yes? That is where I know the name Silas. From Ari's fae sleep."

I didn't answer, merely tugged on Silas's tunic, drawing his chest to mine. "What happened here, Whisper? My folk were Rave, hidden all this time?"

"How do you suppose the first ice queen of the North got the idea for her own people?"

My heart stuttered. Queen Lilianna Ferus. She'd, *gods*, she'd hidden her fae army as phantom guardians of that damn tomb where the Cursed King and my Kind Heart ended his suffering, and their heart song took hold.

"Queen Lilianna had the same idea?"

"She was given the twist of fate in her story by one who'd done the same," Silas told me. His thumb wasn't gloved anymore, and the rough scrape of his calluses on my cheek sent a shiver down my spine. "No more running, Little Rose," he hissed through his teeth. "This is your chance to know everything."

Instinct urged me to flee. His touch urged me to stay. My mind reeled through thoughts of my royals. The flame that ignited meant they were in distress. I thought of Sol's missive. "Will my fate save them?"

I didn't need to explain who. Silas lowered his face, his breath was warm against my ear. "To see your truth will finish the tale. A tale of which they are all a part. From there we take what we know and make our own fate."

I took hold of his wrist, guiding his palm from my neck to my cheek. "You'll be with me?"

He blinked, stunned. "Always. Let your dreams descend. I'll be there."

The words had barely left his tongue before the world faded into abysmal black.

CHAPTER 15
THE STORYTELLER

"Stefan?"

My brother as I remembered him stood over me, smoke billowing from the paper herb roll between his teeth.

"Time to tell the tale, little one. Send them on their path."

I cracked my eyes and woke to the dim light of a rounded throne room. Vines of silver moonvane lined the walls, and an oblong table had been arranged in the center. At one end sat a woman with satin dark hair, pointed ears, and night-black eyes. The Night Folk queen.

This was my Cursed King's grandmother. How did I know it? It would've been right after the shift of the true kingdom. A time when worlds began anew with altered histories, and tensions, and enemies.

When mortals and Night Folk determined they were damned to hatred of each other.

Where were my Golden King's folk? When the worlds shifted, did they fall backward, did they find youth again? Did they live in the turns where their fate could most likely align with the new tale that broke the kingdoms?

I shook away my curiosity and focused on the scene in front of me.

At the other end of the table was a man with icy pale hair, a russet beard, and sharp, cold eyes. His scalp was shaved on the sides, and gold chains and rings glittered around his neck and fingers. A small boy, no older than seven, stood stalwart at his side, dressed in a fur-lined tunic and boots that curled at the toes.

Near the Night Folk queen was another boy. Skin like brown soil, eyes dark like midnight, and sharp ears pierced in black bone studs.

"King Jon," the Night Folk queen said, lacing her fingers over her belly. "We have offered our walls for turns. We want for nothing but peace between our people."

"Peace with Night Folk?" The pale king chuckled. "How could we have peace when your fury coats these walls and have taken from our people all to keep the finer resources for yourselves? You do all this for the simple fact that we do not have the magic in our blood. Do not play games; you will bring us to your courts, only to rule over us."

"Untrue." The queen's full lips pinched. She snapped her fingers and a bone-thin fae attendant scurried to her, bowing at the waist, as he held out a satin pillow. "In fact, we offer a gift of equality."

My eyes widened. Twin battle axes were atop the pillow. The queen selected one, inspecting the sharp curve of the blade. "Twin weapons of equal strength. Forged from the fury in this soil. We wish our Timoran cousins to take one, a symbol of our friendship."

King Jon slumped in his chair, sneering. "A single blade will not feed hundreds of hunters, it will not fill the bellies of children huddled in the snow."

"No." The queen placed the axe on the table. "But our crops are hearty, our furs are heavy, and our lands are open. I urge you to reconsider joining us, for there are omens of the Norns should you refuse."

Her dark gaze landed on me. I swallowed the thickness in my throat when dozens of curious courtier eyes did the same.

"Tell them, little one," Stefan said. He winked as though he knew some grand secret.

"Anneli, that was what you called yourself, yes?"

I nodded before I could think better of it. Truth be told, it was though I knew this conversation by heart. I'd given her my mother's name, and I did not know why I'd not used my own.

The Night Folk queen smiled and beckoned me forward. "Speak of the power forged in these blades."

My consciousness seemed to be locked in another body, another time. I had no power to refuse, no strength to keep my feet from stepping into the center of the room. In truth, I did not feel horribly like myself. My body was not as thin and knobby. My shoulders were straight, and the constant prickle of apprehension on the back of my neck was absent.

In the reflection of a grand window, the only parts of me that seemed the same were the braids of my golden hair.

I said nothing and slipped my hand into a satchel strung over my shoulder. From inside, I removed a goose-feather quill and a glass inkwell brimming in mahogany ink. Somewhere in the distance a voice hummed. The sound of it soothed my heart.

I am searching for something. Each step brings me closer. I let out a breath, repeating the words in my mind as I began to write a tale of hatred, of battle and blood. Of a people who would one day unite after suffering.

Pinched between my fingers, I held the parchment over an open flame. Too far to burn, but near enough it would take a simple flick to turn the tale to ash, then faced the suspicious glare of the ancient Timoran king.

"Find friendship today and you may walk a kinder path. Refuse, and you will be lost in a way you cannot understand."

His angry eyes narrowed. Behind him billowed a dark cloud, some force unseen.

Damn battle lord was here, unknown to everyone.

"Is this some sort of manipulative threat?" The Ice King leaned forward, attention on the Night Folk queen.

"Not at all, King Jon." She didn't falter and held up one of the axes. "She has the power of the Norns, of prophecy. We do not wish unease between us, so will you take peace? Or do you keep our tensions while your people freeze?"

He slammed a hand on the table. The small, dark-haired fae

boy jumped in surprise, the same as the pale boy beside his icy father. King Jon glowered. "Keep your blade. Perhaps in time you will need it. Send your ambassadors for future trade. We are done here."

I watched him and his pale-haired guards storm from the room. Heart racing, I let the tale of war and pain ignite.

"Those blades will bring about a new Etta," I told the queen, voice low and soft.

She tilted her head. "A *new* Etta?"

I said nothing and smiled at the small prince near his mother. "And you, young Arvad, you will be part of it." I leaned over my knees, meeting his dark eyes. "I urge you to keep your heart and mind open to your neighbors in the North."

His nose wrinkled. "I hate Timorans."

"Perhaps there will come a day when you do not."

By the time the final piece of scorched parchment landed on the table, I was all at once in a corridor with Stefan at my side.

"Our time is out, little one," Stefan whispered. "Listen to your heart, listen to the voice you cannot explain." He squeezed my hand. "Until the next tale."

Swift footsteps came up behind us. I screamed as a short blade rammed through Stefan's chest. No, no, no. I couldn't lose him again, I couldn't. I reached for him, but rough hands yanked at my arms and slammed me onto my knees. From the shadows, the Ice King materialized.

A dagger was in his hand. Slowly, he tapped it against his palm. "I do not trust Night Folk fury. But I certainly do not trust the magic of witches."

"Offensive," I spat through my teeth.

The same melodic hum built in my mind. It burned in my heart.

I'll find you, I promised. Why I thought such a thing, I didn't know, but my heart jolted when a voice answered. A broken voice, one that was young and thick with emotion.

Our song here is finished. Sing with me again, Little Rose.

King Jon lifted the dagger. I closed my eyes. A sharp burn filled my throat when the point of a blade rammed through.

I snapped up, gasping. My hands padded over my body. Alive. I was alive. "Silas?"

He was hunched over, a hand to his chest, heavy breaths coming through his nose. He blinked to me, eyes wet. "Do you know what it's like?"

"I don't . . ." My hand covered his over the frantic pace of his heart. Gods, he was trembling. "Silas. What . . . what was that? Did that happen? I-I died."

He winced. "Until the next song. Until the next song."

Silas cupped one side of my face, holding it for a pause, then shoved me back into a dark oblivion.

Brilliant stars were overhead.

"You're certain this must be?"

I sat up, disoriented, and accompanied by Stefan once more. He was dressed differently. A high-collared tunic, wilder hair braided off his bearded face, but that damn smoke was still lit, still puffing around his head.

"Whisper, you're certain this must be?" A woman, thin and pale with fiery hair like my Shadow Queen was looking at me. She shivered in the cold, swollen pillows of skin were under her eyes from exhaustion and bruises, and battle scars covered her skin.

Whisper? I was now called Whisper?

I stood. Hells, my body was different. More meat lined my bones, and pierced in my lips was a bone stud that hadn't been there before. Tattoos of runes marked each of my fingers, and cords of golden hair hung down to my waist.

I was me, but . . . not at the same time.

I slowly drifted to the injured woman's side. She held out a leather pouch, hand trembling.

"It is a curse. We should destroy it."

"It must remain to restore this land one day." I lifted my chin. "Your path of fate is opening, as it is doing in Northern realms. As it will someday do in the isles of fae."

"I don't see how this ends for our Eastern realms. Those kingdoms in the North, the South, the West, they will be overtaken should they win the ring."

I offered a gentle smile. "Trust that there is a path in play that will lead to united lands once again."

"Our people will be destroyed."

"No. This ring will be found and lost many times by your folk, but someday *she* will bring an end to this pain. It will restore the true fated crown of this land."

Recollection sparked in a truth so few of us knew. This moment was a time in the past of the Eastern regions when the bloodline of a first family of memory queens battled with a second bloodline that wanted the power.

This was the queen who'd lost to hateful wars, but there was a tale written here. In distant turns, a woman from the first family's line would take vows with a man from the second. They'd fight to restore the crown. They'd fail.

But from that union would come a daughter. A girl who'd find a boy of shadows, and together they'd pick up this fated fight again.

"It is our damnation to remain in constant battles over that cursed ring." Tears burned in the woman's eyes when she stared at the pouch. "It has destroyed me, my armies. I know I will not live long. Already I hear the call of the Otherworld."

She pulled back the hand she kept pressed to her side. Dark blood fountained from a deep wound. Her thin lips twitched in a tentative smile. "I do not wish to see memory manipulators on the throne, but . . . I have failed."

"There is no failure. You have walked a path of pain through this battle. Their victory is but a small moment, a step toward the fated end."

She closed her eyes and stumbled. Stefan wrapped an arm around her, holding her steady. "I yearn to rest. They made him forget me. They robbed me of my heart."

"You will dine together in the hall of the gods."

"I pray you are right. About it all." Her voice was fading.

Stefan eased the woman to the ground, and I placed a hand on the side of her head. Never had I been a memory sharer, but somehow I knew she would see into the future memories of the bleeding Norns.

It was the gift of the ring, of the queens of the Eastern realms, to garner bits and pieces of past, present, and future memories from the damn Fates themselves.

She'd see my Shadow Queen. She'd see the future of her kingdoms united with a thieving king made of shadows at her side. She'd see the end of this fight she never wanted.

"I see it. The end." With a trembling sigh, she blinked through tears. "May the gods protect them."

"They will know what happened here," I whispered. "They will make your fight worth every drop of blood."

"Will I see him in the Otherworld?" She looked at me, her bright green eyes desperate. "Will I see Sindri at the table of the gods at the dawn?"

Sindri—her mate. How I knew it, I wasn't certain, but I nodded. "He is already free of this world and saves your place beside him."

Her breaths rattled. "May the fated queen have the fiercest devotion of heart."

She let out a long breath, and never took another.

I brushed her hair off her brow, blinking through the sting in my eyes, and whispered. "The queen of your blood has every ounce of devotion. I promise."

When I turned to walk away, I stumbled, landing on my knees, but I was no longer kneeling on frosted earth. Instead, much like it had been in the Night Folk palace, now I knelt before a wooden throne, a cruel-eyed man glaring down at me.

In his hand was the queen's leather pouch. He unlaced the top and tossed the contents onto his rough palm.

"We have the true claim!" Between his thick fingers he held a glass ring, coated in dark runes. The glow of those runes was deadened.

Gods, the same ring had once been in the court of Riot Ode. A relic to be found on a cruel path of fate that would bring battle after battle until a masquerade where a young boy would be stolen from a young girl.

At my side, one of the attendants in the tent looked to me curiously. Warmth spread in my chest. Here was a final piece of this tale that would ignite the steps for my Shadow Queen. The attendant tilted his head when I grinned.

"One day, your house will protect the heirs with the true claim to that ring," I whispered, speaking only to the attendant. "Teach your son of the fallen family, so he will teach his son, and his son, until the end."

The attendant swallowed. He was unsettled, but there was a burn within him. One he might not be able to see. He did not believe his master was the true king of the land, yet he lived on both sides. Much like a man would do in future turns, a man who'd grow in power beneath an enemy while housing a forgotten daughter in his hayloft.

"House Strom," I whispered, "will become the house of royals."

He dipped his chin, confused, uneasy, but there was the slightest twitch to his lips as though he wanted to believe my words enough to smile.

Hot tears gathered in my eyes as the words for the path of fate that would unite Kase and Malin burned through my head. While the bastards of the war camp celebrated and taunted the fallen memory queen, I wrote the words in the dirt.

A song, a tale I didn't think I'd ever truly seen, yet I knew it. From the depths of my soul, I could sing each word of pain and loss, of shadows and crowns.

"We are at the end of this tale, Princess," Stefan said. "Find the voices you cannot explain. Until the next tale."

"Sing my song at the end. Bring me back to you," I whispered to the darkness.

Always, Little Rose.

Silas wasn't here, but his voice was clear and sharp in my mind.

"You will fight to keep that ring forevermore," I said to the wretched royal holding the ring. "You will never rid this land of the true bloodline."

He smirked and tossed the ring, catching it again in his dirty palm. "Watch me, sorceress. Then again, I suppose you won't be able to see much."

The low hum of Silas's voice surrounded the war camp.

I closed my eyes.

"Whisper?" I murmured the name I called the haunting voice. "What was your mother's name? I've forgotten."

My mother? The song in my mind paused. *You remember me.*

"I do." I smiled and spoke the remaining words in my head. *What was her name?*

Another pause, then, *Greta.*

A smile flicked in the corner of my mouth. *I think I shall be Greta then.*

Heartache splintered through my chest. Agony, rich and palpable, burned through my blood. I wanted to tell him not to fret, not to hurt on my behalf. I wanted to tell him many things, but the song began again, one that fitted into the words I'd spun about a shadow king, and a queen who robbed folk of memories.

It was beautiful.

A guard wrenched my head back. A scream slid from my throat, but it faded to wet gasps when the knife rammed through my neck.

In my mind, a cry of anguish broke my heart more than the blade.

Find me, he pleaded. *Live and live again. Find me, Little Rose. Please.*

Phantom aches burned along my throat when I realized I was back in the gloom. I was free of the war of memory workers over a cursed ring.

"Silas?"

"Live—" He stared at the dark ground and cleared his throat. "Live and live again."

"Until death at crimson night." My fists curled. Panic grew, hot and cruel in my chest. "I wrote those words for months before the battle in the South. My daj said those words . . . the night he died."

Silas lifted his head. "If you had no true lifeline, the battle lord could not find you."

No. This was impossible. It couldn't keep happening this way. I dug my fingers in my hair. "Live and live again. I *died* in those . . . dreams, those memories. Are you . . . are you telling me I've . . . died before, only t-t-to live again?"

My voice was shrill, not out of rage, but it had Silas recoiling like I might reach out and strike him. He was unaccustomed to others, that was clear, and he seemed wholly locked in despair when tears dripped onto my cheeks.

"Is that what you're saying, Silas?" I softened my tone. "That I keep dying only to live again?"

He nodded, but kept his gaze trained away.

"But . . . it's not possible. There aren't multiple lifetimes. The Norns have one string, one path, for us all."

"Yes," he said. "The reason the king's final song was against a natural order of fate."

My pulse quickened. "This is why he died, isn't it? To lose the magic of his blood, it would destroy him physically. And my mother! She could write simple twists of destiny, did she offer her strength only to succumb to a weak body and die with an arrow in her throat?"

Silas barred his body away from me and covered his face with his palms. "I *hate* it, Little Rose. I hate that this was the way to save you. Do-Do you know what it's like?" He shook his head, muttering, "She doesn't know. She doesn't know the truth."

His voice was laden in pain, a sorrow so agonizing I felt the ache to my soul. Tears lined his eyes, a wildness was taking hold, a sense of being lost in his countenance, as though the shadows in which he'd lived were pulling him back.

"Silas, we should stop. You don't need to relive this again," I said, a crack in my voice.

Whatever these visions were, they were breaking him. A fierce need to shield him, to touch him, to bleeding protect him, clung to my chest like a boulder crushing my ribs.

"It is too late to stop it," he said in a dark whisper.

I scrambled toward him, reached out my hand, and before I could touch him, fell into nothingness.

CHAPTER 16
THE STORYTELLER

"Greta, I don't know if I can do this."

I blinked my gaze into focus. A tower room perhaps. Near the window, a woman with long, pale hair looked to the stars.

"I've told you, darkness comes at crimson night. There the true fight begins. A fury sleep does not end your battle," I said. "Merely pauses it for a time. Give fate time to unravel, Lili."

My heart jolted when the woman turned around. I knew her. I bleeding knew her well. Liliana Ferus, dressed in a simple gown, stared at me with tear stains on her pale cheeks.

"How can I leave my children? What if . . . what if Arvad and I don't wake?"

"I will do all I can to see to it your path is set. Your children have grand roles to play in these final tales. They will not be alone, I swear to you."

Lilianna took my hands. "Eli will kill you."

I smiled and cupped the side of her face. All hells my hands were . . . they were frail and old. "He can try."

Lilianna blinked; her chin quivered. "Our armies, they'll be cursed, but hidden? Is that true?"

"The Ettan warriors will rise when the blood of the heirs restores this fight. I have seen armies be concealed before. You folk will rise when battles rage again."

The hidden Rave. The twist of fate when the Ettan warriors rose from those horrid shadow guardians at the tomb came from some instinct, some forgotten lifetime where Rave warriors were hidden in the dregs of the West.

My head was spinning.

"You'll look out for my children?"

I nodded. "They will be as my own family. I will not leave them alone. I swear to you."

The moment I moved to embrace her, instead I slammed into a broad body coated in battle leathers.

His face was hard. His skin was flushed red from sun and exertion beneath the long beard over his chin, but I knew those eyes. The blue was the same as the cruel king at the Night Folk queen's table. They matched the innocent boy who'd stood at his side.

"Ice King," I said. "What more can I do for you? The queen and king are dead. You've entombed them. You've destroyed folk I called friends."

The king of Old Timoran paused, a dangerous darkness in his countenance. He'd deluded himself into believing Lilianna Ferus would merely forget all the blood spilled here. The pain of her children, children I would never stop defending.

"You told me my bloodline would reign with Lilianna's." The king gritted his teeth in a vicious snarl.

"I said what I said. My statement remains unchanged. The blood of Eli and Lilianna will rule this land."

He shouted at me, cursed me, and grabbed my arm, yanking me toward him. The force didn't slam me against the Ice King, it tossed me into a cramped room with a table and blades and a disgusting smell of blood.

I let out a shriek of pain when I saw the man tethered to the table. On instinct, out of rage, it didn't matter, I rushed to his side and stroked his blood-matted hair. "Sol . . . Sol look at me."

The Sun Prince was thin—too thin—his cheeks were sunken, his eyes didn't have the glitter of wryness when he lifted his gaze. "G-Greta?"

My heart ached. I wanted to scream at him. I wanted to shout that he was Lumpy, I was his little irritating bird, I was me, but a past I didn't know stole my words.

"I'm going to look out for you," I promised. Distant sounds of a humming wrapped around us as I lifted a rolled parchment from my tunic. "When it is darkest, I'll be there to remind you of your heart."

"I don't matter," he said, voice rough and dry. "He is gone and there is no life for me without him."

I pressed a kiss on his damp forehead, whispering, "In the darkness, a voice small as the song of a bird will guide you toward the song of your heart. This life is not yet done for you, Sol Ferus. It is not yet done for *either* of you. I will be with you, even when you do not know your own name."

I opened my eyes, but Sol was gone. A woman was tied and unconscious in the corner. Herja Ferus.

A guard shoved me forward. "King says to hurry it up. He wants her quiet from now on."

I glared at him and kneeled beside Herja. She'd been battered. Old blood soaked her brow, and her eyes were swollen from beatings. I pressed a hand over her forehead and removed a parchment, the same as I'd done with Sol, and read the words, praying she'd hear.

"Silent you may be, but when he pleads to speak awhile, stay your blade, and find your words." I leaned close to her ear. "You are strong; you have much to live for. Fight, Princess. Fight until your heart sings and take your place when we return to the beginning."

A shadow of a tune filled the room as I struck a matchstick and ignited the parchment into flames before the guards could read a single word.

I screamed when they yanked my hair, but the room spun and landed me in front of three men.

Tied to tables as they waited for death. I touched Tor's forehead. He snapped his eyes to mine, terror lived there, but also agony.

I whispered beside his ear. "Live for him."

A tear dripped from the corner of Tor's eyes. He shuddered, no doubt, believing Sol was dead.

I rounded to the center table, holding the dark eyes of my Cursed King. He was broken, terrified, and kept glancing to the corner.

Let him see her, a familiar voice broke through my soul. *Sometimes it is the only way to have peace when you see the song of your heart.*

Valen was seeing moments of my Kind Heart. A fate tale that had yet to unfold, and my phantom in the dark was singing the tune of it.

You're doing this for him. I smirked to the emptiness of the room. *You're a sentimental bastard, Whisper.*

I knelt beside Valen's table. "Faces in your dreams live, Night Prince. When you see her, you will not recall your dreams, but a spark will ignite in your heart. Follow it, and you will find her."

"Witch," King Eli shouted. "Finish this."

Oh, I plan to, Ice King. I gave Valen a soft smile. "Keep focused on her."

"You . . . see her?" he whispered.

"I am allowing it to be so." More like my own phantom was allowing it to be. "Hold to her."

My heart cracked when Valen took hold of Halvar's hand, of Tor's. They braced for death. They'd be sent to the hells instead.

I removed a third parchment, hands trembling. I'd spent so much damn time constructing these words. They had to be perfect. This would begin the end. The Night Prince burned like a golden bloom against the darkness that polluted his kingdom.

A gentle melody rang in my head as I spoke the words:

> Every day twenty-two, by draw of blood or light of
>   moon,
> Rises a beastly reign to torment you.
> Live for death and gore,
> A lust for blood forevermore.
> No thought for name or past,
> Till she lights the dark at last.
> Royal of beauty, passion, and love.
> The willing one to give of blood.

A choice to make, a way to mend.

Then will the reign of bloodlust end.

In the next breath, heavy shackles tightened over my wrists. Damp stone soaked my bare knees. King Eli sat mere paces away, shadows he couldn't see wrapped around his cruel throne.

"Until the next tale."

I blinked and found Stefan's gaze.

I smirked. "He snatched you too, I see."

"Every time." Stefan was older with peppered hair and a wiry beard. Here, he looked more like Annon than he ever had.

"Kill them." Eli waved his hand and two Raven guards stepped behind us.

We are nearing the end. The next tale is short, I whispered in my thoughts. *One where we finally send the bright king to her. Will you be there, Whisper?*

A broken voice answered, *Always, Little Rose.*

The Ravens rammed their blades through our hearts, and I woke to the sobs of a boy.

I peered around a thick tree. No longer an aged storyteller, my body was thin and dirty, a rogue child without a clan in this land. Neither fae nor Timoran, but this, this moment felt damn important.

"Son, son, look at me." A man with bone beads in his rust-colored beard smiled despite being chained and on his knees.

A naked boy with messy golden hair was tethered to a tree with barbed rope. At the man's voice, he stopped struggling. The boy's face was swollen from sobs. Women, stripped of their clothes, were sprawled at his feet. Gods, my heart ached for him.

"Ari, look at me."

I ducked lower in the shrubs. The man was Petter Sekundär. His contribution to the power of fate in this soil was felt here, but it was passing on. It was passing on to a new path.

His son held his father's gaze, shuddering through silent sobs.

"I am proud of you," Petter said. "I will save you a seat with us in the great hall, my boy."

Ari, my Golden King, cried for his father. He pleaded, he raged, he asked forgiveness over and over as the Ravens lifted their swords and slaughtered Petter and a man at his side. They never stopped until blood soaked the grass and heads were piked in front of the last surviving boy.

"Let him rot for a few sunrises," the lead Raven barked. Darkness coated his body, shadows and hatred. I could almost make out the damn battle lord in the cruelty of this moment.

The Raven gripped Ari's chin and forced the boy to look at him. "Then it's his turn."

"Now's our chance, little one."

I spun around. A skinny boy was there. Stefan. He didn't look old enough to grow a beard.

This tale was important. Deep in my soul, I knew this path of fate would guide us to the end, to the missing piece of my whole soul. But it would fail to take shape if I didn't move and save the boy tied to that tree.

We kept to the thick trees of New Timoran, resting briefly behind thick ferns during the night, and before dawn we sprinted toward the hidden refuge of Night Folk rogues.

"Got anything to shield us?" Stefan asked. "They'll cut us down if we're not careful."

Rogue Night Folk did not hesitate to kill outsiders, even young ones. I removed a slip of rice paper from my tunic and used a stick of charcoal to write a shield of protection. Using Stefan's lit paper herb roll, we burned it to ashes.

Somewhere in the trees was a comforting song. A voice that matched the words on the paper. A promise of protection.

Stefan told me to stay down, then climbed up one of the trees near the tattered archway of Ruskig. He tossed a pebble. "Oi!"

An old man with tangled hair over his shoulders and a beard to his chest stepped out. He yanked a curved knife from his belt. "Get down here, boy."

"There's a Night Folk house near the docks under attack. Killed 'em all. Only the boy's left. He's a fighter, but they're slitting his neck in two days' time."

The man narrowed his eyes in suspicion. "That so? Who is he?"

Stefan peered down at me. I closed my eyes. *A bright king.* He was a bright king for . . . someone important, but . . . not yet.

For now, he was a boy of House . . .

"Sekundär," I hissed back to my brother.

"House Sekundär."

"I know that house." The old man's face sobered. "Once a royal cartographer for House Ferus."

He took a few breaths, then whistled to hidden rogues in the shadows.

"Klock, what is it?" One man said gruffly.

"Gather the people. Night Folk in the vales are under attack."

As the fae assembled to go after the tortured son of House Sekundär, the low melody in the shadows grew louder. I wanted to run toward it. I wanted to touch the one to whom it belonged. Time was running short.

Stefan climbed down, and before Klock and rogue Night Folk could catch the feral children in the trees, we sprinted deeper into the wood, their shouts at our backs.

Deeper and deeper we ran, until Stefan cried out when the earth gave, dropping us into a pit. Silky webs coated our faces. Hairy, bulbous weavers hissed and spat, attacking the intrusion to their peace. When I should be horrified, I fell into a sense of calm.

Stefan winced when one of the poisonous creatures bit at his throat. His chest rose and fell in rough breaths. "Until the . . . the next tale."

I whimpered when the light faded from his eyes and his chest stopped rising.

"Whisper . . ." It took a moment, but soon my body warmed, as though someone had wrapped me in furs. "I miss you."

Do you know me?

A smile tugged on my face, even through the harsh ache of the bites from the weavers. A moment of clarity brought his face into focus—a boy who tried not to smile too often, but when he laughed, his features brightened like the sun.

"Silas," I whispered. My body felt heavy.

Anguished despair cut through my heart. It didn't feel as though it was my own.

"Will you finish the tale for a bright king, Silas?"

He'll find her, his voice was soft, burdened.

"Good. Sing me back to you."

What will you be called?

Each tale, each life, took a different name, a different storyteller. I didn't hesitate, as though the name burned the tip of my tongue, begging to get out. "Calista."

His voice was thick with emotion when he spoke again. *Then it is the beginning of the end. Find me, Little Rose. Find me again.*

I smiled as the heat of the poison flooded my lungs. My head drooped to the side, and a final word whispered off my tongue. "Always."

When my eyes opened once more, swift moments reeled through my head. A small girl playing dice games in Raven Row, her brother haggling with merchants for sly deals, laughter at a game hall.

I was small, barely a girl older than seven turns. I'd been tasting what I thought was my first taste of mead ale when the door burst in and rough traders shouted and shoved, and eventually snatched me off the bench.

I struggled but didn't cry for my brother. When I caught his gaze across the hall, he smiled. Some twisted side of me smiled back, mouthing the word: *Finally.*

The cold bars of a cell sent a shudder down my spine. I squinted against the dark. It reeked of unwashed skin and piss. In the cell across from me, a lump of a man shivered in the cold.

"Hey," I said. "You know, you look like a lump. Mind if I call you Lumpy since you won't tell me your name?"

He tugged the blanket over his shoulders, turning his back to me. "Irritating little bird."

I grinned again. *A voice small as the song of a bird. I promised you.*

One turn of the head and it all shifted. I was looking through new bars, no longer at my Lumpy, but at my Kind Heart.

"Girl!" Her voice was harsh and desperate. "Tell me what you know. You wrote him into the curse."

"I told you I didn't," I snapped. "I'm the fifth storyteller." The *final* storyteller. Every tale came from a different song, a different purpose, and different path. Deep inside I knew it, but how would I explain it to my Kind Heart when I wasn't positive I understood it all myself? "And the first four—dead."

I pressed my head against the bars of the cell, ensuring Elise was listening. "This could start something. It could change the world."

The Kind Heart and Cursed King would restore the first fated crown. From there, we'd finally find the end.

The Black Tomb faded. On my hands and knees, I gasped as my head spiraled through everything I'd witnessed. Blood raged in my head, my chest; it pulsed through every heartbeat like a stampede through my veins.

"I can't." His deep, rough voice broke the silence.

Once more I was in the muddy streets of Raven Row. The night was bloody red, and in the distance, guards traipsed along the glimmering shield against the sea.

Damp mists surrounded me, and it seemed the people, the Rave, even the blood fae, had left me to be alone with him. A few steps to my side, Silas leaned against a broken cask. He combed his fingers through his hair, shoulders shuddering.

"Silas."

He shook his head.

I crept over to his side, placing my hands on the tops of his knees. My body wouldn't stop trembling, but I tugged against one of his arms. "Silas, look at me."

He pulled back his hands. Red lined his eyes; unshed tears brightened them to a dark green. The mask was absent, the cowl he'd used to hide his face had fallen back. A wide, taut scar carved in jagged lines from his brow to jaw. It mangled the skin in a line like a raised spine down his face. How it missed his eye was a mystery, but it looked painful and deep.

Some might call the wound frightening, cursed, even. To me, he was the brightest memory. To me, he was home at long last.

With slow, tender movements, I cupped the damaged side of his face. He blew out a rough breath and tilted his head into my touch. For a long pause, we simply stayed there, heads together, breathing deeper until our emotions calmed.

"Do you know . . ." Silas cleared his throat. "Do you know what it's like?"

With the back of my knuckles, I stroked his cheek. "What what's like?"

His eyes burned through mine. His voice steadied. "Do you know what it's like to watch the light of your *soul* die over and over? Do you know what it's like to burn for lifetimes for another who fears you in the end?"

A sob burst from my chest, and I flung my arms around his neck. He jolted in surprise, but it took mere heartbeats before his strong arms crushed me against him. Silas turned his face and drew in a long breath, as though soaking up every piece of me.

"I didn't . . . I didn't fear you," I said, voice rough. "I just . . . feared that fate would rob me of myself. I feared death. I lost sight of who belonged to my whisper in the dark. You were always there, and I . . . I left you alone all this time."

Silas didn't speak, but I was starting to think sometimes he simply didn't know what to say.

Steady warmth built in my heart the longer I held him, some force tethering me to this man. Something sturdy and unbreakable, a promise that he wouldn't hurt again. A desire to fight off all the demons that came for him, the enemies, the blades; I wouldn't let them near my Whisper.

Silas's shoulders shook, but his tears were silent and tangled with mine. A song of sorrow and fate tied us together and kept us apart in the same breath. I hated it. I hated that he'd suffered. He'd watched Annon, he'd watched me, succumb to death time and again, unable to do anything but carry the tales onward with his voice and my words.

He'd been alone and suffering, and I'd fled from him.

I'd ignored him.

I'd left him.

Truths were clear now. I'd spoken true to my Kind Heart when I told her there were signs of four storytellers before me. What I hadn't known was each one . . . was me.

"How was it possible?" I asked softly. "I looked so different each time, even in my age and name."

"You . . . chose the proper place to join each path and fated tale," Silas said. "You kept each name connected to your past."

"I didn't know my past."

"Your heart did."

My brow furrowed. "But . . . when the tales ended, where did I go? It is like I simply appeared."

"I don't know where you would go. I would feel your soul still in existence, until it burned brighter, and you were there again, ready for another tale." Silas sniffed and tightened his embrace.

So, between each moment, I . . . simply drifted into oblivion? An ache pummeled my skull. "But how did my soul remain? It goes against everything I know of the Otherworld and lifetimes."

Silas hesitated. "Your soul lived on because . . . your soul bond lived. A tether in the darkness, a ballast in the tumult."

Soul bond. My lips parted when I pulled back to look at him. "You?"

He didn't respond, but he didn't need to. Silas, my phantom voice, was the deepest bond. Deeper than the heart, he was a piece of my soul.

"You were left to live this way all to bring me back? You are the bond—gods—you lived such an existence simply to keep *me alive?*"

Silas's eyes burned with something new. "I would do it all again to see you breathing."

Bleeding gods. The pain, the suffering, it was almost too much to bear. Then again, there was more. Devotion, strength, unyielding love. All the brighter pieces of the heart would be needed for him to survive such a wretched existence of solitude and death and darkness.

And he felt them for me.

I had lived different lives, over and over again.

And he'd watched my slaughter, time after time.

Live and live again until death at crimson night. That's what Annon meant when he told me I was ready to find my power. Crimson night shattered the endless cycle, it ended my father's manipulation of a natural life. This was what broke Riot Ode—he'd wiped his daughter from existence, true, because he'd made me a bleeding immortal until I was strong enough to find my power.

It worked; through the lifetimes my power grew. Each fated path added to my voice, it drew me closer to the other part of me. It drew me back to Silas.

"I chose my true name," I said. "Does it mean . . . this is the last?"

"The final tale. There is no new lifetime here. This is *your* fated path, Little Rose."

Hells, like my royals had walked their paths, now I'd unwittingly accepted mine.

I eased back, my palms on Silas's damp cheeks. He held my gaze, unblinking. His fingertips touched my jaw, traced the lines of my chin, my throat, as if studying every surface.

All these turns he'd watched my blood spill, unable to stop it. I could imagine the madness that might come with such solitude and gore. Affection, respect, adoration, *something*, was suffocating me. A sensation that raged through my veins, as though touching him was the only thing that might give me new breath.

My thumb tugged at his bottom lip; I pressed my brow to his. He needed to know. "Silas."

"Little Rose?"

I was not bold. I was wholly inexperienced. But I knew him. Like a piece of me had slipped back into place, I knew he belonged here, with me, his hands on my skin.

"Say the word, Silas," I whispered, tilting my head, "and I would follow you through the lifetimes."

Before courage fled from my body, I held my breath, and kissed him.

CHAPTER 17
THE PHANTOM

MY DAMN BODY WAS SPLITTING IN TWO. FROM THE CENTER OF MY CHEST TO the top of my skull, I was on fire. A beautiful destruction of want and need and wholeness at long last.

Calista's mouth was on mine. A first in every way, and for too many moments I was still as death. Stun bled into want. Unease bled into desire. Fear bled into obsession.

A groan slid from the back of my throat. I cupped her head and bruised her lips with my own. I'd witnessed kisses aplenty in my lifetime. Some were slow, gentle, and tender. Others were violent, wet, and rough. In this moment, I saw the merit of both.

Part of me wanted to devour her. I wanted to bite and scratch and taste my way into her. The other side wanted to study every divot, every curve, every beautiful surface of her body until the dawn.

"Silas." My name came off her tongue in a soft rasp, as if uncertain of what we were doing, yet she couldn't stop.

I wouldn't stop until she demanded it.

Calista Ode took my heart and soul when we were children. First, as the heir I felt obligated to protect out of gratitude for a king who did not toss me to the cruelty of the world. Next, as a little friend. Two strange young ones no one truly understood.

Now, she took everything. My friendship, my voice, my heart, my soul. She could have it all. I was always destined to bow to her. I owned nothing, for everything I had to give had always belonged to the storyteller.

Where her touch had been gentle, her kiss was desperate. Fingers tangled in my hair; she pulled me closer.

I clawed at her waist, taking her braids in fistfuls in one hand, and circled her body with my arm. To claim her mouth, to taste her, was a thrill more intoxicating than the rush of seidr in the veins, drew more sensation than harsh ale on the tongue.

The warmth of her tongue brushed against my lips.

I pulled back, breaths heavy. "Gods, do that again."

Calista smiled and crushed her mouth to mine. The tip of her tongue slipped into my mouth. My blood raced in a raging fire, rich desire added to the thrill of discovering the sweet seduction of her taste, like a forest after rain, fresh and sweet and free.

Her fingertips slipped down the back of the neck on my tunic. She grinned when I shuddered and blew out a rough breath too forceful against her mouth.

A hiss slid between my teeth.

"You don't like to be touched?"

"I like to be touched by you." I took a risk and dragged my teeth and lips across the slope of her throat. "But it feels as though fire is in my skull."

Calista paused her touch, then drew her lips to the sharp point of my ear. "Your touch does the same. Why is that?"

Because our souls were tethered. They'd fought centuries to reunite, and it felt like the whole world was shifting under the collision.

Words seemed too weak. I didn't know how to explain it all. I didn't try and kissed her again. Calista sighed and sank against my chest, her arms choked my neck, and she leveraged each of her slender thighs over my lap.

Damn the hells. Arousal was harsh and cruel with her sweet

body straddling mine. Gods, how did a man keep control when the fiercest desire of his heart rocked against his damn length? Was it even possible? Or did every male in existence lose control in his bleeding trousers?

Did she know she was destroying me? Perhaps that was the whole bleeding point.

I'd never touched a woman. We'd been separated as children who didn't understand such things. Through the centuries that childish love shifted into something fiercer. Something darker. Something deeper.

Desire trembled through me, and if she did not keep her hands on me, I would not be able to draw another breath. Little by little the gentility of inexperience and stun shifted into the passionate, rough kiss. The one that spoke of different things, like tongues on flesh and bodies united as one.

I would never tire of her nearness. After watching time and again her eyes lose the life inside, I'd nearly thought this moment might never be. She'd always been robbed from me in the moments she remembered me.

It was the way of things. Before the curse took her from one lifetime to the next, she would call to me. Speak to me. It was in those moments we would prepare for a new tale. It was then her power would shine and grow and I would sing the final words, sending the paths of fate we put in motion as littles forward to reach the end.

To reach this moment.

Calista's fingertips teased the back of my neck, tangling in my hair. Her nose nuzzled against my skin, then she kissed the puckered scar on my cheek.

A voice cleared behind us.

Calista pulled back, eyes narrowed. "What, Olaf? I'm occupied."

"We have matters to discuss."

I tilted my head in a way I could see the second commander in the corner of my eye. It had been turns since I'd seen the man. Knew he was there, of course, but I'd been bound to the palace where a broken world began. My sole focus was leading Calista Ode back to the first song, so naturally the rest of the world faded into insignificance.

The Rave were buried beneath illusions and manipulations, locked in time, waiting for their princess to call them to arms, or fade as the tale was forgotten and lost.

"You're damn right we have matters to discuss." Calista released me from her embrace and scrambled off my lap. "I saw it all. Do you know how many times I've died, hmm? A lot more than you, so you'll excuse me if these *matters* we must discuss come from him first—" She jabbed a finger in my direction. "And you second. How long will that golden shield hold?"

Olaf blinked through a stun. "Well, it was a defense spell created by King Riot, and the longest I've seen it last is six sunrises."

"Six sunrises. That gives us time to plan. It gives us time to understand what brought us here."

"But—"

"No. No damn buts. I have unanswered questions," she snapped, and yanked on my hand, tugging me back to my feet. "No more guesses. No more half-tales. The lives of every person I love once more hang in the balance. I will not risk them when I do not know the steps to take."

Olaf glanced at me, as though I might reel her back. Fool. I would not stop her voice for anything—her voice was my freedom, my peace, it was the thickest part of my blood that kept my damn heart beating.

I pulled the hood over my face. The Rave slowly gathered close, but instead of watching the argument between Calista and Olaf, they gaped at me. Most knew the king's ward was a puppeteer behind those gates, twisting and turning paths of fate from the shadows. But none had truly seen me.

No mistake, over the centuries, I'd become more ghost than anything.

A thousand gazes seemed to needle against my skin. Unease tightened like a garrot around my throat. Gods, I wanted to leave, wanted to return to the shadows.

I wanted Calista to follow.

"If sea folk emerged once," Olaf argued, "then they will do it again."

"I know. We'll question the sea singer captured by the blood fae and hope we gain some answers on the other kingdoms." Calista gave a wary look to the black flame one of her thieving companions had designed.

Clever, but the way she slumped, the way her jaw tightened, it was a distressing sight for her.

"I need to know how to help them," she whispered, to herself more than anyone. "I need to know how to end this. We guard our shores, do what we can to send word to the other kingdoms. All that takes time. Give me a bit of time to find my place in all this."

Olaf sighed in frustration. "Princess, I know commanding an army is out of your expertise, but we really must—"

"She wants time." It took a heartbeat or two to realize I'd bellowed the words. I stepped between Calista and the commander. "You will give her the time. More than blades are needed to win this damn fight, and you know it."

Olaf blinked, frowning. "Seems you've grown into your voice, boy."

I leaned closer. "You wish this to be the old world—it is not."

"No," Olaf muttered. "You saw to that."

"Enough." Calista tugged on my arm and shoved her way between the two of us. "If you blame Silas for the shift of our world, then you blame us both."

Olaf had the decency to look ashamed. "Forgive me. I blame no one."

"You do," she went on, "but I understand. No doubt you lost many in the fights of old. My father did what he did to save our people, but we must remember this is not the same kingdom. There are more powers than ours now, Olaf. Like us, they are fated to aid in the end of this fight. Guard our land. We will do our part as you do yours."

My heart rushed when Calista curled her hand around my arm, almost possessively. To have anyone care what became of me was a forgotten notion. I could not decide if it made me want to shrink into oblivion, or pull her against me and take her mouth, so no one questioned she was mine.

"We'll guard the shores, Cal." A man approached. Tall, warrior-strong, with strange eyes that looked like ice. I'd seen him a great deal at her side. I envied him. Desired to thank him for protecting her. Perhaps wanted to hate him a little for it too.

"Cuyler." She released my arm and took his. All at once, the unfair desire to hate him grew more potent. Calista lowered her voice. "We need answers from your sea fae."

"Doubt it'll talk. It's horrid." Cuyler shuddered.

"We need to try," Calista whispered. "That battle lord fiend isn't here. I want to know why."

If I had to guess, Calista wanted to know if Davorin had taken a fight to another kingdom. I didn't know what happened in this tale. I only knew it was meant to end back at the beginning. It was meant to end with her.

My palm heated when Calista slipped her fingers through mine. The blood fae was holding an arm toward one of the new stone structures; a gesture for us to follow.

Calista's eyes glimmered with panic and something vicious. "You coming, Whisper?"

I smirked. "Wherever you go, Little Rose."

CHAPTER 18
THE STORYTELLER

CUYLER AND HIS MEN STASHED THE HORRID SEA SINGER IN THE DAMP CELLAR at the Norn's house—or at least, what used to be the Norn's house. It looked more like a blockhouse on a bleeding fortress. Embrasures and parapet walls surrounded the space. Wood and stone grouted together with thick clay deadened the outer world and kept the air cool inside.

More than the old, rotting house transforming into something out of a battle journal, I could not overcome the transformation of the sisters.

Young, almost lovely. Their ghostly eyes weren't so frightening, but it was strange to see their lumps and rolls tighten up to muscle and lean sinews.

I tapped Forbi on her slender shoulder as we trudged down the wooden staircase.

"Are you well, Forbi?" I asked. "There seems to be an urgency, and you once urged me to accept the truth. What happens if I don't?"

"Will the royal her take on the burden should the truth be said?"

"If you're asking if I feel guilty countless folk have been trapped in a dreary existence for lifetimes in Raven Row, then yes. I'm not made of damn stone."

Forbi frowned and let out a sigh. "Tales begin to fade. The part where a dark story grew stronger begins. It begins the part where fate paves *a dark him's* path to victory."

What did that mean? "Davorin's victory?"

"Our tale is clear," Forbi said, turning to continue down the steps. "But without the call, the dark him will rise. Beneath him, we fade."

I was left befuddled, with a touch of bile in my throat. With a cautious glance over my shoulder, I found Silas in the shadows. He stood by no one but me, almost as though others frightened him more than the blood spilled in the Row.

"My delay would cause your souls to fade? Is that what you're saying?"

"Risks from twists and fate. More time, a dark him has more strength."

I pressed a hand to my chest when my heart felt as though it might shatter its way through. "So, because I waited . . . Davorin's fate grew stronger?"

"How could you know, Little Rose?" Silas asked from behind us.

"No." I held up a hand. "No, don't coddle me. I knew there was a path I needed to take, and I ignored it. I fought against it out of fear."

I shook my head. Damn tears. They stung the backs of my eyes and made it difficult to see properly. What a fool, what a weak-spined fool I'd been. The song that broke these kingdoms, the curse, the new story Silas and I had brought into fruition weakened because of my cowardice.

It had given that wretch too much time to strengthen, to grow, to return and attack the people I loved most.

I'd never forgive myself should they be harmed because I refused to move forward.

Out of these fated crowns, I was the weakest.

Elise was willing to sacrifice her own bleeding life for Legion Grey, a cursed beast whose true name was hidden.

Malin was willing to face the tyrants of her land, to accept a throne with a bloody history, all to stand at the side of her Shadow King.

Saga was afraid of her own heart, yet she boldly handed it to the Golden King despite the risks. She faced the man who'd tried to break her, and brought war to his feet.

What had I done? Learned my true name, learned I had a place in all this, then dug my head in the sand for the better part of ten turns all to hide from the feeling, the burn that I, too, had a place in this brutal tale.

Cuyler opened the door to the cellar, the others spilled into the room. Once inside, Silas kept to the corners, his hood pulled over his head. Cuyler strode over to the opposite wall where the horrid creature appeared dry and sickly. His face seemed to rot off his bones, the holes in his flesh revealed his teeth.

Skin flecked off in scaly pieces, and every rib showed through thin, iridescent flesh whenever he drew in a gasp.

Cuyler reached for a water basin and ewer off a wobbly table near a shelf with crates of turnips. "Thirsty, sea singer?"

The creature opened his yellowed eyes, dried lips parted, and his breaths grew harsher when Cuyler poured a long stream of water into the basin.

"I could wet your tongue should you speak."

The sea singer chuckled, rough and raw. He was such a hideous thing. How had I ever felt a flicker of desire? Then again, the song of a sea singer was one of the grandest illusions.

"No?" Cuyler shrugged one shoulder. He lifted the bowl to his own mouth and took a sloppy gulp, intentionally allowing water to spill down his chin. He let out a gasp of relief, grinning. "So refreshing."

"Why speak when . . ." the sea singer began, "when I am . . . dead anyway?"

Cuyler returned the bowl to the table and snapped his fingers. "Good question. You're right, you are dead. But how quickly and painlessly you die is up to you. Where is the battle lord?"

The sea singer tilted his head. "The dark earthen fae?"

"Whatever you call him, he's not one of you. He fled to your watery world like a coward. He's bringing war between our worlds, is he not?"

The sea singer didn't sneer. Truth be told, the poor bastard looked more exhausted than anything. He stared longingly at the bowl and ewer. "He takes enemies back to their truest hatred. To the torment he enjoyed most."

"He's attacking each kingdom in ways he tormented them before." The words spilled from my mouth before I could stop them. I blinked and looked to Cuyler. "I-I don't know how I know that."

"It is his role in the tale," Silas said in a soft rumble.

"What do you mean?"

"Through the histories he used hatred, war, blood. It makes sense he would use hatred in their lands to torment them once again."

A cruel shiver bit its way up my arms. He was right. As little sense as it made, every kingdom, every gift of fate's magic, was an enemy to Davorin. He would try his best to cut them at the knees.

"He's not here," I said, facing the sea singer. "Not yet. Isn't that right?"

The creature drew in a rattling breath, the slightest curl to his pocked, rotting lips flickered on his face. "Not the time."

"He's waiting for a certain moment you think?" Cuyler folded his arms and came to stand by me. "What is it, do you suppose?"

"I don't know," I admitted. "But Davorin is biding his time. He's waiting for something. Where is he, sea singer?"

A hacking cough filled the sea fae's lungs. When he looked at us again his expression was vicious. "The earth fae remains near the Ever Ship."

"I've sailed on that damn monstrosity." I grimaced, but my heart skipped. "Wait, the Ever Ship was . . . your king's ship. He's dead."

"I do not . . . speak lies." The sea singer's chest heaved as he searched for air. His body was battered, soon he would struggle to speak without wetting his lips. I knew enough about the sea fae to know some fared decently on land. Others, like the sea singer, could hardly keep their eyes open when removed from the seas too long.

"What has Davorin promised your people in return for fighting his war?" I snapped.

Three breaths, five. After the sea fae swallowed with effort he spoke. "Revenge."

I shared a look with Silas. He was not there, but doubtless he knew what had happened between myself and King Thorvald of the Ever. The way the bastard had snatched me straight out of Olaf's alehouse, the way I'd left my royals to find their missing littles with my Cursed King's newly cursed blood.

I knew the end of the tale, knew Valen had lodged an axe in Thorvald's chest.

Revenge. The sea folk were here to avenge their fallen king. Doubtless it wasn't hard to convince them to rise, not with Davorin's sly tongue and battle skill.

"Kill me," the sea singer rasped. "Allow me to see the seas of the Otherworld, and I will leave you with one final warning to aid your fight."

Cuyler looked to me until I gave him a quick nod. The blood fae removed a knife and approached the sea singer. "Speak true, and you'll be out of your misery."

The creature let out a breath of relief. He lifted his gaze to me. "When you meet the Ever King again, a word of advice—if you wish to keep your lives, I wouldn't make him bleed."

"What is that supposed to mean?"

The sea singer smirked and merely closed his eyes. He'd given his warning. He would say nothing more. Soon, he choked and spluttered as blood filled his lungs after Cuyler slit a deep gash over his neck.

Don't make the Ever King bleed?

"So, the sea fae have a new king," I said. "Davorin has influenced them. They have reason to despise our folk after that bastard of a king was killed. We are facing a great war," I admitted. "One between land and sea. One between hatred and love."

"His part comes when he returns to his land of old," Danna whispered.

I furrowed my brow. "Davorin's part?"

"Back to the beginning," Oviss added.

Frustration boiled over, but the heat on my skin soothed when a hand rested on my shoulder. Silas had abandoned his corner to stand beside me. Such a simple gesture, yet somehow, I knew it caused him a great deal of discomfort.

Somehow, it made it better knowing he was there.

"I don't know how to help them," I whispered. "I found you because I was out making a promise to protect Lumpy—my Sun Prince. Now, I feel as if I've left them all to the crazed vengeance of a madman. As if I've done this to them."

Silas placed a palm on the side of my face. For a moment it was as though no one but the two of us remained. "Then sing with me, Little Rose."

"Sing with . . ." I swallowed. We had a power together—his song, my words. It crumbled worlds. Perhaps it could be enough to give a new burst of fate to stand on the sides of my royals. Whatever battles they fought, it might help them.

It might protect them.

"I don't have the words," I admitted.

"This is the part of a first bond," Forbi muttered. Her youth was restored, yet the damn woman continued to speak in riddles. I was beginning to think she did it on purpose.

Instead of berating her, I merely sighed. "Explain, Forbi."

With Danna and Oviss at her side, the seers knelt on the damp stone. From inside the pouch on her belt, Forbi removed a handful of rune stones. Danna took out a burgundy candle from hers. Forbi clutched her sisters' hands and began to hum.

The tune was steady, low, and eerie. A chill deepened in the cellar, thick and musty, and pressed against my lungs until I thought it might ache to breathe.

When Forbi's eyes opened, the milky white practically glowed. "The final gift joins at last, a tale of queens for a deadly task."

Forbi's eyes fluttered closed, and Danna's opened. "A dreary foe attacks the gates, hunting for his crown to take."

"Hand in hand, you must stand," Oviss chanted, "all gifts united in our first land."

Forbi hummed. "Sing a tale."

"Bring them home," Danna said, voice soft.

Oviss finished gently with, "Only then will defeat or victory be known."

Next, the three sisters repeated a line, one that was oddly familiar. One I'd heard before when Saga used the sisters' voices to help find her way back to Ari.

Now I saw, it was always aimed at me.

"A caution follows with this tale," the seers said, softly, "should the first bond break, you will fail."

"I feel to say these crowns afar," said Danna, "relive the battles once fought before. A curse of blood, a sea seeking revenge, and a plague of darkness across a land."

"Gods." Silas closed his eyes.

"What?" I gripped his wrist. "What is it?"

"That's what he's doing—he's reigniting the battles that led to the restoration of each crown." He held up a finger for each kingdom. "A curse broken by a choice is again restored. The unification in the East with the sea fae brought them to find the queen's ring, did it not? Yet, it led to a new enemy that would want revenge. And a plague of darkness brought the Raven Queen and Golden King together."

My head pounded in a sick rush of panic. I didn't know exactly what was happening in the other kingdoms, but it didn't take much to guess it was wretched and bloody and dangerous.

"Fight back." Danna said. "Will the royal her let a cruel him crush her head?"

"We need to help them," I said, not to anyone in particular, but more a plea to my own desire.

Forbi rose to her feet. "Then you must sing the songs of fate to choose the soul that will make you whole."

I blinked, looking to Silas. I never wanted to be commanded by the whims of the Norns. It frightened me to know my choices were not my own. But what if, long ago, a path began merely because a little boy and a little girl cared for each other?

What if, before two children even knew anything about heart songs and love of souls, they chose each other?

Silas held out a hand. "I do not know every step. But we have changed paths before. Sing with me, and we might know what moves to take."

I feared what might come of another song between the two of us. From the beginning we'd altered paths, we caused the beginning of the end to a kingdom. Still, there was power here, a boil to my veins, a truth I didn't fully understand.

To sing with my Whisper, to unite my words with his, somehow, I knew it was the only way to save them.

"Careful, Cal," Cuyler whispered. "Your seidr . . . I can feel it. Something is changing. Take care."

He wasn't wrong. There was a heady sense that something was about to change. Perhaps something dangerous. Perhaps it would be as devasting as it was the night we sang a song to save my Raven Queen aunt.

I licked my lips, then reached for Silas's hand.

CHAPTER 19
THE STORYTELLER

HIS TOUCH UNLOCKED A FIRE THAT CONSUMED ME, HEAD TO FOOT. AS though a hook dug into my chest and tethered me to him, there was a sudden peace amidst the fear.

Incoherent words filtered through my head. Silas closed his eyes. A tune, soft and lovely, quiet enough I was certain only I could hear it, built in the back of his throat. His song. My words. This wasn't the same magic as Riot Ode.

"I'm thinking something," I said. "But I don't understand it."

His lips flicked in a cautious smile. "You have the words."

Chest to chest, I embraced the warmth of his skin, the leather and musk scent of his clothes, I found a bit of peace in the chaos, and let the words build in my mind before a string of words formed in my head. A song of unseen paths of fate crossing, of broken hearts restored.

"I don't have parchment and ink," I whispered.

"Does she need it?" Oviss said, head cocked to one side. "A bond burns fiercer than ink."

"A bond burns the tales of fate." Forbi beamed and gestured between me and Silas.

"She has not accepted the bond," Silas said. He looked away for a few breaths. "There are still hesitations that remain."

I wanted the ground to swallow me up. Was I so obvious? Did the crippling fear of fate bleed through so clearly? "I don't even know how."

Silas rubbed the back of his neck. "You will feel it down to your soul. A burn, a connection."

I felt it, the boil in my veins, the longing, the need. But a cloud of fear, of hesitation, of doubt was there like a villainous poison keeping me one step away. I wanted to shout at him, that despite the fear and hesitation, with each passing moment, my mind, my heart, seemed to seek his touch and presence. But Oviss clicked her tongue and removed a crinkled piece of parchment and battered quill from the old satchel.

"Old ways then, royal her."

Ashamed, I took hold of her quill and parchment. With a pinched expression, Danna offered up a small vial of ink.

I blinked to Silas. He was a formidable shadow that brought a strange kind of comfort to my soul. A delight to behold and fear in the same breath. I studied his sharp jaw, a near-straight nose but for the slightest bump that hinted it might've been broken once before. A dark coat of stubble covered his stern chin, and the hint of scars and terror on the other half added a bit of mystery.

I'd always loved a good mystery.

"Write the words, Little Rose. They will still use your seidr." He said softly. "Don't force what is not there."

A crack of guilt, of a strange kind of anguish, fractured through my chest.

I was denying him with every sliver of doubt; I was denying the sacrifice he'd offered by standing by, watching lifetimes come and go as he sang his song, as he aided me along the way. All while he remained lost in the darkness.

For weeks my seidr had left me wanting and empty.

Now, beside him, words flowed through my thoughts. But more than that, it was as if they dripped through my blood. Liquid fire filled me, head to foot, and I could not imagine keeping the words inside, as though each syllable pounded against my ribcage in a frenzy.

A shudder danced down my spine as I wrote each symbol, and Silas's low, sorrowful voice followed.

Gods. I nearly groaned in a twisted pleasure as the burn of seidr bled from my fingertips, his voice, and into the words on the parchment.

Heat seemed to seep through every pour, a radiant calm wrapped around my small corner of the room. A complete song of fate.

I schooled my gaze on the new words. Short, but I had the sense they'd be powerful.

A song of blood keeps life for the one you love.
Trust and let it be, in this a tale of land and sea.

The final words baffled me, but I couldn't recall when a tale didn't. They were vague, but this one brought hope. As if some part of me could sense the peace it would bring to the intended—the Sun Prince.

"I feel as if this is meant for Sol," I admitted.

"It is a start, then," Cuyler offered.

"I always burn them." I glanced at Forbi. "May I use your candle?"

Danna huffed, flicking her fingers toward Silas. "No need for flames of old. When the moment is right, the song of heart will take hold."

My pulse quickened. Silas was the other half of my song, and we were reunited again. Fire likely paled next to the power of the connection in our joined seidr. Kept apart all this time, doubtless the flame had purpose, but now . . . perhaps all we need was each other.

I tucked Sol's song into my trousers and reached for the quill again. "There's more."

Silas's soft voice followed every scratch of quill to parchment. The same brilliant flame ignited in my gut, a desire so fierce I nearly reached out and pulled him closer. It was consuming, confusing, and intoxicating all at once as the words flowed between us.

When shields fall, a heart will call.
Send light to crowns of fate.
When enemies stand on this first land,
Then ends this battle of hate.

I studied the parchment. No time was wasted wondering what it could all mean. It didn't matter. Deep in my belly, I knew it was a path written in stone. No matter what I did, this fight would reach our shores.

Davorin was attacking. He was weakening fated crowns through his ploys and dark games.

"I don't want this battle sod to win," I whispered to Silas. "I cannot stop his return."

"It has already begun," he said.

"I don't want to run. I don't want more funeral pyres. He's harming the people I love." He would come for Silas. A surprising thought, but it ached. Davorin had already tried to murder my Whisper before. The scar was visible forever.

"What is it you want, Little Rose?"

"To understand this feeling. This pull . . . to you."

His jaw pulsed. "Will you deny it?"

"I want to." I admitted. His body stiffened when I stood by his side. "But only because I don't understand it."

Silas hesitated, then held out a hand. "Then stay with me. I will tell you all I know."

Cuyler cleared his throat and faced the few blood fae who'd followed into the cellar. "The princess and Wraith will do their part in preparing these shores against more sea fae and our common enemy. We take our places with the restored Rave. We serve them as fiercely as we serve the fae isles of the South."

His men slammed their fists against their chests.

"We serve you, Calista Ode." Cuyler gave me a small smile, then looked to Silas. "And the Mad King."

Silas's cheeks heated in a flush of pink. He didn't deny it. Another of those questions for which I needed an answer. How had he been here, known as a king, a leader in this dreary kingdom, yet never been seen?

"Come on." I slipped my fingers through Silas's. "You don't say much, Whisper, but I will need you to do some talking."

His mouth twitched in a small smile. "Say the word, Little Rose, and I will tell you anything."

"Good, because I have a feeling, a nasty one, that we don't have much time to figure out what steps we ought to take. I have a feeling my kings and queens are fighting battles, and I'm not certain any of us can defeat them without each other."

CHAPTER 20
THE PHANTOM

"WHAT ARE WE DOING HERE?" CALISTA ASKED OUTSIDE THE CHANGED tenement building where she'd lived time and time again.

Old wooden walls were now packed in clay and stone, part of a fortress near the sea. Still, the door was marked with the same runes as the old door, the last sign this was where she'd lived her lifetimes.

I took her hand and led her inside. She cast a sorrowful glance at the cot where Annon had spent his nights; there was an emptiness with his absence. He could not speak with me, but he knew I was there.

The captain had his ways of offering little comforts, as though he could sense I was fighting to cling onto reality, as if he knew all I desperately wanted was to fall into the shadows of a world where she did not die.

I missed him but recalled better than Calista how desperately Annon wanted to sup in the hall of the gods with King Riot. He took an oath to defend the heir, to see her to her true power, but he wanted to die as a Rave and join his men in the Otherworld.

True, I missed him, but was pleased for him.

Over the sagging mantle of the tiny fireplace, I moved a panel of the wall, then another, and another, until a damp, musty corridor opened.

"What the hells?" Calista poked her head inside. A cool breeze rippled her hair around her face. "How . . . how long has this been here?"

"Always," I said, voice rough. "I-I was bound to the palace grounds, but needed some connection where Annon could pass through to . . . ensure I hadn't slipped into total madness."

"Bound to the palace?" Calista closed her eyes for a breath and flexed her fingers once, twice, then looked to me. "Bound to me. You have been the greatest captive of us all, Silas."

The hair lifted on the back of my neck. Her distress was . . . distressing. I did not want her to think I resented it—how could I? She had always been, even before the world shattered, my friend, my safe one, my heart. The hells had consumed me, no mistake, all these turns. But now, even with the fear in her eyes, it was worth it.

"Part of the curse," I said with a shrug. "The soul bond to the cursed princess was damned to become a spectral, a forgotten piece of the past. Doubtless, the Norns had a bit of fun with that piece of vengeance for the manipulation of the fated paths. It was my idea, after all."

"Your idea saved Saga. It was the boldest idea, Silas."

I faced the corridor, uneasy. "Every kingdom, every crown, had to claw their way through their tale. This is ours, why should we have had it any easier?"

"Our tale." Calista gnawed on her bottom lip. "A first bond."

"Yes. A connected vein of seidr. Unusual, but . . . some would say fated to be." I glanced at the floor. "You *are* the words of my songs. Without your existence, it is nothing more than a tune."

"And you are the spirit behind my words."

I could not sing alone the way King Riot could sing. Somehow our talents, our seidr, bonded into one—her words, my voice became a new vein of fate magic.

Calista cleared her throat and grinned. "Tell me why you've been sneaking around my rooms, Silas. I'm considering slapping you for peeping on me. What have you seen?"

Heat flooded my face. "I never did. As I said, this was for Annon to help bring my presence to you."

"Wait, the roses." She folded her arms over her chest. "That's how he always brought your damn roses."

"You once loved the roses."

"I never stopped," she said softly. "Merely let fear cloud the pull toward them."

No more fears. The games we'd played until now would end.

The corridor wove around new towers, new walls, but soon the damp soil of Hus Rose filled my lungs. A heavy door opened into the mausoleum. A bloody tint to the moon cast scattered shadows around the tomb.

Calista dragged her fingertips over the names of the king and queen. Her chin quivered. "I remember them so well now. It's like a sieve of the past is breaking through the barriers. What age was I when the worlds broke apart? My Raven Queen could never recall. I suppose it's all a little hazy for the lot of us."

"It feels so long ago, but you were nearing your ninth turn."

"And you?"

"I am five turns your senior."

"Hmm, but if I was a soul living numerous lifetimes . . . how many turns am I now?" She arched a brow, almost playfully.

The corner of my mouth curled into a smirk. "I suppose as old as you'd like to be, Little Rose. We did begin this land. We can make the rules."

She snorted. "I feel like we are the youngest, yet . . . we're the eldest other than my Raven Queen. In truth, I figured I was younger during my parents' battles. I appeared so small in my Golden King's dream walk."

"You are *still* small."

Calista rammed her elbow into my ribs. "Being small has gotten me out of more than one tight spot, you sod. All you thick, bumbling men draw more attention than anyone."

"I wasn't arguing the point."

"I think you were."

"And I think you," I said, flicking one of her braids, "still start fights for no damn reason."

Calista's mouth parted. "I do not."

"You do."

"Wrong."

I tilted my head. "Point made."

"You're irritating."

I chuckled. Such a normal sound, yet one so foreign it sent the hair on the back of my neck on end. My smile slipped, and we fell back into a quiet until we entered the palace hall.

When I was silent too long, Calista forced a crooked grin. "You know, back on the Row, I, uh, I didn't mean to lose my wits."

"You lost your wits?"

A splash of pink tinged the tips of her ears. "Yes, when I practically ate you."

The kiss. I cracked the knuckles of my thumbs and turned away. "Then I rather like when you lose your wits."

A heady pressure gathered between us. Desire, unease, a new uncertain path, all tangled in tension.

"Seeing all that," she went on, "It was just . . . a lot, you know? Learning you're an all-powerful being that can't die is quite the accomplished task to take in a day. I need to wrap my head around it, then find a way to rub it in Ari's face, mostly. He boasts about his grandness so often, it's time someone stuns him."

I smiled. "What do you wish me to say first?"

She took hold of my hand and led us to a faded, musty bench. "Tell me about breaking the kingdom."

I looked ahead. Turns of silence, now I could hardly find a way to speak longer than a few words. "Our first true song awakened new paths, alternate paths where the gifts of the Norns and gods-magic were divided among the people instead of held by one throne."

"That was the song we sang as children when Saga was found battered and beaten?"

"Yes," I said. "You . . . you loved her so much, and I only wanted to put your heart at ease, so I sang."

"I always loved when you sang," she whispered, rubbing her

139

forehead. "Something about the sound was so soothing." Calista's eyes snapped to mine. "But you could see things, couldn't you? You didn't always need my words. I recall when my mother was possessed, you were singing. You told her something about her fate."

"I get feelings and thoughts, the same as when you write simple premonitions. To truly change the outcome of fate, to truly build a destiny, I must have your words."

The first glimmer of my seidr came to me as a boy, not long after the announcement of the heir of House Ode. As if my magic was born with her. When I was in her presence, the songs could hardly be helped.

When her power grew even stronger, well, together we shattered worlds.

"We combined words and song when we found Saga, right? That's why it was so powerful?"

I looked away, ashamed. "We'd never truly used our voices in such a way. I never meant for it to break everything, but I told you to add whatever words you thought might make her happy. You wanted the kingdom to grow stronger than Davorin. You wanted your aunt to have the golden king I saw in a dream once. Those desires began the tale of fated queens because it became an alternate path for a raven princess to *become* a queen. It created a world that could rise stronger than before."

"So my Kind Heart and Shadow Queen ought to give us a great deal of thanks for giving them such glamorous titles?"

"I suppose." I offered a small grin. "The first queen opened the way for the rest. As such, the first queen had the longer path."

"The first as in . . ." She looked at me like she already knew the answer.

"You, Little Rose. Your father gave his throne to you. He gave his power away to the first fate queen."

"But my mother—"

"Held seidr, but she could not twist the paths, or sing the songs of a soul the way you can."

We had minor strengths on our own. Dream walking, I'd discovered, was mine. Calista could predict destiny through premonitions like star seers. But together her words and my voice opened the power to unravel the path of fate.

After a long pause, her chin trembled; tears glazed her eyes when she looked at me. "Why could I not know of you? Stef—Annon—knew of you. I think every damn person in Raven Row knew of you. Why not me?"

"A cruel trick of the bitter Norns," I said. "Your path would bring you to rise as a true worker of fate magic, but when your lifeline was shattered, it blinded you from the truth. By restoring each gift, it always led you a little closer back to where you began."

"That doesn't make sense. Annon was always with me, and he was part of my past. He knew my purpose."

I chuckled. It wasn't humorous, more bitter, but I held a great deal of resentment for the Norns. "Your father bested the bleeding Norns. They are cruel, but Riot Ode was sly. He managed to sing a destiny of his captain could walk beside you, so you would not be alone."

She looked at me with a twist of pity. "Stef was tangled in a broken lifetime, but not you. You were cursed to be alone, and I hate it."

"I don't." I swallowed and took a step closer. My hand trembled, slight enough I wasn't certain she'd notice. I pressed a palm to her cheek. "I won't say it has not had its cruel impact, but I knew it would be wretched. Your father warned me. I would need to be the one to hold you here, to guide you back. I was willing and accepted."

Calista shook out her hands. "This is madness. I've always told my royals Raven Row was the first kingdom, and I was damn right. It is." She lifted her gaze with a bit of hesitation. "You are the unseen Mad King, aren't you?"

I studied the grains of the floorboards for a few breaths. "The Western shores needed to be shielded so it could be your home. The ruse was created as part of the shattered world. A ruse with a king, a small, simple system of trade to be inconspicuous. But should anyone wonder too long, should anyone question too much, the wards of seidr would wipe the thoughts clear of the Western Kingdom."

"I don't know how this place even came to be. In my Golden King's dream, the Western seas were empty."

"It was intentional. King Riot needed a place his daughter could return and be safe." My fists clenched; my voice darkened. "A place where the other half of your voice could guide you back, again and again."

"The wards are broken, aren't they?" she whispered. "When I crossed into Hus Rose, I felt the shift. That's when the folk shifted into . . . other people."

"Their true selves."

"But I've always felt an aversion to Hus Rose. Always. If all I needed to do was bleeding cross the threshold, why the hells was I pushed away?"

"It all returns to restoring the gifts, piece by piece. There was a proper time and place. The beginning becomes the last. This tale began with you, but now the other pieces are in place and your path can truly be revealed. I hope we are not too late." Blood pounded through my skull. Emotion pooled in a confusing haze. "The bond should've been found long ago. I should've been found while *he* was weak. *Gods*, do you know what it's like?"

"Silas." Her small hand nudged my shoulder. "Stay with me. Speak to me. Yes, I know I should've been bolder and sought out whatever the first bond meant right after the battle in the South. But *you* cannot keep holding it over my head. We can only move forward now, and frankly, you could've been a little less cryptic. You could've said something like, *come to the palace for answers*, or something better than bleeding *sing with me*."

I pressed my chest to hers. "We were cursed by fate to remain apart. Do you think I could be anything but vague? That is not what aches, Little Rose. It is the truth that you once trusted the voice in the dark, you listened, you accepted it. But it all changed when you got a glimpse at the man behind it."

"What are you talking about?"

"The fae sleep." I made quick work of gripping the back of her neck and drawing her mouth close. The warmth of her gasp kissed my skin. Her eyes were wide, but her palms flattened over my chest.

"Don't lie, Little Rose. You suspected the wraith in the dream had something to do with your Whisper. You felt it, and yet you ran from the sight of me."

"I don't like what you're insinuating. You think your damn *face* is what frightens me?"

When I drew my cheek alongside hers, I took a bit of twisted enjoyment when she stiffened. "It frightens everyone else. Why would you be different?"

Calista grunted in frustration and shoved against my chest again. "Bastard. Scars hardly frighten me. It was the feeling when . . ."

She dragged her bottom lip between her teeth.

"What?" My voice came out rougher than intended, almost desperate. "What frightened you?"

For a moment, she merely studied me, like she was breathing me in. "*You* did, but not how you think. It was this overwhelming draw to the man in the dream. The voice in the dark. I could not resist it; I was consumed the night I saw the memory of Ari's sleep. So consumed I could not even hide the unease from my royals. I . . . I didn't know how to explain it.

"Then, I lost my brother and he mentioned the first bond the same as my father did in the past. It terrified me to think something unknown awaited me, but I didn't know my hesitation was leaving you here to rot."

Tears lined her lashes; she pointed her face to the ground to hide them.

Chaotic thoughts tangled in my skull. They choked off the words, burned through my veins. I pressed my brow to hers, holding her against me. To rot. That's what I had done. I'd decayed, faded; I'd shattered under the weight of helplessness, of anger, of hate and longing. Now, all that remained was a creature she could hardly look in the eyes.

"Do you know what it's like?" I shook my head and glared at the darkness in the corner of the room. "No. She doesn't. She doesn't know."

Gentle hands touched my unmasked cheek. I hadn't realized I'd clenched the whole of my body, until her touch drew out a rough breath and released the mounting tension.

Calista held my face in her palms and peered over my shoulder. "Hey, he's not yours, you damn ghosts."

What the hells? The ghoulish movement from the corners and crevices; my sole companions all this time. There was a fierce piece of me that knew they were nothing but figments of my imagination, but she was . . . shouting at them on my behalf.

"I'm talking to him now, so get gone." Calista gave me a soft smile. "Look at me, Silas. It's just me here now. You're not alone in the dark any longer."

My fingers dug into her arms; my brow dropped to her shoulder. Calista didn't pull away. She didn't flinch. Her palm smoothed down the back of my neck, until my pulse slowed. "I . . . sometimes my thoughts get muddled in the dark."

"I know." Her fingertips traced the line of my jaw. "I hate myself for leaving you here alone. All you've done, all you've been forced to endure, and I abandoned you."

"Little Rose—"

"No." She closed her eyes. "No, it's true, and I don't know if I'll forgive myself for being such a coward. I don't mind if you speak to shadows, Silas, but let me be the one to hold the candle and walk with you through the darkness."

All these turns I'd waited for this moment, when the truth would be hers for the taking, when no walls stood between us, when bonds were found.

She was my mate, my whole being, but she feared losing her own autonomy. "A bond must be accepted, chosen, not forced. You should gather your thoughts, then we can speak more about what moves to make in this war."

"We can't leave the other kingdoms—"

"We do not know how to help them for we are still figuring out our steps," I insisted. We needed to end our tale, we needed to find, accept, and grow in whatever bond was meant to burn between us. But if she did not want it, then we would need to find another way. "While you . . . consider everything you've learned, I will see if we can find a way to set sail to other lands. At the very least, try to send word."

"You'd do that?"

"They have cared for you when I could not be there. I will always fight for them." My jaw pulsed. "Rest, Little Rose. We need to work together to find other solutions."

I did not know what came next. I did not know if we would find each other only to fall in blood against an enemy. I did not know if this was the end of it all.

"Don't go," she said, reaching for me.

I brought her palm to my lips and pressed a kiss in the center. "Gather your thoughts. The steps we take next, we must be sure."

I guided her toward the bed chamber she'd stayed in the first night, then left before I could not. My heart was bonded to hers; every fiber of my being was hers to claim. A piece of the tale, but if she did not wish to accept a fated bond, I would not force it.

I would let her go. I would stand beside her. Even if I couldn't have her.

CHAPTER 21
THE STORYTELLER

Sleep was a ridiculous notion, a mythical thing I'd never find when my blood had not ceased boiling since Silas left me to my damn thoughts.

A bond. He was the first bond everyone wanted me to find. My first song, the boy who'd awakened my magic, my words. The boy who'd watched my death over and over, trapped in cursed shadows, alone for centuries, all so he could help me sing the songs of fate for crowns and kingdoms and . . . us.

He did it all to guide me back to the beginning, to the first kingdom, to him.

Now, he'd left me here to deny him.

That's what it truly came down to—Silas knew I despised fate dictating the desires of my damn heart, so he was willing to let me go. But let me go to do what? Touch another? Kiss another? Bed another? Take vows with some sod I didn't even know? Live alone with Forbi and Danna and Oviss?

With a flurry of kicks, I tossed the furs of the bed off my body and paced near the foot of the bed. Hair stuck to the damp on my forehead, my skin was flushed in prickles of heat, and my bleeding pulse was on fire in my veins.

My royals were under attack, no mistake, but he wasn't wrong. We had our own battles coming to our shores. There was untapped power, magic, seidr, the lot, inside this soil. I could feel it, as though every pump of my heart spewed more heat in my veins. More strength.

I simply couldn't reach it. There was a step to take, one that I knew in the deepest part of my gut would help my family in the other kingdoms.

But was the flame because fate dictated who my heart was destined to love? Was it real?

I dragged my palms down my face, groaning, and leaned my brow against the chilled glass of the window. All I'd wanted was freedom from fate, from darkness, from fear. I'd taken the step, discovered the truth of my existence, now the man who'd unraveled it all had placed my future back in my hands.

"Dammit." I let out a rough breath.

I didn't know what was happening in the other lands, but hot, sharp tears burned behind my eyes. Were they alive? Injured? Was that bastard of a battle lord cutting down their forces?

I wished they were here. I wanted to speak with Saga; she always seemed to know what to bleeding say. I wanted Elise to give me that grin that said it would all be well. I wanted Malin to tease the scowls off Kase's face until we all laughed.

I wanted Sol.

He'd sit beside me and listen to my fears of being a slave to fate's whims. He'd let me rant and rave, then softly give his advice.

I wanted them all, but the wanting for the folk who'd shoved into my heart was a soft ember to the fire burning to find Silas. To feel his skin under my fingertips. To hear the rapid beat of his heart thrumming in time with my own.

While I paced, I caught sight of a torn piece of parchment beneath the crack in the door. The words brought a new thickness to my throat.

Spoke to Olaf. It was horrid, if you must know. I rather hate speaking to folk, but he assured me that signals are being sent to the kingdoms, and the Rave will inspect the sea at the dawn to ensure the water is devoid of sea folk and safe to sail upon. We won't leave them defenseless, Little Rose.

—S

"Gods." I clutched the parchment to my heart. That bleeding bastard and his damn fidelity. He'd stepped outside the gates, stepped into a crowd of folk that likely kept his heart racing, all to see that my royals would be supported.

I turned into the room, aimlessly touching and digging through drawers, as though my hands needed to simply keep busy.

Inside a drawer, my fingers brushed over the ridge of parchment. A book of childish charcoal drawings was inside. Scenes with rabbits with ears that dragged on the grass. Rose bushes with monstrous stingers buzzing about. Sunlight and stick-like horses.

This had been ours. I remembered it so clearly. A book of blank parchment we'd drag about, drawing tales during dull days when he was not required to study with the Rave youth or my father, and I was allowed to wander and explore without irritating nannies.

Hells, even now, I could recall how much I looked forward to the moments with him as a small girl. A soft laugh tangled in a sob as long-forgotten moments flooded through my mind with each page.

Silas, skinny and with his irritated scowl on his face, stood in my doorway. "What the hells are you doing?"

I'd spun around, fumbling with the sash over the dress I was told to wear by a stern-faced servant. "Getting dressed."

Silas let his head fall back and groaned at the rafters before storming into the room. "You hate these stupid skirts."

"I'm supposed to wear it."

"And you're just gonna let folk tell you what to do? I'm not going riding when you're wearing that ugly thing."

I huffed. "S'not ugly, you sod."

"It's ugly. Boots. Trousers. I'll be in the stable if you find your backbone."

My mouth twitched in a small grin as I turned the pages. More memories, more moments, choked the back of my throat.

"Old Mays is outta her damn mind," Silas said when he'd found me with a knife against my tangled curls. He took the knife and dragged a hand down my hair, smoothing out the tangles, after an old cook insisted sparrows would soon take up and nest on my head. "Do you like your hair?"

I nodded.

Silas popped a shoulder in a shrug. "Then don't be stupid and let words make you doubt those things that make you, you."

I could recall so many moments of his brisk, boyish words. His protectiveness. His laughter. The way he pretended not to like picking blood roses but was always the one to suggest we go to the gardens. The way he mocked my childish lisp, then always told me I had a nice voice.

I recalled moments when gentry boys taunted him, calling him names for being an orphan. I'd been hiding outside the walls of the old schoolhouse, listening, as they'd made up lies that the king planned to get rid of his ward since he was so worthless to the royal house.

I closed my eyes and leaned my back against the wall.

"You think the king'll keep you? Why? You don't do anything but eat up his table scraps."

Silas frowned and turned away, trying to leave, but Bragi Helverson was relentless.

He gripped Silas's arm and forced him to wheel around. "Bet your mam was glad to go to the Otherworld."

Silas's face boiled in an angry red. His fists clenched. Bragi wanted it. He wanted the king's ward to react, all so Annon and the other commanders would punish Silas to stable mucking for a month.

"Bet your daj tossed himself over too," Bragi went on, "after he found out what a whore your mam was. You probably weren't even—"

A strangled cry escaped his throat when the first pebble flew from the loft window. Then, another, and another.

"Arghh. Go, go!"

Bragi and his stupid gaggle of bullies tried to flee. Pebbles kept flinging, striking their faces, their arms; one boy stumbled forward, sobbing, when a small gray stone struck him in the teeth.

"Princess! No. Stop this right now. Gods, help us!" A servant had her skirts bunched in her arms, sprinting from the green lawns next to the stable.

Bragi and his wretched gang bolted, bleeding and simpering like little pups.

Silas peeked up at the loft window.

"Your aim needs work, Little Rose," he said. But in the corner of his mouth was a smile.

A smile I never truly forgot. Silas looked at me like I'd saved his damn life. Much the same as I'd looked at him the night Davorin attacked my mother. The way he'd hidden me, brave and stalwart, standing in front of the armoire. The way he'd been forced to leave my father to a fight he couldn't win, and face Davorin. He'd nearly been killed by the strike of that blade, all to keep me hidden, to defend my bloodline.

I closed the book of drawings, swiped the tears off my cheeks. What the hells was there to think about?

So, my heart bonded with the boy who'd always cared for me, the boy who'd always seen me as I was and never tried to change it. What did it matter? I'd picked him before fate bonded us together.

The Norns were the slow ones in making their decision. I was more cunning and picked him before we sang our song of destruction.

So why was I still here?

I glanced in the looking glass on the wall. My hair was disheveled, but manageable. My eyes were red from tears, but I didn't have the patience nor the care to wait for them to clear. In three strides, I crossed the room to the door and yanked it open.

Silas, my phantom, my whisper, he wanted me to decide if my heart ached for him.

It didn't ache for him. It *lived* for him.

CHAPTER 22
THE STORYTELLER

HE WAS WEARING THE BLACK SATIN MASK AGAIN. IN THE UPPER HALL FILLED with the instruments, Silas was alone, facing the window. The light from the moon glimmered over the surface of the masked cheek from where he sat on the bench, thrumming a small lyre.

His dark hair was loose down his neck, falling to his shoulders. He'd removed the cloak and thick leather belt around his waist. Dressed only in a dark tunic and trousers, he almost looked free in the darkness.

Then again, perhaps he was.

I winced at the thought of Silas locked away, watching the world live on without him, with only shadows as his company. My heart cinched in a fierce need to defend him, to shield him from the call to loneliness and solitude.

With gentle steps, I crossed the room, heart racing. He didn't turn, didn't seem to know he wasn't alone. My fingertips danced in anticipation, the need to touch him was fast becoming desperate the closer I came.

One pace from his back, I paused to admire the way his long fingers took to the strings of the lyre. Hardly a thought, more rote motion, and the sound was still a sweet melody, smooth and calming.

I held my breath and reached for the mask. The moment my fingers touched the edge, Silas froze. His breath was rough, but he didn't turn.

"I want to see you," I whispered. "There isn't a need to hide, not from me."

I eased the mask away from the damaged side of his face. The scar was angry and deep, a beautiful reminder that every step this man had taken was for the benefit of my life.

I ran my fingertips along the edges of the puckered skin. Silas shuddered.

"Does touching it hurt you?"

"No." His voice was a gritty rasp. "It's . . . just new."

Touch was a long-forgotten memory for him, and it broke pieces of my heart even more. Slowly, I slid my arms around his neck from behind, hugging his body to my chest and let my cheek fall to the back of his head.

"There is a bond between us," I whispered. "I saw it in Ari's sleep. I saw it burn like a golden flame. It's burning again."

"There is always a choice." The words slid between his teeth as though they were jagged glass in his throat. "Always a choice, Little Rose."

"I've taken long enough to make my choice." I tilted his face and waited for those tortured eyes to hold mine. "You're my Whisper. My voice in the dark. You're mine."

He released the lyre and carefully adjusted on the bench so he faced me, my legs between his knees. Silas raised his hands hesitantly, but soon brought his large palms to rest on my hips.

"This ends the tale, Little Rose. I do not know the outcome. You do this, there are no backward glances. Accept the bond, then you belong to me. The way I have always belonged to you."

Gods, he was . . . *intense*. There was a touch of madness in his eyes, and I didn't want to change it. I wanted to know it, embrace it. I wanted to see all the layers of my whisper the way I suspected I did as a child.

Back then, the bond between us wasn't filled with the burn of desire and need the way it scorched in my veins now, but I recalled a personal love for a nameless boy in my shadowed memories.

"The Norns keep trying to take credit for bringing me back to you," I said, a smirk on my mouth. "But the truth is, Silas, we bested those stupid fates long before they found us. You were mine before the world broke. You've been mine through the lifetimes. You will always be mine."

I kissed him.

Silas jolted, but in a few breaths, took what control I thought I had and claimed it for himself. This kiss was fierce, brutal, almost punishing. Different than the one we'd shared on the Row, this was a kiss laden in promises, of desire, of unshakeable devotion to what we had always been.

Bonded, deeper than the heart. He was mine to my soul.

Silas must've felt the same, for something snapped in his docile, nearly hesitant movements. He pulled away, eyes dark with desire, and tangled my hair around his hands. Silas tugged my head back, altering the angle of my mouth before crushing his lips back to mine.

His tongue was warm, needy. The taste of him was like clean rain, a new delight I would cling to until my last breath.

I wasn't experienced. No mistake, neither was Silas, but my body responded to every brush of his fingertips. I arched into him, desperate for more. Without a thought, I leveraged each leg onto the bench, straddling his hips.

"Dammit," he breathed out against my lips.

"Don't like this?" Gods, I felt I might peel out of my skin if he pushed me back.

Silas's eyes burned with a touch of frenzy. "Like this? Yes, I like this. You're rocking against my damn cock."

My cheeks heated. It was a new word. A little seductive. A little filthy. I liked it.

To torment him a bit more, I slid my knees wider, lowering my core over the strained length in his trousers, and swayed my hips.

Silas coughed. His fingers dug into my skin until his marks would be left behind.

I liked that too.

He groaned and guided my hips over his shaft. "Hells, I'm going to lose my control at any moment."

A sly kind of grin split over my face. "I'm in favor of this plan, Whisper."

No, I wasn't experienced, but my body knew it wanted him. It craved him. I dragged one palm down his chest, the flat planes of his stomach, to the laces of his trousers.

Silas moaned and tightened his mouth, almost like he was in agony, not pleasure.

My hands trembled when I unthreaded the top lace.

"I rarely feel safe in this world," I said softly against his mouth. "But the moment I saw you in the dark, the moment you took my hand, it was as though all the fears faded. Even for a moment."

Silas studied me. He'd given me freedom to touch and tease til now, but dark want in his eyes spilled over. He scooped under my thighs, lifting us off the bench. I let out a shriek, and grappled to hang onto his shoulders until my back struck the woven rug over the floorboards.

"I've clung to a fading reality," he said, dragging his lips across my throat. "Sometimes I do not know what is real, but you have always been my guide in a confusing existence. You are my beacon in the night." He lifted his head and peered down at me. Silas brushed his thumb over the ridge of my cheek. "I would wait a thousand lifetimes for you."

My eyes fluttered closed when he tugged at the shoulder of my tunic with a touch of uncertainty. Silas kept glancing at my face, as though reading my countenance. My stomach twisted in nerves, but my heart yearned for more.

I touched the scar on his face, holding his gaze, urging him to go on.

With the sleeve pulled off my shoulder, Silas kissed the bony ridges. I unlaced the next row on his trousers. The crown of his length split through the top seams.

I swallowed. All hells, he was thick and hard. How would he bleeding fit?

Silas kissed his way back to my mouth. I held the back of his head, holding his mouth to mine, needy for more of his taste. His hips settled between my thighs, and I moaned, seeking the pressure, though it seemed too much, too fierce.

It was as though the surface of my flesh was set ablaze. Heat pooled between my legs, throbbing and pulsing in a way I'd never experienced.

He dragged his teeth along my bottom lip. For a moment he lifted his head, face flushed, breaths heavy, and held my gaze, perhaps looking for any hint I wanted him to stop.

He wouldn't find it. I gripped the bottom hem of his tunic, sliding it over the carved muscle of his back. Silas grinned a little viciously when he shifted, aiding me in removing his top.

Bleeding gods. Muscle and strength was carved across his chest, his shoulders, the slope of his back. I wanted to touch every divot, kiss every surface.

"Is . . . is this strange for you?" I asked. "We've . . . we've grown, but we haven't touched really since childhood."

Silas held one side of my face in his palm. "You were my only friend, Calista Ode. You are still that, but you became the beat of my heart. To touch you is my greatest honor. It is the dream that has kept me living."

What the hells was he thinking, talking in such a way? I'd be blubbering in a pool of my own damn tears if he kept it up.

I tilted my head and kissed him, silencing that horridly beautiful tongue of his.

Silas shuddered as my fingernails dug into his bare skin. One of his hands slid my tunic over my head. Cool air bit at my naked flesh. Instinct drew me to try to cover, until I saw the liquid heat flow through Silas's eyes when he drank me in.

His palm splayed over my belly, frozen. I licked my lips and gripped his wrist, slowly guiding his hand up my ribs, between the cleft of my breasts.

"Gods." Silas groaned, dropping his forehead to mine when his palm covered my small breast. He gripped my hip with his other hand, holding steady as he plucked at the peak of my nipple.

"I want to taste your skin," he whispered, a soft admission, one lined in hesitation.

With my palm, I nudged his face to the other side. "I want you to."

I cried out, trembling under his larger form when his tongue lapped at the hardened point of my other breast. He rocked his hips against the boiling apex between my thighs. The weight of his thick length added a new ache to my core. A frantic need, an obsession to join with him in every way.

I tucked my thumbs into the waist of his trousers and tugged.

"Silas," I breathed out in a rough gasp. What was I trying to even say? I shook my head and simply blurted, "Please."

He lifted his head from my chest, tugging at my nipple with his teeth before releasing me. "Open these legs for me."

With one hand, he pushed one of my knees to the side, spreading me out beneath him. Silas helped my trembling hands shove his trousers down until he sloughed them off. He sat back on his knees and had my pants off in a few rough tugs.

"Calista." His dark eyes roved over my nakedness, head to foot. "You're . . . I-I hardly know where I want to start. I want every bleeding piece of you."

"Promises, promises," I said. "I'd rather you prove it."

"Careful what you ask for, Little Rose." The silky darkness of his voice rumbled through my bones, my blood, to my very soul.

While I settled back on the rug, Silas kept me locked in his heated stare. The tip of his tongue slipped out, wetting his lips, as he watched me recline on my elbows and slowly let my knees drop to the sides.

If I did not feel his passion, his affection to the deepest threads of my heart, I might fear him by the way he looked at me, the way he prowled over me like I would not survive whatever he had planned.

Silas fitted his hips between my thighs. Unable to stop, my body snapped in an arch to feel him, to kill any distance between us.

"I don't want to hurt you," he whispered against my neck.

"I think it's inevitable." I bit my lip and slid my hand between us, curling my fingers around the fullness of his length and stroked once, twice, until the man panted into the crook of my neck.

"Tell me . . . you'll tell me, right? If I hurt you?"

"Silas." I hooked my ankles around his thighs. "I want this with you. No one touches you but me, and no one will ever touch me but you. You can't hurt me, not really."

When he propped onto his elbows, a furrow gathered between his brows. I rubbed it away and guided the crown of his length to the heat of my slit.

In a painfully sensual crawl, he nudged into my dripping center. All gods. My body stretched and adjusted to pull him in, but when he was met with resistance, he hesitated.

"Please." I kissed him. I kissed him for all the turns I could've had with him. I kissed him for the pain he'd endured watching helplessly from the dark. I kissed him to prove how this choice was mine. Not fate's, not a bond; he was mine because I chose him.

He rolled his hips in a quick thrust. Silas cupped my head and held me through the whimper of pain when a sharp burn shot through my center. A hot tear fell from the corner of my eye. He kissed it away.

"All right?" he rasped.

I nodded, digging my fingernails into his hips. I slowly arched against him, the movement soothing the burn.

Silas met my rhythm; slow to build, but it wasn't long before our pace quickened to a frenzied rush, and the slap of skin against skin echoed through the music hall.

My body quaked in his hold. When he pressed his body down, I arched up. Like we were determined to melt into each other. His length filled me from root to tip, and every thrust sent bright shocks of tantalizing pleasure surging through my veins.

"You're mine," he gritted out. Silas bit down on my bottom lip, quickening his thrusts.

To form words seemed too great a task, but the haggard whisper slipped out with each thrust. "I've always . . . been . . . yours."

The candlelight, the heat, the rush of our bodies, it all burned together until a tremble of delicious warmth flowed from my skull to my belly; like molten ore, it spilled between us until I shattered. I cried out his name. My claws left red scratches across his arms as I lost control.

"Silas," I gasped. "Hells. Bleeding gods. There." My body squirmed and writhed outside my control. "There, gods, deeper."

His breaths were ragged pants. Silas straightened his arms and rolled his hips, in rough, furious thrusts. What little control he had left snapped. He pounded into me, wringing out every last drop of my release until his body shuddered. His breath caught and his face heated in a beautiful twist of pleasure.

I rattled the palace with my cries. He was beautifully silent but for the sharp, rough gasps against my cheek as the heat of his release spilled into me.

When his muscles began to quiver, Silas sank over me, both of us gasping and holding onto each other like the darkness might tear us apart all over again. With a sweet kiss, Silas rolled onto his shoulder.

He glanced down and cursed. "You're bleeding."

I looked at my thighs. True enough, a small splatter of blood was there and on the rug. "I hear it's normal."

Silas frowned and hurried to his feet, abandoning the room through a side door.

"Where are you . . . wait, where are you going?"

He was already gone. Horrid panic cracked my throat. Ridiculous, but his swift abandonment ached like a jagged piece of glass ripped through my chest. He . . . he took all of me and simply left?

I leveraged into sitting and hugged my knees to my chest. I couldn't even think vicious thoughts about him, the ache was too cruel.

When the first tear fell, a sort of growl came behind me.

Silas stood in the doorway with a clay bowl and white linen. "I knew I hurt you."

I wiped the tear away, letting out a delirious kind of laugh. "No, I-I-I thought you just left me."

"Leave you?" Silas pinched his lips and knelt beside me, setting the bowl filled with water on the rug. "No, I . . . I figured—*assumed*—it's my duty to care for you since I hurt you."

Gods. This was *it*. This was the sort of devotion, attention, and compassion that had all my damn queens falling head over feet for their kings.

Naturally, Silas wouldn't be accustomed to explaining his actions to anyone. He'd been alone, a trapped observer of the world outside.

Time, that was all we needed. We were together now, both of us content to stay holed away in our own spaces. Perhaps, together we could learn each other until we knew every flinch. We'd come to know every grin. Until I never questioned his quick departure after his length was pulled out of my body.

Soon enough, I'd come to know it meant he'd return with something to worship me even more.

He dipped the linen in the water, then scooted between my legs. "May I?"

My teeth dug into my bottom lip. I nodded. Silas lowered to one elbow, sprawled out onto his side, and cared for me gently. I could not recall a time I'd been so exposed, yet been so safe, so valued.

When he'd cleaned my skin, he pressed a kiss to the inside of my thigh, close to my center. I drew in a sharp gasp and a groan at once. He chuckled and rolled onto his stomach. "Do you like that?"

Like that? His lips . . . so close to the most sensitive places on my body was a new, delirious need I didn't anticipate. All I could manage was a crooked nod as I slid my palms down my body, over my breasts, my belly. Silas watched, a heated shadow in his eyes, until my palms reached my own thighs.

I held my breath and pushed my legs open, wide enough his broad shoulders fit between me, wide enough the cool air brushed against my slickened center.

"Bleeding hells," he cursed under his breath. Silas dragged his lips over one thigh again, his rough palms sliding up my bare skin. "Are you hurting at all?"

I shook my head briskly. Not entirely true. There was a delicious rawness to the flesh between my legs, but I loved it. Embraced it. The sting was a mark he'd been there and fitted my body to his. The way it was always meant to be.

"Are you certain?" he whispered, his breath caressed the folds of my slit.

I whimpered and dug my fingers through his hair. All I could choke out was, "A little."

"Hmm." Silas dipped his head. Gods, his nose ran along my arousal. "Then, I ought to keep my hands off."

"I hate that decision."

He chuckled. "But my mouth can be gentle. I've always been curious about this."

I lost my breath when his lips kissed my entrance. Next, his tongue swiped out and licked me from one end to the other. Unbidden, my body arched into his lips. This sort of thing had never been a thought. I felt a bit naïve, but I didn't think much more than bodies slapping together could be done.

Silas seemed uncertain on the first lick, too, but as if the taste of my flesh on his tongue fueled him, he gripped my thighs, pulling me closer.

"Gods," he said on a breath. "We should begin and end this way every damn time."

I wanted to laugh. We both were exploring together, and no mistake, we sounded like fools at each sensual discovery, but I couldn't move. His tongue claimed me, deep and thorough. The scrape of his teeth sent shivers up my spine, but when he sucked against the tender apex of my core, I shattered like glass bursting into dust.

"Silas." His name slid out in a long, drawn moan, a damn near sob.

I writhed and gripped his hair, seeking for something steady as I rocked against his face. How he could breathe, I didn't know, but the way Silas kept devouring me through the wave, I didn't think he was in terrible distress.

My body jolted as the swell of heat faded. My arms flopped to my sides, my legs went limp. Every piece of my body was spent.

Silas sat back on his heels, grinning. Slowly, he crept over me, then pressed a gentle kiss to my lips.

"I choose you, Little Rose," he whispered. "I always have. Fate be damned. I would choose you even if the Norns told me it was the wrong path."

I stroked his cheek, the cruel scar that twisted one side of his face. I kissed the raised skin from one end to the next, then kissed his mouth for good measure.

"I choose you. You've always been my Whisper, the song of my heart."

He brushed my damp hair off my brow, kissing me there, then looked at me without a shadow in his eye. I hooked my leg around his waist, and opened my lips to tell him the thoughts in my head, the rampant need to tell him that my heart was his, that I felt it more than I felt the urge to breathe.

I didn't get the chance.

All at once, the ground shifted. The palace walls shook.

"What . . . is that?"

Silas clutched me to his chest but looked toward the window. "I don't know. I don't know. Wait." He sat up and looked to me. "Stay here."

He hurried to the window and seemed to freeze there.

I snatched my discarded tunic and scrambled to my feet. "What is it?"

My voice strangled in the back of my throat.

Against the black night a light, like a golden flame, had burst around Hus Rose. From us. In the distance, the shape of the land seemed to be crumbling, breaking, changing.

I clung to Silas's arm. "What's happening?"

"Accept the first bond," he whispered, brow furrowed. All at once, he tugged me against his side, eyes dark. "We've accepted it and found our way back to each other, and I think the tale we started has ended. The kingdom is going back to the beginning. That was where our fated tale was always meant to conclude. Where all our fates were meant to meet."

"Wait, what do you mean, all our fates?"

Silas didn't answer, merely looked to the strange crumble of land in the distance, then looked to me, waiting for me to understand.

"All hells," I whispered when the realization struck me like a blow to the head. The world had once been one. "The kingdoms. They're breaking once again."

My kings and queens, my thieves and crooks. Their lands were shattering.

Silas took my hand. "The words. Calista, the words you wrote in the cellar. This is how we help them, how we can help them."

All gods. The tale that came had something to do with the crowns of fate. We hurried to my discarded trousers. I fumbled with the two pieces of parchment and selected the second one.

"When shields fall, a heart will call."

Silas muttered under his breath, pacing. "What shields have fallen?"

It was unexpected, such a swift, coherent thought. "Mine."

He faced me, confused.

"My shields." I touched the scar on his face. "I've accepted my path, I've stopped resisting the past, and . . . you. I chose you." I studied the other words. "As the land of your enemy restores. Silas, this is the final step, as you said, our tale is ending. From here, fate is unwritten. We need to lead them. We're supposed to be a beacon to the fated crowns. They're crumbling, but . . . this might mean we can lead them to us before that bleeding snake returns to his land."

Silas blinked, then pressed a furious kiss to my forehead. "Then, sing with me. Sing that first tale, Little Rose. The tale of four gifts and four queens. It is time they stand as one."

So rarely did I create a twist of fate without my quill and parchment, but there was something burning within me, like an ability I'd long forgotten.

Wrapped in his arms, the heat of seidr flooded my veins. His voice, my words, it tangled in one burning flame between us. Like in Ari's dream, it was as if those golden bursts of light were splitting in brilliant ribbons from our hearts to distant lands.

Hidden from us, perhaps, but there was an unmistakable fire igniting between us as we fought through the push and pull of fate to weave a final ending of a centuries-long story.

To bring four crowns of fate to the final battlefield.

THE BROKEN KINGDOMS

CHAPTER 23
ROGUE PRINCESS

Castle Ravenspire—Kingdom of Etta

HOLD. *HOLD.* JUST A LITTLE LONGER, HOLD. MY HANDS GRIPPED THE leather-wrapped hilt of the short blade.

"Maj." Livia's little whimper broke a fresh crack through my chest.

I peered over my shoulder. Livia was tucked in an alcove near the great hall with a handful of other littles. Aleksi kept his hand clasped tightly with my daughter's, while two of the Atra daughters clung to their older brother. Aesir was stoic. By my side, Kari kept glancing at her boy with concern he might break, at long last, and flee to find his father.

Across from the children, in another alcove, Metta and the eldest daughter of Kari and Halvar hugged Lilianna's waist.

"Stay down, little love," I told Livia. A few clock tolls before I would've forced a smile to ease the burdens of her tender heart. Now, I could not find the strength to do it.

The door to the hall shook against whatever force was ramming into the wood. I turned my back on my daughter and braced my shoulder against the only barrier between us and . . . a fate worse than the hells.

Kari stood at my side, bracing much the same. Bile burned my tongue to speak this, but the words needed to be said. "Kari, should they enter, should they take me. Promise you'll leave me and get the children free."

"Shut up, Elise," Kari snapped.

Hells, I'd missed the sharp tongue of my friend. In public, as an Ettan warrior, the wife of the First Knight, Kari Atra was often called upon to speak too damn pretentiously. Not like we once did in Ruskig when we were all misfits trying to survive.

Tears brightened her blue eyes. "I'm not leaving you as much as you're not leaving me. And it's not because of your bleeding crown. We're friends. We're warriors. We don't leave each other behind."

I dipped my chin in a stiff nod. Fair enough. Another furious ram of the door and I dug my heels firmer onto the floorboards.

A thousand thoughts whirled through my mind, most of them fell to Valen. Where was he? Was he injured? Did he see an end of this battle?

Did he feel how desperately I wished I could touch him, how fiercely I wished I'd kissed him a little longer before he'd left the castle?

The king fought at the gates with the others. I knew he was alive from the occasional shudder of earth, but it was always distant. Either Valen was growing weak, or they'd pushed the attack into the lower townships.

Since Halvar had discovered the carnage at the docks, the spread of the curse of bloodlust had taken Timoran after Timoran. Only Night Folk and Ettans were spared unless they drew too close. Then, they were slaughtered.

I closed my eyes against the sting. Slaughtered like Mattis.

My cherished friend. He'd deserved a life of peace. He'd deserved to see his child be born. He and Siv deserved to grow old and enter the hall of the gods together. Mattis had never deserved to die in such a way, torn apart and slaughtered in the sand.

I'd lived beside Valen's curse for only a short time. I'd witnessed his transformation, the pain and suffering he'd needed to endure to quench the lust of death and gore.

Short as my experiences with his curse had been, it was enough I never wished to survive it again. Now, it was as though hundreds of Blood Wraith's ran our shores. One difference was these cursed could die, but their lust for blood was never sated until they greeted the Otherworld. They did not sleep. They did not cease fighting.

In my heart, I knew—Etta was falling.

This was a fight I was not certain we could win. We'd sent the warning to the others, and our shores remained empty of Eastern ships. No missive from Ari. Not even the flight of a raven. Calista was silent, though I was never certain which kingdom she was in at any given time.

If she was in the West, she had not responded since the signal was sent seven nights ago.

There was no resentment at the silence of our friends—there was only harsh, jagged fear. I knew Malin, I knew Ari, I knew the story-teller well enough to know if they were silent, they could not come to our aid.

It would mean they, too, were under attack.

I winced when wood splintered. A blade—likely an axe—was snapping through the door. "Lili," I said, eyes closed, desperate to keep my voice steady. "Gather the children."

"Elise, no," she whispered, hugging Metta against her side.

Herja's youngest daughter had only turned thirteen, and sobbed against Lili's shoulder. She'd watched everyone—her parents, her older brother Dain, and Laila enter the battlefield. No mistake, the girl knew Gunnar would be locked in some unknown battles in the Southern Isles.

We all had bid farewell to half our families. There was no telling when we'd be reunited, or if we'd be reunited.

"Lili," I said desperately. "You must get them to the peaks. You're the only one who knows Old Timoran. You're the only one who can get them to the shore on the other side."

Some of our folk, the elderly, the Timorans still untouched, or those with children or tiny infants, had already been led away by three dozen warriors to the Northern Peaks, right near the passage to Old Timoran. The only place the cursed folk seemed to avoid.

Lilianna was a mother to me. She was fierce, she'd taught me how to be queen with gentle instruction and patience as we navigated Etta after the battles. She doted on her grandchildren, she loved her family fiercely.

But it was written in her eyes, as much as it was mine, she knew this kingdom was being torn apart in a way none of us ever could have expected.

She swiped tears off her cheeks and forced a smile to the littles. "All right, loves. You know what we're to do. We talked about it."

"No!" Livia made a rush for me, but Aleksi gripped her hand.

"Come on, Livie," he said, his voice soft and soothing. Broken. A sweet temperament of a boy, but I'd watched every night as his skinny shoulders had racked in silent sobs since Sol and Tor had both kissed his forehead and left to join the fight. Now, he was trying to be brave and bold for his cousin. "We'll meet 'em all over the peaks."

Big, heavy tears dropped from Livia's lashes.

I gave her a small smile and mouthed, *I love you.*

"Stick together," Lilianna told them. Her voice was a wet rasp as she battled fear, a need to stay, to fight beside her husband and children, but also the knowledge that as Timorans we all were more of a liability than an aid here. "We keep to the shadows, loves. It's going to be cold in the peaks, but we'll be back . . . we'll be back before you know it."

Agony ripped through my chest. Kari choked on tears as her four children followed Lilianna toward a narrow doorway that would lead them out through the furthest tower of the castle. She told each of them she loved them, she promised seats in the great hall if that was where they next met.

Aesir pounded a fist against his chest, eyes wet, and vowed to protect his sisters, to make his mother and father proud.

"I love you, my boy," Kari said, voice soft and broken.

Perhaps it was the distraction of our hearts snapping in two, but I'd lost attention on the door. Long enough I did not notice the pounding had ceased. The shouts, the splinters, they'd gone silent.

Until it was too late.

The back door where Lilianna led the children crashed open, forceful enough the wood sagged on the hinges. Men and women, eyes red as the blood moon, shoved inside. Their mouths and teeth and fingers were soaked in dried blood.

Lilianna shouted for the littles to get back, drew a dagger, and rammed the point through the throat of a slender woman. A woman who looked a great deal like the former queen. Hair like golden sunlight, a torn gown that likely had been lovely not so many days ago.

The children shrieked. Aesir gripped a knife. Metta struggled to reach hers and had a large Timoran man rushing for her, teeth bared.

Metta screamed, but the man fell forward, a knife in the back of his skull. Aesir shoved the young princess aside and ripped his knife out of the bleeding Timoran's head, shouting at his sisters to hide.

There was nowhere to hide. The door near me and Kari, again, rattled as the cursed folk surrounded us. Still, there was only a drive to protect our children.

"Get down!" I cried out, swiping my blade across middles, throats, chests. "Down!"

Livia and Aleksi hugged Halvar's daughters in an alcove. Kari leapt in front of them and rammed her seax through the belly of a stout woman with bloody lips and graying hair.

I spun and met the broad body of a tall man. His auburn beard was soaked in days-old blood; his eyes were lost and wild.

"Egil." My blood chilled. Egil Lysander. One of Calder's younger brothers. A cousin of mine who'd hated his father and brother for their cruelty. A man we discovered after the Ettan wars had secretly harbored Night Folk and Ettans in a longhouse on his estate near the old quarries.

Egil was a cousin who'd helped unite our people when Valen and I ascended the throne.

"Egil, no!" I let out a cry of anger, of rage, of hate for what was happening here. My cousin no longer recognized me, all he saw was blood and the need to tear the Night Folk apart and force me to join him. Tears blurred my eyes as I slashed at him.

He hissed and tried to grip my hair. My blade struck his wrist. I struck his ribs. His thighs. I brought him to his knees, only pausing when he lifted a trembling hand.

"Elise." His voice was strained. He clutched his side. "Elise, please, cousin."

My heart stilled. Gods, he was coherent. It could . . . it could fade. "Egil?"

His desperation shifted faster than I could catch a breath. Those bloody lips twisted into a wretched kind of grin. When he spoke again I could nearly hear the battle lord's voice. "Queen of Choice."

Egil made a swipe for my middle. I was swifter. The point of my sword slid through the back of his neck. He coughed and tilted forward, then went still.

I scrambled back, dazed, and desperate to focus. The fight wasn't over. Behind Egil's body another woman lunged for me.

"The hall! Get to the damn hall!" My heart stilled. Valen. They were coming.

A little longer. Hold them off a little longer.

Metta caught sight of Aesir battling with a Timoran boy, no older than himself, but the boy was trying to tear at Aesir with his bare fingernails.

Herja's daughter picked up a jagged piece of splintered wood.

"Metta, no!" Lilianna screamed at her granddaughter.

The girl was already rushing toward the cursed boy, unaware a lanky man had her in his sights. Blade lifted, the cursed Timoran aimed to take the princess down, but he jolted when a blade rammed through the center of his chest.

Next to the man, Lilianna was small, humorously so, but she pushed against him. Blood soaked her wrists, her arms. He struggled to keep upright. When she tried to yank her sword free of his chest, it caught.

"Lili!" I screamed. "Get back!"

Lilianna released the sword, she tried to dodge, but the dying Timoran man grabbed her arm. He bit her wrist, shredding her flesh with his teeth. Lilianna screamed and pounded her fist against his skull.

I came behind the bastard and thrust my sword in his ribs. He roared his pain, but took another bite from Lilianna's shoulder, drawing blood.

It felt greater than an eternity before the cursed man stumbled over, eyes dead and pointed at the rafters.

The door shoved against a few fallen bodies.

"Elise!" Valen shoved. "Elise, answer me. Livia!"

"We're here." My voice cracked.

I heard Valen let out a breathless, "Thank the gods."

In the next breath, Valen burst through, blood soaked, and followed by Halvar, Tor, and Arvad. At long last, Aleksi broke when he saw one of his fathers. The boy lunged for Tor and cried against his chest. Livia wrapped her arms around Valen's waist. He kissed her head, but his dark, midnight eyes found me across the hall.

For a moment, a simple, fleeting moment, we could be at peace knowing we all breathed.

But Valen's eyes widened. "Maj?"

All gods. I whirled around. Lilianna was on the ground, gasping. Kari was gently holding her arm.

"G-Go," Lili rasped, trying to shove Kari away.

"No!" I went to Lilianna's side. Already her eyes were shading to a deep crimson. Her skin was pallid, almost a sickly gray.

She sneered at me, fighting whatever was happening in her blood.

"Lili." Arvad slid to his knees, clutching her shoulders.

She shuddered, face contorted in pain. Then, she lashed. At her own husband.

"*Night Folk.*"

Arvad was a taller build than even his sons. Next to Lilianna he seemed double her size. Still, he dodged, and maneuvered his body behind her, arms fiercely coiled around her waist, pinning her thrashing body to his chest.

"Lil." He pleaded next to her ear. "Stay with me. *Gods*, stay with me."

A firm hand tugged on my arm. Valen pulled me behind him. His eyes were despondent, watching his mother fall under the curse he'd endured, watching her spit hatred at his father, at him, at us all.

Livia watched in horror as her grandmother bucked and thrashed in Arvad's grip.

"Maj, don't kill her," she whimpered. "Please don't kill her. She .. . she can be fixed."

I kept one hand clasped with Valen, and with the other, hid Livia's face in my bloody tunic. We'd heal her. Somehow we'd heal them all. A bitter tear fell onto my cheek. I wasn't going to lose Lilianna. I wasn't going to lose my damn kingdom. Not when we'd battled for peace through too much blood, too much pain.

From the back of the room, the door burst with more of our warriors. Sol, Stieg, Kjell Bror, Hagen, and Laila. Sol embraced Tor and Aleksi, but looked at his mother with a bit of horror. "What the hells . . . no. Tell me they—"

"She was attacked," Valen said, a new hardness to his tone.

Sol blinked furiously. "Then . . . we'll find a damn cure. You were cured."

"By dying," Valen snapped. "*Dying*."

"In the East—"

"Malin is not here to walk our mother . . . to walk her back to us."

Endless nights of fighting, and the stalwart optimism of my king was wavering. I wrapped an arm around his waist.

"I was recently reminded," I said softly. "We do not leave each other behind. We'll find a way."

Valen blinked, then pressed a hard kiss to my knuckles. "Daj."

Arvad's muscles pulsed as he clung to his thrashing wife. Lili's lovely blue eyes were red and hateful. She kept flinging her head back, smacking her skull against Arvad's chest. Already she'd drawn blood on his wrist from biting him. He didn't let her go. He didn't give up his embrace.

"See if you can get her to sleep," Valen's voice was rough, like grit lined the back of his throat.

Arvad's eyes darkened. His jaw pulsed. Next to Lili's ear, he whispered something only meant for his wife, then carefully drew his strong, heavy arm beneath Lilianna's chin. He tightened his grip, his forearm choking off her breath.

She kicked and thrashed. Her skin shaded to a desperate flush of purple as she tried to draw in a sharp breath. Cursed or not, to deprive the lungs of air would silence anyone. Arvad broke. A single tear on his cheek as his shoulders shook, but he didn't relent.

Lilianna's thrashing grew slower, weaker. Soon she could barely pound at Arvad's arm.

At long last, she went still. Arvad let out a shuddering gasp and loosened his hold. He kissed the side of her head, holding his lips in her hair, holding her to his chest.

Kjell went to the former king, and clapped his shoulder. "We'll heal her."

Arvad still kissed her head, but nodded, closing his eyes.

"Come. We can't stay," Valen said, returning to his role as the king. "They're closing in, but we've learned they despise fire. That was not the same for me. So, it's hopeful that this isn't the same curse. For now, we can keep them at bay until we make our way to the peaks. There are sleeping draughts to help with Maj, but we must try to find out what is happening in other lands. We will need Calista to end this."

A glimmer of hope heated my blood.

No sooner had the reprieve begun than the ground quaked.

"Valen." I clung to his arm.

"It's not me." He tugged my body against his side and held Livia against his other hip.

The ground rolled again. It dipped.

"What is that?" Sol shouted, taking Aleksi in his arms and shielding his boy's head as the castle rocked. He pointed out the window.

In the distance, against the eerie red of the night sky, a burst of light broke in the western-most seas. Like a burst of shattering gold, it broke across the sky. Screams filled the hall when the floor dipped.

Valen dragged us to our knees; he tucked my head and Livia's under his arms. With one palm on the splitting floorboards, he tried to use his own fury against whatever was shattering the earth.

As another violent shudder rocked us, he gave up and simply held us close as our kingdom fell apart.

CHAPTER 24
THE MEMORY THIEF

The Howl Sea—Shores of Klockglas

"WHERE ARE THE BOYS?" KASE ROARED. HIS EYES WERE BLACKENED, AND shadows billowed off his shoulders like a dark cloak.

"Hidden." I thrust a dagger into the scaly belly of a fae man who looked as though he had barnacles on his knuckles. The sea fae flooded from the Howl. They hissed revenge, shouted praises to their horrid Ever King that was slaughtered on Eastern shores.

The cliffs just beyond the Howl into the Fate's Ocean, the ones Valen had raised from the sea floor so long ago, were flooded by bursts of dangerous tides. Even the Howl rolled and thrashed in great swells. It was too wild, too deadly; we could not reach the other regions.

Were the Falkyns able to keep sea fae off their shores? In Hemlig, Isak and Fiske had visited to gather new seeds for harvest seasons. Were they even alive? Bard had gone to Furen a week before, Tova and Hanna along with him, and I'd nearly allowed the twins to join them before Sander caught his cough that kept us near the palace.

Another sea fae lunged for me. Their weapons were wicked. Serrated, like the teeth of vicious fish. Some were colorful, with hilts of coral and blades of bone. We'd captured one sea fae with a look a bit like Thorvald. Pointed ears, a sunset glow to his eyes, nearly impossible to distinguish between our fae folk or those of the sea.

I'd robbed him of his memories.

It was worse than I thought.

"Do you see that bastard?" I shouted back at Kase, slicing my sword at a beautiful woman with stormy eyes. She was stunning, hauntingly so. Pale hair and ruby red lips. Her gown was iridescent green like she'd swam through a garden of sea flowers, and it fitted to her body.

She didn't hold a blade, but widened her fingers and dark, jagged fingernails extended.

"He's not here," Kase insisted. His blacksteel blade opened the throat of a fae with a curved sword in hand.

I didn't understand it. Within the memories of the sea fae who'd fallen, I'd seen Davorin. Those memories taken from bone dust from bodies washed ashore meant they'd been in his presence mere moments before they were slaughtered.

Some were killed for refusing to fight.

Their bodies were then thrust through the violent tides of the Chasm of Seas, left to wash ashore from the currents of the Howl or the Fate's Ocean.

Others, the ones we'd snared before death, gave up his influence. His wretched features standing amongst them, empowering them to take revenge against those who had killed their king turns ago.

I'd never forget his damn face. He'd built the anger of the sea folk, nourished it, let it fester. He'd drawn them out of their own kingdom to fight against the fae who'd slaughtered their king. Thorvald could rot in the hells for all I cared. Valen held the Ever King's title with that bleeding gold disc Thorvald kept flicking when we'd been trapped in that damn troll burrow.

Valen had warned the Ever King's brother that every sea folk would meet their end should they step foot on land. Had Davorin emboldened them to try? None seemed to be under his dark trance, not the way the Southern fae had been ten turns ago.

Surely one mimicker was not so powerful he could convince an entire world to rise against us?

I dodged the sea fae's jagged claws, spun on my heel, and rammed the point of the short blade between her shoulders.

She let out a shriek of agony and stumbled forward. Once her face was pinned to the soil, I stepped onto her spine, and leaned over my knee. "We warned your folk, return and you die."

Where I thought she might shed a tear, might whimper, she bleeding laughed. Wickedly.

"Earth fae," she said in a low, hissing voice, like a damn whisper on the sea. "Your time of peace . . . is up. It is . . . time for us to take back . . . the Ever."

Her body spasmed and dulled, as though the life had somehow glowed beneath her skin, then bled out into the tides.

Time for them to take back the Ever? The realm of the sea fae?

They wanted revenge on the East since this was where Thorvald fell into his grave. But the Ever . . . the Ever was a whole damn world as far as I knew.

My stomach clenched. Gods, had they already overtaken the other kingdoms? The warning had come from the North, and Valen was Thorvald's killer. A shudder beneath my feet caused me to stumble.

Time. There was something about this . . . time. My gaze drifted to the blood moon overhead. Crimson and horrid. It appeared, and the battles began. Like Davorin was somehow attached to the omen, it appeared in his presence.

The coward had yet to show his face.

I spat beside the fallen sea fae woman and took up my blade. There was more blood to spill.

Twenty paces away, Kase lifted his palms, inky shadows coiled around his fingers. He pulled his arms toward his chest. Sea fae trudged toward the shore, water dripping from the scarves over their heads, the rings pierced in their ears. They were a damn infestation.

"Dagny! At your back!" Luca's voice roared over the crash of blades and angry seas.

My heart stuttered in my chest. Near a low stone barrier on the water's edge, Dagny fought to be free of the crushing waves, but there were two sea fae with curved swords approaching her from either side.

"No, Dag! Kase, hurry!" I shouted, desperate, a little delirious, as though something inside knew I was too far from her. Kase was too far.

I sprinted for the water. The ring scorched over my skin, hot and sharp like embers in a new flame. My mesmer swirled inside my veins until the surface of my skin ached like someone had taken a torch to my flesh.

Sea folk came close. I used my open palms, mere touches, and they cried out, clutching their heads. Thoughts were too wild, too hurried; I didn't know if I robbed them of their recollection to breathe, to sleep, to fill their bellies? Perhaps they forgot their blood hailed from the sea. It didn't matter, the beauty of my mesmer since claiming the queen's ring was that the initial attack was always disorienting.

It always robbed folk of their wits for a moment.

Trouble was, it drained my own strength. Already, the muscles in my legs barked their fatigue as I carved through the waves. I cursed as I fought to keep pace, but I was passed by Luca. He ran for his wife with a desperation I knew too well. A desperation when the heart knew danger and death awaited the one you loved.

I'd lived it. I'd watched Kase die in my arms.

It was the kind of desperation no lovers should ever experience.

Luca cut down a spindly looking sea fae with a beard to his chest and leapt over a few white capped waves.

Dagny shrieked, slicing her knife at the sea fae, but she stumbled. The sea bastard raised his blade, ready to land the killing blow.

"Dag!" Luca lunged for her.

Time went still. A dagger—or a pain just as wretched—found my heart when Luca covered his wife with his own body and the point of the sea fae's blade thrust deep into his spine.

Without mercy, the sea fae wrenched his blade free and made a rush for the shore as though Luca were nothing more than an obstacle—as if he were simply . . . nothing.

"Luca!" Kase's frantic voice was mere paces behind me. Kryv called for their brother, for the man who'd kept them safe from Ivar as children.

Tears blurred my sight as I cut through the waves.

Dagny's head surfaced and she sobbed as waves struck her over and over. Luca's hand trembled as it reached for her face.

She gave him a small smile. The sort of smile one gave when it was the last. When your heart knew it would be the final thing another soul might see.

"Dagny, no!" I shouted. "Move!"

The second sea fae remained. A second blade. A second enemy.

Dagny hugged Luca's head to her chest and lifted her gaze over his tousled hair. The same damn smile she'd offered her husband, she now pointed it at me.

"Tell him we love him," was all she had time to say before the fae at her back lowered his sword against her throat.

"No!" I doubled over. A reckless move in the middle of battle, but the pain was too consuming. Agony, bitter and sour, robbed the air from my lungs as I watched my friends, my family, fall into the bloody waves.

I couldn't draw in breath. I couldn't bleeding see through the tears. Rage, unlike any I'd felt, sifted through the pain. As though the loss of everyone I loved gathered like a furious knot in my chest, I blamed them all on this wretch, this monster, who'd polluted our kingdoms with his hatred.

For the pain of losing Kase to a cruel masquerade.

For Hagen's lost family.

For Jens.

For Vali.

For our parents who did not get to raise their littles.

Now, for Dagny. For Luca. Two souls who'd wanted nothing more than to live simply until old age dragged them to the Other-world. Souls who deserved to watch their son become a man.

They were gone. Because of *him*.

I trembled in wretched anger and raised my palms. Heat pulsed through my fingertips. The ring burned. All around me, shadows thickened.

Silent and frightening, Kase stepped to my side. He took my hand without a word, and the bond we shared, both as Alvers and our vows sent a shocking rush of power through my blood. Dark power. A kind that could corrupt and consume should I let it.

For a moment, I did.

Billows of darkness with a few sharp flashes of light swirled around us like a wild storm. The sea fae in the waves halted. Rows of enemies, at long last, looked upon our shores with a bit of trepidation.

They only fueled Kase's mesmer.

His vicious, white grin split over his features once two haggard looking fae stepped onto the rocky banks.

"Are you afraid, sea fae?" Kase's rough rasp sent my pulse racing.

Most seemed too stunned to move, others took steps back toward deeper waters. Some dove beneath the surface.

"You should be," Kase went on, a mad look to the glossy black of his eyes. "Did you not realize you've stepped into a realm of nightmares?"

His movement spurred my own. A unified attack, bonded through our hearts and souls, we flung our arms out wide.

A furious gust of shadows ripped through the soft bellies of our invaders like dark daggers. Rows and rows of fae fell as splinters of his mesmer lodged deep in the ribs, the eyes, through the throats, even a few through their open mouths as they screamed, the dark points splitting holes out the backs of their skulls.

Brilliant light from my mesmer collided with the crowns of their heads, ripping through the most basic of thoughts. Breath, survival, a will to live. They were peeled back from their consciousness until the fae could not think to stand any longer.

Fifty paces on either side of the shore, sea fae toppled over. Those rising from the depths of the Howl drew to a halt, watching with a bit of horror as their people stumbled and fell. Dead before they knew what was coming.

Silence fell over the sea for mere breaths before the fae of the sea retreated. They shouted calls for escape. They plunged their horridly beautiful features, or scales, their wretched eyes, into the depths of the Howl.

I stumbled against Kase, and he against me. Such a rush of mesmer robbed us both of our strength, but more than that... the grief was debilitating.

Kase fell to his knees. At his back, the Kryv gathered in a wretched silence as they looked on to where Luca and Dagny had fallen near the shore, arms still linked together. Raum hung his head, hiding his eyes. Lynx clapped a hand on his shoulder.

Ash pressed a hand to his broad chest. One of the youngest of the Kryv had grown taller than most of the others. Ash let tears fall, unashamed, over his stubbled cheeks.

Kase cleared his throat. He wiped one corner of his eye with the back of his hand and rose from the slap of the sea.

"Help me take them back to Felstad. Where we were first truly free." His voice croaked. "Von Grym will know his parents died as warriors. He needs to know they . . . they dine with their gods tonight."

I slipped my hand into his. Kase tended to ignore the existence of gods, but he knew Von would want to believe his mother and father were greeted by those who'd passed before. Kase would want the boy to cling to that faith now.

True, Kase did not believe in the gods, but I'd sent countless prayers to the skies that we'd have a bit of respite from the attacks, a few clock tolls even, to light funeral pyres for Dag and Luca.

It seemed, for now, those prayers were heard.

The pyres ignited the still-scorched stones of Felstad in dancing shades of gold and red. Von stood in the front, chin trembling, tears lining his eyes. A boy. A mere boy of fourteen and he'd now face the world alone.

No. Not alone. He'd always have us.

I rested my head on Kase's shoulder, watching as Jonas slunk next to Von and slipped his hand in the boy's left palm. Sander gently took the right. The two princes held to Von, a boy who'd befriended them, even young as they were. He whittled with them.

Went swimming in the rivers. Visited the Falkyn Nest to cause havoc much like . . . much like Kase and Luca had done as boys.

A tear trickled off my lashes, down my nose, until I tasted the salt on my lips. Dagny befriended me when I was afraid of the Kryv. She fought tirelessly for Von, for Luca. She was bold and selfless.

Luca, all he'd wanted was his family. His friends. His peace.

"Save us a seat," I whispered to the flames. *Every sunrise, I will miss you.*

Kase shifted and wrapped an arm around my shoulders, holding me tightly against his side. I hugged his waist.

To those who did not know him, the Nightrender was a fiend, a heartless shadow. To the rest of us, he was a man who valued nothing over those in his family. Luca Grym was his family. Dagny was both honorary Kryv and Falkyn. She was his family.

He loved them.

He hurt without them.

And he would try to hide it from the rest of us.

I tightened my hold on his waist a little more. "You were his brother, Kase Eriksson."

He didn't take his eyes off the dying pyres, but a muscle ticked in his jaw. "And he was mine."

The pyres would fade through the night. Silence followed the procession back to the open gates of Felstad. Inge mutely ushered us toward the doors where we would soak up what time we had left before a new wave of sea fae, doubtless, returned to terrorize our shores.

We had plans to seal the shores. If we could but reach Niklas and the others across the Howl, perhaps we could manipulate some Elixist warding. Boil the sea so the fae would cook through their innards. Something equally brutal to make up for those they stole from us today.

On my next step, the ground shuddered. The same as it had done at the shore. Kase gripped my elbow and whirled toward the shore. Perhaps he had the same thought—had the North arrived?

Nothing, until . . .

"What is that?" Lynx asked.

A flash of strange, golden lightning burst across the sky.

"Raum, what do you see?" Kase gestured to his Kryv. Raum's eyesight and mesmer had only gained potency over the turns.

Raum stepped forward, eyes narrowed. "I-I can't tell exactly, but it looks like a burst of just . . . *light*. It's from—gods—it's hailing from the West."

Calista. My pulse quickened, but I had little time to fret over our storyteller. In the next breath, the ground lurched again. More violent. A sick crack below us gave way to the truth that our foundation, the damn bedrock beneath our feet, was crumbling.

Kryv moved swift as shadows and reached for the young ones. Lynx snagged Von, while Inge shouted for Hob to shield their daughter.

"Jonas! Sander!" Kase shouted, one hand on me, the other arm open, beckoning to our sons. "Come to me, now. *Now*."

The twins sprinted for us. No sooner had they wrapped their skinny arms around their father's waist, the soil shook with such force that we stumbled to our knees, and Klockglas seemed to sink into the sea.

CHAPTER 25
THE RAVEN QUEEN

The Court of Hearts—Southern Kingdom

ARI'S LONG NIGHT FOLK LEGS COULD OUTPACE ME BY THREE STRIDES TO ONE. I fought to lengthen my gait, but with the violent shudders in the soil, it made the journey worse. My heart was screaming for speed. We needed to reach the burrows. I needed her in my arms.

All at once, Ari yanked me off our path as the ground sunk into a deep crevice.

"What's happening?" A pointless question. Ari knew as much as me.

For days the isle had, once again, succumbed to the wild plague, only worse. Fae folk thrashed and writhed in spitting rage until the healers tended to them with Niklas's elixirs. Since the battle of the isles, every kingdom was well stocked with the wards against Davorin's dark glamour.

Still, when it caught their blood, the wild plague was vicious and unforgiving.

The ground rocked again. Ari tucked my head to his chest, his breaths harsh and swift, as though he could not fill his lungs before he needed to reach for another gasp of air.

When there came another pause in the shift, we wasted no time before we sprinted toward the trees again.

All around us folk abandoned the Borough walls. At the command of their king and queen we would head for Whisper Lake. It was the only flat ground close enough to the Court of Hearts where few trees could topple over us, where knolls wouldn't give in.

"This . . . isn't Valen," Ari said through strained gasps as we ran.

At first, we'd thought—we'd hoped—the North had arrived to aid us in the rising battle. It would mean they were safe; it would mean the warning they'd lit on the torches had passed and they'd come to aid the isles.

There were no Ettan ships. Only shifting earth and a gold burst against the blood-red sky.

There was no Davorin.

Ari had not slept, he'd hardly eaten. Since the flame ignited as a warning, he'd traipsed the gates tirelessly, the heirloom blade in hand, waiting for Davorin's strike. Only the essence of his glamour was here, but no true sign of the battle lord.

Lack of sightings of him meant little since Davorin took pleasure in the torment. He was here. Somewhere.

I could sense it to my very soul.

The thought added a burst of desperation to my pace, and I quickened each step until we reached the tree line.

I let out a strangled cry. "Ari, there. Gods, hurry."

"Dammit." Ari released my hand the instant he caught sight of Gorm sprawled on his belly, a hand down a wide hole. Magus and the Court of Serpent guards surrounded the blood lord, shouting commands and shielding their heads from falling branches.

In the trees, Gunnar Strom and other archers fired at the borders of the burrow when feral fae tried to rush against us.

Eryka's eyes were white like the blaze of stars, her face pointed toward the sky, and she kept repeating the same words. "Back to the beginning fate will lead. Who rises in the end, is yet to be seen."

I shook my head, peeling my attention off the star seer, and dropped in front of the entrance of the troll burrow.

"Gorm, where is she?" Ari skidded next to the blood lord.

"The troll folk are caved in on the opposite side," Gorm said. "The princess is too deep to reach."

"What!" I leaned over the edge. "Mira? Mira, speak to me."

A whimper replied.

Ari mimicked Gorm and flattened on his belly. True enough, the troll burrow was deep. Magus hung a lantern over the king's head to chase away the shadows of the opening. Perhaps a dozen paces down, Mira sobbed at the bottom of the burrow, surrounded by rocks and massive clods of dirt.

The trolls, Dunker and a few of his rowdy cousins, were tasked in watching the princess, tasked with hiding her from Davorin should he show his damn face. Rune kept to the trees, Gorm and Magus watched either entrance.

If the burrow did not cave in from the shudders, soon enough the wild fae would claim us all. The rancid tang of blood spilled over the area from the endless arrows slicing through flesh, through Gorm's blood fae on foot, using their blades much the same.

Ari reached a hand into the tunnel. He grinned, wide and white. A forced grin, but to Mira it would be her familiar father who loved nothing more than to make her laugh with his jests and taunts.

"Come on, my girl," Ari said. "Maj and I were having a race through the trees. Thought you might want to join."

I bit down a cry when the ground shifted again. Mira sobbed. Ari's jaw pulsed, but he returned the smile again.

"Mira," he said, firmer. "Come on, now. Time to leave the burrow. You must stand, climb as high as you can, and reach for my hand. Look nowhere else but me. Maj will help you."

I pressed my palm on the soil, urging the land to sprout roots, vines, anything of use for our daughter to take. Until my heart stilled at her words.

"I c-c-c-can't," Mira wailed. She screamed, a sound that shattered my soul into broken pieces when a violent roll of the soil cracked the distant windows in the Borough.

"Mira," Ari said, voice rough. "Take my hand. Now."

"Daj," she whimpered. "It's m-m-my foot. It's stuck."

No. A sick rush of bile burned my throat. A few more violent quakes and she'd be buried. No matter how desperately I pleaded with the isles, they would not cease the movement. It was becoming clearer, a different power, a different glamour was at play here.

"Saga." Ari tossed me the heirloom sword. He maneuvered to his knees and started to slide through the hole.

"Ari, no."

He paused, only long enough to flicker a quick grin. "Back in a moment, sweet menace."

A promise was buried in his words. A promise we both knew he couldn't keep, yet it mattered little. Either Ari or I were going in that damn hole, and the only reason it was him was due to those long, bleeding Night Folk legs.

His mussed head of golden hair disappeared into the burrow. I closed my eyes, pleading to the night for his return, for my girl to be unharmed.

Gods, one more cruel shiver of the bedrock and they'd be trapped. My family, the two people I cared most for in the whole of the world, would be lost to me. Hot tears of hate, of fear, of regret, scorched through my veins.

Davorin was my tyrant. I'd brought him back. In more than one way I could not help but feel as though this scourge, this pain, was the fault of my foolish young heart. To think, I once thought I knew love with that bastard.

The love I had now with Ari, all I'd ever known before my husband was mere infatuation.

I took Ari's place at the top of the hole and blinked through the billows of falling dirt as Ari skidded his way toward Mira. How long had she been trapped in the dark? The trolls could burrow away from the cave in, but Mira could've been trapped there if Rune and Gorm had not sent the signal.

"It looks to be the ankle," Gorm said plainly.

He was flat and direct in most cases, but I'd known Lord Gorm long enough now to catch the flickers of anxiety in his tone. It was there. He valued the little princess. Not only because she was a royal and Gorm honored the royal house, but he . . . he truly cared for her.

Like a strange, gentle uncle who never understood the meaning of her jokes.

I lifted the lantern, feeding more light to the darkness. Pebbles and bits of dirt struck my face. I didn't blink. I hardly breathed until Ari reached Mira.

She sobbed and gasped. Danger was all around, but he took a few breaths to wrap her in his arms, to kiss her head, to assure her he'd be there.

"I'm not leaving you," he said.

Ari slapped a heavy mound of dirt. "Get out Dunker. Damn troll. They're still hanging around as if that's useful."

No doubt, the trolls could not stomach leaving their royal charge. Still, it would've made a great deal more sense if their hefty claws dug out, came to warn us, or dug a new hole to better reach Mira.

The ground shook, enough Ari had to brace against the dirt cavern walls. He hunched over Mira, creating a shield over her small body. Gorm's heavy palm gripped my lower leg when the edge of the burrow gave and nearly tossed me down the flume with the rest.

"Mira," Ari said when the shudder lessened. "I'm going to lift this stone, and I need you to move." He held up a hand. "No, I know it hurts, but we cannot stay here. You are strong, like warriors. Besides, think of how you'll be able to boast of your strength the next time you see those pesky twins."

Mira coughed, and if I had to guess, she almost laughed. It was a delight of her existence to prove to the Eriksson twins she was brave and cunning.

"Ready. One," Ari braced his shoulder under the stone. "Two. Three."

He grunted and the stone shifted. Mira cried, gasping, but dragged herself away until another angry quake rocked the ground.

"Ari!" I stretched my arms into the tunnel. "Hurry, gods, please hurry."

In the next breath, Ari scooped Mira up, he maneuvered her onto his back. "Head down, Mira. Keep your head down."

His fingers dug into the walls of the tunnel. I cursed and stretched out my hands as the sides gave slightly against the quaking. Gorm held my ankles, but I leaned deeper into the tunnel, desperate to get my hands on them.

"Go to Maj," Ari commanded. "Mira, go, go."

She reached her skinny arms over his shoulder. Our fingers hooked, then slid apart. Ari cursed, his muscles flinching as he held steady on a ledge of the tunnel, trying to balance and ease Mira toward the surface without falling backward.

"A little more, my girl." I was practically tumbling into the tunnel. If not for Gorm, I would spill over the side.

Mira slapped for my hands, sobbing, but in the next attempt her palm landed against mine. I pulled her up the side. Gorm pulled my legs. Like a rope of bodies, we dragged Mira free of the tunnel. She collapsed in fitful tears against my chest.

At the next shudder, half the tunnel caved in and my heart stopped.

"Ari!" Gently, I guarded Mira at my back and dug through the dirt half-covering the opening. Ari had pressed his body against the side of the wall to avoid the spill. His skin was coated in damp soil, his body trembled from exertion. Those beautiful, soft, golden eyes held mine in the dark.

"Don't you dare," I said through clenched teeth.

"We're out of time. This earth is going to give in and you need to take her from here, Saga," he said softly.

"We fight these fights together, don't you dare give up on me." I reached my arms into the tunnel, no thought for the cracks in the soil, the snapping of trees. No thought but having my husband's hand in mine, his arms around me.

"Together. You promised me, Ari Sekundär." I sank deeper. Once again, Gorm gripped my legs. "This is not where our story ends. Now climb your ass out of this tunnel."

Constant shudders sent more stones, more debris into the troll burrow, but soon Ari tightened his jaw. He began his climb, careful as he went. All around him soil was breaking. The strength and sturdiness of the burrow was failing.

"Saga," he gritted out when it felt as though the whole of the isles were flipping upside down. "Go, *gods*. Go."

"Give. Me. Your hand." I was bathed in dirt. Clumps of it hung on my lashes, blurring my sight, but he was mere paces away. A few more movements and I'd have him.

He cursed, but reached for a jutting root. In a swell of shuddering soil, the burrow split in half.

"Ari!" I screamed. The crack was taking him in. "Take my hand. Jump!"

With no options left, Ari released his hold on the dirt wall and jumped across the crack, arm outstretched. I let out a cry of agony when his hand clasped my palm, yanking my shoulder painfully with his weight. In an instant, I grasped his wrist with my other hand.

"Climb," I whispered, voice rough. "Help me."

Ari was hanging over an open pit, all the walls caving in. He swung his body until his feet found purchase in what was left of the wall. Over my body, a thicker, broader form reached into the tunnel.

"Hold tight, My King," Gorm's gravelly voice followed. "I'm vastly stronger than the queen, and I will be taking hold of your tunic. It must be done."

Gorm didn't wait for a word before he reached over me, close enough now to grip the back of Ari's top. Together, we heaved. The extra tug was enough to draw Ari to the edge, where he could hook a leg on the ledge and roll out of the tunnel.

His tunic was half-peeled off his back, his face coated in dirt, but he was bleeding free. In two breaths he had my body pressed to his.

"Foolish woman," he gasped against my throat. "You could've been trapped or hurt or—"

"Stop talking." I choked my arms around his neck, breathing him in. "Don't you ever again tell me to leave you, understand me? It will not happen, you damn fool."

Ari kissed my throat, then let out a shuddering breath once Mira nuzzled her way between us. He held us both, kissing our heads, my cheeks, Mira's forehead.

"All gods." Gorm shook us from the moment of relief. The blood lord did not gasp, not in such a way. He was rarely taken by surprise. But he was stunned now.

I lifted my gaze and cried out in fear. Ari positioned me behind him; I covered Mira with my body. The forest floor snapped and bent, great bursts of dirt and rock shot into the air like the bursting geysers in the Court of Blood.

But beyond them was a cloak of night. Shadows like clotted ink devoured trees, ferns, anything in its path was devoured. The darkness was speeding our way, too swift to outrun. We'd be taken.

This was the moment I'd always feared.

The moment our stories ended.

"I love you," Ari said, holding his arms around me and Mira. He ducked his head. "To the Otherworld, I love you."

His words were the last thing I heard before our world was swallowed up in cruel darkness.

BEGINNING OF THE END

CHAPTER 26
THE PHANTOM

THE WORLD FELL INTO AN EERIE STILLNESS. AS THOUGH EVERYTHING—
sound, air, movement—all of it ceased for a few breaths.

Calista let out a sharp gasp and slumped against my chest.
During the song, we'd both lowered to the ground, too overtaken by
the strength of seidr. Whatever we'd done, it reminded me too much
of that night we'd found the Raven Queen tied to a bed, bloody and
battered.

By attempting to be a beacon, or guide for other kingdoms, we'd
once more done something drastic.

"Silas." Calista lifted her head, her eyes fluttered open. "Do you
feel strange?"

I nodded and tugged her body closer. "It feels like we've . . .
unraveled something again."

"Like a new path that wasn't there before has opened."

Exactly. My limbs were heavy, my pulse weak with exhaustion,
but I managed to peer out the glossy window toward the main Row.
"Dammit," I hissed under my breath.

"What?" Calista said, keeping a hand on my chest but leveraging
to her knees to look outside.

"The Rave," I said. "The shield they created is weakening."

194

Between the gilded swords on the shore, the flicker of their burning shield against the darkness beneath the waves was dying, like an ember in a rainstorm.

"Because of us?"

"It was the warning," I said, a deep, wretched kind of foreboding gathered in my chest. "The tale ended, and the kingdom once more returned to the beginning. It is his land he is returning to. I think . . . this is a path that was destined to happen, but whatever alternate fate we just opened, we must find it. Quickly."

Calista blinked, lips tight and bloodless. With a curt nod, she scrambled toward our discarded clothes. Gods, what I'd do to stay tangled in her limbs, peaceful, unburdened to the end of our days.

We dressed. My palms smoothed her wild braids. She helped secure the mask over my scar, as though she knew it caused a great deal of distress to be seen without it. Together, we abandoned Hus Rose through the front gates and sprinted down the newly restored cobbled stones of Raven Row.

"Hold," Olaf barked, marching down the line of Rave warriors.

In the distance, a dark current over the surface of the sea bubbled. Like a pot slowly boiling, the water bubbled, gurgled, and hissed.

"Even the Chasm of Seas is different, more defined," Calista whispered, gaze on the tides. "I . . . I remember it looking much the same as a girl."

I slipped my fingers into hers. "Your daj always watched it, despite normally peaceful trade with sea fae, he always held a wariness about the Chasm."

"Do you suppose he sensed this?" she asked, voice low. "Even then, do you suppose he sensed there was fate tangled with us and the fae of the sea?"

"It is always possible." I didn't truly understand the depth of Riot Ode's power. The king had tutored me, guided me when my own song tangled with his child. But there was always a sense that the last king of fate could feel a great deal more than he let on.

"You brought us back," Olaf shouted. "Now we fight for our land as we did long ago."

"What is he going on about?" Calista asked.

"Cal!" The blood fae who guarded her appeared from behind one of the towering buildings, blade in hand.

"Cuyler." She released my hand and went to the blood fae. "Did you see anything shift? We saw the land moving."

"Anything shift?" His pale eyes widened. Cuyler pointed behind us. "Yes, I saw a *shift*. Look. Tell me that damn peak in the distance wasn't there a few moments ago, for I'm convinced I've lost my mind."

I spun around. True enough, frosted peaks took up the northern skies. Lusher forests filled the darkness of the night well beyond Hus Rose.

"Bleeding hells," Calista said. "The kingdom . . . it's grown."

"No, it hasn't grown. It's restored," I corrected. "Look at it, Little Rose. This is . . . home."

"Home?" Cuyler forgot any trepidation for me and came to my side. "You mean the original kingdom? But the fae isles were split from the old kingdom of House Ode, right? Etta, even the regions of the East. I saw them break apart in King Ari's dream—" He paused and glanced at me. "Well, I suppose you already know it since I'm quite certain you, Wraith, were the one leading Ari through it. Which, I have many questions about."

He wanted answers. I doubted I'd be the one to give them. There was a strangling kind of panic that came when folk spoke to me. A panic I never truly knew was there until I stepped beyond the gates of Hus Rose.

I didn't understand it.

With Calista I could speak fine enough. With this blood fae, I shrunk to the shadows, taking a step away from him.

"Silas was there." Calista rested a hand on my arm, gave me a soft smile, then faced Cuyler. "He was Ari's Wraith. It is his skill beyond seidr—to dream walk, much like my Shadow Queen does with her tricky memories."

I let out a breath of relief. How did she know the words had been throttled in my throat before they'd even formed?

Olaf approached, sweat soaked his brow, the hint of damp and brine was laced into the threads of his clothing. Apart even this short time, he already looked younger, stronger, much more like the Rave captain he'd been in Riot Ode's army. The silver from his ratty hair had faded to the dark brown, his eyes had less yellow to the whites, and more vibrancy bloomed in the paleness.

"Shields will be broken within two nights, mark me," Olaf said. "That quake, it was not an act of the earth. It's added shoreline and absorbed much of our strength to hold. We need more defenses if another attack should come. What happened in Hus Rose?"

My skin heated. Could they smell or sense that I'd left them to guard the damn shore while I tasted every surface of Calista's body? It didn't seem fair that I indulged in pleasure while others stood out in the night, blades ready.

Still, something had shifted. The connection we'd built must have been the final piece. A true bond had formed in those heated moments, one that had clearly shifted our world as a whole.

"Any sign of the battle lord?" Calista asked.

Olaf let out a sigh and faced the sea. "Not yet. But the Chasm, you see it there, it is more . . . lively. Sea fae have always been rather antagonistic, even during peaceful trade turns. They like to think of themselves as superior."

"Don't we all," Calista answered, but she faced me. "Silas, there is something coming. I *feel* it."

"Same," I whispered, and pressed a hand to my heart, a signal that the feeling was within me too.

"You're different." Olaf narrowed his eyes at me.

"They are, aren't they?" Cuyler offered and started to circle us. "I can't place it, but Cal, even you seem different."

Gods, how much detail should I give? Was it common for folk to divulge every movement they made as lovers? In order to properly defend us, did they need to know what I'd done with *my mouth*?

Calista's hand fell to mine, squeezing gently, and the calm of her touch soothed the rage of taut panic. Her long-awaited acceptance of me, of us, seemed to give her some uncanny insight into my emotions. For she, again, spoke before I drifted into a suffocating unease where shadows would take me to a dark reality I struggled to escape.

"Our first kingdom began to shatter when a bond was formed between me and Silas," Calista said. "We all know this. Gifts of fate have been scattered and gathered. What happened in Hus Rose was a final piece of a wretchedly beautiful story," she said, looking at me. "No more secrets, no more hiding the bond that brought us all here. I've found it, accepted it, and it ended that alternate path we opened so long ago. It has brought us back to where my father began his battle."

"That makes a bit of sense. It feels like the battles we fought beside the king," Olaf said. "If I'm understanding, by breaking the kingdoms onto that new vein of seidr the two of you opened, Riot gave us time, yes? Time for the gifts of fate to grow stronger."

"You would know, Rave," Cuyler said. "You were there. Were you losing the battles?"

Olaf paused to consider it. After a moment, he nodded. "The battle lord was a terrible foe. His dark glamour overtook everything, and he knew the Rave like he knew his own twisted mind. We *were* his army, after all. We could rarely hide a move from him, so yes. I think even the king knew that defeating Davorin with our blades alone would have been a damn near impossible feat."

Calista closed her eyes for a few breaths. "I've harbored guilt since I saw the way my parents sacrificed it all to keep me alive, but it was not a sacrifice to them. To divide the power of fate was my daj's answer, his way to keep his people free and living. Daj . . . he was not a selfish king, true? With his power, I mean. He wasn't power mad."

"No," Olaf said, a slight smile in the corner of his mouth. "No, Riot Ode viewed his seidr as a duty, not a call to riches and prestige. He was a mightily fair king, My Lady. He would never have passed on that duty to you—" Olaf spared a look to me. "To the both of you, if he did not know you would rise with the same justness he and the queen shared."

"Folk I love—these other royals—they are honorable much the same." Calista hesitated. "Sort of. The Shadow King is quite proud to be a thief. Be aware of it."

Olaf smirked. "You have walked the path you were meant to walk. Your power is yours, but you face the fight of your parents. Our command falls to you. Well, I suppose if the bond is reunited, it falls to both of you."

I winced. Hardly able to speak, how was I to give a damn army any kind of command?

"I know little about armies," Calista said. "Silas was a boy when our worlds faded. He might know more about the Rave, but I doubt he knows how to lead an army."

Calista wasn't degrading me—her smile told me she was shielding me. I dipped my chin and stepped closer to her side.

"I think that is where we are lucky to have so many kings and queens in this game," she went on. "They each will bring a talent, a thought, a strength, that perhaps the final throne does not have." Calista hooked her palm around my forearm, her gaze only on me, as she lowered her voice. "For that is what we are. The final throne."

Four queens. Four battles. Four fates.

"Agreed," Cuyler said. He faced the new distant peaks. "What I want to know is what bleeding happened, though."

"Forbi said the battle bastard would return to his old land," Calista said. "I think it is because there is no longer a song of Riot Ode keeping him out. Just like Saga was shielded, I think there have been slight advantages that have kept the kingdoms safer from his influence."

"You," I muttered under my breath.

Calista tilted her head. "What do you mean?"

"You helped guide them. Protected them. You formed bonds that did not need to be so strong for them to find their fate. You could've been a distant worker of fate, but . . . you made them your folk. You were their advantage."

Her brow wrinkled. Calista stepped into my side and let her head fall to my shoulder. "Then so were you."

I always viewed my involvement in the other kingdoms merely for her sake. But the more I thought on it, the more I realized, through the turns I, too, had grown respect for folk I'd never truly met beyond the Golden King.

I sang fierce songs, pushed my limits, telling myself it was all for her, but in truth, I didn't want her heart to lose them. I wanted them to live, to grow stronger, because I wanted Calista to have her damn people again.

"So, if I'm understanding all this," Cuyler said. "There are no longer any wards, any protections against the battle lord. Your father cursed the lands, cursed you, to keep you safe, right?"

"I think so," said Calista. "I think a new tale is beginning. One where either he rises victorious, or us."

"Three damn hells," Cuyler said, almost exasperated. "This bastard is like a pest that never dies."

Strange, but I almost laughed. I swallowed the sound, uncertain if this was a moment, if that was a comment that warranted laughter. There was much to learn in the ways of . . . people, and I didn't know where to bleeding start.

Calista snorted, convincing me I was correct in assuming it was a little humorous.

"He's more than a pest, he's a damn disease. I plan on making certain our blades are the antidote to be rid of him." She rolled her shoulders back. "We don't know when he'll come, but we can be bleeding sure he will. He is already spreading his pestilence. We must prepare, but . . . this new path we created—" She glanced at me. "Is not meant to be walked alone."

"Should we send word to the other kingdoms, then?" Cuyler asked. "I don't know if it will get through, but we can try."

Calista shook her head. "Cuyler, I don't think there are other kingdoms. Look at the shoreline, the peaks."

"Where are our folk, then?" A bit of strain was in the blood fae's tone. No mistake, his thoughts were with his people in the fae isles.

"Silas," Calista looked to me instead. "When they began to break, we tried to be a beacon to them. Is it possible we brought them here?"

"I don't know, Little Rose." I was walking a new path with everyone else.

"Those peaks—" Calista gestured toward the northern cliffs. "Those look similar to the landscape in Etta. And . . . the forests—"

She turned in the opposite direction. "What if the fae isles have returned to where it all once was? What if they're here?"

"How would they survive such a shift?" Cuyler murmured, a little more broken than before. Truth be told, I didn't think he meant to say it out loud.

"We sang a tale," Calista said softly. "A song meant to guide them here. They have always had a place in this fight. Four . . . four queens. Four thrones. We're to stand as one now."

"I suggest we protect our shores," Olaf interjected. "While also, perhaps, sending out a search. Gods know we could use more warriors."

"I'll go." Cuyler lifted his pale gaze to me, then Calista. "I'll take my men, we'll search for . . . for whatever might be left."

"He'll be there," Calista said, a crack in her voice. "Your father will be all right."

Cuyler's jaw tightened. His smile looked forced. "Give us time to gather a few supplies and we'll be off."

"Be careful, Cuyler. I have no guide on what will happen from here. Silas?"

I looked to her and shook my head. "Our fate is in our hands now, Little Rose. How our paths unfold is now up to us."

In our hands, and I didn't know if we'd be the ones to fail or rise as victors at long last.

CHAPTER 27
ROGUE PRINCESS

Somewhere in the West

RAVENSPIRE WAS DIFFERENT. A FEW BROKEN BEAMS FROM THE SHIFT, BUT . . . there. Surrounded by blossoms of moonvane and new trees. Aspens like Etta had always had, but more evergreens, a few spiked plants that seemed only to grow in the fae isles.

What was missing were the normal borders of Lyx, the lower township near Ravenspire. And the docks. Where was the damn sea?

Valen shuffled through our chamber. Tables were overturned, a few cracks were in the windows, but most of our belongings were here, and it made little sense.

The damn kingdom had been swallowed by a night so thick I could not see my own hand in front of my face. As the soil had shattered, we'd lost sight of it all. I was certain we'd wake in the Otherworld but instead we were . . . somewhere else.

I couldn't even orient myself in this new landscape, yet somehow, it felt a great deal like home. Trees blocked our view, but we couldn't remain here not knowing what faced us in the wood.

Valen handed me an additional dagger and strapped one in a sheath on the small of his back. He tucked a few bits of copper *shim* to a pouch on his belt, his axes, and the wrapped disc we'd won from the death of the sea king.

Valen rarely left it unguarded, unsettled by the threat from Thorvald's brother ten turns ago to return. Truth be told, there was a strange, fading power to the gold talisman. Like it was slowly dying.

"Ready?" He asked, taking my hand.

I squeezed his fingers, nodding, and followed him out of the castle to the crowd gathering in the cracked gardens. The cobbled paths, bowers, and fountains had toppled in the earth shift. Most of the plants remained unscathed, but like everything else, seemed different than before, lusher, more vibrant.

A cart had been loaded with supplies and Lilianna. Our horses and charges fled during the shift, so the front was pulled by Ettan warriors, Arvad, Kjell, and Dagar Atra. Arvad hadn't left Lili's side. We'd anticipated the need for sleeping draughts, but something else was keeping her body at rest.

In truth, every cursed Timoran seemed to have fallen under some kind of sleep spell.

We'd emerged in this new Etta with Timorans sprawled about, coated in blood. For now, they were all safely locked in the cells, sleeping. Lilianna would remain with us. If we found a way to help her, we could help them all. Until then, we had some sense of safety from at least one threat.

Valen went to a few knights with the orders to keep guard on the palace where our elderly, injured, or those unable to lift a blade would remain. A few gates were crooked and bent on their hinges, but still strong. With archers and watchmen in place, it was the most we could offer them for safety.

I stepped away from Valen and went to the woman staring at the sky, her hand on her belly.

"Siv," I whispered.

Siverie peered over her shoulder, a glisten to her eyes. "Do you think he's here, Elise? I don't want to leave him behind."

My throat burned. I wrapped her in my arms. "He's always with you, Siv. Gods, he loved—no, he *loves* you. He'll always be here, no matter where we are."

She'd sniffed when she pulled back, wiping a few tears off her cheeks. "I should come with you."

Siv was heavy with their child. I placed a hand on her belly and smiled. "I need you here. Protect these people, protect your little. We'll return, I swear to you."

"You . . . you and Valen, everyone who's going out there, you're all I have left."

"And we'll be back." I trapped her face in my hands. "Don't you dare have that babe without me."

Siv let out a broken laugh and hugged me tightly. I refused to be the first to let go. Siv had been without Mattis barely over a week, and I suspected the shock of it was still settling. No mistake, if ever we found time for peace, the pain of his absence would come with a wretched vengeance.

When Siv released me and returned to the inner gates of Ravenspire with the others, I crossed into the gardens to those going out into the wood.

The rest of us, most of our armies, and the royal littles (for I doubted there would be any chance we could leave our young ones without the comfort of their families after what they'd seen) would trek for the light in the distance.

Our kingdom had shattered, but the same golden shimmer we'd seen before the break remained in the red sky.

Perhaps it was a ruse, a trap set to lead us in like a moth to a flame, but somewhere inside it felt . . . safe. Like home.

"We travel with little light," Valen said, his voice lifting over the caravan. "Until we know what we're facing, blades out, instincts sharp. Littles are kept on the inside." The king took in his nephews, his nieces, his warrior's young ones, then at last, his own daughter. Valen kept his gaze on Livia as he finished his instructions. "You all run if we command it, no question, no fighting. You run. Aesir."

Halvar's son snapped to attention.

Valen gripped the boy's shoulder. "You're the oldest of those not of age to fight. You'll lead them if it comes to that. Can I count on you?"

"Yes." Aesir dipped his chin. "Always, My King."

Burdens lined my heart. One look at my girl and it wanted to snap in two. Livia fought to be bold and brave, but there was a significant tremble to her chin as she clung to Aleksi's side. I wanted nothing more than to assure her it would all be well, but in truth, I'd never seen this. I did not know what was happening, or what we faced in those trees.

"May the gods be with us," Valen said with a touch of despair.

I took hold of Livia's palm, bending down to kiss her knuckles, and positioned her on the inside. I stepped next to Valen, blade in my free hand.

He leaned in and pressed a kiss to my throat. "Don't break your promise, *Kvinna*."

Protect yourself. At all costs. The plea of Legion Grey seemed so long ago. I could hardly process all that had happened since a handsome dowry negotiator stole my heart. Unknown as our future was, I would not go back. I would never change the path that led me to Valen Ferus.

"I promise."

Valen took out one of his axes. "Then, let's find out where in the hells we are."

My legs ached, like splinters of bone were jabbing into my boots. Our path led us down hillsides. It was as if Etta had landed on a damn mountain, and the gilded sheen to the sky kept leading us down.

Those pulling the cart kept taking shifts with others to keep up their strength. By now, I had Valen's axe in one hand, a sword in the other, while he stood on the inside of me, holding Livia in his arms.

Nothing had leapt from the shadows. No beasts appeared, other than a few hares, shy deer, and the tails of white foxes. What had changed, however, was the hint of the sea at long last. Brine and sand and cool wind washed through the wood the closer we trudged toward the beacon of light.

"Should we make camp?" Herja slipped beside her brother, the bow strapped over her shoulder, a bit of respite for her tiresome grip.

"Probably wise." Valen let out a sigh. "I don't know how much further we have to go to reach the shore."

Herja stroked a hand down Livia's head, a weary smile on her face. "I'll let those in the rear know. The littles will sing your praises."

Valen leaned in to whisper against my ear when she left. "I think some of the young ones are doing better than me."

I cracked my neck side to side and took a seat on a fallen log. The moan slid from my throat involuntarily when blood rushed to the aches of my feet.

Valen grinned. "Perhaps they are doing better than you, my love."

"Careful how you mock me right now, King. I'm tired enough to get a bit violent."

He kissed my lips quickly before gently settling Livia at my side. She whimpered in her sleep, then flopped her head onto my lap, her body crooked and oddly positioned on the log.

We all looked a little disheveled. Tor's hair had slipped from the braid down his head. Sol's face was coated in dirt. Even Halvar hunched as he leaned against a tree, blood and innards still stained on his tunic.

Stieg aided Valen and Hagen in delivering water down the line. Most took the pause to stretch the soles of their feet, their backs, and to relieve their belts from the weight of blades.

I closed my eyes and let my back slump against the trunk of a nearby tree, holding Livia a little tighter.

A branch snapped behind me. My heart leapt to my throat when a distant, low rumble of a voice followed. Someone was in the wood.

In the next breath, I had Livia tucked behind the log, awake and trembling, as I lifted a blade. "Who's there?"

At my voice, Halvar rushed to my side, next, Tor.

Valen was swift to return, axes out. "Show yourself."

The night thickened. Like more weight filled the shadows between trees.

"Show ourselves." A rasp, low and gritty, followed. "I do despise demanding royals."

I let out a rough breath of relief when from the darkness, a familiar face appeared. Like us, a blade extended, eyes pitch as the night, but Kase Eriksson smirked.

"Kase," Valen breathed out, dragging his fingers through his hair. "Gods, what . . . how are you here?"

"I could ask you the same." The Nightrender was not a warm man, at least not to others, but when Valen hooked an arm around his neck, Kase clapped my husband's back with as much relief.

"Elise? Herja? Gods, it's the North!" Malin's vibrant red hair broke through the trees. Each of her hands was clasped in one of her boys'.

"Mal." Hagen rushed for his sister and had her wrapped up in his arms in the next breath. He laughed when the twins hugged his hips.

Their brother, Bard, stepped from the shadows and clasped fore-arms with Hagen, a look of relief on both their faces in knowing they were all still intact.

"Look at you little creatures." Hagen lifted each of the Eastern princes into his arms. "You've grown a full head since I saw you last."

"Maybe me. Sander's still bony," said Jonas. His darker hair was on end, and his pale cheeks were coated in a new layer of dirt. Sander had more auburn waves, like his mother, and didn't even attempt to argue. He merely hooked his skinny arms around Hagen's neck, hiding his face.

"Livie!" Jonas wiggled out of Hagen's hold and raced for Livia. "Gods, guess what? You'll never guess. Our bleeding kingdom broke. *Broke.*"

"Ours too." Livia wrung her hands together.

"Alek!" Jonas said with relief when my nephew joined them. "Oh, good, Metta, Dain, and Laila are alive. Maj was really scared they got hurt. She was scared for you, too, obviously." Jonas gave quick embraces to his cousins from Herja and Hagen, then returned to his playmates.

Sander seemed content to hide in Hagen's arms.

Malin came to me, quickly embraced, then pulled back. "So, the same happened to Etta, the shadows?"

"The shift?" I returned.

Malin nodded. Her shoulders slumped, weary as mine, and dirt soaked into her freckles. "Elise, everything . . . everything has changed. The Howl, it's gone. How does a sea disappear?"

I shook my head. None of this made any sense.

"We left some folk behind," she said. "We decided to look about, to catch our bearings. Thankfully we found you."

"We've done the same. We have wounded and—"

I didn't get a chance to explain about Lilianna's predicament before Kase spoke.

"Safe to say we've all experienced something similar? The sea attacked us, said they were there because that was where their king died."

Valen's jaw tightened. "They should've come for me."

"Sounds like you had your own worries."

"That we have. Is Niklas with you? My mother, she has need of his skills."

Kase shook his head. "We've found a few of our folk who were in other regions when the shift happened. But . . . no Falkyns yet."

"Have you lost anyone?" I whispered, taking Malin's hand.

Her face fell, and even not knowing the names, my heart ached for them.

"Yes," she said. "Both . . . both Luca and Dagny. They fought for each other, died together. You?"

All gods. I closed my eyes. "Many Timorans, and warriors, and . . ." I tightened my hold on her hand. "Mattis."

"No."

It took a few moments for us to describe the events that took place in our kingdoms. All horrid, all strange and confusing.

"We need to be on the watch for Ari, Saga, and Calista," Valen said at long last. "For now, I'm assuming whatever spell brought us here, brought them as well."

"I think you're right, Uncle Valen." Dain swiped his dark hair out of his eyes, and sheathed a short blade, gesturing at the treetops. "Or do you suppose that bird up there looking at us is simply a normal raven?"

CHAPTER 28
THE RAVEN QUEEN

My smaller heart thudded in my rounded chest. They were there. All of them.

"Saga?" Elise stepped forward. She stripped a short fur cloak off her shoulders and held it up.

It'd do. No time to fret over a little flesh.

I flew into the shrubs. Elise let out a ragged laugh and rushed to the bush, gently tossing the fur over the top of the hedge, then stepped back as my body peeled into my true form. Feathers shifted to fingers. Bones stretched and repositioned. My legs lengthened with my spine until I reached a hand and wrapped my front with the fur.

"Saga." Elise flung her arms around me. Her body shuddered. Sobs. We were all holding in bleeding sobs.

"You're all here?" I whispered. "You're all truly fine?"

Elise's eyes burned. "Most of us."

A cinch gathered in my stomach, but I was soon drawn into the kingdoms. Over my shoulder, I looked to the trees. "Rune, where are you?"

The rustle of leaves followed shortly. From a distance away, shadows shifted, and the length of Rune's glistening wings came into focus under the red moon. He landed in a crouch in the next heartbeat and folded his wings.

"We heard movement," he said. "And came to investigate. Gods, it's a relief to know it's you."

Herja shoved through her people and took hold of my arm. "Gunnar and Eryka?"

"They're safe," I told her. "Eryka has said a few things."

"As always," Kase grumbled.

Malin used her elbow to shove his ribs, then looked back to me. "Any idea where we are?"

Oh, I had an idea. And it made little sense. "We took to the skies to get a vantage point," I said. "I quickly learned I didn't have need of one. This land . . . this is my home. My first home. The land in which I was born."

Heady silence stacked over the gentle breeze through the leaves. Valen was the one to speak. "When you say the land in which you were born—"

"The first kingdom. The one we all saw in Ari's memories." I hugged my middle, keeping the fur over my breasts and thighs. "This is the kingdom of my brother. I swear to you, from the peaks to the distance to the shore, this is home."

"The kingdoms broke," Elise muttered and held a hand to her head. "They broke once, now if this is right . . . it's as though they've gone back."

Rune came to my side. "We went to scout around to get our bearings and for Ari to draw a map. Come to our camp, just through there." He gestured to the southern wood. "We found a pond with plenty of fish, and we can plan how to reach the sea. That is where the light shines."

"Any sign of the storyteller and Falkyns?" Kase asked.

I grinned. "Niklas found us."

"Hells." Kase's chin dropped, and I suspected it had a great deal to do with the fact that he did not want the rest of us to see his expression in the moment.

"But Cal," I said, voice soft. "I have not seen her. Not yet."

"It could be her at the shore, if something is there." Sol Ferus stepped beside his brother. "I agree, we need to make our way there."

"Follow us," I said, slipping back toward the shrubs. "He will bluster his words, as you know, but Ari will be extremely relieved to see you all."

I led them through the trees in raven form. Rune kept to the tree-tops with me, watching for threats from above.

The forest was still and quiet but for a few curious creatures. My mind still hadn't gathered the possibility of what happened here, but I knew this land. The falls, they'd be half a day from our position. There, we'd find the hot springs like the ones that had been in the Court of Blood. In the other direction were wild fruit trees with colorful pomes and spiked fruits and berries where we could feed kingdoms for months. Where we could gather and make all manner of sweet wines and ales. In the center knolls were where quarries had once been, where the smiths stocked their iron ore and masons found their granite.

The sea was close. Doubtless it would have the same shoreline with pebbled beaches, herring and silver fish, fat from blue algae that grew on the black stones at the bottom of the coves.

All of it was familiar. It made little sense.

The barest flicker of a flame cut through the trees. I let out a cry and dove toward the small camp. Niklas, Junie, and their Falkyns had arranged traps and wards that kept Davorin's dark glamour out. Still, every face was tense, everybody seemed ready to lunge and attack.

Ari shot to his feet with Mira asleep in his arms. Which of the two refused to part with the other, I didn't know. Since pulling her from the burrow, Ari hadn't taken his hands off the girl. Then again, nor had she. The only time she seemed to breathe at a normal pace was when both her little hands were clasped in mine and Ari's.

Gorm, Magus, our folk who'd joined us in the journey to explore beyond the altered isles, rose at the sight of me.

The Falkyns watched with curiosity, sharpening their blades or checking the wards endlessly.

I slipped behind a shrub where I'd abandoned my clothes while Rune landed in front of the king.

"Well? Anything?" Ari asked.

Rune folded his wings, grinning, and accepted Bo's subtle hand when the tracker went to his lover's side. "Oh, we found a great deal."

I slipped my gown overhead and stepped into the camp before I'd finished tying the belt. I pecked Ari's lips, but he kept his face close. "I learned quite swiftly after you left, that I cannot do that again. I'm not certain I've taken a breath since you flew away, sweet menace."

Gods, I'd never tire of this man when he allowed the sincere vulnerability to snap through the surface. I kissed him, slowly, Mira's body pressed between us.

"It is a good thing I did," I whispered against his mouth.

"Tell me why, though, for I doubt I will agree. Any place without you is never a good thing."

"Because she found us." Valen's voice snapped Ari's face away.

The Night Folk king grinned a little slyly as the others filtered in behind him. Now, like Ari, Kase and Malin carried exhausted twin boys. Valen had Livia perched on his back. More and more, folk from both the North and the East filled in with their blades, littles, and a thirst for battle in their eyes.

"Ah, finally decided to join the fun, Nightrender?" Niklas tossed a pouch between his hands.

Kase glowered and eased Sander onto a grassy plot of land. "I come with armies from the North. Seems like you are the ones joining the fun, Nik."

Niklas chuckled. Relief burned in his eyes at the sight of the Kryv and the Eastern folk. But the sight of the somber boy walking between Isak and Fiske, Niklas's face shadowed. "Where are Luc and Dag?"

Kase's eyes shaded black. I wasn't certain he could control it. In a rare tender moment, he brushed a lock of Sander's hair off his forehead. "We'll speak about things soon."

Niklas blinked, scratching his head as his chin fell. Junius clasped his hand, a palm over her mouth.

Doubtless, they already knew there would be a somber tale to tell.

"Gunnar." Herja shoved through the procession.

"Maj." Gunnar released Eryka's hand and sprinted for his mother. He swallowed her in his arms. Soon, Hagen hooked an arm around his son's neck, then embraced Eryka much the same. Gunnar laughed and teased his sister, donned in her warrior's gambeson, then embraced Dain and young Metta.

"For a moment, we can be at peace." Herja kissed Gunnar's cheek, smiling.

Ari gently eased Mira into my arms, then crossed the camp in four strides toward Valen.

"I keep trying to think of something grand and hilariously amusing to say." He paused, and clasped Valen's forearm. "I'm afraid I must disappoint us all and simply say it is a great relief to see you, My King."

Valen pulled Ari into a quick embrace as best he could with his daughter still clinging to his neck.

Ari tapped Livia's nose. "Been a frightening adventure, Princess?"

"Etta broke," she whimpered.

Ari's smile flickered a bit, but as he'd always been able to do, he hid the disquiet masterfully. "I see. Well, the good in all this, is now it seems we're all much closer together. I know for a fact the Nightrender is especially thrilled by this turn of events, don't you think?"

Kase groaned. "Soon, I will demand that Valen or your own wife build me an isle of solitude to escape your voice."

"Then what, pray tell, will bring you immeasurable joy each sunrise when I call out to you?" Ari laughed when Livia, at last, snickered at Kase's scowl. He grinned at the Night Folk princess. "You shall see us all the time now."

Livia's smile was weary, but there all the same.

Ari gestured to Mira in my arms. "You know, all the other littles seem to be asleep. You're the only one awake, Princess."

Valen hiked her further up his back. "What do you say, little love? Care to sleep by Mira? Better than the smelly boys."

Livia nodded, eyes heavy with fatigue. Valen cast Ari a significant look, one that hinted we'd all be speaking shortly, no mistake, of a great many drearier things, then went to settle Livia on the grass where I laid Mira.

Once the young ones were sleeping around the pitiful fire (we dared not draw too much smoke to our location) we huddled close together, three differing kingdoms. Royals, warriors, thieves, it didn't matter what we were.

"We all saw the same thing," Elise said. "A flash, the darkness, then we all woke here. Is the Borough intact?"

Ari nodded. "For the most part. Are you telling me Ravenspire is here?"

"Every damn gate," said Elise.

"Our Nest is above ground," said Niklas, "and it's a travesty that I will remedy as soon as I can borrow the claws of a troll."

"Same with the Black Palace, though we did lose the courtyard, and Felstad is made of even more ruins," Kase said, flicking a twig into the dying flame. "Our sea is gone. Our regions are one land, one area. It is as if we fell asleep and awoke with our entire kingdom rearranged."

"Think of when it all fell apart," I offered. "We saw it in Ari's fae sleep. I've no doubt the people of old awoke to a new world."

"The difference was they had no memory of a before," Malin offered, her hand wrapped tightly in Kase's.

Ari knelt and traced out the land with a stick in the dirt. He lifted his gaze to mine. "You're certain this is the general area of where we are?"

"I saw the sea. From there, I can gauge our vicinity," I said. "The golden flares are coming from the shore."

Ari brushed off his hands. "Are we in agreement that we go toward it?"

"Should we go in a small group?" Kase offered. "We have children with us."

"I don't know if it is safer to keep them elsewhere," Elise said, "We don't know what we're facing. How do we protect them if we do not know?"

For a moment we all seemed to consider the notion. Sol cleared his throat and spoke. "There is something that feels almost peaceful about that light."

"Could be a fae trick, Uncle," Gunnar said.

Sol tilted his head. "I've thought the same, but where is Cal? The West is the only piece missing. What if she is there? Is her home not by the shore?"

"I'm going to just say it," said Valen. "Calista is the daughter of the king who split our kingdoms. What if she is the one who has restored them?"

"Not such a far stretch," I admitted. "Calista's journey was meant to grow. My brother saw to it she was protected. We all know she had a path to find, so it might be that she has found it."

"How do we explain the attacks on our shores?" Valen asked.

"We don't," said Ari. "Davorin has shown us new tricks. His glamour is there, his presence, but it's almost like he is there in a mist. Nothing tangible. I don't know where he is and it's horrifically maddening."

"Same with the sea fae," Kase said. "Mal saw his likeness in their memories, but he never showed."

"I say we rest," Elise interjected. "Even for a few tolls. Then tomorrow, we do not stop until we reach the sea and find Calista."

All at once, Bo shot to his feet. "There is someone out there."

He squared to the trees, head tilted, a hand on the hilt of his sword.

"Our camp is warded," Niklas said, voice soft. "Remember, no one can reach us if we stay within the borders."

"Does that count for arrows, Nik?" Gunnar whispered as he took hold of his bow.

"Let's hope so," was all the Falkyn said.

"Back to the beginning," Eryka muttered again, like she'd done before our world shattered.

The hair lifted on my arms when branches snapped. Trees shifted. Raum stood beside Bo, eyes narrowed as he peered into the shadows.

Soon, the Kryv's mouth cut into a grin. "It's blood fae." He looked to Gorm. "I think one of them looks a bit like you."

Gorm stalked to the edge of the camp in the same instant dark figures stepped into the firelight. Faces masked, spears in hand. Cuyler pulled down his mask at the first sight of his father.

"Daj. Thank the gods." Cuyler hurried over the borders of our camp and clasped Gorm's forearm.

Always formal, always on duty, still, Gorm clapped the side of his son's cheek. "Good to see you safe. Where is the princess?"

Cuyler found me and Ari. He dipped his chin. "My Queen, My King. I was sent to find you. We suspected you would be here. All of you." His pale eyes scanned the weary camp.

"Suspected?" Ari folded his arms over his chest. "So, Cal is behind this?"

"She was guiding you. The lands were breaking, and she did not know what would become of you. She did what she could and sang . . . or used seidr to bring you here."

"She's all right?" Sol stepped forward.

"She's . . . well. There are some changes with Raven Row and Calista. Are you all well, at least as well as can be?"

"Most of our people are scattered across this new land," I told him. "The Night Folk have need of help with Queen Lilianna."

Cuyler's mouth tightened. "We have refuge, room enough for us all, by the shore."

"The light is Cal, then?" Elise asked.

"It is. Rest for now, but there isn't much time. I think . . . I think we are facing the return of our enemy." Cuyler glanced to me.

Ari stiffened at my side, and his voice took on a violent rumble. "Then he will face us all. But his head belongs to Saga. More than any of us, she deserves that." He pressed a kiss to my hair. "I promised you, sweet menace. He returns? Then he will not be leaving with breath in his lungs."

The truth was, if Davorin was returning, then either he or I would be greeting the Otherworld. I would fight to the death to rid this bleeding world of the battle lord.

GIFTS OF FATE

CHAPTER 29
THE STORYTELLER

A GLIMMER OF GOLD, THAT WAS ALL I HAD ON WHICH TO LAY MY HOPE AS THE dawn spilled into the dusky, red satin night. My legs dangled over the edge of a parapet wall; I gazed out on the turbulent sea.

Soon. A voice in my head spoke the truth of it. I liked to think it was my daj, maybe Stefan in his big burly Annon form over there in the Otherworld. All I knew was something was to change, and it was to change soon.

All night Olaf and our Rave had planned how to guard up the shores. I'd helped lay spiked fences. I'd aided the Norn sisters with their odd warding spell casts. I tried to find a song, words kept creeping up my throat, then dying once they reached my tongue.

In one breath, I wanted the sun to rise. In another, I wanted to run back to Hus Rose and hole away with Silas and never face what the dawn might bring.

According to Olaf, with a new length of land to manage, shielding every port, every cove, and every bit of the kingdom would be impossible. We had new peaks, new isles, places I certainly didn't remember. I'd been too young to have every speck of land memorized.

Olaf and many of the Rave warriors knew well enough, there were plenty of areas our enemies could rise and overtake.

"I know the battle lord," Olaf had said, hunched over an old, tattered map he'd pulled from one of the towers. A part of the fortress I'd guess was his old alehouse. "He'd often lead ships upriver and take the peaks, then descend from behind since he is quite skilled at navigating rocky terrain. Likely the reason you told me he set up his battle camp in the peaks of the old Southern Isles, true?"

"He overtook it, but I thought it was because he'd learned a blade for my Golden King was hidden there."

"Possible," Olaf offered. "But he favors mountainous ranges since most folk find it more difficult to navigate. He trained us often on unstable ground."

"And he knows the Rave will know him."

Olaf grinned a little viciously. "Exactly. Which is why I expect the attack to come here. Straight on. We should set our defenses on the shore."

"All?" Silas asked.

"All. We do not have great numbers; we will need every blade." Olaf's thumb dragged away from the old north cliffs on the ancient map. "He has joined, somehow, with the folk of the sea. I'd say he'll come head-on. Here at the docks. Look for swimmers and skiffs approaching in narrow coves or in the shadows since sea fae have larger vessels than us. They won't be able to bring them all into port."

Memories of the dead Ever King's ship that ripped me to the East still lifted my skin. Then again, I wasn't convinced it was the actual vessel that turned my insides—it was more that pushy bastard named Thorvald. He had few manners, and certainly didn't know how to calmly ask for favors.

"Their ships are beastly monstrosities," I said with a bit of theatrics, but it suited. "Like vicious deep-sea creatures that sail above the surf and below it, too."

"I remember them similarly," Olaf said. "They might not be able to take the rivers out of sheer size. So, the docks are where I'd suggest placing the most protections."

I'd agreed, but it was half-hearted. Protections, even at the docks, wouldn't be enough, and we all knew it.

What could we do? Spread ourselves thin, or put most of our attention on the main gates of our new fortress of Raven Row? I stared down at the lines of shields, the spears, the blades. The Rave were unmoving. Across towers and parapets and walkways, they all kept time in their steps. What I'd give for a bit of distance between us and the bubbling chasm.

So many wrongs could happen. So many lives could be lost. I was no warrior. By the hells, at times I hardly felt like a woman. I felt naïve, despite my turns of life. I felt uncertain, as though all this time I'd been more reliant on the nudges of fate and not my own seidr, and I'd never noticed.

Now, the ending was unwritten. It could go either way.

I closed my eyes, it seemed as though a thorny ball flailed about in my belly. The worst of it all was all this new, bleeding land, and none of my royals had shown their faces.

Had they been crushed? Were the Norns so cruel that they'd rip them away without a chance to fight? Was it my fault for waiting so damn long? The burn in my chest was unforgiving. Brutal, really. I felt as though I might crush beneath the weight of it all if I could not catch a glimpse of them soon.

"You can speak of your troubles to me."

I whipped around. Silas, buried beneath a hood, mask hiding his scar, leaned one shoulder against a tower wall at the entrance to the parapet.

A smile tugged at my lips. I patted the space beside me, then watched as he crossed over to me and dangled his long legs much the same.

I let my head drop to his shoulder. Slowly, he tipped his head, so his cheek rested on top of mine.

"I don't know if I can do this," I admitted.

"Do what?"

"Fight. I barely survived the last battle. I had one bleeding job to do: hold Malin's ring and summon the others through the damn

Nightrender's shadows. I dropped it. *Dropped it.* Then practically exploded."

Silas chuckled softly. "I know. You sang. It was us connecting. Your seidr was too powerful for that leech to touch."

"Leech is such a dull name for him. Dig deeper next time."

Silas's cheek moved on my head, and I took a guess that he was grinning. "Can I speak true, Little Rose?"

"Always."

"I'm not certain I can do this either."

I lifted my head, holding his stare. "You are strong. You've always been a fighter."

"For you," he said. "I fought for you."

My brows tugged together. "You trained with the Rave, with Annon."

"I was a boy, *a boy*, when our world changed. Since then, I've . . . I've battled shadows, Calista. My first real kill was that sea singer at the docks, and only because I've practiced and observed the proper way to snap a neck for centuries. I am no warrior, not like your kings and queens."

My palm slid over the top of his hand, lacing our fingers together. "Yet you never ceased calling to me. You knew this would end in a battle, and you never shied away. How do you do it without fear?"

"I never said I have no fear," he told me. "I have been afraid every damn day since I stood between you and that bastard with his sword."

My eyes stung. All this crying was growing rather ridiculous, but it couldn't be stopped. Something about this bleeding man had my heart sobbing at the memories we shared and the time we'd been forced apart. I touched the small bit of his scar that jutted beyond the curve of his mask.

"I face this with fear," he said, voice low and soft. "But I will face it head-on."

"How?"

Silas shifted and took hold of my hand, lifting my knuckles to his lips. "Because I fear the loss of you more than a battle. Should I remain hidden, should I ignore this fight, I've no doubt I would lose you. I won't again." His eyes clenched shut. "Do you . . . gods, do you know what it's like?"

I hugged his head to me, his forehead on my shoulder. My fingers slid under his hood, pushing it off his head, so I could run them through his hair. I pressed a kiss to his brow. "I don't know what it's like, Silas."

"My words are nonsense," he murmured. "Ignore them."

"They're not nonsense," I told him. "What did I tell you? I don't care if you talk to shadows, or if thoughts come out that you cannot control. I don't know what it was like then because my heart's song was kept from me."

Silas went still, then slowly lifted his gaze back to mine.

I rested a palm against his unmasked cheek, my thumb tugged on his bottom lip. "But I know what it's like now. I know what it feels like to find that side of your heart you never knew was missing. Should I lose you, I would be broken down the center, a walking half of a soul for the rest of my days."

I kissed his cheek. Silas let out a soft sigh and closed his eyes.

"You're right, though," I said. "To lose you now would be worse than any battle. I'm afraid you'll need to be satisfied with your grand champion being utterly inexperienced on the battlefield."

He grinned, and I thought it might be the loveliest of things. "I have a champion?"

"Obviously. You use your tongue rather magnanimously, and I would like to keep it from now into the eternities."

The skin visible on his face flushed with a bit of pink in the rising dawn. "No arguments from me."

Together, we laughed. Then words, another tale burned on my tongue. This time, they grew clearer. My seidr was coming swifter, stronger.

Silas grinned. "You feel it?"

"There is a song of fate here, some twist trying to break through, but I can't quite grasp it."

Silas cupped a hand around the back of my neck, drawing my forehead to his. "It will come. You have the words, Little Rose. You always have."

I tilted my face until our lips brushed. Gingerly, Silas kissed me with a touch of tender hesitation, like it was something we hadn't done before. I didn't mind. The slow claim of his lips soothed the ache in my heart. It added a bolster against the fear desperate to pull me under.

This kiss was a slow build. Tender and soft in the first heartbeats, then little by little it built to something deeper, something with a greedy fervor. I hummed in need when Silas's tongue slid against my lips, parting them until I tasted the clean warmth of his mouth.

He tugged me closer, one arm slipped around my waist; the other slid through my messy braids. I dug my fingernails into his shoulders, clinging to him like the slightest breeze might tear us apart.

How was it I could go so long not knowing a bit of my heart was so near? It seemed vicious and wretched. Yet to have it now, to know the cost we'd paid to claw our way back to each other, made moments as this more precious than air in my lungs. It made them richer than the grandest treasury.

These moments would be my safety, my hope, and my shield against what was to come. These moments were where I would find the courage to face every sunset, and rise, blade in hand, with every sunrise. I would fight for these moments, for they were too beautiful to lose again.

Silas's hand slid down my waist, curling around one of my thighs, readying to leverage me over his lap on the ledge, but his hand stilled at the haunting bellow of a ram's horn.

We broke apart and faced the sea.

"Bleeding hells." My lips parted. "Silas . . ."

He hurried to his feet, jaw tight. Silas tugged me back to standing,and nudged me a bit behind him. His hardened stare was unyielding on the thrashing tides of the dark Chasm line.

Our time for respite was at an end.

The water grew more violent. It tossed and thrashed. From beneath the tides, vicious spikes and strange masts of black and pale and blue sails broke through the water. Those horrid, massive vessels with decks and stairs and three masts instead of one shot toward the dawning sky like fatted whales breaching the surface.

One after the other, they rose and aimed their bowsprits at our shores.

Skulls and daggers dotted the sails. Some had coiled, skeletal serpents. All were swift and vicious. All were packed with dark, moving figures. Sea fae. Doubtless, the sort like Thorvald who could command the sea, yet walk our shores with blade in hand.

"There's so many," I said in a soft gasp. Blindly, I reached for Silas's hand. A heavy weight gathered in the pit of my belly. Worse than the moment I joined the ruse against Davorin ten turns ago. There was something in this moment that told me . . . it was the end.

One side was not leaving this battle alive.

Silas squeezed my fingers. "There are many, but their power lessens on land. We've fought for this moment, and I am not about to give it up easily."

"I understand them now."

"Understand who?"

"My royals. For I am going to the shore, I am going to stand with the Rave, to defend the Row, and it is because I am unwilling to give you up. It is because I am standing with you, Silas. Their heart songs, their *hjärtas*, were the reasons behind my royals' every move. I understand them now."

His jaw pulsed once, twice, then he kissed me. No hesitation. No shyness. One feral, lasting kiss before he broke away and tugged me along the parapet wall to the winding staircase of the tower.

Horns rattled through the sturdier Raven Row. The Rave warriors, few as they were, lifted shields off their backs. In one, unified roar, they heaved the shields over their shoulders and placed them in front of their bodies. The first row of warriors crouched low. The second lifted their shields and stacked them on top of the first to form an impenetrable shield wall.

On the towers, archers tightened their bowstrings. A warrior on either wall traipsed along, dipping their arrow tips in oil wells. They'd rain fire down upon the sea; we'd watch them burn.

The Norn sisters laid out runes near the sea, and a brilliant, emerald flame burst from their spell. It slithered across the shoreline like a fiery serpent, adding another barrier between us.

"The sea comes." Olaf approached us as he secured vambraces on his wrists.

"Davorin?" I asked.

"Not that I see, but we know he's there, waiting. He sends the first wave now."

"You were right, Olaf," I said. "He is bold. They attack head-on."

Olaf faced me, and he rested his hands on my shoulders. His touch brought with it a sharp shock over my flesh. I shook it away and had the decency to hold his gaze.

"You have been concealed from your truth and power for a great many turns, My Princess," he said. "But Captain Annon never once doubted that you would rise to this moment." Olaf flicked his gaze to Silas. "Both of you. Your place, boy, is as valued here as hers."

I nodded briskly. "We look to your wisdom, Olaf."

"You shall always have it." He grinned, younger than he'd been in all my memories.

I reached back to Silas and took his hand. Facing Olaf again, I straightened my shoulders. "Then defend our shores. Until the last Rave falls."

CHAPTER 30
THE PHANTOM

Until the last Rave.

A haunting memory of Riot Ode demanding the same spilled through me like a poison I couldn't escape.

Riot Ode said that command, and he never left the battlefield.

I flicked the latch off the sheath of the blade on my hip. A strong seax. I'd cared for it all this time. A true Rave blade. A dagger paired with it remained at Hus Rose, but this would serve well enough now.

It had kept me company, and I knew, somehow I bleeding knew, a day would come when I would raise it in battle. With the emptiness of my existence, I had little else to fret about. I'd nearly grown obsessive caring for the blade, growing accustomed to the hilt, the weight.

The sword would be strong. It'd serve us well.

Calista looked to my movements, watching with a stoic expression as I unsheathed the blade. She swallowed thickly; I could see the movement of it in her throat, and I slowly took out a dueling pair of knives. Good for throwing and quick movements. Both of which she'd developed into strengths.

Another horn blared into the dawn. The Rave archers shouted

from the walls. I watched as the igniter leveled a torch against the arrows, setting them ablaze.

Commands roared from several of the higher ranked captains on the walls. They shouted at their warriors, much like Olaf shouted commands to the whole of the Rave. Arrow points aimed toward the fading starlight. Pale blue burned against the last stars fighting for presence in the sky.

Now, the peace of the dawn burned in anger and fire.

Shouts from the approaching ships grew louder. Strange commands floated to us across the thrashing seas, a few were hums and ethereal songs. With their singing, the sea thrashed more. A thought flooded my head, spilling to my chest, as though some connection drew my seidr toward the sea.

"Calista," I whispered. "Listen to them, can you sense it?"

She closed her eyes for a few breaths before they snapped open. "There is power in their song."

"Their magic—it hails from their voice. Like ours."

She grinned with a perfect touch of violence. "Then I suppose we ought to aim our blades at their throats."

I spun the sword in my hand. A new determination to slit as many throats as I could thrummed through me with every beat of my heart.

"Olaf!" Calista shouted. "Take their tongues and their ability to sing."

The captain arched a brow, then grinned. "As you say."

He roared the commands down the line of Rave. The archers altered their positions. Instead of raining fiery arrows on the ships, they would hold. They would aim at the actual sea folk to rid them of their power.

"Sing us a song," the seer, Forbi, said with a light playfulness in her tone. She practically danced about with her sisters, casting more rune spells that ignited emerald fire across the shore.

Calista stepped into the center of the Row. I followed, taking hold of her hand. Her skin was flushed as if flames boiled in her veins. It sparked heat in my blood, a need to release some burst of power. The same always took hold when our seidr connected into one fierce song.

"I have words," Calista murmured. "Sing with me?"

"Always."

Calista turned into me. We dropped our blades and laced our hands together, brows touching.

> "A tale of old, returns anew.
> Brought forth by bonds that bind the few.
> Love of choice. Devotion of heart.
> Honor and passion brought the start.
> In dawn's soft light, a path is growing.
> To bring about a gift so cunning.
> In realms of darkness, the plan is spun.
> To end a game long ago begun.
> Find each place for which to rise.
> As gifts of fate greet darkness on the tides."

Her voice was soft, yet strong. I held her close as each word drew out more melodic sounds. My voice joined with hers. Low, deep, and dark. It intertwined with her words in a tune not heard before, but one that was silk over the tongue. It was a harmony that burned in my throat until my body trembled against the sting.

With each word our seidr tangled, almost vibrant enough I could make out the threads spinning tightly into a knotted rope of a path.

A new tale. We were singing paths that had never been seen before. Our power could twist fate, but it did not bring guarantees. We were merely opening a way to give us a chance, to puzzle out the words, to find out steps, and make our plans.

Should we succeed, then the power of a fated path was brilliantly fierce.

Should we succeed, there was chance even a fae as strong as Davorin could never come close to overtaking us.

Calista slumped against me when her words ended. My tune faded off, and the burn throbbed in my chest as seidr took hold of the new song, and pulsed it into the bleeding soil, into the damn universe, to make it so.

"Gods, I feel like I might topple over."

I encircled her waist with my arms, keeping her upright. "Deep songs are taxing, but look."

Calista lifted her gaze to the shore. Subtle, but there was a glimmer of brilliant light. Like chains between the Rave warriors, seidr flowed through them, bolstering them, granting strength.

"Is that us?"

"It's seidr. Your daj used to do the same during battle."

Olaf's laughter drew my attention. "Quite reminiscent of Riot Ode."

"See," I said. "His song would bolster his warriors, alter the hearts and desires of his enemies. I don't think we'll suddenly see those ships turn around, but our song is strengthening our folk. Like the king kept his folk safer and sturdier on the battlefield, so will this."

"I don't need to write it anymore, right?" she asked softly.

I placed a hand on the side of her face. "Ink and flame served as a tether between us once. But we're together now. Our voices will burn the words into the unseen fate of this world. Together, we are stronger than any bit of ink or flame ever was."

Her chin quivered and she looked to the sea. "Yet we've not seen anyone from the other kingdoms. I'm not so certain we did much good."

True enough, I'd expected the royals from other kingdoms to be there, yet we stood alone. Still, the burn from the seidr just now was forceful enough I fought the urge to double over. The last time I'd felt such a surge of power, we'd shattered a world. I had to hope it would aid us now.

I lifted my sword from the ground and handed Calista her knives. "We don't know what fate has in store. What I do know is I will fight with you—to the end if needed—on this day. That is what I can do right now."

Calista gave me a smile, soft but powerful. She spun one of her knives, then faced the shore. I didn't need to ask her plans. I knew. In the same step, we rushed toward the line of Rave warriors together.

The *thwang* of bowstrings rose over the commands of Rave officers. Fiery arrows sliced through the morning light. From the edges of the newly fashioned fortress, warriors shouted as the flames in the sky acted like a beacon leading us forward.

The flood of Rave shields and blades created a formidable barrier along the shore. Still, a fleet of ships barreled through the dark waves. Shouts and hisses spat back at us when the arrows met their marks.

A few bodies toppled into the tides as fire from the arrows devoured the flesh of their spines. Tides frothed with iridescent fins, and hauntingly lovely voices filled the air.

There was a tug at my gut, a need to follow the voice. Slight, perhaps, for me, but more than one Rave lowered his shield; more than one man staggered forward to the sea, as though caught on a hook and lured into the tides.

"Hold your bleeding positions," Calista shouted. "What the hells is wrong with you? It's shrieking!"

"They cannot stop," I said, gritting my teeth against the sensual pull.

Blood rushed in a heady desire, and my bleeding pants tightened. Hells, I wanted to drop my sword—a most inconvenient time—and press Calista's lithe body against a wall until I stretched and filled her. Until her screams breathed against my neck again.

I shook my head, desperate to focus.

"Damn sirens," a Rave near to us roared. "Archers, keep your bleeding heads and aim at those tides. Silence them!"

A siren's call.

Calista narrowed her eyes at me. "You like that sound, do you? Well, cover your damn ears, Silas."

"Don't be jealous, Little Rose. My needy thoughts are of you."

"Ah, how flattering."

I obeyed her word and covered my ears against the sweet song. "Forgive me, but it's truly impossible to ignore."

"Well, they sound wretchedly odious if you must know the truth. An awful voice, really."

"Until one of their male sea singers returns. Tell me if you find it so simple."

Calista puffed out her lips and rushed for the line of struggling warriors.

"Keep your heads," she shouted. "Fill your ears with bleeding mud, you sods!"

Shouts riled more creatures of the tides and smaller skiffs and boats, carrying more sea folk. The larger ships had wild sails that cracked and snapped in the sea winds. Folk with blades tight between their teeth climbed on the ropes on the rails, a few started to dangle over the sides, ready to pounce on the land.

The smaller rows of sea folk met rune fire from Forbi and one of her spell casts. The fae screamed when bits of the fire licked up their damp arms, scorching their flesh in deep, pungent wounds.

Deeper in the surf, a fae with stringy and dark hair emerged from the waves. His skin was a soft color, almost bronze in the light, and there was a touch of red to his eyes. A blue scarf covered his head and kept his hair out of his eyes, and his ears were pierced in the lobes all the way to the sharp point of his fae ears.

It seemed, for a moment, that his hellish eyes found me in the tangle of warriors.

He grinned and opened his arms wide. A low, rumbling voice filtered down the row of sea fae in the surf. More voices joined. Beautiful in their own way, but their beauty was a poison, a blight that would destroy this land. Was responding.

In the next moment, waves churned in heavy, violent walls, taller than the shield wall of the Rave. As though the water answered to their voices alone, the song of the sea fae lifted the water over their heads in a massive, curling wall.

"Get back!" Calista screamed.

Olaf echoed the command. I sprinted to Calista's side, tugging on her arm, drawing her away from the sea wall.

Sea water crashed over the line of Rave. It devoured Forbi's spell cast. It pummeled a hole through our defenses in one strike.

Water flowed down Raven Row, striking me at the ankles. Sea fae cheered and roared their advances. The ships seemed to catch the winds at the exact moment. Bleeding gods, they kept coming. More thrashing tides, more skiffs, sloops, and multiple-mast ships rose from the dark current of the Chasm.

"Silas." Calista's eyes were wide with fear. "Why is our song failing?"

I didn't know. Seidr was meant to be strong in these moments. King Riot always used his voice to shield his armies except . . . except when Davorin fought against it.

"He's here," I said softly. "Somewhere. His glamour will be focused on corrupting the hearts of the Rave. Even if they do not realize it, their hearts will falter and the seidr will not be as strong. The darkness of hate always digs into the light of the heart."

Calista's eyes scanned the shore. "I see no sign of him."

Nor did I. An invisible foe. A power unseen was one we could not fight.

"Little Rose," I said, voice low, grip tight on the hilt of my blade. I kept my focus ahead. I watched as sea fae tumbled off the sides of their ships and spilled into the water, fierce on the attack. "I need to tell you, whatever happens here—I have loved you all my life."

"Gods, I hate that. I mean, I love it, but I hate that you're saying it because you think we're going to meet the Otherworld."

"Better to say it than get there without telling you."

She snorted. It was rough and wet, like she battled a lump in her throat. "I love you, Silas. You're my Whisper, my comfort in the darkness. I suppose if we meet the gods today, we can cause all manner of havoc there."

A grin teased my mouth.

Blades and roars lifted from the onslaught of sea fae. The heavy metals of their strangely curved swords collided with the sleek iron and steel of Rave blades. Our warriors were vicious, and held a potent glamour of their own. Some were illusionists and twisted the sea fae with their tricks of the eye. They'd cast grand holes in the ground, drawing a pause in the assault long enough for archers to fill the bellies of the sea folk with their arrows.

Other warriors held abilities that were closer to the Night Folk or the Raven Queen. They could tangle moss off the stones into taut ropes, tripping the fae at their ankles. There, they'd rise with a blade in their spines.

Most Rave were common fae with mere connections to the earth and its gifts. They could compel thoughts, but only briefly, and normally not when their focus was on the battle.

But battle was where the Rave's strengths truly were revealed. Perhaps they felt the weakening of our song and strengthened, instead, their boldness in the fight.

The strikes of their swords held purpose and aim. They cut at the crooks of necks. Sword points filled the spaces between ribs, slicing into lungs and hearts. The Rave kicked at tender knees, then another would thrust his sword through the backs of throats.

Olaf shouted positions, yet it seemed wherever the captain tried to place his Rave, they were attacked by more fae from the depths.

With each blow, and each failed attempt to draw them back, it seemed as though sea folk were lying in wait and knew just where to bleeding strike. Sea fae were menacing, almost endless, and they knew the blade much like the Rave.

Sea fae weapons were different. Curved swords that looked damn near rusted or made of rough-cut bone that sliced through the wall of warriors.

My muscles ached from clenching, but I held fast to Calista's side as a few slippery fae, damp and sodden, shoved through the Rave. They rushed at the warriors lined at the fortress walls.

They aimed for us.

Calista ducked a strike from a bulky fae. She rammed the point of her knife in his thigh while she was tucked low.

A man with pasty skin and gold rings in his ears lunged at me. His sword struck the edge of mine. True to my word, I was no trained Rave. I knew a few maneuvers from my time as a Rave youth in Riot Ode's court. My skill with the blade, fair or horrid, came from practice in the darkness of my solitude.

No mistake, it was sloppy and disjointed against the fae. His blade caught my arm; the sick slice of steel in flesh turned my stomach. I pulled back, not wasting time to inspect the wound, and jabbed my sword into his middle.

The fae dodged. He spun quickly and lobbed a downward strike for my neck.

I narrowly avoided the blow but managed to snag the point of my sword against his hipbone.

"Earth fae," he hissed and hurried back to realign his steps. "You don't stand a chance. So few numbers against the dark one? Against the whole of the Ever?"

My lips curled. "That dark one you follow so willingly, did he tell you how a few children nearly sent him to the Otherworld?"

For a moment, a bit of confusion flashed through the bright crimson eyes of the fae. He sneered in the next breath. "I suppose I'll have to gnaw on a few of those young ones to make sure it never happens again."

He sliced his blade against mine again. Calista's shriek pieced my heart. Beside me she backstepped swiftly, blood on her lip. The fae against her was swift. But so was she. One knife struck the man's shoulder, the other his belly.

She let out a furious cry as she ripped it free and finished the bastard with a rough thrust to the soft point of his throat where his voice would be. He went silent.

The sea fae in front of me nicked my thigh. I kicked his ankle and shoved him back. Calista sprinted for us and in the next move had one knife rammed into his ribs.

The sea fae roared his pain and spat at her face, stumbling away. "You keep your bitches here? Weak."

"Well, this bitch just stabbed you," she said, giving him a cruel wink.

Blood boiled in my brain. I didn't think. The movements came damn near rote. In one hand, I twisted the sword point down and shoved it deep through the fae's back until the sharp point emerged through his lower belly.

He gulped through a fountain of blood spilling over his lips. His body slammed against my spine when I wrenched the blade free. I kicked him off once he slumped forward and watched the blood pool beneath his corpse.

Calista's shoulders heaved. Her eyes burned in a new kind of rage. But a shadow crossed her features when she took in the attack. More ships. More fae.

We were fighting a losing battle.

I held out my hand, ready to face the end with her at my side. I didn't know why our song did not work. I didn't know why fate had abandoned us. Perhaps it was punishment for what we unraveled so long ago, the fate we had manipulated.

I suppose it didn't matter anymore. So long as I left this world for the next with her beside me, I would accept our destiny to love endlessly in the great hall of the gods.

CHAPTER 31
THE STORYTELLER

I was going to die here. Odd, but there was a peace within me. What I'd feared most, the short life of a storyteller, didn't seem so daunting. Perhaps it was because now I knew the truth—I'd died before. It wasn't so terrible.

Perhaps it was the peace knowing Silas was at my side at long last.

The thought brought a swell of comfort. I'd walk with him to the Otherworld. Truth be told, it was almost exciting. I wondered who would greet us first. My parents? Stefan? Maybe some of those my other royals had lost along the way.

Shoulder to shoulder with Silas, bloodied knives in hand, I rushed for the shore.

The waves rolled near the chasm. Over the barrier between the two worlds, more water thrashed violently. A bit of black spilled from beneath the surface, like ink bubbled from some undersea well. Then amidst the darkness, rich, bloody crimson rose toward the surface.

The sea fae slowed their assault. They roared with a twisted bit of glee at the sight.

There was a knot in my belly. Whatever was coming was of great importance to the sea folk.

Through the violent boil of the Chasm, a dark, jagged point emerged. The bowsprit was sharp and angled, opening like the jaws of a coiled sea serpent. Spines like actual broken pieces of bone followed. Each piece jutted off the round belly of the new ship like bony knives.

My breath caught at the sight of the first mast. Thick, crimson sails stitched up in rough pieces of canvas and whatever hardened creatures the sea folk added to strengthen them were a horrid memory.

The Ever King's ship.

There was too much distance yet to see who manned it now, but it didn't matter. The inky seas spilled around the royal ship, and it took little to guess what creature was rising along with the strongest ship of the sea.

Rave braced for the new attack. The sea folk seemed empowered and faced the shore with a new thirst for violence burning in their eyes.

Horns wailed from the towers. Archers prepared to fire, doubtless until the last arrow met the soft flesh of an enemy. There were simply not enough of us to battle them and win. We would fall today, but we would fall with blades in hand, with passion in our voices, with as much sea fae blood sprayed on our faces as we could manage.

Silas blew out a sharp breath. I braced, knives at the ready.

Sea fae that were already on land fought the Rave, Olaf among them. The captain swung and battled with ferocity in every jab, strike, and thrust, yet no strikes seemed to rid the land of the sea fae. Like a plague, they appeared from the waves and rose onto the shore.

The space I could fight lessened as the Rave stepped back, huddling around us; more sea fae rushed the land. One fae would strike. I'd block. Another would aim to take out my feet. Silas would chop his sword.

A blade sliced across my ribs. I cried out, fumbling.

"Calista!" Silas's terror-lined voice broke down to my soul.

A sea fae, two heads taller than me, with eyes like dried blood, took hold of my hair; another gripped my wrist. They grinned wide enough I could see the sharp points of their canines showing through. I never understood why the sea fae had damn fangs. They didn't drink blood. Maybe they tore their fish apart, raw and feral-like.

I held their eyes; I'd look at them as I died.

In the next breath, inky shadows curled around my legs, scaling my body like a dark cloak. Darkness filled the spaces between me and the sea folk.

My heart stilled.

The two sea fae watched the ribbons of shadows thread around their limbs, their throats.

They had no time to consider moving away before the darkness tightened like a garrote and yanked their necks to the side in a horrid angle. They convulsed on their feet, then toppled over.

For a moment I was stunned, until I took note of the flopping corpses of other sea folk. Shadows slithered away, leaving their broken bodies in the muddy walk of Raven Row.

I followed the retreat of the shadows and nearly cried out in a broken sob of joy when the Nightrender—that wonderfully frightening Shadow King—stepped onto the row. His eyes were the blackest of black, and he wasn't alone.

My royals. My family. They spilled into the gaps behind him, a wave of their own. Too many—as in they had bleeding young ones. All their littles were in the throes of the battle. My gaze landed on Mira, tucked close to Saga's side.

I looked to my aunt, panic in her eyes as she took in darkness on the sea. If Davorin got his slimy hands on Saga's daughter . . . all gods, I blocked off the thoughts of what he might do.

"The battle lord comes!" I screamed at them. "He rides with that bleeding ship and we can't hold against them."

Valen shoved through the crowd. I pressed a hand to my chest, tears blurry on my lashes when Sol followed. His face was as stone, but he gave me a swift nod.

"Pull the fighters back," Valen shouted at me.

I didn't hesitate. "Olaf! Pull back. Pull away from the sea."

Another horn blasted into the dawn, and at Olaf's command, all the Rave captains down the line of warriors barked their orders to move back. Some sea fae remained trapped among us, but after the brutality of the Nightrender, most fought mightily hard to reach the shores.

Silas was among those who cut them down as they fled.

Gods, he was brutal yet unsure. He killed without thought of skill or finesse, but he killed with passion.

Rave surrounded us. Olaf joined, leaning over his knees, gasping. "What is the move?"

"We must place barriers between us." Valen approached, eyes wild with his fury.

"Wise," said Olaf, "if I recall, the sea fae have a fear of too much heat. We ought to set a row of torches."

It seemed too simple a plan, but I didn't know the sea fae. I was too young to remember much about the days when my father and our realms of old traded with the sea. I did recall tensions were always hovering around the two lands even then. For all I knew, the sea fae might grow sickly near fire.

But my unknowns shifted when a sharp, bitter voice broke over the crowd.

"Liar." Junius Tjuv stepped forward. Niklas followed close behind, his eyes narrowed at Olaf. Gold rings lined his fingers and dug into his skin as he cracked his knuckles.

Niklas was swift and shoved Olaf fiercely. Knocking him back at least five paces.

"Hey, stop it," I began, but paused when Olaf laughed.

"I've always found a bit of fascination with the body magic. A lie taster." Olaf clicked his tongue and began to stagger back to his feet. "It would be a useful gift."

Before I had time to move, Olaf's head tilted back, mouth spread open. A burst of billowing blackness shot toward the sky. Screams followed. Silas yanked on my arm, pulling me back even further as the shadows gathered into a solid form, as they misted over broad shoulders and long legs.

Shouts—most, I was certain, were curses and roars from Ari—turned to chaos at my back when Olaf's body fell into a heap. He moaned, but it was swiftly cut off when Davorin lifted one leg and stomped viciously on the man's head once. Twice.

"No!" I screamed. Stupid of me to try, but it was horrid watching Olaf's skull shatter under the force.

"No?" Davorin's eyes flashed. "You would have a traitor to his lord live? The Rave are *mine*, little princess. Now, where is my raven? Her first."

Never again. Ari was not the only one who promised Saga this bastard would not touch her. With Silas's hand in mine, anger, swift and potent, flooded my veins. Deep in Silas's chest a sound rumbled, and when I screamed the simple word—*shield*—much like that day on the shores of the isles, my skin burned.

A blast of power burst between us. Bright and fierce.

Davorin covered his face, a wall of darkness surrounding him like black stone. This time, he was ready. He knew us. Knew what to expect. As promised, this scourge of a man had returned more powerful.

Davorin laughed and began to lower his arms, but hissed his anger when Valen shoved in front of me and Silas and slammed his palms on the cobbled stones.

In a great roll of the earth, Raven Row began to crack. Davorin struggled to keep his footing. The split in the earth widened into a deep scar between the shore and us.

Without a command, Tor sprinted down one edge, Sol on the other.

"The earth bender!" A sea fae man still ten paces off in the shore roared his rage. They knew who'd slaughtered their king. But I took a bit of pleasure in the look of fear in their eyes as the snap of stone and soil roared over the violence of the waves their ships created.

A divide, deep and jagged, built a new kind of barrier. The gap was large enough it would take a running start to leap across. No doubt they'd build planks, but it would keep them at bay for a time.

It was made even better when thick fury spilled off Sol's palms and blue flames ignited on Tor's. My Lump and his consort directed each other as they spilled their bonding furies into Valen's gap. Brilliant bursts of blue flames shot into the air with a dizzying pyre that would dissolve anyone who'd try to cross it.

With slow steps, I approached the edge. Through the flames, I held Davorin's hateful gaze. His nose wrinkled with disdain.

"Again," I shouted. "Bested. We all look forward to sending you to the hells."

One corner of his mouth curved. "What a mouth you've gained, little one. When I have my hands on you, I'll be sure to silence you the same way I silenced my raven. You share blood; I'm sure you'd love it just as much."

He gripped his damn length over his trousers. A disgusting hint at what he meant. Silas curled his arm around my shoulders, holding me against him with a delicious sort of possessiveness. Davorin laughed, as though we'd behaved exactly as he'd hoped, then backed away from the flames. He was blocked from us. For now.

Sol wiped his brow with the back of his palm when the flames burned fiercest. Tor draped an arm around his waist, and they waited a few breaths, as if ensuring their magic would hold, then turned into us.

No waiting and with no real warning, and I flung my arms around his neck. The Sun Prince squeezed me against his body, his face against my neck.

"Gods, it is never a dull moment with you, girl." He held me tighter. "I've been sick with worry over you."

"You." I smacked my palm on his back, tightening my hold. "I get a bleeding missive about dreary things, then a damn flame bursts on my tower. No other word from any of you lot. Only the knowledge that somewhere, you're under attack. If I didn't love you so much, Lump, I'd be hating you right now."

"You're all right then?" Sol pulled back to inspect me from head to foot.

"No. I'm not. I'm not all right. I've learned a great deal about myself. I'm rather powerful, you ought to know."

"I already figured."

"Well, good, because I am. Oh, and now I have a bleeding *hjärta* whom I love to his soul, so I bleeding understand how you all get so bleeding mad over your lovers." I was rambling and couldn't stop. Panic, fear, rage, all of it collided in my chest like a torrent of emotion that could not be caged.

Sol lifted his gaze to Silas for a breath. "All right. That one's a bit new."

"Yes, it is new. In truth, I rather like that part," I said, rambling. "But now that . . . *creature* weakened us right under my nose. He was commanding the Rave positions and killing them with the sea fae, and I didn't notice. I'm supposed to lead them."

"The Rave?"

"Yes, my father's army." I waved my hands between us. "They've been here all along, but that's not important right now."

Sol pinched his lips and gave my shoulders a little shake. "Cal, slow down."

I blew out a long breath and gripped his wrists from where his hands rested on my shoulders, as though he could steady the race of my pulse.

"That creature is a fae of deception," he said firmly. "You couldn't see the truth. We're damn lucky to have Junie, or none of us would've seen him."

True. It was true. Davorin knew how to hide in plain sight. He'd been doing it for centuries.

"We tried to twist fate," I said. "We tried to offer protection and bring you to us, but the song wasn't holding well. That's why he's here. How long has he been here?"

"He's been tormenting all of us through illusions, or spell casts, so I don't know. But we're all here now. You can breathe. We have time. He cannot get through our pyre, you know that. We have a bit of time."

I closed my eyes, nodding. "How long will the burn hold, do you think?"

"Through the night," Sol said. "Maybe into the next day. You agree, Tor?"

"Should hold," said Tor, glancing at the blue flames again.

"We didn't anticipate a battle," Sol said, a little breathless. "I know this is probably a lot for you to take in, but we have our children, Cal. My mother, she's hurt; she was possessed by that bastard. Now, to get her back, Nik needs time with her. Now that he is here, is there anywhere we can go to get them all safe? He will be out for them, Mira most of all, I'm sure."

All the littles. Mira. Lilianna. I knew Lilianna in such a different way now, my heart was racing at the thought of any of them being so vulnerable. Was anywhere safe?

"Hus Rose." Silas's soft, timid voice was the response. He kept back, no doubt, the sudden crowd unsettled him, but he'd offered us a place. His eyes were on me. "Hus Rose. It's warded."

"It's perfect." I gripped Sol's arm. The Sun Prince was wholly intrigued by the sight of Silas. He said nothing, but I could see the way his mind spun with theories and questions as he studied my masked Whisper. "Hurry. Hus Rose is the palace here. It's like a damn fortress with wards and rooms and protections. We can keep them safe there."

Sol blinked and rushed back to the royals.

I was embraced briefly by Saga. Her hands shook, but she kept a steady expression.

I took her palms in mine. "He's not going to touch you."

"No," she said with conviction. "He's not. He's not touching any of us. Never again."

She turned toward the littles to gather her daughter. We all sensed the urgency. We'd embrace, cry, discuss everything later. Silas kept his head turned away from the others, but he shoved through them to reach the gates of Hus Rose first.

"Is anyone . . ." Ari pointed, following Silas with a befuddled expression. "No one is going to say anything about this one? Later, I suppose. By the by, I claim the right to stab Davorin no less than twenty times before Saga takes his head. Just so we are all quite clear."

I would laugh if the whole of Raven Row wasn't on fire and the shores were infected with enemies.

"Cuyler!" I caught sight of the blood fae in the crowd. He rushed to me and took hold of my hand. "Hells, I'm glad you're back."

"What do you need, Calista?" he said without hesitation.

"We need more warriors. Davorin took out a great many. We need healers for any wounded."

Cuyler nodded and gestured for his watchers at his back. "We'll see to it, Cal. Trust us at the gates, give us that burden. You and the Wraith, take the littles to safety, they've all been through a great deal. Then we'll plan this . . . battle. We're truly at war again."

My jaw tightened. "We are. But we will fight to the end, just like my Shadow King says."

"Go." Cuyler gave me a reassuring look. "Your warriors are here to fight for you. For you all."

I followed the crowd of royals and littles toward the gates. Silas had a hand on the iron bars, and with a low hum, he paused. The lock clicked and the wardings at the first gates fell away in a rush of wind.

Silas turned around, nervous and obviously unsettled. "Inside, there are rooms aplenty."

That was all he said before taking a long step to the side, slinking into the shadows of the knobby trees and tangles of branches. I hurried to his side.

When I clutched his hand, his palms were trembling. I tightened my grip. "You are magnificent, you know."

He snorted, watching the folk of distant kingdoms traipse the gardens of Hus Rose. "I said five words. I'm a marvel."

I chuckled. "I cannot imagine how overwhelming this is after so long alone. Yet, you have not once ceased trying to overcome the unease. To me, that makes you magnificent. Accept it."

He grinned and lifted my knuckles to his lips.

"Hello, my lovely storyteller." Niklas Tjuv approached with all the confidence of a man who'd not had his world torn to bits, who'd not survived battles in his own land. Between his palms he tossed a sack of some elixir. "That was rather frightening, wasn't it?"

"I could've done without it."

"Well, it seems we will work together again."

"Good," I said. "You're one of my favorites. That's an honor, by the way."

Niklas beamed and pointed at Silas. "This one brings a slew of questions, doesn't he? But first, Lilianna Ferus, she's overcome with a manipulated curse of bloodlust, much like Valen."

"Bleeding hells."

"It's a nasty bit, but I know how to end it. No death and dying on this one since it stems from that battle creature's dark glamour. Thanks to our impressively cunning skill last time, I know how to ward against it. Still, to avoid her slipping from me and devouring us all, is there a safe place to work where she'll be separated from the littles?"

"Silas?" I turned to him.

"Ah, one question answered," Niklas chimed, still wholly unbothered.

Silas hesitated. When he spoke, he spoke to me, not the Falkyn. "There are . . . there are catacombs and cells in the gardens. Plenty of thick walls."

"Perfect." Niklas's smile widened.

By now, I suspected the Falkyn was hiding his own unease to better aid in Silas's clear discomfort at all the royals.

Silas cleared his throat. "I'll . . . I'll lead you there." He lifted his gaze to mine. "I'll meet you in the upper room."

"Do you wish me to come with you?"

He seemed ready to shout a resounding, desperate *yes*, but he took in the wandering royals, the children, and shook his head. "Help them first."

"We'll be back before you know it, Cal." Niklas winked, then faced Silas. "I can be silent, stoic, or quite pleasant in conversation. I'll leave it to you to decide, Wraith. But I must say, I'm glad I get to meet you before Ari. No doubt he'll take all your time soon enough."

Silas's face paled. I bit my cheek to hide my smile. He was trying, and even if he hadn't been alone most of his life, my royals were overwhelming in the most beautiful ways. Once they learned all he'd done—they'd draw him into their arms and hearts, and he wouldn't have one damn chance to refuse.

245

"You all better see this." Cuyler waved from one of the walls surrounding Hus Rose.

There were a few pegs that created makeshift staircases so folk could walk atop the flat stones. Valen, Stieg, and Sol followed me to the higher alcoves on the walls, high enough we could see over the pyre wall.

My stomach lurched. "The royal ship is here."

I was certain they called it the Ship of the Ever, or the Ever King's Ship, or some other pretentious name, but those blood-red sails were at our shores. The sea fae that manned the massive vessel were disembarking with blades, rope, and torches in hand.

Davorin stood back, his eyes locked on Hus Rose. On us. The distance might've been tricking my eyes, but I swore to the hells that mimicker was grinning. Like he knew all the secrets of our world.

Low, distant chants and songs from the sea fae cast a haunting tension across the shattered roads of Raven Row.

From the royal ship, a man descended from the gangplank, a boy was by his side. The boy kept his face pointed down, and the man would occasionally stop and swat at the boy's head if he stepped too close.

Atop the man's head was an odd hat, made of three points, likely stitched in leather. He approached Davorin and muttered something. The battle lord hardly looked away, but the sea fae glared at the burning gap between us.

"That is Harald," said Valen. "Thorvald's brother. I remember him."

"He's the bastard who threatened to return," Sol added.

Valen nodded, jaw tight. "In ten turns. This is no coincidence."

"Davorin played his hand well," Sol said, voice rough. "We sent him to the sea. We bleeding sent him to find a new army. One filled with folk who despise us and will willingly fight for him."

In this moment, I despised the Norns. They were cruel. Ari would blame himself somehow, no mistake. But as Sol told me, Davorin was slimy. A trickster. His moves were too unpredictable, and he had centuries of battle knowledge to use against us.

A gloomy tune rose from the royal ship when another boy, taller than the first, emerged. He paused at the top of the gangplank, taking in the broken Row. It was too far for me to gauge his expression, not to mention his head was covered in another one of those funny hats. But he was dressed in a black tunic, a thick belt on his slender waist, and the golden hilt of his sword caught the gleam of the morning light.

Crewmen shuffled around his back like a sort of shield.

The crewmen were the source of the gloomy tune. Their voices were ghoulish and dreary. Almost a touch mad.

I tilted my head, catching a few words.

. . . a man he's not, we work we rot . . .

"Gods," Stieg said with a small gasp. "That boy there. He's . . . he's the prince of the Ever Kingdom. Erik. That's Thorvald's son."

Bleeding hells. My stomach tightened. I kept my sights on the boy as he walked, a bit stilted, down the plank. He kept his shoulder back in a smug confidence, and he had an . . . air about him. A darkness. But there was something more, something that almost tugged against me. Like he was important to know, to watch.

My Cursed King let out a long sigh at my side. "No, hear the song they sing after him?"

I strained to listen to the rest of the rumbling tune.

. . . no sleep until it's through. A sailor's grave is all we crave. We are the Ever King's crew . . .

Valen frowned. His face was weary, his shoulders burdened when they slumped forward. "He's not the prince of the Ever any longer. He's now the damn Ever King."

"When you meet the Ever King again," I whispered, repeating the warning from the captured sea singer. "If you wish to keep your lives, I wouldn't make him bleed."

Valen and Stieg looked at me, brows raised.

"What does that mean, Cal?"

"It was a warning. We were attacked by sea singers. One of them warned us not to make him bleed."

Stieg cursed. "Because his blood is poison. That was why the Black Palace took him as a tiny boy. But not only is his blood poison, it can heal great ailments. The boy must sing for his blood to heal;

247

that is why Ivar and Britta tortured him, because he never broke. He never sang a word."

I swallowed the scratch in my throat. Why was he important?

There was a connection here, some pull to my own seidr, and something told me this boy king had a part to play in it.

CHAPTER 32
THE PHANTOM

We didn't have much time. The whole of a damn sea kingdom was at our gates. Davorin had returned. How long had he been close to us? I should've known. I should've been sharper. Once, I'd been skilled at sensing danger.

I hadn't even considered Olaf was not who we thought.

Now, the captain was dead and the battle lord was ready to claim his bleeding throne.

"What do you think he offered the sea folk?" The man, Niklas, asked at my back.

He'd told me I could choose silence as we descended into the catacombs, but in truth he'd asked a great many questions. Most had not seemed necessary for an answer, an occasional comment on the eeriness of the bones jutting from the walls, but this one was direct.

"What do you mean?" My reply was sharper than intended. This was why I kept quiet.

Niklas seemed unbothered. "I mean, how did Davorin entice an entire kingdom to fight his war?"

"They must get something in return."

Niklas clicked his tongue, as though considering it. "You heard them shout about Valen when he cracked the road." All at once, he snapped his fingers. "That must be it. They called him out by his power, like it was a mark. You know, they threatened to return to take Valen. Perhaps they've been promised him in return for their service to Davorin."

"The Night Folk king is not a man one can easily take."

Niklas chuckled darkly. "I know. It makes it almost entertaining, a little humorous. I want to say, I'd like to see them try, but honestly —I don't. I want them to all disappear and leave us in bleeding peace. I was quite happy, you know, almost lazy. These last ten turns have been the first I can remember living without the constant threat of enemies. I mean, we all knew Davorin was still out there, but we had peace. Now . . ." His words trailed off.

I paused at the bottom of the staircase in front of an arched door. "Now?"

Niklas's bright eyes were burdened when he lifted his gaze. "Now, I've lost two fiercely good friends. I've watched another boy become an orphan."

Heat gathered in my chest. The familiar tug of seidr. Calista strengthened my gift, and I could not truly twist fate without her, but there were always nudges. Weaker versions others would call their gut feelings, but for workers of fate, it was always the voice of a new path.

Something about what he had said, brightened my own power.

"You should take in the boy," I said without thinking. To think would be wise. I was not a fool and knew my words could be brisk and strange. Perhaps it was rude to say such a thing.

I didn't know much of anything about the Falkyn, only that he'd been critical in restoring the Golden King.

Niklas lifted a brow. "Why would you say that?"

"Never mind." I opened the door.

"No, why did you say that?"

"I don't know."

"Hmm. I don't need my wife to be here to know you're lying."

Irritation rolled up my throat. "I don't know why I spoke; it was just a thought."

Niklas was pensive by the door. "It is a possible thought. One I think I will consider once all this is over."

"You know this boy?"

"Of course, I do. As I said, his mother and father were dear friends."

I shrugged, done speaking.

Apparently, the Falkyn, was not. Niklas rubbed his chin, bemused. "I don't know why those words are . . . settling so deeply. It's almost strange."

It was seidr. I wasn't going to explain it. A new path was broadening for the man and he could feel it. That was all.

"Here is the room," I said. "Will it do?"

Niklas took it in. Walls made of bone and rock surrounded us. In the center was an old, wooden table with a layer of dust thick enough to coat my entire body. It reeked of musk and ancient air, but he nodded.

"It'll do just fine, I think." Niklas placed his hands on his hips and took in the space once more, then spun on me. "I will need access to a stove or fire. Possible?"

"The cooking rooms are old and empty. They're yours."

"You never eat or what?"

"I eat."

"Hmm." Niklas had a mischief about his gaze. "You don't speak much do you? Odd. For I'm quite certain you are the Wraith from Ari's dream, and you spoke enough there."

Dream walking was not reality, another part I wasn't planning to explain. Mostly because speaking was growing uncomfortable. The familiar dampness gathered on my palms and my scalp prickled with the urge to duck away.

Niklas didn't press and waved his hand about, gesturing at the arched ceilings of the catacombs. "No time to waste, I suppose. I'll go speak to Arvad."

I jolted when he clapped me on the arm, like I'd witnessed folk do when they were attempting to be friendly. He flashed me a quick grin, told me to take a moment to go rest before the royals of every kingdom bombarded me with questions, then disappeared back up the staircase.

Centuries of solitude, now I had whole royal households as my damn guests.

My chest grew tight and my skin heated.

Other folk were thrilling in many ways. I was glad they were here. It was the right step, a unified front and all that. But the noxious, painful pieces that came when too much chatter, too many bodies were close by, had me also wishing the lot would find their own space and leave me to be alone with Calista.

I shook away the unease and followed where Niklas had gone up the stairs, anxious to find the only person in the entire palace that brought me solace.

Calista wasn't in the music room. I thumbed a few strings on a lyre out of habit to soothe the race of my pulse, and went to look for her.

Folk strolled the corridors of the palace now. I avoided them. Truth be told, they seemed to avoid me, but curious gazes followed me as I strode past. I leaned into the shadows, seeking their dark reprieve. Most of those wandering about looking for rooms didn't look familiar. Then again, I knew so few faces. Only those who'd truly stood closest to Calista all this time were recognizable. These unfamiliars were likely members of the thief guilds, other warriors, or possibly servants.

I kept my gaze schooled on the woven rugs in the halls until I rounded into the corridor with Calista's bed chamber. Not a moment too late, for when I stepped into the hall, Calista backed out of the room. Soft steps, movements like a whisper, she gently eased the door closed.

In a breath of relief, without a thought, I wrapped my arms around her waist from behind and let my brow fall to the back of her head.

She jolted with a little strangled squeal, whirling around. Calista snickered and smacked my chest a few times. "Don't startle me like that."

"Sorry." Now, I pressed my brow to hers. "You make it easier to breathe."

Something about my words drew a small smile over her lips. She kissed the hinge of my jaw. "You weary of socializing?"

I balked. "If you call muttering a few words to the Falkyn, then avoiding every other soul in this damn place socializing, then yes. I'm quite finished."

"Shhh." Calista pressed a finger to my lips. "You're normally so quiet. Lower your voice."

"Why?" No one was around. Finally.

"We have exhausted littles in my bed." She gestured at the door. "The only way we could get them to part with their parents at all was by promising they could all sleep in my magical room." Calista wiggled her fingers.

"There's not magic in—"

Again, she pressed her finger to my lips. "Silas. Hush. There is, and if you want them to sleep so we can make plans, you will agree with me."

I dipped my chin and murmured against her finger. "As you say."

"My royals are all meeting in the hall." She gave me a cautious look. "Do you wish to join? You don't have to, I can tell you what is said."

I gripped her waist and kissed her softly. Why it mattered so greatly that she would let me be alone should I need it, I didn't know. But it did. It was as though she took me as I was. As though she truly did not mind if I wanted to dwell in darkness. It burned through my heart to know, broken and unsettled as I could be, she finally knew of me again. She finally . . . wanted me.

"I wish to join you."

"Really?" There was a heady kind of relief in her voice, her eyes.

"I should be there. This is . . . this is our fight."

Calista let her shoulders slump a bit. "Thank the gods. I'll admit this to you alone, but I'm terrified."

I wrapped her in my arms and tucked her head under my chin. Calista hugged my waist.

"That battle sod, he terrifies me. He's . . . he's a nightmare to me."

"He won't touch you."

"He could. He *did*. He was so close. Hells, the way he toyed with us and we didn't even realize it is horrifying."

"I know." I pressed a kiss to her head. "But we know his games now. We're all together. Our song, it brought the kingdoms together. He is strong, but so are we."

She squeezed my waist a bit tighter. "This is why I want you with me. You think you do not have clever words, but your words always speak the right things to my heart. So, obviously, my reasons are utterly selfish, but who the hells cares?"

I chuckled and took her hand. "Lead the way. I can promise you, I will let you do all the talking."

Calista smiled. Dark as the future appeared, her smiles were swiftly becoming the brightest part of my days.

CHAPTER 33
THE PHANTOM

THE CURSED KING. HIS MORTAL QUEEN OF CHOICE. I COUNTED THE FIRST familiar faces on my fingers, subtly, at my side where no one would notice.

The Shadow Queen. Gods, I hated that ring on her finger. The damn thing took a particularly brutal death for Calista to set it on its path. The Shadow King. He seemed as bothered with all this chatter as me.

There was Calista's Sun Prince. I respected him the most. He'd been like Annon had been—a brother. Even locked in madness, I knew through the bond with Calista that the Sun Prince protected her.

Next to him was his consort. The pyre fae.

I narrowed my eyes. There was something burning from Tor. A nudge, a path unseen. With Calista near, I could damn near see when significant paths of fate might fall into place. And I felt something with the pyre fae. His life could possibly change. Soon.

The dreary part of these senses were that I did not know if it was a change for good or ill.

My gaze swept over to the far side of the table where Niklas bent beside the first Night Folk king to be tangled in one of Calista's paths. Arvad. The father of one the final fated royals.

Arvad abandoned his chair, followed by two other men, and swept from the hall with the Falkyn.

I hoped they found a way to heal Lilianna. She had played a grand role in the steps that brought my mate back to me.

Perhaps, the notion of speaking with them sent my head spinning, but I would always honor them. I would always value them for the dangerous roles they played in this tale. The way they aided Calista on her own path without even knowing they did so.

My attention went to the head of the table. The Raven Queen. She'd been a princess when last I saw her as a boy. She'd always been kind to me. We had spoken some when I was still her brother's ward.

I doubted she'd recall it. Curses had a way of tangling thoughts into confusing memories.

Upon a glance at the final seat at the table, my chest cramped. Instead of no one taking note of my secret assessment, I was met with the burn of dark, golden eyes, folded arms, and a general sense of annoyance.

The Golden King looked like he might want to toss the drinking horn in front of him at my head.

Calista led us into the room. Under Ari's scrutiny, I hung back, half-drenched in the shadows of the alcoves and doorways. While the others embraced Calista, inspecting her for dreary wounds, my blood turned to ice when he rose from his seat and crossed the dim hall.

Ari said nothing for a moment, merely kept his arms folded over his chest, and faced the room, shoulder to shoulder with me.

Then, "I'm ready now."

I didn't know how to respond, so I said nothing.

"Whenever you are," he went on. "I'm ready."

Cautiously, I turned to face him. "For?"

"Oh, for us to discuss the lovely bond we share. Or did you think me so dense that I wouldn't realize you are Wraith—the man who walked me through a damn fae sleep. If you thought such things, that's rather foolish. You know me well enough to understand I am too impressively sharp not to notice."

"I do not recall much sharpness, but I recall an aggravating tongue."

Where I hoped to offend enough that he might leave so I could hide the trepidation in my stance, my tone, my damn face, the Golden King failed me. He was neither offended, nor keen on my disquiet. Well, if he was, he did not let it stop him.

Ari laughed. "Such a somber sod you are. Why do you not speak to me? After all that happened in that sleep, I face you here, yet you say nothing."

I stared at my hands. "Dream walking is not the same as the waking world."

Ari's face softened. "Where have you been, Silas?"

"You recall my name?"

"Do I recall your name?" Ari didn't look at me with the fear of some. He didn't even pay mind to the hint of the scar on my face. "You are the man who saved me. You brought me back to my wife, to a daughter. To life. I would be lost if not for you."

"I revealed a few truths."

"Ah. Another modest hero, I see. Someday you bleeding fools will learn to boast your strengths and feats instead of claiming them as menial tasks. Let us not diminish what you have done, what I know you did."

"And what did I do?" My eyes narrowed.

"I know you fought to find me again when Davorin overcame me in that sleep. I don't know how, but you were distressed when he appeared. I'm certain it was you who found a way to keep us reeling, to keep him away from me long enough to survive it. So, yes. I remember your name. Though, I do like Wraith. It's rather intimidating, don't you think?"

As they often did, words failed me.

I closed my eyes when Ari placed a palm on my shoulder. "Where have you been?"

"Here," was all I could say.

"With the hidden Rave?"

"With silence."

He hesitated. I didn't want pity, but when I looked, it wasn't there. Only understanding, perhaps a touch of sympathy was written on his features, but not pity. "I see. Not really, but I'm sure I will see soon enough. I'm guessing you haven't had much company all this time, though."

Gods, I almost smiled. Like an instinct. "A few ghosts."

"Explains why such a crowd seems to frighten you more than battle. Since this is the case, I'll make you an offer: should you have something to say, but do not wish to speak, then you tell me. As you know, well and good, I am marvelous at speaking for others. Over others. Around others. Really, anything you ask of me, I'm sure my tongue and voice can handle it."

Ari winked, clapped a hand on my shoulder, then returned to his seat beside Saga.

By now, all eyes were on us. Most followed Ari as he traipsed with all the arrogance I remembered of the man, then like one head, gazes landed on me.

"I'll just say it," Calista said, waving her hands. "That way none of you sods will be so brazen like this fool—" She opened a palm to Ari.

"Check your words, Cal," Ari said. "I'm no fool. Merely the boldest of us all."

"Or the greatest pest."

"It is a possibility, I suppose."

She snorted. "Before you all start to bother him, this is Silas—my father's ward. Yes, he is the man from Ari's fae sleep. Yes, he is my Whisper. Yes, he is the first bond that everyone so vaguely put out there—"

"I knew it." Valen slapped the table and pointed a finger at Ari. "Fifteen silver *shim*, you bastard."

"When the hells did we even make such a gamble, My King?" Ari looked affronted.

"At the docks when we left Gunnar's vows. Kase, tell him."

"I recall the bargain included a day of Ari not speaking," said the Shadow King.

"Then your ears would bleed from longing," Ari snapped back. "But it doesn't matter, King Valen has made this up in his head."

Valen balked. "We said the ward was connected to Cal."

"Exactly. We said. Truth be told, *I* said. You all followed. If anyone is to win such a gamble, it is me." Ari leaned against Saga until she wrapped her arms around his shoulders from behind, her palms on his chest. With a nod and wave, he said, "Carry on."

Valen leaned closer to his own wife. "He's acting too much like the king he was when we first met."

Ari cocked his head. "Magnificent?"

"Annoying."

Ari grinned like he'd, at last, won the game.

How did Calista keep up with them all when they spoke like this?

"Go on, Cal." Sol Ferus seemed to be the calmer voice of reason. "What's happened here?"

"As I said." Calista glanced over her shoulder. "Silas is . . . well, he's mine. He's part of me, my power and his are one. We brought you here because . . . once the first bond was restored, the song that broke us apart was ended. The world returned to the beginning. I didn't know it would happen, but I wanted you all safe."

"We saw the beacon," the choice queen—Elise—said gently. "You did lead us here."

"Eryka." Saga glanced to a pale woman who was half asleep on the shoulder of a lithe-looking man. A woman with a scar much like mine carved down her face. Only she did not hide it.

She fluttered her misty eyes, looking to the Raven Queen.

"You keep saying that same thing," said Saga. "Back to the beginning."

"Stars speak when they speak," the fae woman returned.

"We've heard it a great deal too," Calista offered, then paused for a moment. "And the tale was always meant to return to the first bond that began it. I've been . . . well, I've . . ."

Her voice kept trailing off.

I am terrified. Her words were a poisonous dart to my chest.

Unease was heavy on her shoulders, the way they slumped, the way her spine curved, it was clear. There wasn't a moment of thought or hesitation. It was as though my feet moved on their own accord, with a strange desperation to ease her burden more than I cared for my own.

I touched the back of her arm. Calista jolted, but the smile was damn near instantaneous. It brightened the room, chased away the night.

She let out a long breath and leaned into my side.

"I don't know how to say it," she admitted. "In truth, I'm still wrapping it all up in my mind, but . . . I am your storytellers. From the beginning, it has been me. I've been on this path, searching for my heart bond since the world shattered."

I squeezed her arm with what I hoped was something reassuring.

Sol rose from his seat. "What do you mean, you are our storytellers?"

She licked her lips and held his gaze, unwavering. "I mean, I met you before those cells in Ravenspire, Lump. I saw you as a small boy, a little heartbroken that you had a new tiny brother." She chuckled and cast a look toward Valen Ferus. She drifted to the Shadow King and Queen. "I mean, I was there when a queen's ring was lost to her enemies."

The Shadow Queen's mouth parted, but whether it was stun, or confusion, she didn't speak.

"And you." Calista looked to Ari. "I was there when a boy needed rescuing after slaughter, so he could free the heart of a beloved aunt who had been lost to me. So he could rise to his destiny as the fated Golden King."

Perhaps, for the first time in our acquaintance, Ari Sekundär did not speak.

"That is what I mean, Lump. I've always been there." Calista looked to Elise Ferus. "That is what I meant, Kind Heart, when we met in that tomb, and I spoke of storytellers before me."

"Cal," Elise said, a catch to her voice. "You told me those storytellers were killed."

With a jerky sort of nod, Calista forced a quivering smile. "And they were."

"Bleeding gods." Sol's eyes went wide. "Live and live again. That was the curse your father cast. You cannot die."

"I assure you, I can," she said, rubbing a hand over her slender throat. "I have. A few times, as it turns out."

"And you didn't know?" Saga rose from the table like Sol, but approached Calista, taking her hands in hers. "You didn't remember?"

"Not until the final moments." She flicked her gaze back to me and took my hand. "That is when I would find those whispers in the dark. When the song of fate would take over and finish the tale."

"You both have been dying over and over."

I clenched my eyes. The blood, the pain, the fear, watching it over and over again was a plague in my mind I feared I would never escape. No matter how much I touched her, kissed her, held her, it would always be there.

Calista's voice shook. "Silas did not fade. As a cruel gift of the Norns for what my father had done, he was left to finish the tales, and wait for it to begin again. He was left to . . . guide me back. Annon was cursed to walk with me. Makes a bit of sense now, doesn't it, how he told me we'd said goodbye before."

"Cal." Saga stole her from my grip. I wasn't particularly pleased, but stepped back to let her embrace Calista. "I don't understand the purpose of it?"

"Same purpose as your curse, so that ugly sod out there couldn't find me. Hard to track the bloodline of House Ode if it does not have a true existence."

"Bleeding hells." Sol sat back in his seat again. "You were Greta. Is that what you mean?"

Valen scrubbed his face. "You were the enchantress."

Calista looked away as if ashamed. "We had to do things, you understand, don't you? We had to cast the words of your heart song. None of them were simple or kind or easy. Fate was punishing us for manipulating the whole bleeding world. To find our way back, we would have to fight. Your curse wasn't only to keep you alive and safe from that wretched Ice King; I knew it was the way for you to find my Kind Heart."

"Calista, if you think we are angry, you're wrong." Valen took hold of his wife's hand and kissed two missing fingertips. "I would not change the path that has brought us here. It is pain-ridden, filled with loss, but our lands did grow stronger. We are stronger. None of us would give up our families for a bit of comfort, right?"

"Some of us would not be here," said the son of the Night Folk princess—Gunnar, if I recalled it correctly. He took his star seer's hand tightly.

"Speak for yourself. I could've done without the separation from Tor," Sol said, but there was a lightness in his tone as he returned to his chair and placed a hand on his consort's leg. "I'm simply saying, the curse of madness was quite disconcerting, little bird."

Calista let out a wet chuckle. "Apologies, Lump. You always were the clever prince."

"Debatable," Valen muttered.

"Had to be something with your mind to satisfy that old Ice King."

"So you were there," the Shadow Queen said, holding up the silvery glass ring. "Those legends of the first and second families of memory workers. You were there."

"They were losing," Calista said. "The first family. I said the words, Silas sang the song, and it set the ring on a bloody path back to the proper heir. Without the song, the ring might've been lost. Perhaps, never restored, and the hatred from our wretched battle lord would've consumed a fated gift of devotion. I am sorry your folk were killed, your majs and your dajs, in order to reach the end."

At that, Calista cast a hesitant look toward Ari who had hardly budged.

"I wish I could've stopped what happened, Ari," she admitted. "That sod is cruel, and I think he sensed your importance; he knew the importance your maj and daj played in the court of House Ode. He took his revenge on them."

The smith's daughter. The cartographer. I was there that day when House Sekundär found its song. I hated showing the truth to him, yet was glad Ari got to see his folk again.

"You sent the rogue Night Folk to free me," Ari said, voice low.

Calista nodded. "We did. It was the final death before I ended up in the cells of Castle Ravenspire, restored to my true name."

Ari dragged a hand through his hair. "I always wondered how they found me in the damn nick of time." He gave Calista a small grin. "Now, I know."

Saga sat beside her husband again, gently twirling his hair around her fingers until the tension seemed to fade from his shoulders.

"To find my way back," Calista said, hugging her middle, "the gifts of fate needed to be restored to the new paths Silas and I sang on that horrid night we found Saga. The ones you all saw that have brought us together."

"All right," the Shadow King said. "Well, now what? What happens now that we are back to the beginning?"

Calista slipped her fingers into my hand. "The curse is done, the tale is ended. Now . . . we face this end at the mercy of new fates, new paths."

"So should you fall in battle . . ." Sol began.

"I wake in the Otherworld, Lump," Calista admitted. "The same as all of you, so don't bleeding fall."

"Maj will want to know this," Valen said, looking at his brother and sister. "She began our tale, she was the one who arranged for Etta to sleep under our curses."

The Shadow Queen rose. "May we see it, Cal?"

"Take it." Calista tapped her head. "But then we all must rest. We won't have peace for long, and we all know it."

As if summoned, one of the fae warriors entered the hall while the queen took hold of Calista's memories. They gave the report. Sea fae were claiming the shores, led by the darkness of the battle lord. He told the royals it would be a matter of time before they attempted to take Hus Rose once the pyre burned out between us.

"Their Rave are still in position," said the warrior. "Archers are trained on their rising camps. There are two Western spell casters securing the wards around the gates. Should we do the same with Elixists and any fae from the isles?"

"Hells, why are you all looking at me?" Calista said when those at the long table faced her.

Elise grinned. "You are queen here, Calista. We all have a say now. So what say you?"

Calista gave me a strained look. "I say we'd be wise to protect our gates. For now, we keep Davorin out, but we find a way to sneak up behind him. There is a tale here. A way to end this, I can feel it. We simply need to find the path."

CHAPTER 34
THE STORYTELLER

LET THE DREAM DESCEND, SILAS.

"Silas." His name was soft on my tongue. My lashes fluttered. Pitch coated the room where there had been a sliver of light when my eyes closed.

I propped onto one elbow, a heavy weight around my middle. The smile came at the sight of his strong arm still draped over me like a new growth on my own body.

I peered over my shoulder. Silas slept, the mask removed, his chest bare. Gods, he was a bit of a delicious marvel. One worthy of stone, no mistake. One I ought to commission that bleeding earth bender of mine to design into a statue.

I bit back a laugh. I was certain Valen would not agree to any commission of the kind, but it would be entertaining to detail, in every salacious term, how I wanted the chiseled edges of Silas's muscle to shape.

Then, between his legs, Valen, it must be made to size for it's magnificent.

I could imagine the horror on my Cursed King's face, an image which promptly drew out a chortle that fashioned more into a wet gurgling noise in my throat. Silas shifted in his sleep, then settled again with a sigh.

With care, I shifted so I was facing him. He looked so peaceful during sleep.

Let the dream descend, Silas.

My brows furrowed as I lifted one fingertip and traced the edges of his jaw, the curve of his lips. I must've been dreaming of him, and it was sticking with me.

The other royals had witnessed Silas unraveling the memories of the lifetimes, sat still and stoic for a time, then we all scuttled away to find a bit of rest before blood and death found us once again. I hadn't expected to sleep so long.

A flash in the night caught my eye through the gap in the thick, black shades. I skillfully maneuvered free of his arm, a chill struck my skin at once, but I wrapped one of the furs over my shoulders and went to the window.

My stomach lurched.

Beyond the gates, Tor's pyre was not as vibrant, not as tall. Along the shores, into the docks, even a few of the outer towers of the fortress that butted to the sea, tents and shanties lined our shores.

Mammoth ships filled every bend in the shore, every distant tide. Sea fae were everywhere. Soon enough, they'd rise against us. The dawn would still be tolls away, and a new pressure gathered in my chest, like an omen, heavy and fierce.

This day was when new fates would be written.

This day, something would change.

I cast a lingering glance to Silas in the bed, then slid into a simple pair of trousers and one of his oversized tunics. With my belt, I tightened the fabric and secured my knives. There was little time, and if this was my last approaching sunrise, words needed to be said.

I placed a blood rose beneath their names and sat back on my knees, staring at the symbols carved in stone.

"I wish you were somehow, I don't know, *here* again," I said, voice rough. I closed my eyes, imagining their faces, from both memory and from those moments I saw in the fae sleep.

Since learning the truth of my bloodline, I often imagined Riot Ode laughing. I imagined Anneli being the one who brought it out.

In my heart, I knew they were a love that would live on. A love meant for sagas and dreamy tales.

Still, I wished they were here.

"I wanted you both to know," I said, a thick rasp to my voice. "That . . . that I'm grateful to you. I know all that you did to keep me breathing." I chuckled softly. "Rather creative, a little horrific, but still quite the sacrifice."

Tears burned behind my eyes. I traced my mother's name in the stone. "I remember you loved to laugh and loved sweet things over the savory. Always with the berries and cream before the meat. I remember you let me braid my own hair because I wanted to try when other majs would've been horrified knowing their little, precious girls were running about with manes on their heads."

I let my forehead drop to her name. "I remember you taught me how to be afraid and fierce, all at once."

I pressed a kiss to her name, then looked to my father's. A tear fell onto my cheek. "And you, King. I remember the tales beneath the stars. The way you taught me the kingdoms, the lore, the magicks through starlight. I remember you were gentle when some fathers were not. Proof of it was when I first heard you bark an order at the Rave and I nearly pissed myself." I laughed and used the back of my wrist to wipe away another tear.

Always with the tears.

"I didn't know you could get so loud because you never did—not with me." I flattened a palm against his name. "The point is, I . . . love you both. Part of me feels like I always remembered you, like I always remembered all of it, just hid it away. But your sacrifice, for me, for our people, hasn't been forgotten. Who knows, maybe I will see you soon and we can talk about this life together." Thick, knotted emotion burdened my words. "I hope I've made you proud."

"You have, Little Rose."

I spun around toward the front of the mausoleum. Silas had the misfortune of being fully clothed, but he looked at me with those dark, glassy eyes.

I grinned sheepishly, and wiped more tears. "Wanted a few words. In case they're the last."

He shook his head. "You're rather morbid."

"Realistic, I think you mean."

I kissed the petals of their roses once more, then went to the entrance. My chest butted up with Silas's as I strode past. "You should be sleeping."

"Your tiny form brings a great deal of surprising heat. It was cold."

"I'm not tiny." I shoved his shoulder gently.

"Like a twig on a tree."

"You should talk. You try to move like a phantom, yet you're ridiculously thick around the shoulders and your feet might as well be the paddles of two oars."

Silas's teeth flashed white and bright when he laughed. "That is not even close to the best you can do, Little Rose."

"Yes, well. I'm tired."

On the gates were a mixture of Rave, Ettan, and blood fae warriors who strode along the new parapets across the fortress. Gunnar Strom had a bow strapped over his shoulder, his attention on the sea. Beside him was Eryka.

Perhaps they were restless like me. A blood fae paused at the young prince. Cuyler. Again, did anyone sleep here?

"I've run from this and run toward this in every memory I have," I said, voice soft. "This day is what we have all been both avoiding and building."

Silas pressed his chest to my back, one arm curled around my shoulders, tugging my body to his. "You feel it?"

"Do you?"

He nodded. "The end we've all foreseen."

"Words came for you," I told him, turning in his hold, so I could rest my cheek on his chest. "Well, I'm not certain. I woke with them in my mind."

"Seidr?"

"I don't know." Hells, sometimes it was bleeding impossible to figure what was my power and what was a simple thought. "*Let the dream descend*. That was all I thought."

"Hold to it," he said. "It speaks to me."

"Think it's meant as a tale? A twist? A premonition."

"Yes." He chuckled. "I've learned that sometimes the tales and the songs begin small. Simple warnings that you give so well. But when there is power to the words, we ought to hold them close for later. They could build into something larger. It'd be a shame not to remember them."

"Likely it will be vague as always until the last moment."

"Possibly not even then for the Norns are rarely accommodating."

"Such true words. Those wenches." I closed my eyes, embracing the slow cadence of his heartbeat. "Dawn comes soon."

Silas hugged me against him in response.

"I like this moment," I said, gliding my open palms up his firm chest. "In the quiet, with you."

Silas freed a rough breath when I slid my hands beneath his tunic to his bare skin.

"They're certainly over too soon."

I didn't want to be melancholic, but the thought was there— would we have these moments after dawn came? Time was fleeting, and I didn't want to miss a single instance with Silas.

"Perhaps . . ." I kissed his throat. "Perhaps we should drag it out a bit more."

His gaze slammed into me, a tumultuous storm of need and desire. Silas checked the walls once, then grabbed my palm and hurried us deeper into the gardens behind the palace.

Once we were deep in a thicket of flowering shrubs, I opened my mouth to ask where we were going, but Silas silenced any words by pressing my back to the trunk of an oak tree. He hesitated for half a breath, then kissed me. Brilliantly forceful. Silas kissed me like if he did not the whole of the world would crumble yet again.

He urged my body closer until our hips, chests, knees, all of us knocked into the other. I whimpered when the strain of his hard length pressed into my center.

"Time runs short," he said, pressing kisses down my throat. "What we do with what is left, I leave in your hands."

In another moment we were shredding the lower half of our clothes away. I fumbled with his belt, the laces of his trousers, until I could shove them down his hips enough his hard length sprang free.

Silas had less patience, less finesse, and tore the waist of my trousers trying to slip them off my body. He spared me a heated look, then lifted me under my thighs, wrapping my body around his. Skin to skin, I thought my soul might split in two. Soaked and starving, I rocked my hips.

With a bruising kiss, Silas claimed my mouth. His tongue slid between my teeth at the same time as a finger slipped inside me.

He took the gasp from my tongue for himself, and added another finger until I bit down on his lip to keep from crying out his name for the whole palace to hear.

He pumped his fingers in and out, deep and slow. My body quaked. I burned for him, for all of him.

I shook my head. "More. I need you, I need more of you."

A low, gritty growl was my response. He removed his fingers and dragged the tips over my thighs, over my lower belly, as though marking me with the evidence of what he could do to me.

"More of this?" he rasped. "You need more of your mate, Little Rose?"

He shoved my back firmer against the tree, so he could release one of my legs and grip his length. In beautifully cruel strokes he teased my entrance with the crown. "Is this what you need? Need me to fill you until all you feel is me?"

"Gods," I said. "Where did you learn to talk like this?"

He grinned. "Comes naturally with you. I'm still waiting for an answer."

"Yes. I want you inside."

Silas slid the tip inside. He kissed me, sweeter than before, and whispered. "We don't have much time, so I'm going to need you to come fast. Come hard."

Damn the gods. I wanted him to crack my body in half and fill every vein with more of him. This passion, this obsession, was heady and vibrant. No wonder everyone on these palace grounds could hardly see reason when their *hjärta* was threatened.

"Ready?" Silas's breath was hot against my ear.

I couldn't catch a breath and simply nodded, clawing at his shoulders. Silas rammed his length inside to the hilt. I moaned when he offered no respite, merely tightened his hold on my thighs and pumped into me deep, hard, and fast.

My breasts bounced against his chest with each thrust. I hooked my ankles at the small of his back when the heat of my release built, then snapped in one vibrant wave.

I couldn't stop rocking against him, desperate to squeeze out every last piece of pleasure.

"Calista," he moaned, wildly thrusting into me. "Again, do that again. Gods, you feel so perfect wrapped around me."

His tongue tangled with mine. My core throbbed, but I kept rocking into his length as he deepened his movements. Silas kissed me, his teeth trapped my lip, then in a few more breaths, he went still. A heavy moan hummed from his throat to mine as his length twitched inside.

His release dripped down my thighs, it dripped onto the soil, and I loved the whole sight of it. Like we were staking claim across the palace. This was our kingdom. Our world. Our home.

But this man, he was mine *alone*.

For a moment his forehead pressed to mine, and my arms remained locked around his neck. A tinge of gray was chasing away the velvet black of the night. The precious bits of peace were fading away.

My heart ached when voices lifted from within the palace . Distant glides of steel and leather rippled into the thicket as warriors roused and prepared.

"There must be movement at the shore," Silas whispered.

I forced a smile, desperate to suffocate the disquiet in my chest. There was no choice—we faced a battle today. Run and be killed, fight and be killed, or . . . fight and claim back our land for good.

Silas kissed me, a mere whisper of a kiss, and slid out of me. He helped me gather my tattered trousers, and fastened his belt. When we laced our fingers together, he kissed my knuckles, his eyes locked on mine. "I love you, Little Rose. I always have."

"To the Otherworld, Whisper."

CHAPTER 35
THE STORYTELLER

I QUICKLY GATHERED MY OLD TROUSERS FROM THE UPPER ROOMS AND adjusted the laces around my waist as Silas and I hurried toward the great hall. Whatever was about to happen, torn clothes from a beautiful, rough-handed moment in the thicket wouldn't do.

Commotion rose from the hall. Royals, warriors, their guilds, and a few confused, sleepy littles bustled about, strapping blades, muttering plans, inspecting old maps of the first kingdom with the guidance of the Golden King and Raven Queen.

"Auntie Cal." Livia Ferus hugged my waist. "Your room was magic. Not one nightmare came."

I gave Silas a smug grin and stroked Livia's dark, silky hair. "Told you."

A boy with messy hair standing on end approached, munching on a juicy blood pear. "This where you're living now, Cal?" His grassy green eyes flicked to the dark rafters overhead. "Sorta dusty like, but there's a lot of rooms."

I released Livia and mussed the boy's hair even more. "Keep out of trouble, Jonas."

He puffed out his lips.

I grinned and lowered my voice. "Or at least, don't get caught."

273

He took another bite, smiling and showing off a missing tooth he must've recently lost in the back of his mouth. "Never do. Unless Livie—" he glared at the Night Folk princess. "Tattles."

"I don't tattle, Jo. You're just not as tricky as you think."

He rolled his eyes dramatically and sloppily licked his fingers. "You're a tattler when you don't get whatcha want. A big, blubbering baby."

I chuckled when Livia attacked. First, she hooked her arms around the boy's neck. Jonas tugged on her messy, sleep tossed braid. She cried out and tugged on the new piercing in his ear.

"Hey!" Jonas said through a grunt. "That'll bleed, Livie!"

"Aww, big, blubbering baby."

Jonas grunted and sprinted after her, eyes black as his father's, when Livia took off squealing in an odd kind of delight.

"Will he hurt her?" Silas whispered.

"No. Just watch." I patted his chest and made it to the count of five before three more littles snapped into action and chased after the other two—all on varying sides of the war. Mira sided with Livia this time. Sander, unsurprisingly, did as well. I suspected only because he liked to torment his brother.

"Ah," I said. "Alek is on Jonas's side this time. Usually he's with Liv."

"Do you sense it?" Silas whispered beside my ear.

His words drew me to a pause. Long enough I felt a heat gathering in my chest, a sign that words wanted to shape. A path of fate that would lead to a heart's song was here.

It was coming from the littles. All hells, one of those young royals had a fated path taking shape.

"Oh no." My shoulders slumped.

"Could be a good thing," Silas said. "Might mean our fates do not end here."

"Let's go with that option." My stomach burned in sharp, bile-soaked waves. Unable to shake the notion that everything would soon change, I would cling to any hope that led us to think we would emerge out the other side of this battle.

We left the youngest among us to torment and live freely for a little longer and joined the rest of the crowd gathered in the center of the hall.

"Flame's nearly gone." Niklas was going around to everyone and handing them something. "Find a place to wear this unless you want that creature to wear your skin."

He paused at me and wiggled a bracelet made from twine. "Ankle or wrist, Cal. Make sure it's secure enough they need to cut off your limb to remove it."

"More of your elixirs?"

"Same ones from the fae isles. The wards to keep him from mimicking our likeness or possessing us. But if you recall, he can also absorb the different magicks of folk. This'll see to it he can't."

I tightened the bracelet until it cut into my skin. Niklas handed one to Silas with a nod, not a word.

"You made these in one night?" I asked.

Niklas offered a dramatic gasp, as though he were affronted. "What do you take me for, girl? I've had these bleeding prepared for turns. We all knew this damn nightmare would be back one day. If you sang us here, many thanks for keeping my stores intact during the shift. Then again, I have complaints about my nest being above ground."

I chuckled. "Win us this fight, and I'll dig you a bleeding new Nest."

"Done." Niklas winked, then moved on to others, seeing to it that everyone bore his tricky ward somewhere on their person.

Folk who'd stand in the battle were given clay plugs meant for the ears. Cuyler had been the one to warn the warriors of sea singers and sirens. Wretched songs of lust and desire would not be our undoing. To step into the Otherworld because we'd died from an untamed ache between our thighs would be horrifying once we faced those who'd fallen in much grander ways.

Warriors across the realms secured blades—seax, axes, short blades, bows, arrows. Halvar Atra barked his commands at the Ettan warriors. Kase and Malin were more subtle, tucked close with their thievish kind of people; likely they were trading schemes, ploys, tricks, any sort of idea the Eastern realms might have.

Then, there was Gorm and Cuyler and the lord of the Serpent Court. The skinny young fae who'd pleaded for sanctuary with the Court of Blood so long ago had thickened to a man. A beard coated his face, and he was clearly respected by his forest folk.

Ari and Saga spoke with the Rave. I grinned. Many of the warriors leveled Saga with the respect of their personal royal. She was, after all, once their princess.

Odd to see the crossover. True, the royals addressed their own folk, but there were a great many who had started to behave like our army was one entity.

It was. For we were one, at long last; the people of the fae realms were one again. No jealousy pitted us against each other for having different abilities. No order of who held more power. We were one people, with different talents, different strengths, all of us were fighting for our freedom.

"Archers." Herja Ferus, donned in battle fatigues and leather straps for her bows and knives, stomped in front of the line of warriors. "We take the towers. We will be the ones defending the palace of Hus Rose. Not one damn sea fae gets through."

Gunnar Strom followed his mother. Playful and sly in most instances, Gunnar looked closer to a damn assassin. Donned in black from head to foot, his hair was covered in a black cowl, and on his neck was a black fabric that could be pulled over his mouth.

A thieving prince, born of Etta, but Kryv in his heart.

Beside them, Valen helped Elise fasten her sheath a little tighter to her belt. She secured the braids of his hair to ensure nothing fell in his eyes. Valen's father looked at me across the hall.

My pulse quickened as he approached.

Arvad Ferus looked a great deal like his sons, but for piercings in his ears, and a bit more scruff on his chin than Sol and Valen. "I was told the truth only this morning."

I swallowed thickly. "Disconcerting, isn't it?"

"You could say that." Arvad rested a hand on the hilt of his blade. "I remember the storyteller who guided my mother. I will never forget Greta. Which is the real you?"

"This." I gestured to my figure. "I have always been me, merely different faces in different times."

Arvad crossed his arms over his chest. "I never knew such power existed, but I am glad we had you on our side."

"I am glad for the same now."

The former king scanned the hall. Time was fleeting. Warriors were in their final leathers. Blades were secure. Soon, we'd stand at the gates.

"How is Lilianna?" I asked.

Arvad dragged a hand down his face, worry written in every line. "Sleeping. But all our cursed fell into a strange sleep when the kingdom shifted. Niklas says we wait to see if his elixir clears the dark glamour in her blood. I am told it takes time. I am told I will need to be patient. Anyone tells me that again, I might kill them."

I offered a look of sympathy. "I hope when she wakes, her world will once more be safe again."

I hoped we were all alive.

A horn echoed over the hall. Halvar stepped in front of the doors that would lead us to the gates.

"Four kingdoms have united this day to fight common enemies, but we have always been united. We all know the truth of our world. We all know what has brought us here. Alvers, Night Folk, blood fae, mortals, we all stand together to fight for our kingdom. One land. One people."

On the final word he raised his sword and the hall erupted into cheers and roars. From the isles of the South to the peaks of the North, folk raised their blades, ready to bleed, to die, for the freedom every bleeding soul deserved.

"Come with me for a moment." Silas took hold of my hand and ushered me to an alcove in a hallway that led to the staircase to the upper floors. From the narrow space, he removed a blade wrapped in fur. "I have saved this for you."

"What is it?"

"It was Annon's. He gave it to me before the king cast his curse, knowing what would happen. He wanted you to have it when you took your place in this fight."

The blade was made of fine bronze toned steel. Black, polished onyx lined the hilt and guard, and silver lined the edges. A stunning weapon. Not too heavy it would ache in my grip too soon, but made to strike, and strike hard. Behind it, Silas took out a short blade and blacksteel dagger.

"And those?"

He smirked. "These were mine."

"Ah, when you pretended to be a Rave."

"I was a Rave youth. Same thing."

I snorted and pecked his lips. "Not even close, Whisper."

Strapped with our weapons, we returned to the hall in time to witness warriors bidding farewell to their families who'd traveled with them, to the royals doing much the same with much more somber little faces than moments ago.

Mira cried into Saga's stomach, while she clung to Ari's hand, linking the three of them together. A few ladies from the blood court and serpent court were there to attend the little princess. Along with two watchers from Cuyler's men.

Gorm stood beside his son. They both dipped their heads when I approached.

"Gorm," I said. "You ought to know, Cuyler has done every irritating duty to impeccable standards. You ought to be proud."

Lord Gorm was not an expressive fae, but his mouth quirked in a small grin. "Then I shall be, My Lady."

"Also, I've demanded the use of My Lady be dropped from all languages."

"It is a title that came with the blood in your veins," Gorm said plainly. "Like your blood cannot be drained, a title of royal cannot be dropped unless you are ousted. I have no plans to oust you, so the title remains."

"Then as a royal, I alter the rule."

"You cannot declare a change to a rule, My Lady. It takes discussion and counsel, and I will once more remind you—the title is made by your blood. I have no intentions of draining your veins, so alas, the title remains."

"I've made it a rule, and it's done. Titles are finished."

Gorm sniffed around me, then shook his head. "Your blood has not changed. You remain, My Lady."

I rolled my eyes and looked to Cuyler. "I gave it a good try."

Silas followed close behind as we made our way to the others. Livia fought to keep her chin from quivering as Valen kissed her cheek and Elise pressed a kiss to the top of her head.

Sander was mid-promise to Kase and Malin that he would keep watch on the others and keep them away from windows. Jonas, the boy of mischief, was also one who felt a great deal. He'd turned away from his family, face pointed at the ground, greatly interested in the knife he kept spinning.

I held my breath when Silas paused, then turned to the boy. What was he doing?

Slowly, Silas knelt. "Boy."

Jonas lifted his bright eyes. "Wraith. That's what Daj calls you."

"You can call me that," said Silas. "You do not bid your mother and father farewell?"

Jonas's mouth pinched. He shook his head.

"Why?"

"Because."

My heart cinched at the subtle croak in his small voice.

"It's hard to say goodbye," Silas said, voice soft. Almost uncertain. It was as though, all at once, he realized he was speaking, and the discomfort of interacting with others was taking hold. "Sometimes it feels like there may not be another hello."

Jonas blinked rapidly, then slowly nodded.

By now, Kase and Malin were watching, listening. Malin pressed a hand to her heart. Kase's eyes were shadowed. The slippery Nightrender thought we hadn't figured out that meant he wanted to hide.

Silas held out the dagger he'd taken from the alcove. "This was given to me by a man I greatly respected when I was no bigger than you. He often left to fight battles, and he told me when he left, there would always be another hello. Even if it takes place in the Otherworld, he would be there waiting to say hello. No one who leaves through that door today will ever truly leave."

279

A tear dripped onto Jonas's cheek.

"Keep it." Silas handed the dagger to the boy and curled his small, dirty fingers around the hilt. "I'm placing you in charge of this place. I've lived here for centuries, and I think you'll like it."

"Why's that?" Jonas hugged the dagger to his body.

Silas's mouth flinched like he might smile. "There are plenty of places to hide and play tricks on others. I think if you inspect the music room on the upper levels, you might find ways to make folk think there are haunts chasing them."

A new kind of delight brightened Jonas's eyes. No mistake, a dozen ideas were already whirling through his head about how he could torment all the littles.

Silas rose from his knee. "I'll be back for that dagger."

"I'll keep it safe," Jonas promised. He ogled the blade with a touch of admiration, then looked back to Silas. "Why don't you show your face?"

"It was injured."

"Daj has lots of scars on his back, since he got rifted as a boy. That means his skin got all torn apart. You can show your face. We're not scared of scars. I've even got this one—" He jutted out his skinny wrist, complete with a white scar in the center. "Fell down the bleeding stairs, though, so it's not that great."

With care, Silas reached a hand to the back of the mask. He paused, unsettled. In truth, I did not think the mask was to hide the scar out of shame. More like the mask had become a safe place for Silas to merely hide.

He pulled it away and Jonas tilted his head to glance at the wound. The boy grinned. "That's pretty big. Bet it'll scare that stupid bit—"

"Jonas," Malin snapped, and Kase used a quick flick to his boy's ear.

His shoulders hiked up in surprise, as though he'd forgotten his family was behind him. "I mean that dark fae out there, I bet it'll scare him."

Silas gave a small smile, hardly there, but I took note of it anyway. Jonas turned into his mother and now clutched her waist in a tight embrace, the dagger still in hand. Kase studied Silas for a long, drawn pause. My Shadow King blinked, clearing away the inky pitch over his eyes, and held out an arm.

For a breath, Silas merely looked at his hand, then clasped Kase's forearm.

"Doesn't need to be said?" asked Kase.

"No."

"Well, I'd like to hear it," I said. "Go on, Shadow King, tell him that it means something in your secretly soft heart that he comforted your boy. Those were the most words I've ever heard Silas speak at once, so go on. Speak your weepy gratitude."

Kase smirked and released Silas's arm, eyes trained on me. All he gave me was a stern, "No."

He returned to his family, pulling his twins tightly against him for a final farewell.

Outside Hus Rose, a horn blew. Then another. Silas stiffened and clutched my hand. "The pyre is fading."

I closed my eyes. It was time.

Shouts echoed through the hall. Every ruler of the varying realms snapped their warriors into line with others. Those remaining behind in Hus Rose with the littles and injured began to gather their charges. A few wails from the children made me want to scream myself. Scream in rage at Davorin for all the pain he'd caused.

I clenched my teeth to muffle the sob in my throat as I watched young Aleksi be tugged away from Sol and Tor by a woman with gentle eyes. The boy was fighting damn hard not to cry, but the tears were there in his gilded eyes.

Only when the boy was out of sight did his fathers bend. Sol's shoulders curved. Tor gripped Sol's arm, as though he might keep him steady.

Sing the words.

I turned to Silas. "Did you say that?"

"I didn't say anything."

Sing the words? Like a strike to the back of my skull, the thought came. I fumbled into the pocket of the trousers, the same ones I'd worn after finding Silas again. When the parchment was in hand, I let out a squeal of relief.

"His song." I wheeled on Silas. "This was the song for Sol, remember? I said the words felt like they belonged to him. But I wrote them down because . . ." I lifted my gaze to him. "I hadn't yet accepted us. Danna said sing it in the right moment. I vowed I'd always protect him. Help me bring them back to their son."

I wanted to have songs for all my bleeding royals, but I could not discount there was some path twisting here. I'd felt it since I laid eyes on Sol and Tor, since I first received his worry-laden missive.

Silas stepped close and cupped a hand under my palm, holding the parchment with me. "You have the words, Little Rose."

I closed my eyes. Silas dropped his brow to mine. The words were soft, barely audible, and his voice was smooth. Deep, low, powerful.

"A song of blood keeps life for the one you love. Trust and let it be, in this, a tale of land and sea."

Before Silas, written tales created a tether between us. The flame sent the words to his voice. Now, together, the small parchment ignited in a black flame on its own. I startled but held firm and finished the tale. At the final word, Silas's gentle hum faded, and the last corner of the parchment turned to ash in our hands.

Seidr filled my veins. Something had been cast. Something had been done. I glanced over at my Sun Prince. He still looked to where his boy had been taken away, but I smiled.

Whatever happened, I had a feeling fate would be on his side.

"Pyre is gone!" Stieg shouted near the window.

My pulse quickened. I took hold of Silas's hand. I never was one to draw much attention to myself, but I turned into the hall and lifted my voice. "Now, let's go kill this bastard and his bones are scattered in every palace of this realm."

CHAPTER 36
THE PHANTOM

OUTSIDE THE AIR WAS DARK, DREARY. SMOKE BILLOWED FROM THE PYRE THAT was quickly fading in the crevice Valen Ferus had built. But smaller fires were lined on the edges of the sea fae camp. They'd claimed our shores, and now it would be up to us to shove them back to the sea.

Raven Row was vastly different than it had once been.

Tenements and grimy alehouses were now stone towers and walls, and the spindly trees that once surrounded the Row were full and plentiful. Knolls offered various terrain. We had little time to plan and plot how this battle would be won, but if we could but hold them off today, we could better know what we faced. What their weak points might be.

Warriors lined the gates, their shields raised with blades out.

The three eccentric rune seers danced behind Calista and the front line, as though wild cats ready to pounce. They were youthful now, their haggish appearances gone with the curse over our world, but they remained as irksome as ever, muttering nonsense that wasn't truly nonsense.

Trouble was, their words only made sense in the moments in which they were happening.

"This is the part where dreams descend."

Calista spun around. "Forbi, what did you say?"

Forbi tossed her long braid off her shoulder and dropped a few bone chips, burned with glowing runes on each side. "Let the dreams descend and find the end."

Danna spun around, chanting the same words in a sing-song tone, until she added. "Gifts of fate unite this day, used with purpose to end the pain."

The rune seers danced away, casting their spells alongside the casters of the forest clans in the Southern Isles. Added defenses. Small curses—a spell of stumbling feet, of disillusionment, of a constant bleed to the nose.

Simple pauses that could turn deadly if a fae stumbled enough.

"Silas." Calista took hold of my hand.

"I know." I kissed her knuckles. "A dream descends. There is a path to take here, we must simply find it, Little Rose." I faced her, one palm on her cheek. "We're not alone here. These words, these paths, I like to think they are the king, the queen, and the captain fighting this fight with us. I like to think they're guiding us."

She closed her eyes and leaned against my palm. "I think you're right. They're here with us."

Once we shoved our way to the front of the gates, I pointed my attention to the ships. The royal ship and its crimson sails were the most wretched. Dark laths and spiked edges. The various vessels beside it weren't much better.

"Flanks!" Valen shouted to his army. "Take the flanks! Try to trap them in the center."

If we could herd the sea folk toward the center of the Row, then Valen would split the earth beneath their feet.

It would be taxing for the king. It'd drain his fury, but we would follow with blades, with fear, with illusions.

"What sort of power do you think those slimy sea fae carry besides lust songs and thrashing tides?" Calista whispered.

"I don't know. I never learned a great deal about them. We only know the boy king has poisonous blood, yes?"

Calista winced. "That is what I'm told. Don't make him bleed."

I was not in the habit of making boys bleed, but should that boy king try to touch her—his blood, poisonous or not, would spill.

Maybe it would be wise to block the sea fae from the sea completely. Drag them into the pit of the earth, then pummel fire at their bleeding ships. How long could they last on land before the drier air caused the land sickness where their skin cracked and they grew weaker?

I gripped the bars of the gates, studying their movements. Already lines of sea fae were arranged in orderly units, much like us.

From the upper towers along the fortress edges, Gunnar Strom and his silent, cursed princess mother were seeing to it endless quivers and fresh arrows were available. The archers and the warriors along the walls on the inside of the palace grounds would be the final line between enemies and Hus Rose.

"Being that you were locked away as a boy, I feel it's within reason to ask if you handle a blade well enough?" Ari stepped beside me, his gaze ahead.

I cast a quick look at Calista. She fiddled with one of her knives, but I had few doubts she was listening.

"I can fight. You likely fight better. Don't let that rush to your head."

"It is there," said Ari. "Nestled and warm beside all my other astonishing attributes." His face sobered, and he gripped my shoulder. "Keep to your fight. You cannot let anything else distract you, or you could become a liability to others and yourself. You hear what I'm saying?"

Ari was not subtle. Nothing about the man worked in subtleties, and he tipped his head dramatically toward Calista.

That was a problem, one for which I had no solution.

"If she is in danger, I will not look at my fight. I will join hers."

Ari let out a long sigh. "It was worth a try. Can't say I blame you. None of us would do it differently either. Don't die, Wraith. You need to live long enough to become utterly enamored with me like all the rest."

I was not witty but planned to say some sort of offensive remark. All jests and taunts choked off when the final plume of pyre smoke

285

receded, as though the earth were drawing it back inside the crevice in an instant.

Blood burned through my veins. Through the fading clouds of ash and smoke, Davorin's pale, cruel grin met us. He'd lined his eyes in kohl, runes lined his lips and throat. He looked every bit the battle lord of my childhood, only more wretched, more like a creature than a man.

Sea fae split as one of their own, a man with long hair past his shoulders, rings pierced in his ears, and two horrid, curved blades in either hand, stepped through. At the sea fae's side was a lanky boy, tall enough he looked like he was caught between being a man and still a boy. His face was bruised, his lip crusted in old blood, and there was a slight tilt to his body. It was as if he were angling away from the man yet did not want anyone to take note.

He was not the boy king, but clearly another expected to fight in a man's war.

"You have bits and pieces of armies," Davorin's calm, dark voice lifted. "We have a kingdom here to stand against you. Lay down your blades and only a few will shed blood." He smirked, knowing damn well no one would set their swords aside at his request. This was his game: toy with his food, then strike as though he offered mercy and his victims refused. "The only blood for which I will take—the Golden King."

Ari scoffed but didn't take the taunt.

"And one of the seidr workers." Davorin's gaze fell on me. "Preferably the boy. I'd like to see if Riot Ode's daughter screams like her aunt."

Ari and Calista seemed to have the same thought and grabbed me in the same breath. Calista's hand on my arm, Ari's on my shoulder.

"Let him have his fun," Ari whispered. "Take out that anger in blood, Silas. Another wise battle lesson from me to you."

A response to Davorin came, harsh and furious. "Any other pointless demands, you bastard?"

I nearly laughed when I realized it was Elise Ferus who'd spoken. To Davorin, the Queen of Choice would be a mere mortal, a woman whose life was only extended by the mercy of the fae folk. She'd be a simple kill to him.

Truth be told, I thought he'd be quite wrong.

The flush to her cheeks gave up the rage in her heart. The swift way she spun a blade proved she'd been taught well. The fire in her eyes revealed the determination to slaughter on behalf of her people.

Davorin chuckled with condescension. "Yes, actually. Give me my little raven. It's been too long since I've tasted her."

I slammed my palm against Ari's chest when he made a move for the gate. "Let him have his fun, Golden King. Take out that anger in blood."

Ari's jaw pulsed, but he stilled, a murderous kind of look in his eyes.

"The Ever Kingdom stands against the earth realms." The sea fae beside Davorin shouted, a wicked sneer on his mouth. "In the name of the king, we have come to claim your land and—"

"We've no wish to hear you, Harald," Valen shouted. "We recall you well enough. If a king declares war on another kingdom, then let *that king* speak."

"I speak for the king of the Ever."

Davorin chuckled, as though the heated words were a bleeding thrill. His smile faded soon enough when a firm voice cut through.

"You do no such thing." The fae parted again.

"The boy king," I said, nudging Calista's ribs. She nodded, and blanched. "What is it?"

"Why is he important?"

I studied the boy as he trudged forward. Young as he was, his people moved aside, almost fearful.

In the new dawn, the boy had removed the hat. A black, silken scarf was tied over his head. Like Harald, the boy had gold rings pierced in his ears, but like me—there were scars written on his skin. One through his lip, more down his throat in cruel gashes of raised, pale flesh. He walked with a slight limp, but the way he clenched his fist, I suspected he fought hard not to.

"Erik." Stieg moved toward the front of the gates. "Do you remember me?"

The boy king halted. His eyes were like the red of the moon at night. They narrowed. "Warrior."

"There doesn't need to be war, Erik. There doesn't."

He chuckled. There wasn't anything friendly about it. With a quick breath the boy king opened his arms and raised his voice. "I am Erik Bloodsinger, King of the Ever. Unlike my uncle, I am not here for petty squabbles of earth fae."

"Boy, cease this talk," Harald spat. "We spoke before—"

"Do not address your king with such careless words, *Uncle*." Erik practically hissed at the man.

There was hatred between them. Hatred Davorin loved.

"Why are you here, King?" Valen asked, giving the boy a bit of respect.

Erik faced the Night Folk king, drew his sword, and aimed the point at him. "You. For the death of King Thorvald, I am here to challenge you for the power of the Ever."

"We came for the earth realms," Harald spat, trying to keep his voice low, but anger drove his tone loud enough the wind carried it.

Erik ignored him. "There is nothing I could ever want from the earth fae but the power you stole."

"I would give it back, should you wish to speak peacefully," Valen said.

"Give it back." Erik chuckled bitterly. "The mantle is bestowed by the blessing and curses of a sea witch. Such a thing cannot be *given* back when it was conquered. I've given you the honor of my warning, King. When we meet next, it will be with blades in hand."

"No, it won't," Calista whispered, then shook her head like she hadn't meant to say it.

A burn grew in the back of my throat. The sense of a dormant song. Whatever she was feeling was beginning to carve into my blood.

The Falkyn's wife, Junius, if I recalled her name, leaned into Valen. "He's speaking true. This war is not truly brought by him, but he wants revenge for Thorvald."

Valen sighed with a bit of disappointment. "As you say, Ever King."

"Willing to meet our demands?" Davorin stepped in front of Erik Bloodsinger.

The boy king shifted aside; he pinned a dark glare on the battle lord.

Valen stretched his palms. By his side, the Shadow King did the same, dark coils of night wrapped around his hands.

"Your demands are rejected." Valen answered for the lot of us.

In the next breath, the Night Folk king slammed his palms onto the cobbled walk, and the world bent and snapped.

The battle began.

CHAPTER 37
THE STORYTELLER

THE SEA FAE SCATTERED AS VALEN'S FURY CARVED THROUGH THE COBBLED roads of the fortress.

Davorin shouted a command, and a row of sea fae lined up along the shore. Like they were prepared for the earth bender to act, with a low, eerie hum the fae lifted their arms. The tides thrashed and rose in a fierce wall of water at their backs.

"Walls!" Halvar shouted in the same moment the sea fae tossed their arms forward and the crash of violent waves slammed onto the land. It filled the cracks of Valen's broken' earth. It offered new canals for sea singers to poke their heads from beneath the roads. Merfolk and their jagged teeth sneered from the narrow rivers of sea flowing through Raven Row.

Gentle songs from the singers called to our folk. A few staggered forward.

"Inge." Malin's thieving companion snatched hold of his wife's arm. "Stop."

His woman battled against him, pleading for relief. "Jakoby, don't you hear them? How beautiful." She moaned in a wave of pleasure.

"Kari." Halvar pointed a finger at his wife when she dropped her blade. "Kari, hold there."

Elise rushed to the woman, but even my Kind Heart was wincing against the lure of the song. I knew the damn feeling. Bleeding sea singers.

"Seal the ears from the tides!" Eryka shouted on the parapet wall beside Gunnar. Her eyes were a foggy white.

"Listen to the star seer!" I shouted back. "Use those plugs for your damn ears! Sirens and sea singers are among us, you sods!"

The trouble with plugging the ears deep enough to avoid the song of the sea was we had to pause. Blades had to be shifted. It gave the sea folk time to move forward. With a trembling roar, more sea fae rushed down the Row.

The bastards could practically walk on the water carving through the streets. They slammed into the shields of the front line of warriors. Sea singers kept their calls, and others brought their blades.

Steel collided. The slice of cutting blades against leather and flesh trembled through my chest. I jabbed at the belly of a man twice my size. He cut at my throat. I dodged, and when I righted again, Silas's blade had cut through half the man's neck until I could nearly see bone.

Davorin roared for more sea fae to take the watery canals, then bled into the soil between the cobbles. His dreary shadows overtook sea fae. The battle lord used their bodies to drift closer to Hus Rose. One by one he'd seize control, kill and brutalize our warriors, then slip into the next stupid sod.

Until he came up against my Shadow Queen.

Malin spun around, blade in hand, the glow of her ring bright on her finger. The sea fae chuckled darkly. Davorin's voice bled from his throat. "A queen of devotion."

"Malin!" I cried her name when Davorin swung a blade at her.

She was quick on her feet. From somewhere in the fighting, Kase called for his wife. Shadows coiled around sea fae, ripping them away. Still, he was too far.

Malin swung her blade, catching the sea fae in the chest. The moment the point broke the flesh, Davorin spilled from the fae's mouth and finished the bastard off with a slice to the sea fae's throat.

With a violent kick, Davorin shoved the body away. Over his shoulder, I caught sight of the narrowed eyes of the boy king. For a pause in his own fighting, the sea king took in the dead fae at the feet of the battle lord, then lifted his hatred toward the back of Davorin's head.

His lip curled, then Erik Bloodsinger dove back into the fighting.

Malin's blade slashed against Davorin's. He laughed, delighted. The battle lord struck, she parried. He kicked at her leg, Malin cut at his throat.

A promise was made long ago to a dying memory queen. I vowed her line would live on, I vowed her sacrifice would be worth the pain and loss. I revealed the faces of Malin Strom and Kase Eriksson.

They brought her peace.

I wasn't about to break that promise now.

I dodged a strike and tried to get closer to Malin.

"Little Rose." Silas cursed and shoved me aside when another of the young sea fae appeared from the edge of a canal. A boy who'd been nothing but mist before, all at once, was there, knife in hand. As though he'd materialized from droplets in the damn air.

He had smooth, dark skin, ferocious, stormy eyes, but the boy looked wholly terrified. Like he was attempting to find someone else and found me instead.

He jabbed his blade, and only then did I take note of the way one arm hung limp at his side, the way his body was battered. Did his sea magic tear him apart when he turned to bleeding mist?

Silas lifted his sword, the fae boy flinched.

I did not revel in the thought of killing young fighters who, no doubt, were forced to be here. It seemed, nor did Silas.

"Leave here, boy. Live another day and remember who let you go." Silas shoved the boy into one of the deep canals before he could swing a blade, then gripped me under the elbow. Silas didn't try to stop me from racing toward Davorin, he merely joined me.

By my side. As he'd always been.

Davorin had a hold of a curved blade from the sea and cut at

Malin's neck, only this time she stumbled backward. With one knee, Davorin pinned her down. "I wonder what will happen when one gift is wiped away?"

"No!" I cried out. "Malin you are a queen of fate. Your tale is here. It's here."

I closed my eyes, the hum of power bled in my blood.

"You have the words, Little Rose." Silas's soft voice was there.

I clung to him. Somewhere amidst the chaos, the bastard of a battle lord called for our necks. What was happening, I didn't know, all I knew was my blood was on fire. I knew Silas was near.

I knew a promise needed to be kept.

"Shadow Queen!" I called, eyes clenched shut. "The beacon of a crown beckons you through. Step from darkness and take back what has always belonged to you!"

Words said before. Words I'd promised during a different time, a different battle. They were a reminder of what games had brought us here. Silas's deep, soothing voice blended with mine until the heat of our heart song coiled like mists of gold.

A few sea fae gasped. Some backed away.

Others were entranced enough to approach, possibly to kill us. They could try. I felt as though I might be able to melt their bleeding brains should they dare touch me. When I opened my eyes, Davorin looked at me with hateful resentment, then lifted his blade over Malin again.

Only now, she was grinning. The ring burned like a golden flame on her finger. Even her golden-green eyes were alight in something new. She ripped a blacksteel knife from her boot and tried to slash the point across Davorin's leg.

The blade didn't seem to do a bit of damage to his flesh, but it startled him enough he shifted to one side, giving Malin room to kick him off.

She spun the blade in her grip and rose to her feet. "You thought you could pin me down and he'd sit back and let you?" What Davorin hadn't noticed was the coiling darkness around their ankles. Malin sneered. "Then you do not know true *devotion*."

The sea fae shuddered around her. Some collapsed in screams

and fits. I grinned. Their nightmares were attacking their damn minds.

More shadows surrounded Davorin and Malin, growing taller. Thicker. Until Malin held out a hand. From the shadow wall, Kase emerged with Kryv, with Ettan warriors, with Niklas, a handful of his Falkyns, and their crooked blades.

Kase tilted his head. His sword rolled in his grip as he looked at Davorin. "You're afraid your wards won't hold?"

Wards? What wards?

Kase's eyes flicked to Davorin's skin. Barely visible beneath his tunic were inked symbols. All hells, did he have some kind of protection against him?

If he did or not, that didn't bother Kase and Malin.

"Shall we find out if they do?" The Nightrender locked his fingers with his wife. Together their power was fierce. The magic of that cursed ring combined with his wretched gift of fear and darkness billowed like a dark wave over the battlefield.

The stun was delicious to behold.

I laughed with a new kind of cruelty as Kase's wave of nightmares rose higher and higher.

Davorin let out a roar of frustration and dissolved his murky body into the soil at the same moment Kase and Malin flung their arms out and pulsed the darkness against the sea folk.

In a sickening crunch of bone, countless sea singers, merfolk, and battle fae twisted in unnatural angles.

They tumbled to the ground, convulsing.

Those whose fear of death hadn't taken their lives screamed as the fiery gold of Malin's mesmer dug into their eyes, their ears, their noses. They shuddered and pleaded for it to cease. Still holding tightly to Kase, Malin balled a fist, and dozens of brilliant webs of her mesmer crawled back to the glow of the ring.

The sea fae fell. Most with horrified expressions and a look of stun in their glassy eyes.

Doubtless, she'd robbed them of the memories to even know their own names.

In the next breath, Falkyns and warriors took those trembling fae to the Otherworld with swift swipes of knives and swords and a few curious looking powders. Niklas took a great deal of pleasure in painful deaths.

"He's unnerving," Silas muttered, watching the Falkyn lead laugh as he dusted a sea fae's mouth with an elixir that seemed to thicken until the poor bastard suffocated on his own tongue.

"He is." A grin split over my mouth. "We need to remember the gifts, Silas. That is how we fight this battle—everyone must remember their gifts."

He offered me a poignant look, then nodded. "Those words matter. Keep those words, Little Rose."

CHAPTER 38
THE PHANTOM

THE ARCHERS RAINED ARROWS AGAINST A THRONG OF SEA FAE WHO'D managed to strike at the gates of Hus Rose. They'd taken the rivers and streams in the forest and emerged on our side of the battle.

Herja Ferus shouted her commands from above. Her consort stood with their daughter, a unit of Ettan warriors, and a few of the Nightrender's Kryv guarding the entrance. With his arms open, the brother of the Shadow Queen opened his arms wide. Hagen Strom, as I understood it, was a type of shield with his magic. So was the woman on his opposite side, a silent Kryv who held back the forces of the sea singer voices, the flinging waves the folk kept using to break in.

"Speak clearly, my love," Eryka said, a little curl to her mouth when Gunnar took a place beside his mother on the parapet.

The thieving prince tugged down the mask covering his face. "You wish to fall on your blades. The lot of you."

A mere boy when these battles began, now Gunnar Strom was a man, vowed, and stronger with his dark mesmer. I'd seen it change and shift through glimpses of my connection to these fated battles.

He was a little horrifying. Hardly any of the sea fae arched a brow as they took a knife, a dagger, one even gathered a shard of glass from one of the windows, and rammed the points through their flesh. Eyes, throats, bellies, it didn't matter, their minds belonged to the prince, and he took it without a flinch.

I raised my sword, embracing the heat and energy of the armies at my back.

Archers shouted from the towers as sea fae began to retreat. More fiery arrows arched across the sky. Deep in the trees, to either flank, warriors shouted as the pyre roared below, the flames reaching for the silver moon like a beacon leading us forward.

The flood of our armies shuddered across the damp soil. Sea fae were no simple foe. They filled the canals, the edges of Raven Row. For folk of the tides, they knew how to hold a blade well enough.

I kept catching sight of the boy king. With all his venom laced toward Valen, the Ever King kept his distance from the earth bender.

Then again, there was something there. As though another force kept them parted. Something unseen.

"I sense it too," Calista said through a grunt as she rammed the point of her knife through a spindly fae with mossy hair. She kicked his body into the canal, watching a bloom of dark blood spill out over the surface. She nodded toward the Ever King. "There is a time and place. That's what I keep thinking. Paths are soon to cross, and I don't understand it."

"We never do." I dropped my sword against a sea singer. Without the trance of his voice, his horrid face was carved in threads of rotting flesh and sunken cheeks and bloodied eyes. He stumbled under my sword and fell beside one of the water-filled crevices.

Like the waves sensed the loss of one of their own, a white-capped curl rose and devoured the dead sea singer into the depths.

Another wave of burning arrows assaulted the towers of the fortress along the edges of Hus Rose. Screams mingled with bodies falling from walls they'd been attempting to scale. The collision of steel and blood burned between two sides.

My sword struck a fae's short blade. The man had ghastly deadened eyes, as though no color could find them. A shard of bone pierced his nose, and his teeth were shaved to resemble the merfolk with their jagged mouths.

Our blades locked, spun, and dodged until I sliced the back of his leg. At my back, another came. And another.

Focus forward. Ari's words reeled through my brain while I kept Calista in my sights. We were tossed into a cruel existence as children, but through the lifetimes, we'd managed to gain a bit of know-how when it came to the sword.

She preferred knives; they fit her smaller figure, but she managed Annon's old sword well. Her cuts and stabs went to ribs, to thighs, the back tendons of the knees.

I fought without the same skill as the royals and warriors, but in a matter of moments, my face was splattered in hot, sticky blood, and my muscles throbbed for more.

Ari fought nearby. Sea folk dropped to his feet screaming in terror. His fury molded their brains in illusion and left them defenseless. Saga stepped behind her husband and called the roots and branches from the trees and wood nearby.

This land, by all accounts, was the land of her birth. It would respond to her glamour the same as the isles.

When the fae were entrapped, Stieg and Lynx—one of the Nightrender's Kryv who could force folk into a slumbering calm—moved in to slit their throats from behind. Halvar and Tor—they used blade first. Wise. Too much exertion on mystical killings and we'd exhaust our magicks before it was over.

Davorin and Harald pressed the army of sea folk forward. Davorin was a bleeding fool, but he was wretchedly skilled with the blade. The battle lord brutally took the heads, the throats, the hearts of warriors. His frustration curled over his lip whenever he tried to overtake them with his dark glamour and Niklas's protections held.

"Take them." Harald's voice roared over the fighting.

I shuddered. A line of horridly lovely women stepped forward. Skin smooth as satin, lips painted in blood red, and eyes like precious stones and metals. Some silver, some glistening emerald, others like a sapphire sea.

They clasped their hands. Their voices were sweet and sharp, but as the sound spread, warriors, a few Falkyns, and forest fae choked up blood.

"They're cursing them!"

I didn't know who shouted it, but they weren't wrong. The women were clearly spell casters of the sea. Their damn sea witches.

"Shut them up!"

I thought that command came from Ari. From the edges of the fight, a cluster of huldrafolk approached the sea witches. Huldra were seductive and could pull out lust as viciously as sirens and their male sea singer counterparts.

Cuyler, his men, and the tracker of Ari and Saga's court joined. Overhead, a winged blood fae swooped down. He clutched a sea witch's face between his palms. She hissed and thrashed, trying to curse him, but soon her skin brightened. It cracked and split. Where soft flesh had been, now her face hardened into clay stone.

"Rune!" The tracker whooped and rushed to his side. He kissed him fiercely, then together they attacked with Cuyler and his men at their backs.

I dodged a lazy strike from the bruised boy who'd stood beside Harald at the gates. He had the same reddish tint to his gaze like most sea fae, his hair was tied off his neck, and like the king, the boy kept a red, silken scarf tied over his head.

When I faced him entirely, he jolted at first, eyes on the scar on my face.

"Want to know how I earned this scar, boy?" I took an assertive step closer. "That dark fae your folk follow gave it to me when I was younger than you. When two children defeated him." The boy blocked my weak strike, but there was a new fear in his eyes. "Go home. Don't fight for him. He is weak."

"I don't fight for him." The boy slashed his blade again. "I fight for my king."

"Your king?" I chuckled. "He does not even fight for the same reason. He seeks the earth bender."

"And I seek to keep him alive."

Odd. There was hidden affection between the young king and the boy. A boy who shared characteristics to his king. To the king's uncle.

I took hold of the boy's tunic. He writhed and tried to lash at me, but his lanky body stood no chance. I drew his face close and the sea fae boy froze. "He's your blood?"

The boy didn't answer. The young king did.

"Tait, you damn fool." Erik Bloodsinger pressed a palm near one of the canals. "Drop him, earth fae!"

Young, but the water grew violent under his touch. The sea king cursed me, glared at me, and tried to throw me off balance with a rush of waves.

I merely grinned and faced who I assumed was Harald's son, the king's cousin. "Go home. You have a fate to face, boy. It radiates from you, but you cannot face the path the Norns have devised for you if you are dead. Nor can he."

I tilted my head toward the Ever King. Young heart songs lived here. Hard to differentiate to whom they belonged, but my seidr screamed in heat and the urge to form a song around the sea folk.

This war would end long-fought battles, no mistake, but I wondered if the end of one tale would open new ones.

I dropped the young sea fae into one of the canals. He never surfaced. With a bit of hope, I prayed that he took his young ass far from here.

New rushes of sea fae emerged from crevices. Sea singers, witches, men with blades and the voice to harness the waves. Valen and Sol fought near the edges. Without a word, the brothers fell into a violent rhythm.

Valen pressed his palms to the soil. His fury would be weakened from breaking the Row, but it still had power. He crumbled the banks of the crevice, smashing the sides closer together. Sea fae scrambled to be rid of the shifting edges, desperate to avoid getting crushed.

But when they emerged from the water, Sol held out his palms. Dark, sticky fury spilled off his hands and dug into the soil beneath their feet. Blackened veins coiled around the sea fae, poisoning them from the bottom up until they thrashed and choked on spittle.

Use our gifts. I sliced my sword against a fae trying to flee. He fell at my feet.

Calista was near Tor and Elise. Safe. Alive. Bleeding stunning how she struck and killed.

Smug grins faded from the faces of the sea fae. Now, they simply looked terrified as they fought for their lives.

"*Slaughter* them," Davorin roared.

For some, a new energy latched onto the sea fae. They dug their swords deeper, fought with a wretched anger, and slashed their blades into the fray without mercy. Across the Row, I caught the gaze of the battle lord. His lip curled. He'd been aiming for Saga, but Ari's illusions locked the bastard in a wretched confusion that kept him altering course.

Soon enough the Golden King would fatigue. The Raven Queen would not be able to hold her strength against the bastard.

Davorin cut his blade through spines—earth folk and sea folk alike—and made his way toward me. Toward Calista. He wanted our throats, perhaps our power. He'd want us to turn this war in his favor.

Our gifts. Use our gifts.

"Don't forget the part where the dream descends."

I spun around. One of the seer sisters, Oviss, flashed an eerie smile, saying nothing more before she bolted away. I had no time to think long on the notion before Davorin shouted angrily. His dark glamour spilled over the canals of water, darkening the tides.

These turns he'd been hidden beneath the sea, no mistake, he found a way to take on pieces of their abilities.

In frustration, he flung the water at a row of Rave warriors. Cuyler was among them. The tracker and his lover. Even some of the forest folk from the isles.

Davorin faded. Like a drop of ink, he slipped from his fae form and bled into the wild currents, wrapping the tides around the warriors in a dark, watery cocoon. All hells, he'd devour them soon enough.

With a fierce jab of my sword into a dark streak, the wall of water faded. Our warriors fell over. Some in puddles of blood.

"Blood fae!" My heart quickened. Cuyler wasn't moving. He was Calista's friend. He'd protected her. "Blood fae, get up."

He didn't budge. Nor did one of the fae from the Court of Serpents.

"Rune!" the tracker shouted and scrambled to the winged fae.

I didn't have time to see the outcome before pools of black tides spun wildly and shaped legs and shoulders until Davorin returned, ready to strike. His blade crashed on mine. I spun and cut at his ribs.

He drew his sword against me, I met the edge and blocked the strike. Faces close, Davorin hissed, "You think you stand a chance? Don't forget who marred you, boy."

"Don't forget who made you nothing but mist, you bastard." I pressed my brow to his. "Two children. Some battle lord you are."

He grunted in frustration and kicked me away. Davorin held no mercy and flung his blade against mine, over and over, no reprieve. All I could do was mark his strikes and try to block.

"Silas!" Calista screamed my name when I fumbled backward.

Tor released a blast of pyre beside her, trying to keep a new swell of sea fae back, and as a signal to Herja and Gunnar above. The archers readjusted their arrows to the center of the Row. They aimed at Davorin.

The battle lord dodged a fiery point, but a second arrow pierced his shoulder. Or, at least, it should've. The point seemed to peel out of his flesh.

What the hells?

Davorin's grin was wolfish and cruel as he tossed the arrow aside. "You cannot touch me, boy. Give yourself up, and this battle ends."

I took a step back, avoiding the swift strike of his sword, but the point caught the side of my ribs. A flash of pain burned through my side. Instinct to flee from the pain took hold. It was how I survived whenever Calista died. A way to flee from the heartache and anguish was to let my mind slip into shadows. Here, in the middle of a damn battlefield, I wanted to slip away. To escape the burn of his strikes.

I gritted my teeth, blocked a second strike, but stumbled to my knees.

Davorin raised his blade again.

"Do you know what it's like," I murmured as the peace of darkness threatened to drag me under. *Stay. Focus.*

"Silas! Lift your sword. *Your sword!*"

Somewhere in the haze her voice was there, calling to me. Calista Ode. My first friend. My princess. My heart song.

I blinked. *Stay. Stay with her.*

"Silas!"

I snapped my eyes open as Davorin swung a deep strike. My blade met his. The blow knocked me back; it pressed the edge of my own sword against my chest as he reared over me. With both hands, he shoved against his hilt, trying to dig the edge of my sword into my flesh. His body weight, his strength, left my arms trembling.

"I'll drain her of her blood," he hissed close to my face. "Just to make absolute certain every drop of Riot's bloodline is gone. I'll do it slowly, until she pleads for death."

These were no weak threats. Davorin was not a man who killed quickly, he was not a man who let those who wronged him die an honorable death. Should he gain the upper hand, he'd take Calista. Lock her away, drain her of her life. He'd slaughter Ari, claim his daughter and the Raven Queen.

He'd say he would forgive the fae folk of the other realms, but the Alvers, the Night Folk, they'd be left to rot as slaves of his new sea fae, no mistake.

"You won't be able to alter her fate in the Otherworld, boy." His teeth gleamed in a sneer.

An eerie hiss fell over the Row, followed by the shrieks of sea fae. A bit chaotic, but voices rose over the battle in fierce panic.

"King's blood."

"Been wounded."

"Move, *move, you wretches.*"

Their cries and shouts added to the chaos nearby. A few fleeing sea folk stumbled, knocking against Davorin.

"Fools," he spat and lost his hold on the sword against me. I shoved back, rolling away, and scrambled to my feet. Behind me, the genesis of the commotion was clearly surrounding the boy king.

Erik Bloodsinger wore a vicious smirk, but kept a hand pressed to his side, clutching a gash on his ribs.

Poisonous blood.

His own people fled from him rather than help him. Then again, he didn't seem surprised. The boy trained his gaze on me, a narrowed expression written on his face. Hand pressed to his ribs, Erik faded into the alleyways of the fortress, never looking away. As if he wanted me to see him. As if he were telling me to get off my ass and take back my chance in this fight.

Bleeding gods, had he cut himself on . . . purpose?

Davorin hissed and cursed as sea fae fled to avoid their own king. I didn't understand how his blood worked. If they touched it, was it fatal? Did they need to ingest it?

However it killed, the sea folk feared it. And their fear kept the battle lord distracted long enough for me to ready my stance and my sword.

But my blood chilled at Calista's voice. "Tor! Tor behind you. No!"

She screamed near the edges of Raven Row. Sea fae were rushing toward the shoreline, but from one of the broken canals Harald emerged, eyes on Calista and the pyre fae casting defenses around her.

Torsten had his back turned. Harald raised his blade.

I gained a single, worthless step by the time the bastard rammed his sword through Tor's spine. Like a coward, he struck from behind and forced the tip of his curved sword through the front of Tor's chest.

"No!" Calista screamed.

"*Tor.*" Sol's pained bellow soaked into the Row. The Sun Prince was locked in a horrified stun as Harald pulled back his blade. Tor stumbled to his knees, blood dripping from his chest and back.

Harald grinned, as though he knew he'd destroyed someone of note, then fell back into the blood-darkened tides of the canal and out of sight.

I quickened my pace until I dropped down at Calista's side. She draped herself over Tor, sobbing. I helped her roll him onto his back.

"No." Her voice broke. "I sang your song. Stay with him, Tor. Look at me."

She clasped his cheeks in her hand. Blood dripped over his lips when he coughed. His eyes were hazy and unfocused, he looked around, as though searching for someone. Searching for Sol.

Sea fae were descending again. Regrouping from their fear of the king's blood. We'd be struck, killed. I had to move her, but Calista clung to Tor, desperate to keep his eyes open.

Calista cried out in anger, fear; a bit of despair.

"I sang your song!"

At her final word, the ground shuddered violently. I braced with my palms. Then, much the same as the night the world shifted to the first land, a golden strand of light encircled her. It rippled out like the pulse of a heart.

The strand of light shoved back the sea fae, a gilded ward much like the Rave had created at her command. It shielded Hus Rose against its enemies. It shielded Raven Row. The pulse of Calista's power covered us, our wounded, our dying, from the enemies.

We had time. We had a chance.

Sol skidded beside Torsten. "Tor! Tor, look at me."

He took his consort's hand.

The flicker of a smile crossed Tor's bloody lips. "Sol."

"I'm right here." Sol pressed Tor's knuckles to his lips. "You stay with me. Nik . . . Tova, they can . . . they can heal you."

Sols' gaze fell to the blood soaking Tor's tunic.

"Sol." Tor coughed. "Tell Alek . . . tell him I love him."

"No." Sol shook his head violently. "We promised him a hunt in the peaks. Don't break those promises, Tor. Don't you dare."

The Sun Prince tightened his hold on Tor's hand.

"I love you," Tor whispered. "Always . . . always have. I'll save . . . I'll save your seat, Sol Ferus."

"Tor." Sol's voice broke when Tor's eyes fluttered close. "Torsten."

He shook his consort's shoulders. Tor's chest rose in fading breaths.

"Niklas!" Sol shouted in a rough cry of anguish. "He needs . . . *save* him."

It wasn't long before Night Folk fae, before Valen and Ari and Sol's father were there, lifting Torsten's limp form off the Row, shouting chaotic words, and taking him into the trees on the edges of the fortress.

The gleam of Calista's ward burned bright, giving time for others to collect the wounded. The fallen.

"I sang his song," Calista whispered, tears in her eyes. "This doesn't make sense. I sang the song, but he's . . . he's gone, Silas. You saw that wound. It's . . . too deep."

I knew death. I'd witnessed Calista's over and over again for centuries. My stomach burned in sick, in an ache for folk I hardly knew, yet felt as though I'd always known. Whether it was the entanglement of our fates or as the silent voice in the shadows as they became Calista's new family, I didn't know.

But I knew them.

And in my mind—we'd just lost one.

CHAPTER 39
THE STORYTELLER

THIS COULDN'T BE HAPPENING. I DIDN'T UNDERSTAND. THE SONG HAD burned in my soul, so this *shouldn't* be happening.

"Calista," Silas's haggard voice followed as we raced into the trees where folk were taking the wounded, the broken. Where they took Tor.

"I need to get to him."

Two clearings were already filled with fae, running about trying to tend to those we'd been able to drag behind the wards and barriers.

Warriors stood watch in the trees. The injured we were able to reach were laid out between them. Tova set to work along with Niklas and Elixist Falkyns. She was one of the few Mediski Alvers who knew how to heal the body, at least well enough to keep most folk breathing.

The Norn sisters aided with their hums of rune spells to cast away pain and blood.

I wanted to vomit at the sight of Gorm pacing near Cuyler's head. Blood coated my Blood Fae's—my friend's—face. I could hardly make his features out beneath the gore.

A compress made of healing oils and blue moss was wadded into a clump by Tova. "Hold it; stop the bleeding."

"His eye?" Perhaps for the first time, I heard the blood lord's voice waver.

Tova shook her head. "I don't know. You speak in absolutes, Lord Gorm, so I'll be frank—stop the bleeding, or he's gone."

Gorm's pale eyes shadowed. He took the moss and knelt by his son. Soft whispers, words not meant for us, came from the blood lord to his warrior son.

Next to them, Hagen Strom gripped his brother's shoulder as Tova fought her own tears and stitched up a festering gash on Bard Strom's throat. Deep and dangerous should it bleed much longer.

I blinked through the tears and kept running toward the center clearing.

In the corner of my gaze, the dead were laid out and tended to by Raum, Isak, my Shadow Queen's thieving friend, and his wife.

Pain was hot and cruel and carved through my chest as I took in the fallen. Magus of the Court of Serpents stared blankly at the tree-tops, his spell-caster mother's body at his side. The eldest serpent sister dropped to her knees, her bloody blade across her lap.

The woman's big, owlish eyes were soaked in silent tears as her folk crossed both Magus's and Yarrow's hands over their chests, daggers in their lifeless grips. The woman placed a kiss to each of their heads.

I kept running.

Ettan warriors with their thorns and roses embossed on their gambesons were laid out. Falkyns and huldra and blood fae. So many of our people.

A cruel fissure snapped through my chest at the sight of the once-cursed tracker from the South. Bo sobbed against the unmoving chest of Rune—the winged fae who'd befriended Saga and my Golden King.

They'd taken so long to love each other after the battles in the South. Now, their time was stolen too soon.

A tear fell onto my cheek. No more. No more *hjärtas* would be lost.

I forced my gaze ahead and ran for the crowd in the center of the trees. Where was he?

The gleam of the wards near the shore were still bright. How long we'd be separated from the sea fae, from Davorin, I didn't know. I couldn't think. I could hardly breathe.

My skin was on fire. Unseen flames licked down my arms to my fingertips where the lingering burn of seidr faded. I ignored the bite of pain and sprinted toward the crowd, the anguished cries in the center of the clearing.

"Stop the bleeding," Sol shouted, his voice thick with agony. "Tor, stay awake. You look at me."

My Lump was hunched over his consort, one hand behind his neck. Elise, Arvad, and Valen had their hands on Tor, trying to stop the wretched fountain of blood bubbling through the wound in his chest.

"Tor," Sol's voice cracked. He pressed his forehead to his lover's brow. "Stay here. Alek needs you. I need you. *Please*, dammit, open your eyes."

Sol buried his face into the crook of Tor's neck, cradling his consort's head. Tor's chest was barely moving, and every breath he did take rattled in wet blood. Bile burned my throat—the Other-world was opening its gates.

Everyone else knew it.

Ari's face was hard as stone. He clung to Saga's hand without mercy, and looked nowhere but Torsten Bror's unmoving, bloody body. Kase's eyes were black as midnight. Malin and Herja tried to help in stopping the bleeding, taking Elise's place when my Kind Heart would hurry away, sobbing without trying to stop it, and snatch up more moss, more stained linens.

Halvar lowered to one knee beside Tor's legs and gripped his friend's ankle, like he wanted to be there as he stepped into the hall of the gods. Kari kept a hold on her husband's shoulder. She didn't speak a word, but what she knew would happen was written in every furrow of her face.

Valen cursed. His own desperation was bleeding through. Tor was his Shade, his brother, his family.

Sol pled—gods, he was damn near exhausting his voice with his pleas—for Tor to open his eyes, to wake up.

A strong hand took hold of my palm. Silas, face dirt-soaked and bloody, pulled me into his chest.

In his arms, I broke. "We sang the damn song." I pounded his chest, shoulders shuddering. "His song was there. He was . . . he was supposed to be safe. You saw it. Seidr wrapped around us, and protected us, and . . ."

"I don't know, Little Rose," Silas whispered into my hair. "I don't understand it. I felt the same."

Gods, I hated the Norns. I hated them. I wanted them to burn in all three hells. How could they—how could they rip my Sun Prince's heart again? How could they rob a boy of a father who'd suffered so much to find his love? A father who'd never hesitated to take in an infant fae who'd have been left to the wilds of a battle torn world?

I hated them.

The burn of my blood, of my cursed magic, felt as though it might split through my skin and devour the world in one breath.

I'd welcome it if it took away this pain.

"Tor?" Sol's voice was clear. He paused. Slowly, I turned to look. All gods. Sol pressed a hand over Tor's chest. He looked to his face again, fear written in every despondent crease. "Tor. No, keep breathing, gods, keep breathing."

"Son," Arvad said, gently trying to take Sol away.

The Sun Prince swatted at his own father and held Tor's face, pressing desperate kisses to his cheek. "Please, keep breathing. He's breathing, right?" Sol lifted his wet eyes to his brother.

Valen sat back on his heels, sweaty and broken. "Pulse is there, but—"

"Then he's alive," Sol shouted. "Don't stop. Why are you stopping? Where is Niklas?"

"Sol," Niklas's voice came from the edge of the clearing, he was mixing pungent herbs vigorously. "I . . . I can bring comfort. I can't bring back the beat of a heart."

The Sun Prince was slipping into desperation and held his trembling hands over Tor's chest. Elise kept a steady hand on the wounds, as did Malin. Valen joined, though he wore a despondent expression.

I hated myself, but turned away, unable to watch the final moments.

Stieg, Frey, and his brother Axel were some of the warriors standing guard. All the men kept their heads down. Stieg faced the trees. One of Valen's Shade himself, Torsten Bror was a brother much like he was to many of us.

This shouldn't be happening.

I hugged my middle and fell to my knees. Why them? Why did it have to be *them*?

"He mean something to you, Warrior?"

Stieg let out a shaky gasp, sword raised, but his stun was pointed at the trees overhead.

Silas stepped in front of me protectively and watched as branches rustled. I rose back to my feet, looking over Silas's shoulder as someone climbed over the thick oak branches.

All hells.

The boy king and his crimson eyes peered out of the leaves.

I drew a knife. The wards must've slipped. I would not let these sea fae bastards take this moment from Lump. He deserved peace as he bid farewell. He deserved so much more than this.

"Leave, Erik," Stieg said. "We looked out for each other once, remember? I'm asking you as that fellow prisoner to leave this be."

The sea king tilted his head and flicked his gaze to the scene in the center of the clearing. "His heart still beating?"

Stieg hesitated. "I don't know."

Erik Bloodsinger was a tall boy, slender and lithe, but still a boy. I doubted he could grow a whisker on his chin yet. But there was a captivating, sinister aura about the sea king—one that was breaking into something like reluctant compassion.

"Does he mean something to you?" he asked again.

Steig glanced at Frey, then back to the boy. "Yes. He is like a brother to me. A close friend."

The warriors took a step back when the sea fae king slid from the low hanging branch. When he landed, he winced, and rubbed his left thigh. Silas took hold of my arm, but I wasn't afraid. Not anymore.

"Do you feel it?" I whispered, patting Silas's arm.

He hesitated, then nodded. "There is a tale here." Silas glanced at the Ever King. "Weren't you wounded?"

"Don't know what you mean." Erik didn't look at Silas, he rested a hand on the hilt of his curved sword and kept his focus on Stieg. "I'm in your debt for saving me a time or two, so I'll do it to repay you."

Stieg arched a brow. "Do what?"

"What do you think?" Without another word Erik lifted a hand to his mouth and scraped the meat of his thumb across the sharp, slightly elongated point of his canine tooth until a trickle of blood coated his skin.

Stieg's mouth parted. "Bleeding gods, you'd do this?"

"What are you talking about?" I snapped.

Steig took a step—a feckless step—toward the poisonous sea fae. "Erik can kill with his blood, but remember what I said, he heals too. You'd sing, boy?"

"If it squares us."

"Why should I trust it when you fight with our enemies?"

"I made my reasons for being here clear," said Erik. "If he is dying anyway, what does it matter?"

"Will you sing?" Stieg pressed sharply.

Erik's scar through his lip went taut against his smirk. "Aye. I'll sing. But it squares our debts."

Like a hand struck my chest, I let out a gasp. My fingernails dug into Silas's arm. "A song of blood. A song of blood, Silas."

Silas narrowed his eyes at the fae boy. "Bloodsinger."

The Ever King glared at us and took a step behind Stieg toward the clearing.

"A song of blood keeps life." I couldn't finish the thought, my words were too breathless, too damn hopeful.

Hand tangled with Silas's, we followed close behind as Stieg led the sea fae toward Torsten.

Nearly there, Erik paused. His shoulders rose in sharp breaths. "I won't do it near him."

Erik pointed at Valen. The Night Folk king looked weary, lost, but he had enough thought to draw a blade and stand. By now, others had noticed an enemy had descended into our death camp. Not just anyone—the damn sea king.

"Stieg?" Kase said, a deep growl to his voice. "What is this?"

Stieg blew out a breath. "The Ever King has offered his healing blood to Torsten."

"Lies." Ari snapped. "There is no reason a minion of Davorin would do such a thing. Little bastard's probably possessed by him right now."

Erik narrowed his eyes but said nothing.

"He's not." Junius, haggard, sweaty, bloody, and locked in wretched despair at the sight of Tor, emerged from the trees. She stood beside Niklas, who still fought to mix his herbs, but didn't look at the Ever King. "I wanted to see him…but…the boy king is not lying. He is here to heal."

Ari's face softened. He looked to Saga, almost hopeful.

"He has reason," Stieg insisted. "Payment for protection I offered during the Eastern battles of the Black Palace."

"Won't do it with him near," Erik seethed again. He closed his eyes as if battling some internal thoughts that were vicious and cruel. "Get him gone, or I challenge him, and your like-a-brother dies. Your choice, Warrior."

"We sang the song, Cursed King," I said gently. "Before the fighting, there was a song for Lump. I sang it. A song of blood brings life for the one you love. Those were some of the words."

"And the rest?" Valen snapped.

I swallowed. Hells, this was the path, the twist of the song of seidr. The more I thought of the tale and its song, the clearer it became. "Trust and let it be, in this, a-a-a tale of land and sea. Let it be, Valen."

Stieg looked at his king imploringly. Valen hesitated, but slowly rose and stepped away from Tor's unmoving form.

He dropped his axes. "As you say."

Erik gave a slight hiss at the Night Folk king as he shoved his way toward Torsten.

Sol lifted his tear tracked face. His deep blue eyes seemed to shade to a cruel black when he saw Erik. "Get him back. You don't touch him, sea fae."

"Lump." I rushed to his side. "Did you not hear Junius? This is part of your song; I feel it. That's why the wards went up. Torsten has a song. Let it be."

"Out of time, earth fae." Erik glanced at Tor. "He's half in the Otherworld. Can't bring back the dead, now, can I?"

"Son," Arvad tried again. "It's the only chance you have."

"He could kill him." Sol gripped Tor's tunic.

"He *is* dying," Silas broke, and pointed out the truth none of us—Sol most of all—wanted to admit.

"He will," Arvad added. "He will die, son."

"No, he—"

"Moments," Arvad said with more force. "You have moments. I've been around enough death to know when a soul is leaving the body, Sol. This is a chance. A gift of fate."

Sol's mouth tightened. He trembled as he fought to keep the anguish from spilling out. With a furious kiss to Tor's forehead, he whispered softly against his consort's ear, then stepped back as Erik replaced him by Tor's head.

"Keep everyone back," Erik told Stieg. "I can't lose the song or he's a dead fae for certain. It'll look like I'm killin' him. I'm not."

Stieg took a place between Erik and our folk, then watched with a bit of curiosity as the boy lowered to his knees at Torsten's head. He winced. There was a pain in his leg, and the Ever King fought to hide it desperately.

With the blood on his palm, Erik placed it over the flow of gore in Torsten's chest.

Accustomed to Silas's voice, his low, silky rumble, it was a bit of a shock to hear the smooth, higher sound of the Ever King. Sea fae found power in their voices. Almost like seidr. Perhaps it was a bit of proof we were all connected. We were all fae folk, if we could look beyond our bloody skirmishes, we might find true peace someday.

Erik closed his eyes, bloody hands over Tor's wound. His voice grew in intensity. A hum from deep within his chest. Slow, haunting, steady.

Until Torsten's body spasmed.

"Stop!" Sol roared. Arvad wrapped his arms around his son's shoulders, holding him close. "Stop it."

"Lump." My voice cracked. "Let it be. Let it be."

Blood spewed out of Torsten's mouth the longer Erik sang. The boy's shoulders slumped. His voice grew softer. His fingers trembled. The song was draining him.

A little more, sea fae. A little more.

I clung to Silas's arms, unable to breathe, unable to move, until Tor's body ceased spasming. Until the blood stopped flowing over his lips.

Erik stumbled. He caught himself on one of his hands before he fell to the side. Stieg went to the young king's side, propping him up. The boy swatted him away and wiped his lips with the back of his hand.

"Wound's closed," he said, weaker than before. Erik didn't try to hide the limp as he stood and rubbed his upper thigh. "That's all I can do. Hope you didn't wait too long."

Without a word, the Ever King began to trudge back to the trees.

Before I could think, the words came. "Your story is only beginning. Take care with the hearts you claim."

A furrow creased between his crimson eyes. He said nothing to me, but turned on the crowd. "Consider my debt square, Warrior."

"Erik," Stieg said, holding a hand out. "You don't want this fight. You can end it, don't listen to Davorin. He's a spineless bastard who will give you no loyalty."

Erik ignored Stieg and looked to where Valen kept to the edge of the trees. "My debt with your warrior is clear. Tack on the blood hair woman too." He flicked his gaze to Malin. "Seeing how she took me out of that room. But with you—it will never be cleared until blood spills."

"We don't have to be enemies, boy."

"Is that what you told my father right before you killed him?"

315

Valen sighed. "You were young; you do not know all the reasons."

"Don't tell me what I know. I know what he did to your precious little seer fae. I also know I will never forget the sight of him tumbling into the sea." Erik stepped into the shadows of the trees. "Consider this truce at an end."

The Ever King faded into the darkness in the same moment Torsten drew in a sharp breath.

CHAPTER 40
THE STORYTELLER

S OL HAD T OR WRAPPED IN HIS ARMS. I WASN'T CERTAIN WE'D EVER BE ABLE to pry them apart. Torsten was still bloody, still looked like he ought to be on a funeral pyre, but when we inspected the wound, as the boy king said—it was closed. Nothing but a blood-smeared mess on his skin.

Whatever path of fate came with Torsten's song, still held. Rave, Ettans, and Falkyns traipsed our small camp, taking shifts on who'd stand watch.

Herja returned to the walls with the archers. Hus Rose remained untouched.

The sea fae had settled for the night from scout reports. It seemed, for now, we could rest.

The mood was somber in the trees. Few folk spoke about what happened in the battle. Most coupled off or burned offerings for their friends who'd fallen. Kings and queens visited those in their individual armies who'd been wounded or killed.

Saga led a prayer to the gods for Rune, Magus, and Yarrow. Ari handed the new Serpent Lady a talisman from her brother and promised the support of their crown as she navigated her new title.

"Cuyler." I touched his shoulder in one of the healing lean-tos that had been hastily erected.

The blood fae stirred, a mossy bandage still wrapped across his eye. He forced a grin, but it was more a wince. "Cal."

I didn't try to hide the disquiet and took his hand. "You almost died, you sod."

He chuckled. "That I did. Seems I'm short an eye."

"For certain?"

"Well, it's not in my head anymore, so."

I let out a wet laugh when he beamed. "You bleeding idiot. It's not something to smile about."

Cuyler sighed and closed his uninjured eye. "Well, it'll be quite a tale to tell. The more battle scars one has, tends to attract all manner of blood fae women."

I rolled my eyes, leaned over, and pressed a kiss to his sweaty forehead. "Don't lose the other one, you fool."

"Ah, but two missing eyes might very well attract two women."

I shoved his shoulder, glad he at least had his wit, then made my way back to the camp.

With Herja at the gates it gave Gunnar and Eryka a bit of respite. Gunnar inspected Bard's scar across his throat, then mocked Tova the way she kept her hands all over his uncle.

"All I'm saying, Tov, is it's about bleeding time."

"Shut it, Princeling."

Gunnar frowned. "What have I said about that name?"

"Eryka," Tova snapped, clinging to Bard's arm. "Take your stupid husband away."

Eryka gently took Gunnar's hand. "They'd like time alone."

Tova rolled her cat eyes. "All gods, not like that. He's *injured*."

"But his tongue and fingers are not," said Eryka. "Those are some of my favorites."

Tova's eyes widened. "Bleeding hells, how do you handle her mouth?"

"Masterfully." Gunnar wrapped an arm around Eryka's shoulders and kissed her head. "I'll be visiting Uncle Tor."

Bard chuckled, tangling Tova's fingers with his. "I'd leave him and Sol alone for a bit. They left half a clock toll ago."

Gunnar's eyes widened. "Right. Good advice." He jabbed a finger at Tova. "Let my uncle sleep, you fiend."

"This is why." Tova faced Bard. "You asked why I hesitated—this is why."

Bard Strom simply laughed, holding the wound on his neck, and kissed her knuckles.

Heart lighter, I returned to the main circle. A small fire kept the site warm enough. My Cursed King was wrapped around Elise nearest the flame. Their foreheads were pressed together, bodies covered in a fur wrap, and it looked like they were whispering words to each other.

Kase and Malin kept with the Falkyns. Niklas and Junius had lost several of their guild, and as they always did, the Kryv were there to mourn with them.

"All right, Cal?" Ari said, eyes pointed at the sky.

"Not really. You?"

"Not even close." Ari rubbed the back of his neck. "I keep seeing his bleeding face, the way he hunts Saga. I can't wait until his damn head is off his shoulders. I don't think I will sleep until it's done."

I gave his arm a squeeze. "It will end soon, Golden King."

"I've been thinking." He didn't take his eyes off the sky. "Should . . . should anything happen to me or Saga, will you take Mira?"

"Ari, don't."

"I need to know she will be shielded from that ass. Please, Cal. I plan to live and chatter and aggravate the lot of you for centuries, but if my plans are robbed from me—after watching Tor nearly . . ." Ari shook his head and finally pinned me in his gaze. "I saw the way your seidr shielded Tor. Will you do the same for my daughter if the worst should happen?"

His eyes burned with need. He *needed* to hear it, needed me to give him one sliver of peace.

I tossed my arms around his shoulders, awkwardly hugging him from the side. "I've always been there, Ari Sekundär. I saved you once, so I'm not letting you die now, but my answer is yes. Should the Norns be the wretches they are and steal one of my favorite parts of this dreary world away, yes. I will guard Mira with my life. I'll guard all your little irksome royals."

Ari cleared his throat and patted my back. "Thank you. Now, if you'll excuse me, I need to rest beside my wife. I have this wretched feeling if ever I fall asleep, I will wake up and realize all this has not been a horrid nightmare, and is, in fact, still a battle."

I smiled, watching him go, shoulders slumped as he searched for Saga.

I did the same. Silas remained on the edge of the camp. He stood alone in the shadows, muttering under his breath. I only caught a few words as I approached.

"Dream descends. Never again." He laced his fingers behind his neck and started to pace.

My heart ached for him. There were moments when the shadows that consumed him overtook his thoughts, where he got lost in the swirl of fear and unknowns. I knew it, accepted it, and vowed to be the one to always pull him back.

I reached a gentle hand out and touched his arm. Silas jolted in a startle. His eyes were a bit wild, but after a few breaths he took in my face. "Little Rose."

Silas swallowed me up in his arms, holding me close. I wrapped my arms around his waist and fell into the slow, steady beat of his heart. A peace found only here, only in his embrace.

"Are the shadows taking you?"

Silas let his head tilt, so his lips were pressed to the top of my head. "I keep having a thought that makes little sense and it gets . . . frustrating."

"What is it?"

"Dreams descend. You've said it, the rune seers have mentioned it, and it won't leave me."

I stroked my hands up his back. "Maybe we should rest our minds, and it might be clearer."

Silas's body seemed to relax into mine. He nodded. "Stay with me?"

I nudged his ribs with my elbow. "Where else do you think I'd be sleeping?"

His smile sealed the final bit of peace I needed to hold me through the darkness of the bloody night.

A hand was shaking my body like I was a damn dried leaf in the wind.

"Cal."

"Go away."

"Wake up."

I cracked an eye. "Kind Heart, this is unbecoming of you. You're usually much more thoughtful than this."

Elise snorted, but there was a bit of exhaustion behind it. "We're gathering to plan. Our scouts brought something back."

Silas shifted at my side, lifting his head. His arm fell from the place it had been wrapped around my waist, and I felt emptier than before. Elise's insistence didn't give us much time to dally.

We brushed off the dirt and twigs and joined the others near the fire. Junius laughed and nudged Tor's ribs when he and Sol emerged from the trees, Sol adjusting his belt. Tor didn't even hide the flush to his face and simply held tightly to Sol's hand.

Frey and Axel and Raum were already explaining what they'd seen.

"The battle lord is never unprotected," Raum said. "He has wards about him, sea fae guards, and he seems to have absorbed enough of their power that he can crawl back to the sea much the same as he did before should it come to that level of desperation."

"He has vulnerabilities," Saga insisted. "Ari's heirloom blade for one. It will kill him."

"Not if we do not rid him of these new rune wardings," Frey said.

Saga frowned. "How do you know he is shielded against the blade?"

"We all saw him," Valen offered. "Every time a blade struck him, it wouldn't break his skin. He's like a damn shield."

"But my sword was created to slaughter him," Ari said.

"Come on, Ari," Axel said. "This battle lord knows what that sword can do. He's known for ten turns how close he came to death. You think he did not prepare?"

"So what," Ari barked with a tone of frustration he rarely let loose. "We just drop to our knees? We just accept he can't be touched?"

"We're not saying that," Raum insisted.

Niklas cleared his throat. "The way they have explained it to me, from what I've read of wards and protection spell casts—our best bet is to carve out those rune shields from his damn flesh. Spells were cast by sea witches. Fearsome creatures. Almost as impressive with their potions as Elixists."

"We can't assume," I said, glancing at Niklas. "Don't you need to know where a spell originates to better understand it?"

"Yes."

"Then, we better know for certain sea witches were—"

"Calista, sweet Calista." Raum gave me a bemused look. "You offend me. I see practically everything as though it were in front of my damn face. I saw the markings. Saw those beautiful witch folk adding more along his wrists and arm. He's warding his body, and we can be certain, he's accounted for the fatal blows of Ari's blade."

"Dammit." Ari turned away, pacing, his hands on his head. "Then what do we do? Don't tell me that bastard is unkillable, I won't accept it."

"There will be a way," Valen said firmly. "We'll find a way. I'll cut off his damn arms if I need to."

"Good plan," Raum said, "except, as I said, he's always under watch from the sea fae at Harald's command—"

"Not Erik," Stieg interrupted. "It's interesting, but Davorin plots with Harald. I think he has little influence over the boy king."

"But does a boy king have influence over his people?" Kase offered.

Raum let out a sigh. "I don't know. I can't tell. They look at him with fear, but also look to Harald with the same fear."

"Erik Bloodsinger is hells bent on avenging Thorvald," Valen said. "He will not be an ally."

"Perhaps not," Stieg said, "but if he holds little love for Davorin, perhaps he won't put up too much resistance if we happen to corner the bastard. You heard yourself, the king is here for you. This is his uncle's war."

"I don't care for the way everyone disregards this boy," Elise said, taking a step closer to Valen. "Yes, he's young, but we know what his damn blood can do."

She cast a look toward Tor. "I'm unspeakably grateful for what he did, but he will not use his blood to heal Valen. It will be to kill him. I don't want to depend on a boy capable of killing my husband, thank you."

Valen pulled the queen against his side, pressing a kiss to her head.

"I agree with the queen," Kase said. "Better to find a way to get Davorin vulnerable and take him ourselves. I'd be glad to cut his bits off. I'd leave some for you to finish him off, Saga, I swear it."

Saga looked pale. "We were depending on the heirloom blade."

"It is still an option, sweet menace," Ari said. "We just need to find a way to break those protections on him."

"We need to get him vulnerable, unfocused, maybe even while he is sleeping," Niklas said. "What I know of flesh wards is that the magic within them is connected to the will to live. Distract that will, get the mind in a restful state where it is not locked within constant surges of adrenaline—the skin could soften. The wards might be penetrable."

"Oh, is that all? Get the bastard drunk? Get him asleep when he's surrounded by a damn sea kingdom?" Ari's frustration was locked on his tongue. Soon enough, I suspected our Golden King might start lashing out with violence.

"If he is warded against a blade, how do we cut at his skin?" Saga dragged her fingers through her hair. "He's had ten damn turns to plot how to avoid that blade and our different magicks. He *knows* us."

"Not all of us."

I startled. Silas stepped forward, fingers flicking at his sides, a hint of his nerves.

"He knows you, Wraith." Ari pointed at Silas's face. "The proof is in that bleeding scar you ought to flaunt more than you do."

"Riot Ode hid a great deal of what Calista and I could do together. He knows our power is connected, but he does not know how deeply. He does not know everything I can do. He never saw me with you, Golden King. He invaded the dream, but never saw me."

"What are you saying?" Ari folded his arms over his chest.

Silas looked to me; he took my hand and squeezed, like I was the sure place to keep him steady before he went on. "Use our gifts. That is what Calista keeps telling us, and I think it's . . . I *feel* like it is the path to take. Gifts of fate began and ended this long fight to reach this moment. Fated queens have risen to power across the realms. We've been given these gifts. We ought to use them."

"What gifts are you expecting to use?" Elise asked.

"All our magicks, but . . ." Silas paused. "To do it, I have an idea. Calista and I create songs that ensnare paths of fate between us. It is how we've broken them before, and it is how we restored these lands. We sang a song and that new twist of fate was entrapped by our seidr; it yielded to our heart's desire. It is possible that we might have a way to keep our battle lord ensnared long enough for all our gifts to play a part in this battle."

There was drawn silence until Saga spoke. "Are you saying you have a plan, Silas?"

He tightened his hold on my hand. "Yes."

"Going to share?" Kase muttered.

I glared at him. "You do much the same when you plot. Don't deny you love to leave those bleeding pauses to let us wallow in your cleverness, Shadow King."

Kase shrugged and didn't deny it.

"Falkyn," Silas said.

"Wraith." Niklas tossed a pouch of some wretched elixir between his palms. "What can I do for you?"

Silas licked his lips. "Do you have an elixir for a deep sleep?"

I drew in a sharp breath. "All gods."

With a tight grin, Silas met my wide stare. He nodded, like he knew I understood what he was thinking. "Let the dreams descend, Little Rose."

CHAPTER 41
THE PHANTOM

Dawn broke through the trees when the Golden King smashed his way into the small lean-to I'd claimed with Calista.

"Up," Ari said, kicking at my boots. "Something's happened in the sea fae camp. Need to see if we need to alter plans."

Calista snapped up at my side. "I'll kill them all if they've gone and done something that makes us shift our moves. We spent all bleeding night roving over every damn detail."

I agreed, but kept quiet, snatching my sword before we followed the others to the edge of our small camp. Seidr wards from Calista's blast over Torsten were fading, but still a glimmer caught the gray dawn when we reached the edge of the trees, crouched low.

What cover we needed fell to the hands of Kase and Ari. The Nightrender draped us in darkness with our own bleeding fears, and Ari used his illusions to twist the shadows to appear natural. Mere phantoms in the trees.

The sea fae camp was moving about, some frantically, others stood still on the edges near one of the canvas tents.

"The battle lord," I whispered near Calista's ear. "By the shore."

Davorin had his arms folded over his chest, a taut frown on his stony face. The man was like a pestilence, a sliver of darkness in the

325

dawn, a stain on what might be bright and lovely. He brought with him an aura of pain, and I could hardly wait to rid the bleeding world of it.

"There." Ari said, voice rough from somewhere down the line. "Who is it?"

Sea fae emerged from the tent, a body held on long furs between them in the makeshift cot. Someone had died.

My blood froze when a boy emerged after the body. Then another. Erik Bloodsinger followed the procession to the sea with haughty arrogance.

"All gods," Calista said. "That's *Harald*. He's . . . dead."

Unbidden, a grin split over my face. No wonder Davorin was fuming—his loyal, high-ranking sea fae was gone.

By the looks of the young sea king, there was no disruption to his day at the death of his uncle. Erik waved a hand, and a billow of waves snatched the body of Harald and devoured it in the waves. Without a backward look, the boy king strode off into another tent, wholly unbothered.

"Come on," Kase muttered to the rest of us. "This is not a hinder-ance to the plan. If anything, it is a bright morning."

"Strange, hearing such optimism from you, my dreary friend," Ari said. "But I shall take it. Davorin meets his end today."

There was an inspiring viciousness buried beneath the levity of Ari Sekundär, but I embraced it. My life held little meaning for centuries, but today—to my bones—I felt if I succeeded, all the pain, the ghosts, the shadows, the agony, would be worth it."

A hand slapped against my arm. The Nightrender glared at me with his inky black eyes. "Come on, Wraith. Let us see if you can hit those marks."

*

"What if it doesn't work?" Calista's forehead was furrowed in worry as I strapped the sword to my waist. "What if he ends it straightaway?"

"He won't get the chance. You know he'll want to make a spectacle of it. Offer ransoms and bargains. He'll want to use this against the Raven Queen and Golden King. We'll have time."

Calista gripped my arm, her fingernails dug into my skin, and for the first time I caught sight of the glassy tears she was trying not to shed. "What if. You're. Wrong."

I leaned down and pressed a kiss to her lips, slow and tender. My hand cupped the side of her face when I pulled back. "We're bonded, Little Rose. To the soul, and that is key here. I am not leaving this battle without you, believe that."

Calista closed her eyes and leaned into my touch for a few breaths before snatching her knives and leading us back to the clearing.

Midday was approaching. The last tolls of the night were spent plotting and marking the next moves. With Harald gone, we needed to act before Davorin grew frustrated with the boy king's lack of enthusiasm for battle, and more obsession with hunting Valen.

Left too long, Davorin might try to overtake the whole of the sea fae by killing the king. Some of the plan depended on my suspicions about Erik Bloodsinger.

The sea fae were an obstacle, true, but Davorin was the head of the snake that brought them here. Cut it off, and the rest would die.

Seidr boiled in my blood. Calista feared the next steps, but I saw the flash in her gaze, I saw the way her body seemed to burn as much as mine with the pulse of our power.

This was the step. It had to work.

What would it be like to live . . . free at last?

The thought was almost too damn overwhelming to even imagine.

"All right." The Nightrender rose from drawings in the dirt. A plan for movements, for marks, as he called them. Saga aided in the landscape. Ari and his knowledge of maps aided in distances and realistic expectations of movements. Kase glanced at the drawing again. "This will move fast. Our different magicks will be stretched. Do not exhaust yourselves before the right moment."

The crowd nodded.

327

Halvar Atra and Raum from the Kryv would take the left and right flanks with the warriors. Hagen Strom, his son Dain, and daughter Laila were returning to Hus Rose to aid Herja and the archers.

Eryka kissed Gunnar. Glistening tears tracked her pale cheeks. "I will miss your scent while you are gone. Blood is such a wretched smell and somehow, when you are near, I only breathe in you."

Gunnar kissed his wife, long and hard. "I will miss you. All of you. Stay down. Stay safe."

"Make him pay."

Gunnar added another tender kiss to her forehead. "I've been waiting to do just that since the day he put his hands on you."

Calista had informed me of the beatings and torture Eryka had endured when she'd been captured by Davorin in the isles. There were personal debts the bastard owed us all. Somehow, we did what we could to fit them all in, to find a way for everyone to take their bit of blood today.

Eryka stood with Tova and Isak and Fiske. They would guard the wounded. Isak was added for his ability to blind any enemies who'd come close, and Fiske for his premonitions.

Gorm bid his son farewell. Cuyler was aggravated no one would let him join, despite a damn hole in his skull still bleeding where he was missing an eye.

He wasn't alone. Most of the wounded who were asked to remain back had complaints. We'd all fought to be here. To sit out and be nursed tenderly while we fought to end this at long last, seemed wholly unfair.

Gunnar came to stand by me, a small knife hidden in his boot. The thieving prince flashed a grin. "Ready, Wraith?"

"No."

He chuckled. "This is why I like you. Direct. To the point."

"I am ready in some ways," I admitted. "In others, I have a great deal of fear."

Gunnar dipped his chin. "That's the thing I learned when I ran with the Kryv—all of us are always afraid. Use it to bring you back to

Cal. Out of all of us, if anyone could traipse into the Otherworld to shout at you for dying too soon, it's her."

I smirked. A new sort of ease was beginning to shape around these royals. One I never thought I'd fear. I still took comfort in solitude, but speaking a few words, sitting amongst them, wasn't so taxing any longer.

Malin approached, a somber expression on her features. She unfurled her palm and held out the queen's ring. "It will move swiftly once this is in play, Silas."

I nodded and slid the ring on my smallest finger. Heat from the power within it burned into my skin.

"Keep up, Ari," Gunnar said, tethering a silken scarf over his head. There was still blood in the fabric from one of the fallen sea fae who'd once worn it, but it would only aid us now.

Ari tugged a cowl over his head, frowning as he secured the heirloom blade to his waist. "Keep your steps as they ought to be, and I will not lose you."

"We need to go." Kase tilted his head to the sky. "Much longer and they'll be readying to make their moves. Get him isolated, Gunnar. Then, Wraith, do what you must do. This ends today."

Calista stood a few paces away from the others. The royals had bid their farewells if their hearts were leaving.

I had not.

Scrutiny, other gazes, other folk, for the first time did not cross my mind when I went to Calista Ode. I trapped her face in my palms and kissed her. Long, deep, a lasting sort of kiss that I hoped would bring her back to me soon.

Her lips trembled when she pulled back. "I don't need to threaten bodily harm to make sure you return to me, do I?"

I grinned. "Threaten you'll never touch my body again and this will be over in the next clock toll."

She gave me another quick kiss. "I love you. Bring us to him, Silas. I'd like to get on living our last lifetime together."

"Consider it done, Little Rose."

I kissed her cheek, and slowly released her hands before returning to Gunnar. What was left of him anyway. The only recognizable part of the thieving prince was the sharp amber of his eyes. Soon enough, that began to fade to the stormy red of the sea folk.

Gunnar's rounded ears were now sharply pointed. His hair was longer and knotted at the base of his neck, and silver rings were hooped in the lobes of his ears.

Ari slunk into the shadows as Gunnar tied my wrists in a thick rope that looked a great deal like the rigs on their ships.

"Shall we, Wraith?"

I nodded and fell into step behind Gunnar Strom, his new captive.

On the edge of the sea fae camp, we paused. Gunnar took a flacon of ale from off his belt and took a long gulp. Twenty paces away, Ari should've been perched, keeping watch. More than most of us, Ari and Saga deserved to have this nightmare end. I was determined to see it done.

"Let's go," Gunnar said gruffly.

I kept my head down, tethered arms outstretched, and stumbled behind Gunnar as we crossed the fading seidr line into the tents of the sea fae.

"Oi!" Gunnar shouted to a trio of men who stood around a small fire pit, smoking paper-rolled herbs. "Where's the king? Look what I snagged. Drunk off his ass and stumbling about. These earth sods heal with the harsh ale."

Gunnar barked a laugh and yanked on the rope, causing me to fumble on my feet.

The sea fae converged on us, one had a curved blade leveled at Gunnar's throat. "What House?"

What the hells did that mean?

Gunnar laughed again and swatted the sword away. "Go get the king and the earth fae battle lord. Don't hesitate."

Weight added to the air, a fleeing moment, but Gunnar's mesmer gathered swiftly. Another breath and the three sea fae blinked, their eyes glassy and disoriented. They turned around and guided us toward the center of the camp. Perhaps what unnerved me the most were not the differences between us and the sea fae—but the similarities.

They sat in groups. Friends? Family? Men held horns and tin cups of steaming drinks. Sea fae looked worn and weary much like us.

In truth, they were fighting because they were led here to fight, to avenge a royal. Could they be horribly blamed for the act? Should any of our royals ever be snatched, I had few doubts every damn realm would rise up to save them or avenge them.

We emerged from between two tents.

"King Erik," said one of the men in front of us.

The lanky boy turned around, a tin mug in his grip. His eyes flashed in surprise at the sight of me, followed promptly by a wash of frustration. I fought the urge to grin. It made me more certain he'd been behind the chaos that knocked Davorin away from me.

Not out of the kindness of his shriveled sea fae heart. If I had to guess, I'd say Erik Bloodsinger was raised to cherish the notion of clearing debts.

I'd let the other boy live, after all.

The king did not want to show he was soft on anything, but he'd been uneasy at the thought of the other boy dying. It was clear in his rage, in his struggle to reach him.

I let the boy live, so the king let me live.

Now, no mistake, his risk was all for naught.

"This be a dreary day for the House of Kings," the man went on, "but we brought you one of the earth fae."

"Not just anyone. Look at the sod," Gunnar murmured, a new, thick accent that matched the fae of the sea. "He be one who keeps nearest the royals."

"What do we have here?"

Gooseflesh lifted on my arms. I hated the reaction to the bastard, but wretched and spineless as he was, he was still a horror from my boyhood. He was still the man who ripped away the king and queen from me—two royals who'd come to treat me as a member of their household.

This bastard was the one who'd stolen Calista away.

Davorin slicked his hands through his hair, dark eyes locked on me. He lowered his palms and slowly unsheathed a blade. "I asked for your blood. Well done."

He looked to Gunnar, not considering for a moment he was anything other than sea folk.

"We're not to be killing him straight off, are we?" Gunnar huffed and looked to the young king.

"Who are you to question?" Davorin's voice was icy and filled with hate.

"I'm . . . I'm not, it's just . . ." Gunnar leaned in, lowering his voice. "He was using one of the earthen fan's strange trinkets. Think he wanted to bring them shadows that draw out their armies again."

Davorin's brow arched. Gods, I prayed those rune wards on the battle lord's flesh only shielded against the blade. I prayed the next words would take and burrow into the bastard's blood.

Gunnar's whisper grew rough, demanding. "Just look at the ring on his finger."

Unbidden, Davorin's gaze fell to the queen's ring. Greed and desire burned in his eyes.

Gunnar cleared his throat and went on, directing his words to the sea fae who hardly seemed to notice he'd addressed Davorin. The thieving prince had frightening magic, and I was glad for it.

"This scarred sod seems to be thinking his folk'll come for him," Gunnar said to the boy king. "Isn't that what we want? The earth bender?"

Erik tilted his head. "Aye."

"We want the realms," Davorin hissed.

Erik Bloodsinger ignored him and studied Gunnar with a new scrutiny as the prince rambled on.

"So, if he's dead, what's to stop the earth bender from sinking us into his pit? If he's alive, they'll try to snatch him back, right? We'll be able to lure them out."

I held my breath when Gunnar faced the sea fae and battle lord without blinking. Now was the moment where we'd be found out, or our plans moved forward.

"You'll let him live. You'll place me as guard over where you keep him." Gunnar didn't flinch. He kept his body squared to Davorin. "You'll keep that desire for the ring on his hand."

There was a flicker of Gunnar's eye color. As though the sea fae red was fading. Dammit, Ari would be fatiguing. We needed to move before Davorin noticed.

"Am I understood?" Gunnar finished.

Davorin glimpsed the ring and a twitch came to his mouth.

"Is it your word, sea king, that the prisoner remains breathing as bait?" Davorin asked, arrogance dripping in his tone.

Erik tilted the cup to his lips. "It is. Take him to Harald's tent. You." He paused in front of Gunnar. "What house are you from? Bones?"

Gunnar swallowed. "Aye."

"What is your voice?"

Dammit. We knew so damn little about the sea fae.

Gunnar shifted on his feet, uncertain. "Not skilled enough to say, My King."

I held my breath. Was it even believable? Did unskilled magic exist in the sea kingdom?

After a suffocating pause, the young king shrugged. "Lack of voice doesn't seem to have stopped you from scouting well enough."

"Aye." Gunnar dipped his chin.

With a wave, Erik turned away, back to his lonely corner of the camp. "You have the honor of guarding him then."

"Many thanks, My King."

"We'll use him as bait at nightfall."

When Gunnar turned me toward the empty tent from which the fae had taken Harald, I caught the gleam of Davorin's grin.

He had no intention of honoring the young king's word.

And that was exactly our hope.

Gunnar shoved me inside the tent with a final, significant glance and stepped outside. It took longer than expected, but soon, muttered voices came from outside the tent. I had my back turned to the flaps, heart racing, when the canvas stretched and another body entered the tent.

"I wondered if you'd be trapped as a little all this time." Davorin chuckled with a bit of wickedness. "But look at you, the king's ward is all grown up."

I turned over my shoulder.

Davorin paused at the edge of Harald's unmade cot. Blood stained the furs and linens. He'd been killed? No mistake, Davorin had a hand in it. What kept him from killing the boy king? His poisonous blood, perhaps?

"Why do you keep fighting here?" I asked. "You've never won. You won't win. You should've lived out your days beneath the sea."

"Never won?" He chuckled. "Have you lived a happy life, boy? Or have you been locked in a wretched existence to hide from me? The way you all have been fighting to reach this moment, so have I. Now, I am home. My kingdom is restored. Curses are ended. The outcome of our fate rests in our hands. I intend for it to fall in my favor."

"We hold the gifts of fate."

He grinned. If Davorin were not so horrid, he would have a comforting face. If he did not have such hatred, he might look kind when he smiled.

He was a tyrant who was ugly and putrid at all angles.

"Gifts of fate." The battle lord approached me and gripped the ropes on my wrists. "Yes, I know. Thank the gods, these stupid sea fae do not know the things they ought to notice. Like this."

He yanked the queen's ring off my finger with such venom it scraped the skin, drawing blood.

"I've seen what this can do. Was that the plan, boy? Bring your fated royals through shadows to you?"

My jaw tightened.

Davorin smirked. "I wonder what would happen if I brought them to me."

He slid the ring on his finger. The runes along the edges glowed in a vibrant flame. Davorin removed his hold on the ropes and studied the ring.

"Many thanks, boy," he said. "I'll ready the sea fae. We'll watch for those shadows and meet them when they arrive."

"It's a good plan," I said. "But it'll never work."

Davorin's steps staggered a bit. His eyes widened. I hoped he sensed the heaviness by now, I hoped he knew something was shifting inside his blood.

"You see," I went on. "Another thing those sea fae—and apparently you—don't know, is how to detect a highly concentrated sleeping elixir. One that happens to be on that ring. Shame that your greed is so predictable."

"No . . ." Davorin took hold of a tent post. "You wore it."

"True. But you were kind enough to leave so much of your glamour behind to be studied by Elixists all these turns. Seems one of our own knows exactly how to hone his potions for certain magical imprints. Like yours. No one wearing that ring will sleep . . . except you."

"What did you do?" Davorin fell to one knee.

I lowered with him. "Let your thoughts go, and let those dreams descend."

CHAPTER 42
THE PHANTOM

I STEPPED OUT OF A LAYER OF DARKNESS TO DAVORIN FLAT ON HIS BACK, EYES opening slowly.

"You could've had so many things in life," I said.

He snapped up, disoriented. "Where . . ."

To his left was the old palace of House Ode. There were the gilded fountains that had once decorated the lawns. To his right were the gardens that led to the wood.

"You still dream of it," I said, taking it in.

"What have you done?"

"How do you think the Golden King lived in such a vivid dream"

Davorin's eyes burned like hot coals. "You have seidr, not the weaker body magic."

"Weaker?" I chuckled. "That is one of your shortcomings, always viewing the other clans as less-than. Who stands against you now? Every vein of gods-magic. You know as well as I there are individual strengths, powers that grow. Look at your own dark glamour."

"A dream walker." Davorin scrambled to his feet. "You cannot hold me here forever."

"True, but I can for long enough."

Davorin let out a cry of frustration and lunged for me. I stepped aside, swifter than he'd ever be able to move. "The beautiful thing about dream walking is I cannot be harmed. I become a phantom in your mind."

He raged, searching for his blade.

"You won't find it." I grinned. "I am interested to see what lives in your dreams. Or are we in a nightmare?"

I shoved against his chest and in a breath, the lawns faded into the throne room of the old palace.

"Ah." I chuckled when I looked at the thrones. "A nightmare then. No less than you deserve."

Davorin's breaths came sharp, his face was flushed and angry. Above him on a golden dais, Ari sat like a true, arrogant king. His hand was clasped with Saga. The gown she wore was revealing. Slits along her thighs, low hanging necklines, and thin straps.

Revealing with a purpose—to show the scars across her flesh, the scars Davorin had left behind. Scars she carried with grace and held no pain for her any longer. He was a forgotten nuisance. Not even a bother in her regal life. She sneered at Davorin, still on his knees, and rose to sit on her husband's lap.

"Could've been you," I told him. "Should have honored her the way they honor each other. You will never forget them, even when you are in the hells. To them, one day, you will be nothing but a distant memory, lost amidst the thousands of new, joyful moments in their long, happy lives."

Davorin cursed and lunged for me again. I turned and tossed him into another scene.

The Night Folk clans, laughing, their littles all around them as they feasted beside a glittering lake. Plentiful. Happy. Joyful.

"The curses, the anger, the enslavement you brought to their clans—it only brought them together. They chose unity. Enemies chose each other."

"I'll kill you," Davorin seethed through his teeth. "You cannot touch me. You think you can get close to destroying me? I assure you that you cannot."

"Hmm. We'll see." With a heavy slap to the back of his head I tossed him forward again. He landed face down in the courtyard of the Eastern palace.

Ribbons of gold and red lined the branches of the trees. Two boys wrestled each other in overgrown, mossy cobblestones. The Shadow King and Queen laughed with their guild, with Falkyns in the center. A place where wretched masquerades once took place, now was a place of laughter for thieves and an inseparable family.

"Strange how you tried to break two lonely littles, only to help them find the devotion of a family larger than they ever imagined."

Golden light shimmered toward the edges of the courtyard. Images of Kase and Malin faded. Davorin was gasping, like the anger, the rage of seeing the rise of every kingdom and throne was breaking him piece by piece.

I grinned toward the shimmer. "You've lost, battle lord. A man who could've had it all. Friendship, armies at his command, love— you gave it away for hate and greed. It was always meant to be your downfall."

"You can do nothing."

"So certain?"

My grin widened at the new voice. I reached a hand for the shimmer of gold, and a misty image of Calista stepped forward.

Davorin's face contorted with rage. "How is she here?"

"She followed her heart song and found me," was all I said.

"No. This is not Riot's seidr!" Davorin's lip twitched.

"Who said anything about the fate king?" I asked, head tilted. "He paved the way for his girl to find her own power and she has. Curious isn't it? I think Riot knew exactly how powerful she'd become. I think he knew *my* soul, *my* gifts, would be hers. The same way hers bond with mine."

Davorin clenched his fists. "Soul bonded? It's not been done. It's not possible but in sagas of the gods."

"Then the fates must truly wish you to lose this battle." Calista popped one shoulder. "For soul bonding has happened to us, you bastard. Silas's soul sings to mine, and I will find his—even in your dreams."

Somewhere, distantly, the tang of hot blood burned in my throat. Davorin cried out, clutching his wrists, batting at his chest.

A sneer curled over my lips. "Ah, if I had to guess, the thieving prince is nearly finished."

"What are you doing?" Davorin bellowed.

Calista squeezed my hand. "We're coming, Silas."

"Sing with me, Little Rose." I faced her. "Trap him here. We finish this now."

The spectral of Calista glanced at Davorin. "You will not be able to move. You won't be able to lift a blade until we are finished with you."

She faded into nothing but emptiness. I closed my eyes, embracing the burn of her heart calling me back, calling me toward wherever she was. Davorin still swatted and raged at the phantom pain on his limbs.

"Wake up, battle lord. Your fate awaits." I slammed my palm against his chest. Different from a fae sleep where Ari had to fight his way free from the glamour that held him captive, this was nothing but a simple sleep. I could demand it to end at my leisure.

I demanded it now.

I woke with an ache in my skull and the reek of flesh and gore in my lungs. Gunnar's illusions had faded by the time Davorin's eyes opened. He spun a bloody knife, a cruel grin on his face when the battle lord shifted back but cried out in pain.

With a shock of horror on his face, Davorin looked at his bare chest, his arms. He'd been stripped and slashed.

"Seems like those sea witch runes don't do much good if your mind is at rest." Gunnar chuckled. At his feet were lumps of bloody flesh, inked in spells and runes that would've kept Davorin protected from our glamour, mesmer, and fury. They would've protected him from a blade created to kill him.

"Didn't know how far to cut. I tried to get to the bone, just to be safe." Gunnar tossed the knife into the soil underfoot. The point landed close to Davorin's feet. "That's for my wife."

Blood dripped down Davorin's skin, draining him of strength. Still, he reached for his blade.

Sing with me. I closed my eyes, a deep sound rolling from my chest. The words Calista demanded in the dream remained fresh in my mind. Warmth surrounded my heart, as though some deeper piece of me knew she felt the pull to the vicious song where she was in the moment

"Damn you!" Davorin was flung backward. The wrist he'd used to reach for Gunnar's blade snapped and cracked at a sick angle. Sweat pooled over his brow against a faint glimmer of gold that seemed to shackle his skull to the ground, seemed to clamp his jaw shut.

The ground shuddered. It rocked and cracked. Screams from the sea fae rose.

Gunnar and I stood shoulder to shoulder. Davorin winced against whatever tether Calista's words had placed around his functions; he watched helplessly as the bit of bloodied earth beneath us shifted and ripped apart from the sea fae camp.

Harald's tent tilted. Gunnar shoved the canvas aside. I knocked out the poles until the flaps, ropes, and posts tumbled into a crack in the bedrock.

I wanted the sea folk to see this. I wanted them to see it all.

"Silas!" Across the new cracks in the camp, Calista sprinted for us.

Her wild braids were like gilded chains in the sunlight. Her whole countenance seemed to ignite in beautiful light. Perhaps it was only me who could see the burst of her power in her veins, but she was damn radiant.

Amidst the dust and bursts of soil and pebbles, Calista sprinted for the space. "They're coming! Sing with . . ." She let out a cry when she leapt over a widening piece of broken earth. Calista hardly took a breath before she sprinted for us again. She collided against me, arms around my waist, breaths heavy. "Sing . . . sing with me, Silas."

I lowered my brow to Calista's and wrapped her in my arms. Davorin raged, unable to move through the dream song binding him in place.

"You have the words," I whispered. "We finish this now."

Calista's long fingers dug into my waist as the slow, deep tone of

340

my voice tangled with her simple words. A song of safety and protection. A song of justice and the summons of the gifts of fate.

> Four thrones of fated light,
> Rise and claim your fight.
> Each with a place, have it be known.
> Rid lands of hate and claim each throne.

Davorin's head cracked against the ground when another violent shudder knocked the posts of what was left of the tent. Blue flames rushed along the edges of the broken camp. It surrounded the bit of earth we'd robbed away to keep Davorin separate from them.

It ensured they'd keep a distance and left the battle lord to face his enemies.

At the sight of the pyre, sea folk ran about in chaos.

Elise and Valen emerged through the smoke and flames. The queen held a blade, shielding her husband as he lowered to the ground, closer to the edge than before. His dark eyes were locked on the sea folk, then to us.

Doubtless, Valen Ferus was going to attempt to trap everyone in place until the end. Taxing, but determination was carved over his face.

All the gifts.

As if Elise understood the toll it would take on his fury, she gripped his shoulder, the blade in her other hand. Fate was fickle. Elise Ferus was mortal, a non-magical being, yet her simple touch always seemed to burn through the Night Folk king like an amplifier of fury.

Cracks and ravines and bursts of jagged stone devoured the camp. Sea fae scrambled toward the water's edge. Some were speared by Valen's assault. Others fled for the trees, desperate to break away from the earth bender.

Some fell to their knees, grasping at roots or stones, cursing the gods.

"A queen of choice," Calista shouted at the battle lord. He dug his fingers into the soil, cursing and trying to escape the violent shift of earth. "Their power lives in the earth of this land. It strengthens us, fuels us. And you did not defeat them!"

The ring on Davorin's hand brightened again. A wall of darkness surrounded the camp. Any of the sea folk who readied to fight, who thought they might show a bit of boldness, lost their backbone.

Blades dropped. Sea fae raced away from inky shadows, keen to escape the horrors of the land.

Some succeeded and reached the water. Waves rose, swallowing them out to the depths where they called forth their fierce ships. Others were locked in the ring of shadows and met with every warrior, thief, and Rave from each realm.

At the edge of the broken earth, the Nightrender stepped out, his hand clasped with his Memory Thief.

"A queen of devotion," Calista roared, her hands still clasped tightly around my waist.

Davorin didn't try to stand against the rage of mesmer. He met her eyes with hatred in his.

"They have the power of body and mind. They protect us, heal us, they know what it is like to survive cruelty, how it only makes us wiser, slier, and a tad trickier."

The deadly shadows encircled some of the sea folk caught in the darkness. With a simple tilt to his head, Kase snapped their bodies. Rifters from the Alver folk killed more. Hypnotiks tormented their minds, holding them steady until Malin's brighter mesmer coiled with her husband's darkness. More than one fae jolted at the touch of her mesmer.

I hoped they forgot how to breathe and suffocated slowly.

"But my favorite," Calista shouted, a grin on her lips.

Blood dripped from Davorin's nose as he fought against the bands of our fate song. He was weary; the wounds on his skin were clearly draining him.

"My favorite part is when a queen with the gift of cunning—" She bowed her head in condescension. "Outwits a sod like you and brings his end with the most honorable lovers you'll ever meet."

Calista and I pulled apart.

Davorin let out a rough gasp, free of the bonds, and staggered to his feet. He gasped and spat blood.

Doubled over his knees, his eyes burned in dark hate. He pointed a finger at Calista. "Your head is *mine*."

On his first step, the ground shifted again. A rocky ledge stretched through the blue flames, shifting into a vine and sod-coated bridge. A call from the land, not from Valen, but from a queen whose power spoke to the spirit of the kingdom.

Ari and Saga crossed Tor's river of flames and onto our isolated bit of earth. Davorin's chest heaved. He reached for Gunnar's knife and curled his hand around the hilt in the same moment Ari drew the heirloom blade.

"You barely left me anything," Ari said, glaring at Gunnar. He turned his fiery gaze on Davorin. "We never did finish what we started at the shore that day. I rather detest never finishing a fight." Ari rolled the blade in his grip. "Shall we?"

Davorin lifted his knife, and gasped when the force of Ari's strike nearly cracked the blade. A few swipes, a few jabs; the battle lord held his own against the Golden King. But loss of blood and a lack of his protections was taking its toll.

Ari swiped the point of his sword across Davorin's middle. A deep, festering gash dug into his stomach. Davorin cried out and stumbled to one knee.

Blood stained his teeth as Ari closed the distance between them. The light, playful countenance of the Golden King shifted into something wretched and cruel. He swung the sword against Davorin's shoulder.

The battle lord cried in pain, dropping his grip on his own blade.

"You threatened my daughter." Ari slashed again, striking Davorin's ribs. "One mistake."

The wounds were scorched, gangrenous; they were infected the longer they festered on Davorin's body. He shuddered, spitting blood out of his mouth. Ari didn't slow.

He cut a gash on the lower half of Davorin's back. "You tormented my wife."

A stab through Davorin's hip. The battle lord jolted and gasped, trying to draw in more air.

Ari left the blade pinned in Davorin's body, gripped Davorin's hair, and wrenched his head back. "Tormenting her, touching her, *harming* her," Ari snarled beside Davorin's ear. "That was your greatest mistake."

With more force than was needed, Ari dropped his grip on Davorin's head. He ripped the sword from his back.

Davorin cursed and cried out. Ari dragged the bloodied tip across the soil and paused at his wife.

He kissed her quickly, then handed her the blade. "He's yours, sweet menace. However you see fit. His end has always belonged to you."

Saga gripped the hilt of the heirloom blade. The magic of it wouldn't fester the same as it did for Ari, but it would kill well enough.

Davorin lifted his head. He held Saga's gaze, even tried to sneer. It was hard to tell through all the blood.

"I feel nothing for you," Saga said. "You are a pitiful creature who could've had it all, and you destroyed it. What a horrid life you have lived in your crusade of hatred. A crusade you could never win. For our brutality was even greater than yours. It went to the darkest pieces of our hearts. It burns for the ones we love."

"Ah." Davorin coughed. "But I did love you so well, little raven."

Saga did not take his bait. She grinned with the same viciousness as her husband. "You were wholly disappointing. The only man who satisfies me in every way is Ari. He bests you by all accounts." Saga leaned closer. "He always will, and I swear to you, your name will never cross my lips again."

Davorin's eyes darkened. He opened his mouth to spit more harsh words, but choked on a gasp when Saga slammed the point of the blade through the center of his throat.

A look of stun painted his face, as though he thought she might not actually go through with it.

"Burn in the hells," she whispered, twisting the blade a little more in his neck. A bubble of blood erupted over his lips. Saga yanked the sword free with a grunt.

Davorin's body wobbled for half a breath, then he fell face down. Unmoving. Bloodied.

Dead.

CHAPTER 43
THE STORYTELLER

It didn't seem real.

I could see the blood, could smell the refuse in the air. His body wasn't shifting. No dark glamour dug into the soil. He was there, unmoving, bloody, and gone. Still, my mind did not want to accept it.

Until Saga's gasps drew me from my own stun.

She dropped the blade and stumbled into Ari's arms. He clung to her, kissing the side of her neck, gripping her hair.

"He's . . . he's gone. He's gone." She kept gasping the words against her husband's chest.

"You were terrifying," he whispered back. "Beautifully terrifying." Ari kissed her. His hands on her face. "I need to be alone with you soon, it was such a sight."

Saga gave a wet, broken laugh. Her shoulders slumped and she clung to him again, almost shrinking, as though the countless turns, the centuries of pain, were crashing over her.

Truth be told, I think the lot of us felt the same.

I leaned into Silas. He mutely hugged my body against his. As Tor pulled back the pyre, even Elise and Valen held hands, both on their knees across the gap. Exhausted, maybe a little lost on what to do next.

Kase and Malin were, oddly, the most joyful. They laughed against each other. Laughed and held tightly to a new dawn. A new existence.

The ring of glowing seidr used to tie Davorin on this small bit of broken earth faded as the song we sang drifted into nothingness. Shadows pulled back.

The sea fae camp was in ruin. Tents were toppled. Fae were still fleeing through the tides. Ghastly ships appeared from beneath the waves, distant and too close to the Chasm barrier we'd never be able to catch them. Not at the speed their strange vessels could travel.

The ones trapped under the blades of Rave and our other warriors looked about at the broken soil and slaughtered battle lord with a touch of horror.

I grinned, taking it all in.

The gifts of fate. Together, those twisted paths Silas and I naively created, united at long last to end the battle my father, my mother, our people, once gave their whole lives to fight.

Lifetimes in the making, victory was finally ours to claim.

Much the same as the battle in the isle, the cleanup and organizing afterward was nearly as exhausting as the actual fighting.

It took the whole of the day and well into the night to gather the dead sea fae and return their bones to the sea. Funeral pyres were lit for our fallen. Too many, in truth, but we took a breath to honor the fallen. To walk amongst them, to remember them, and sing them into the great hall of the gods.

The most joyful part of the battle was reuniting with those left behind.

Livia Ferus shoved out of the doors first, nearly tripping a few of the blood fae watchers set to guard the little royals. She was sobbing and running, and she never stopped until she flung her arms around Elise's neck. When Valen approached, still soaked in ash and sweat, she opened her arm to squeeze his neck too.

Aleksi greeted Tor and Sol like he thought a warrior might, stalwart and steady—at first—but in three breaths the boy crumbled and cried until Tor scooped his skinny body and carried him into the palace.

Jonas and Sander were already chatting about all they'd seen when Kase and Malin took hold of their hands, leading them back to the hall.

"There are ghosts here, Maj. Swear to the gods," Jonas said. "Oh, and I saw lots of shadows. Scared the piss outta Sander."

"Did not." Sander shoved his brother. "You're the one who said you needed to sleep with me the whole time."

Jonas shoved back. "Did you cut off his head, Daj?"

"No," Kase said, pressing a kiss to the boy's head. Perhaps not an affectionate man to others, but the Nightrender became another person entirely around his family. "Saga was the one who cut him down."

Jonas groaned. "Mira's never gonna stop boasting about it then."

I chuckled and watched as Mira hardly seemed to care that her mother was the one who ended Davorin's life. She cared more that she had both her parents' arms wrapped around her, holding her close.

Silas kept close to my side as we helped bandage the wounded. We aided Niklas in passing around his elixirs.

Elise's cry drew our gazes across the hall. Elise, Herja, honestly most of the Night Folk clan, sprinted toward the doors when Lilianna stepped inside, a little pallid, but grinning and no longer trying to rip out her family's throats.

Herja's youngest girl clung to Lilianna's waist. Livia hugged her grandmother's arm, and Alek took the other. Through the embraces, Lilianna found my gaze. Once her family released her, she approached, almost cautiously.

"Arvad . . ." She cleared her throat. "He told me the truth."

I smiled softly. Every moment was clear in my head. Our letters. Our interactions. Our plot against the icy King Eli. I was the one who warned her of a crimson night because my Whisper warned me of the blood moon.

I was the one who told her of the fury sleep, the way to hide her warriors since I knew deep in my heart, through the whispers in my mind, that another army was hidden much the same.

"Strange, isn't it?" That was the best I could say. What was there to say? It was unbelievable in many ways, but it was true.

She smiled. "No. The more I think of it, the more it makes a great deal of sense. You have always had strength. So did Greta. You have pulled us—everyone—through the most trying ordeals of our lives. Battle after battle, you gave us ways to escape, ways to survive. You are truly a queen of cunning. I could not ask for a more fitting title." She cupped one of my cheeks. "Nor a truer friend."

Lilianna pulled me into a tight embrace, and I let a tear fall as I clung to her, much like I'd done before I sent her to sleep all those turns ago.

When the moon perched at its highest point, it was pearly white. Cold, blue light replaced the bloody tone of our nights.

I tilted my head and soaked it up.

Davorin's head was spiked in the hall of Hus Rose. Some of the littles shrunk from such a sight. The ones who did not were expected. Aleksi and Jonas spent the better part of a clock toll spewing curses at the bastard and fighting invisible battles as though they were there.

When the doors opened to the great hall well after midnight, a hush descended.

Stieg, Frey, and Raum returned with two boys coated in dirt and grime.

"Gods," I whispered, clinging to Silas's palm. "It's the sea king."

"That's his cousin with him. The boy I shoved into the water."

Erik Bloodsinger looked about the hall. He caught sight of Davorin's head. If I hadn't been watching the young sea fae, I would've missed the flicker of fear in the boy's eyes.

"Found what's left of the sea folk," Raum said, tugging on the cousin's arm.

"They're all that's left?" Kase narrowed his eyes. "Where are the rest?"

"Dead or long gone through the Chasm."

I scoffed. "They abandoned their king. They abandoned boys to their enemies."

Stieg offered a look of sympathy to the Ever King. One Erik promptly ignored.

Valen rose from one of the chairs at the table. "Will they dine with enemies? I'm certain they're hungry."

Stieg shifted uncomfortably. "I've been told countless times that the Ever King will surely poison our ale and food. He assures me we will not see it coming."

Valen's jaw ticked. It was clear he did not want to punish a boy who'd saved Tor, but there was more than one life to consider. "Then they'll be more comfortable in the catacombs. Agreed?"

It was with hesitation, but soon enough the lot of us agreed. A cinch tugged at my chest as the sea fae boys were led through the hall. It felt wrong, almost cruel, but what could we do? Bloodsinger was quick, he was filled with hate, and he knew how to poison the whole damn palace if given the chance.

As he was led through, the young royals stopped to gawk, to catch a glimpse at a king who looked more like them than their parents.

Livia leaned around her father, watching the boy. More curious than the princess's stare was when Bloodsinger glanced over his shoulder. Whether he sensed the eyes of another on him, or something else, he quickly found the Night Folk princess.

Livia peeled her gaze back to the table, cheeks flushed in embarrassment. Erik narrowed his eyes, almost confused, before he was dragged out of sight.

"Tired at all?" Silas asked and pressed a kiss to my hand.

I leaned my head on his shoulder. "Yes. I think I should like to wash and sleep for days. I hope you feel the same."

"Why do you hope?"

I paused, tugging on his hand, and drew my lips close to his. "Because washing requires no clothing, and sleeping requires your body close to mine. I hope you are agreeable to this plan."

A sly curve to his lips lifted the scar on his face. "Always, Little Rose."

CHAPTER 44
THE PHANTOM

VALEN AND STIEG KEPT PACE ON EITHER SIDE OF MY SHOULDER.

"All the ships have left," Valen said with a touch of disgust. "They simply left, like spineless sods."

I felt much the same but didn't see the need to repeat it. The spiral steps took us into the catacombs. The final cell door was guarded by a Rave warrior. At the sight of us, he dipped his chin and stepped aside.

"Certain about this?" I asked.

"No." Valen shifted. "But I am told I must try."

Stieg smirked. "Elise is persuasive."

"Yes, she is."

I shoved the door open with my shoulder. Light from the day brightened the cell, but it was still a prison. A miserly fur mat, a bucket for waste, and another for water. Half gone already. No mistake, the boy had been dousing his skin in the water more than wetting his tongue.

In the corner, Bloodsinger glared at us. Chains on his wrists, his bare feet dirty and bruised. On the stone floor beside him was a rolled scrap of parchment. The boy promptly tucked it away beneath his leg.

Valen let out a sigh and stepped forward. "King."

The boy said nothing.

"We've come to negotiate peace. That is what kings do, after all."

Again, nothing from the boy.

"Your folk are gone. They've sailed back through the Chasm, but you don't seem surprised."

Erik's lip curled. His hair was tousled and dirty, and he kept scratching the back of his neck, like the ends irritated the skin there. Based on the number of scars on his flesh, it was probably likely the skin did aggravate him, even more so away from the sea like this.

"Your uncle was killed, I am told."

Of course, we knew Harald was gone; we witnessed it, but it was a way to gauge the indifference or fear of the young king.

Erik's mouth flinched. He turned to study the bones built into the wall. "What a pity."

I glanced at Stieg. The boy seemed hardly bothered by Harald's sudden demise.

"Since you are the last line of authority in the Ever Kingdom, I'm here with a formal offer from every realm—a call for peace between our folk," Valen said.

"No."

"No thought? No consideration?" Valen shook his head. "Boy, I killed King Thorvald, we both know this, but his death did not come for no reason. Cease this vengeance and let our folk be peaceful again. I have the talisman of the Ever, I know it gives me a bit of power over that kingdom. I will shield these lands from the sea fae if I must. I will see to it the Chasm is warded forever if you choose to wallow in your threats."

Erik paused for a few breaths, then leaned his elbows over his bent knees. "Tell me this, earth bender." His voice was rough and dry as scorched grass. "Would you make peace with the man who slaughtered your father?"

"The man who tried to slaughter my father, the man who nearly slaughtered my entire family," Valen said, "I despised him. I sought revenge against every descendant of his line. If you think I do not understand your anger, you're very wrong."

"Then why are we speaking?"

"Care to know how it ended for me?"

"No."

"Well, you are in chains, so I'm going to tell you whether you want to hear or not." Valen crouched, holding the Ever King's stare. "I took vows with a direct descendant of my enemy's line. My queen was the best choice I have ever made in all my many turns."

Erik snorted. "There are no queens of the Ever. You've nothing to offer me. Might as well save your breath, earth bender, I've no interest in your tales."

Valen shook his head and rose. "I've spent time these few days reading any lore we could find on this talisman of your father's. We've determined it is most likely a power from a sea witch, true?"

"Powerful sea witches," Erik snapped.

"If that is so, then it is a temperamental gift," Valen said. "A type of magic that is rather unforgiving. It does not like to be lost from the one to whom it once belonged."

"Witches are damn arrogant," the boy muttered, and the way he curled his face away, I wasn't certain he meant to speak.

"How are you so certain the power of that talisman will even answer to you, Erik Bloodsinger?" Valen asked. "It has been under our watch for ten turns, and now, it will remain here indefinitely."

"It does not call to you," Erik said, but there was a touch of worry in his tone, like he might not be certain.

"Does it call to you?" Valen studied the boy, but the young king merely returned his scrutiny with a glare. Valen opened his arms. "You're right, the power within it does not call to me. It is nothing but a thin, gold disc. I feel no power over your kingdom. I only regret that blood had to be shed between us. I do not want your title, Ever King. I want to guide a young royal in peace between our worlds. Nothing more. No conditions."

Erik leaned forward, eyes burning. "Then you do not know the ways of the Ever. The death of an Ever King does not happen. It is a crime against the kingdom I will never forget, nor overlook."

Vengeance, hatred, it was as though viciousness had been branded in the boy's blood. The Ever Folk rose to avenge a fallen king. Doubtless their world was one made wholly of righting wrongs through blood and war.

Valen's shoulders slumped slightly. "Then, you remain here, King Erik. Until we know what to do with you."

The boy turned back to the wall as though hardly bothered. Tension in his neck, his shoulders, the way one foot tapped, gave up the truth. The young king was frightened, and he did not want anyone to know it.

Valen abandoned the cell first, me close behind. I paused in the doorway when the boy's raspy voice broke the silence.

"Warrior?"

Stieg halted. "Erik?"

"Did you kill the other boy?"

"Harald's son? Your *cousin*."

"Just . . . did you kill him?" Erik snapped. He didn't turn around.

"No, Erik," Stieg answered softly. "We're not the monsters you think we are."

When the boy didn't respond, Stieg followed me into the corridor. The clang of the door slammed at our backs and the Rave stepped in front again.

"The boy is lost," Stieg said as we began to trudge the stairs. "He is doing what he thinks is right by avenging his father. It's natural. We'd all do the same, but Thorvald was a monster. You weren't there, but he looked ready to throw Erik onto his blade when he saw the damage Ivar and Britta had caused."

Valen rounded back down the bend in the stairs. "Did you both see the parchment in the cell?"

"I noticed," I admitted.

"Someone is speaking to him. They're delivering missives."

"You think there are hidden sea fae?" Stieg asked.

"Possibly. Kase has sensed nothing, no fear, no glimmer of apprehension except from the two boys. Raum has searched, and nothing." Valen's dark eyes narrowed. "Perhaps someone else is trying to gain his trust."

"Valen," Stieg chuckled. "You sound like you already know. Who are you thinking?"

"I'll be on the watch tonight," he said without responding. "I want to see for myself."

It was my night to make rounds around the fort. Valen still insisted he'd be there. I wasn't going to argue. Calista would be there. Everyone else could join. I was certain I'd hardly notice them, for my eyes would be on her.

Elise yawned and let her head drop to her husband's shoulder. "I'm not cut out for watch duty, it would seem. Tell me why we're here again. I thought this was the job of skilled warriors."

Valen grinned. "Are you turning into an adventureless queen, my love?"

Elise pinched his side. "Watch your words, Valen Ferus. I am the one always asking to travel, while you are content to stay holed away in your comfortable castle."

I could understand the Night Folk king on that piece. I'd be content to remain holed away for another turn if it meant Calista and I were undisturbed and unthreatened for once in our damn lives.

Calista tugged on my hand. "I think someone's slinking through the grass over there. See the way it's moving."

True enough, there was an odd sway to the long snake grass leading to the tower with the cells. Valen leaned over one knee, watching as the intruder wove their way toward the tower until they emerged on the rocky edges of the tower walls.

"Dammit. I bleeding knew it." Valen rubbed a hand down his face. "Recognized that little swirl she puts on some of her symbols."

Calista bit down on her bottom lip, to keep from laughing, I thought. Now was not the time to aggravate the king.

"Is that—" Elise squinted. "Bleeding gods, what is Livia doing? We need to get her."

"Wait," Calista said. "We're watching. He can't hurt her. Let's see what she's up to."

I cast her a furtive look. She had reasons to watch this play out, as much as I did.

Valen frowned. Elise still seemed aghast. Together, they watched their daughter, draped in a dark fur over her frilled nightdress, tap on the bars of Erik Bloodsinger's cell and lean close. I never saw the young king, but clearly, she was speaking to him. After a moment she dug into a small leather satchel and pulled out . . . a book.

"She's . . . *reading* to him?" Valen seemed more confused than before.

Elise pressed a hand to her heart, smiling. "That girl is too bleeding good for this cruel world. She's befriending him, Valen."

"Why?"

Elise blew out her lips. "She knows the tale of Thorvald, and likely knows who that boy hates the most. You know your this is Livia's way of making certain another battle does not take her daj from her. This must be why she's not sleeping well."

Valen's jaw tightened, but he gave us a quick look. "Livie's been having wretched nightmares."

"The littles have never known war," Calista said. "This whole ordeal was frightening. Are you satisfied that no sea fae are sneaking in to speak to the boy?"

"No, I'm not satisfied," Valen said. "Now, I have a tender-hearted daughter trying to befriend a boy who'd like to slit my throat. If he doesn't alter his words, another thing will be torn from her soon enough."

Valen had his answers. He offered us a farewell, and took Elise's hand once they had a promise that we would keep watch on the Night Folk princess until she returned.

"So," I said, wrapping my arms around Calista's waist. I pressed a kiss to the crook of her neck. "Are you going to tell him?"

She snorted. "You mean, am I going to tell him that a bleeding heart song is growing between his beloved daughter and a boy from an enemy kingdom? No. I think I will let that path open however it is meant to open. I'm quite done meddling in fate."

I chuckled, embracing the heat of a song burning between the two of us the longer the two littles were close to each other.

Calista had the right idea. Twisting fate had done enough damage to our lives. I, for one, planned to live as far from tales and tricks of the Norns as I could.

I planned to live, for the first time in lifetimes, in peace with my rose by my side.

EPILOGUE
WESTERN KINGDOM: THE STORYTELLER

APPARENTLY, SILAS AND I NEEDED TO BE CORONATED.

Gorm, that logical fool, was the one who insisted until we all caved. The blood fae was soft spoken, but damn unrelenting. It was a true gift, a power no one could manage without bending beneath his insistence on what must be done because that is simply what is done.

I tugged at the collar of the satin gown Saga had brought from the new Borough in the Southern realms. My hair was out of its rough braids for the first time in what seemed forever, and I finally relented and agreed to wear the silver circlet Gorm had fashioned for me turns ago.

Silas was across the bed chamber, and I might have liked to stare at him the whole of the day rather than be seated on a bleeding throne.

A clean, deep blue tunic with dark trousers. Silver runes stitched the hems of his sleeves, and his hair had been braided down the center of his head, like a bleeding warrior. No mistake, he was my favorite sight of all.

Hus Rose was promptly decided on as a neutral fortress. It would be a gathering of realms. Here we fought for our folk, our lands, so here we'd gather as one land, every turn, perhaps every two. If Silas had his way, it would be every five.

In the center knolls, Silas and I would take our place. Already, plans for a longhouse all our own had been mapped out and designed. Ari had a great deal to say about it, insisting there be rooms aplenty for when our royals decided to drop in from time to time.

Silas spun a silver band around his center finger, once, twice.

I chuckled and took hold of his palm. "Unsettled?"

"Always."

"About truly taking a place as king, or something else?"

"I don't much care what folk call me. I'll leave you to do all the talking anyway." He grinned, but a pink flush tinged his cheeks. "I've never left Raven Row. At least, not for centuries. It's strange to think, soon we won't be here."

I took his hands in mine. "We can stay here if you'd rather."

"No." He kissed me quickly. "No, I want to leave. I am a prisoner in many ways when I'm here, Little Rose. Still, it's unsettling, and I feel ridiculous about it."

I stroked the sharp line of his jaw. "It's not ridiculous."

"A bit." Silas finished securing the blade on his belt. "We literally survived a war of worlds, and what frightens me is a new dwelling."

"Well, when you put it that way."

He tugged on the end of my hair like he always did when we were littles and ushered me to walk ahead of him toward the great hall.

The hall was truly a sight. A raised dais had been positioned at the far end. Blossoms and vines of berries donned the edges. Atop the platform were eight bleeding thrones. Simple for now, but Gorm assured every royal house the fortress would be fitted with proper thrones soon enough.

I didn't think any of us cared where we plopped our asses.

Already, my royals were seated in their places. Elise and Valen both wore circlets made of silver and moonvane. They had their fingers laced, and kept their heads close, whispering through grins.

I never knew what my Cursed King and Kind Heart snickered

about, but it brightened my soul to know they were once more at ease and laughing together.

Kase seemed ready to bolt if one more fae or warrior dipped their chin in respect. He, in fact, had managed to find a way not to wear his black crown. Malin smiled when we appeared in the doorway, her gown was like liquid silver. I smiled back. This was the moment —I could recall it now—but I knew this was the moment I'd shown the dying memory queen all those turns ago.

A true queen of fate seated beside her king amidst the united thrones.

Ari and Saga both wore dark circlets of raven's wings. Saga waved once she saw me, but Ari was too distracted with his daughter. Mira seemed content to sit on her father's lap, playing tricks with their illusion magic, laughing as they kept trying to outsmart the other by making pebbles appear and disappear in Ari's palm.

Seats in the hall skidded as folk rose. Sol and Tor stood near the front. My Sun Prince strained to catch a look at the two of us, grinning. Lilianna and Arvad stood hand in hand beside them.

I was their storyteller. I'd been the one to guide them once, but somewhere along the way we'd switched places. They guided me, taught me, loved me. The fools had already dragged me into their family before discovering the truth, but even more now, they treated me as their own.

Like their blood family.

Gorm and Elder Klok from Etta stepped in front of us.

"To a king and queen of fate," Gorm said, bowing his head.

"To the king and queen," said Elder Klok. "For a queen of cunning who united us all."

The two men marked our foreheads in runes with goat blood. Then, they left us to take our places among the others. Silas clung to my hand. He'd removed his mask, and even knowing how little scars bothered our folk, he despised scrutiny; likely worse than the Nightrender.

I clung to him much the same. My pulse raced. Hard to imagine we were finally here after all this time. This was the ending my father, my mother, my Rave brother, had all sacrificed their lives for our lands to reach.

Silas held my hand as I stepped onto the dais, struggling with the damn gown. I'd much prefer trousers, but for one bleeding day I supposed I could manage.

Once he was on the dais with me, he took my hand again, and as Gorm had instructed before dawn, we sat as one in the center thrones.

"To the kings and queens!" Gorm shouted again, then took to one knee.

"To the kings and queens!" Folk rumbled after, every land, every kingdom lowering to their knees (except for Niklas and Junie, but I thought it was more to draw out Kase's deeper scowl than anything).

I looked to my sides, taking in the faces of my royals. I refused to cry, but the sting was there.

My folk. My family. They'd fought for me. They'd saved me. Much more than I'd ever saved them.

I faced Silas, grinning. I would always love my royals for their bold choices, their will to love so fiercely. Without them, I would never have found *him*.

Feasts followed. A final night of celebration, for tomorrow the trials of the remaining sea fae would be had. Dreary works. Most of our captives were young fae. All the grown folk left them to be at the mercy of enemies.

It seemed the Ever Kingdom did not know the meaning of loyalty. Not like it was known here.

I snuck a glance at the table where the young royals ate with each other.

"Livie," I said, crouching down by the sneaky princess. "What's that you've got?"

She flushed and held up a silver charm in the shape of a swallow.

"Bought it from a forest fae. Thinking of making a necklace with it. Maybe an arm band."

"What's the meaning behind the bird?"

She popped a shoulder, studying her little charm. "I just like it."

I lifted a brow. She was clearly wanting me to cease with the questions. I pressed a kiss to the top of her head. "Looks beautiful. Giving it as a gift?"

"I don't know. Maybe."

"Well, if you do, whoever receives it will be fortunate."

Sun split the hazy clouds over the sea. What looked to be a storm hovered over the thrashing current of the Chasm of Seas. The black streak of darker water never faded, never stilled. Sometimes it seemed like the sea knew its king remained on land and would not calm until it took him back.

Now that the coronation was finished, the sea fae were at last set to be returned to their watery kingdom. Two weeks since Davorin's death, two weeks since they'd lived within the tides.

I anticipated a bit more landsickness, but the young king held his head high as Niklas strategically took a bit of the boy's blood.

Erik Bloodsinger sneered at the Falkyn. "Boils in the veins. Sort of makes folk froth at the mouth right before it fills their lungs with blood."

He nodded at the blood on the Falkyn's blade. Niklas was bold, but even the Falkyn lead knew how deadly the king's blood could be and dropped it into one of his vials with care.

"This elixir I've created will ward the Chasm against you, boy," Niklas explained. "You'll never step foot in our realms again, understand? Your people are to be locked in your kingdom for good."

Erik never lost his arrogant, boyish smirk. "We'll see."

My stomach turned when the sea fae captives were brought before every royal seat on the dais by the shore. Sick that our only captives were two boys. Battle worn and hardened, but boys abandoned by their own people.

Cousins, yet they didn't look at each other, they hardly seemed to acknowledge they were not alone. I wasn't certain they even cared for each other, despite sharing blood.

Stieg led Erik Bloodsinger through the center of the crowds, Halvar led Harald's son. Either he'd been injured in the battle, or still bore a wound from his torture at the Black Palace, but the limp to the king's leg was noticeable and Stieg knew it. Where the warrior could've shoved the boy to the ground, he let Erik lower to his knees of his own accord, in his own time.

When the Ever King lifted his head, a bit of twine slid from beneath his dingy shirt. At the end was the glimmer of a charm—a silver wing of a bird in flight.

Well, damn.

One glance at Livia standing between her mother and father, and it was obvious the girl was the most unsettled of us all. She couldn't even lift her gaze to look at the young king.

Harald's son shook Halvar's grip off and the First Knight allowed it.

We'd discussed how to proceed in the early hours of the morning, but in truth, the way all my royals, the way Silas and I, hesitated, I wasn't convinced any of us knew how to go about this. Sol and Tor looked squeamish whenever they glanced at the Ever King.

Everyone but the young royals knew what Erik Bloodsinger had done for Tor.

"What is your name, Harald's son?" Ari was the first to speak.

The boy didn't speak until Halvar nudged his shoulder.

"Tait," he rasped. "Tait Heartwalker."

"These names, Bloodsinger, Heartwalker," Ari muttered, then looked back to the boys. "Tait Heartwalker, a royal of the Ever—"

"I serve the House of Kings," Tait snapped. "I do not claim the seat."

"I have no idea what you're talking about, nor do I truly care. Truth be told, boy, I'm tired. I'm wholly tired of this fighting. I'd like to simply rid our shores of any enemies and go home to my magnificent palace, and live out my days with my stunning wife, and delightful daughter, undisturbed."

Ari *was* tired, we all were. Now, the Golden King would begin to ramble.

Saga took hold of Ari's hand, looking like she might be fighting a grin too. Instead, she addressed the enemy fae. "For raising blades against our folk, we banish you to the Ever Kingdom. Should you rise and walk upon our lands again, boy or not, you will not be shown such mercy."

Tait kept his red gaze steeled on the ground.

Silence went on long enough I began to squirm in my seat. At long last, Valen rose from his seat. He strode toward the young king.

Erik Bloodsinger never looked away.

"You did not challenge me, boy. Was that not your purpose for being here?"

"The opportunity was taken . . ." Erik said, his crimson eyes flicked toward Torsten before he returned his smug smirk to the Night Folk king. "By other things."

"You must wait ten turns again? Remember, we spoke already of that temperamental power. Perhaps it will not want you."

"I suppose we'll find out."

"It won't happen," Valen said. "As we've already said, the sea fae will never rise through the Chasm again. We will ward up the barriers between our worlds."

Valen lowered to a crouch again, his voice too low to hear, but I knew what he was saying. He told us he would do it. He'd offer Erik Bloodsinger a place among the Night Folk.

Valen was an enemy to the boy, but my Cursed King was no bitter soul. He knew what it would mean to a boy to avenge his father, cruel as that father was. We'd all witnessed Harald's rage. If Erik was raised by such an uncle, it was a wonder the boy did not try to bite and lash against us all.

But more than that, he knew his daughter's open heart had tried to befriend the boy. She wanted peace, and as doting as a father as he was, Valen wanted to grant her that. Even if she didn't realize it,

Valen was trying to keep a peaceful existence for his girl. Even if it meant welcoming an enemy into his clans.

For a moment, Erik studied the Night Folk king, as though confused. He cast a quick look to the dais, then back to the king.

Was he considering it? Would he stay among us? Would he demand peace between our worlds?

The notion of it was so foreign, I almost couldn't fathom it, but my grip tightened on Silas's hand in anticipation all the same. Silas chuckled and threaded our fingers together. Peace. We might have it. The Ever King was young, but he still had the title of king.

We could guide him, help him navigate his folk into allies with us, not enemies.

Then, Erik's sneer returned. He lifted his voice loud enough we could hear. "The Ever will never be at peace with the earth fae. I will never stop, never cease fighting against this realm, until I hold the heart of my father's killer. Until everything he loves is in the hands of the Ever Kingdom."

The red in Erik's eyes burned. Did he bleeding want to get his throat slit?

Valen's shoulders curled a bit. He shook his head and rose back to standing. He'd done all he could do. The king wanted peace, no mistake, but the boy kept threatening his life, now his family. Everything Valen loved? It was his wife and child.

Valen wouldn't keep threats near them.

"You leave us no choice. Erik Bloodsinger, you are banished to your kingdom. The wards on the Chasm will be built with your blood. Even if sea folk found a way through in some distant time, *you* will never be allowed to cross. You, Ever King, are a prisoner in your own realm. A merciful prison, but a prison all the same."

"Maj, I don't think it has to be this way." Livia whispered. "I don't think Bloodsinger means it."

Elise took her daughter's hand but didn't falter as Valen leveled his word on the sea fae.

"Livie, sometimes no matter how much we want peace, some folk are not willing to do the same."

Livia's chin crinkled. She let go of her mother's hand and rubbed a spot on her arm below the crook of her elbow. When the guards gathered the two sea fae boys, the Night Folk princess closed her eyes and turned away as the warriors led them to the shore.

I didn't know how fate would unfold for the Ever King. I didn't know if the faint song between his heart and a princess of his enemy would die or build. But my Kind Heart was right, he brought this act on himself.

Valen had offered a road to peace, and the Ever King was determined to remain a threat.

"How are we supposed to make certain they're gone?" Kase asked. "Drop them in the sea and hope they swim away?"

"Look." Malin gestured to the sea.

Erik and Harald's son had stepped into the tides to their knees. The waves rose, lapping around them when Erik raised his hands.

"You thought we were alone. The king is never without his ship." Bloodsinger waved his hand, and a fierce thrashing gathered near the borders of the Chasm's current.

From below the surface the sharp, jagged bow sliced through the tides like a knife. A fearsome sea serpent made the bowsprit. Crimson sails snapped in a new wind. Crewmen bustled about, pulling on the rigs of the numerous masts, humming their eerie songs. The black laths glistened like onyx in the sunlight and aimed one side of the hull toward the boy king.

My eyes widened when a great side door clanked on chains and opened. Harald's boy didn't wait, one flick of Erik's hand and the boy took his leave, letting the tides pull him under and toward the Ever Ship.

Wind wrapped around us in a fury, as though the vessel had brought with it new storms.

"Until we meet again, earth bender," Erik shouted into the storm.

"Won't happen, boy," Valen fired back. "You've seen these realms for the final time."

All the king did was grin, flashing his teeth, then let the waves pull him under.

In the next breath, Niklas hounded Falkyns and Rave warriors to prepare the shields. They watched in a new kind of tension as the strange side door closed on the Ever Ship, and slowly the massive sails, its decks, its horrid sea serpent bow, sank beneath the waves.

The Chasm barrier awakened in violent tides and white foam. It was our only hint the Ever Ship was being pulled through the current, pulled back from where it came.

In the instant the Chasm calmed, Niklas demanded the wards be placed. Fiery streaks shot across the surface of the sea, colliding with the dark barrier. A wall of thrashing water burst toward the sky all along the edges of the kingdom, even curving out of sight on the far reaches. Every border would be shielded against sea fae.

It would take a fierce act of fate to break the guards against the Ever Kingdom.

For another month we remained at the fortress at Raven Row. Soon, battle fatigue shifted to games—archery, axe throwing, feasts.

Until the next full moon rose, white and bright, and it was arranged for every royal to return to their new realm. Their new pieces of the kingdoms. Where we'd rule together, thieves, mortals, fae, and fate workers who never wanted to need their damn seidr again.

The distance between realms and royal houses no longer took weeks or crossing seas. Three days, four at most, to reach any realm in the kingdom. We'd be seeing a great deal of the littles through the turns. I'd be seeing a great deal of all my royals until my last breath, and the thought of it added a bit of warmth to my chest.

"Ready, Little Rose?" Silas draped a satchel strap over his shoulder and held out a hand.

I took in the music room. The tagelharpa, the lyres, all of them had been packed away and would ride with us to our new palace. Still, there was an ache about leaving Raven Row.

True, the fort would remain. Rave would always be here, watching the shores that remained nearest to the Chasm of Seas.

Even with the wards in place, there was always a lingering threat beneath the waves.

Gorm was the resounding voice here, a trusted Captain of the Rave. Raum, Tova, Bard, even Malin's thieving friend and his family would live in the Row. A few Ettans would take the rooms in the fortress, some of Halvar's brothers and their families. Bo insisted he could not stomach leaving the place where Rune had died and would be one on watch of the waves.

A piece of every realm would be here to trade, to exist, to stand united in the same land, as one people.

I gave Silas a small grin and took his hand. "I'm ready."

Rave dipped their chins as we strode through the corridors of Hus Rose. It would be built into the fortress eventually. A space large enough we could all gather, not only the royal houses, but folk of the courts and their families.

Once a turn, it was already decided, we would gather again. We'd keep our kingdom safe through royal councils; we'd celebrate peace.

Outside, Silas and I faced Hus Rose as the gates closed against us.

"Ready, My Queen and King?" Cuyler winked from the head charge that would lead a coach to the center knolls.

"What have I said about titles, Cuyler? If you're our First Knight, I refuse to hear it every damn day."

"I know," Cuyler said, adjusting the strap hiding the scar and missing eye. "Which is why I plan to toss them around most liberally to irritate you."

"We ought to leave him here," I murmured and made my way for the coach.

Silas chuckled and followed me inside. Doors closed, shades drawn, I was in his lap, arms around his neck.

I kissed Silas, hard and greedy. He clung to my waist, holding me tightly.

When I pulled back, I pressed my forehead against his, stroking my fingertips down the scar on his face. "Thank you for never giving up on me, Whisper."

He kissed my throat, burying his face against my skin. "You're my peace, Little Rose. You're the one who chases away the darkness. Say the word and I'd follow you anywhere."

I kissed his lips softly. "Tell me now is when we finally get to share each day, tell me now is when we share one lifetime together."

Silas's brow furrowed. He brushed a hand over my cheek, swiping stray hair off my brow. "I swear it, Little Rose. Each morning, each night, every beat of my heart is yours. To the Otherworld."

"To the Otherworld, Whisper."

He'd been mine since my first breaths, and he would be mine beyond my last.

EPILOGUE
NORTHERN KINGDOM: ROGUE PRINCESS

"I HOPE SHE IS FREE OF THE MARE DEMONS TONIGHT," I SAID, WAVING AS Sol, Tor, and Alek rode away on their horses. Livia rode beside them, laughing with her cousin as they tried to out-trot the other.

Valen wrapped an arm around my shoulders, holding me against his side. "She'll be all right. I sent a draught with Sol should she need it."

Nearly six months after the death of Davorin, Livia still had wretched nightmares. She'd scream, pleading for us to survive. She'd cry for her Uncle Tor—as if she knew what had happened, though we'd all vowed never to speak of it. How would we explain to Aleksi his father had come so near death, only to be pulled back by a boy we'd banished in the tides?

The sea fae king might feel it a sense of honor to avenge his father, but the same emotions lived in our realms. Alek would feel indebted. Truth be told, Sol and Tor did. They despised how our battle ended with the boy who'd saved Tor as a prisoner in the sea realms.

They understood. Erik Bloodsinger felt no loyalty to us. He'd healed Tor not out of love for him, but as penance to be repaid to Stieg.

To the sea king, that debt was square. Doubtless if the king faced Stieg on a battlefield now, the boy wouldn't hesitate to attack him.

Harald was a wretched man. I was glad he was gone, but I couldn't fathom what he'd burned into his nephew's head about the horrid earth fae they hated so much.

I turned down a corridor, but Valen tugged me in the opposite direction, laughing. "Still forgetting the directions, Elise?"

I groaned. "Hells, I'm never going to get accustomed to the shifted walls of this bleeding castle."

During the shift of lands, Ravenspire remained intact for the most part, but there were a few differences. Whole rooms turned in the opposite directions. Even the damn peaks were out a different window. The Ribbon Lakes were less ribbons and more ponds where we'd fish and spend warm afternoons.

The townships and docks of Mellanstrad were shifted into one flat township now. And the peaks had more caves and forests where a few of the Timoran people and Night Folk with the urge to hunt took up residence.

Our closest friends remained in the lower cottages and homes around Ravenspire. Siv and her boy were always close. She named him Mattis and often told him, even as a tiny babe, of his father who'd died to protect our world.

Halvar, Kari, and their brood lived in the eastern wings of the palace. Herja and Hagen opted for a large longhouse beyond the gardens. The same as Tor and Sol took up the longhouse nearer to the ponds since Livia and Alek had a love for swimming.

Another worry I kept hidden about my girl—she was too drawn to the water. After witnessing her draw to the sea king, it was always a concern. Likely a worthless one, since sea fae were locked away.

Valen's grip tightened on my hand as he closed the door to our bed chamber behind us. A sly grin crossed his handsome features when he pulled me close. "Alone for the first time in a while, my love." He pressed a kiss to my throat. "How should we spend our time?"

A grin split over my lips. "I could take something sweet. Maybe we should head to the cooking rooms and—"

"Wrong answer." Valen's teeth scraped against my neck. I sighed and tilted my head, giving him more access. "Anything that does not include my mouth on your skin, Elise, is the wrong answer."

A heated tremble rippled up my arms. Since the day I fell in love with Legion Grey in that old schoolhouse, my heart had never ceased beating for this man. All the battles, the fears, the scars, the damn curses we'd survived—it was worth every step to end in Valen Ferus's arms.

"I think I like your answer," I whispered, tracing the point of his ear.

I kissed him, desperately. Gods, I would never tire of this man's taste, his kiss, his passion. Sweet or greedy, it didn't matter. A touch, a kiss, a smile from Valen sent my body aflame.

"I hope you weren't planning on remaining clothed," I rasped against his skin when his teeth scraped over my throat.

The glossy midnight of his eyes flashed like dark flames. "Not a chance."

The gown I wore was simple, laces down the back, and Valen's hand made quick work of unthreading them, baring my body to him.

He groaned and slid a rough palm between my breasts, down my belly, until his fingers teased the sensitive folds of my core. I gripped his wrist, urging those clever fingers into the slickened center.

"So wet, *Kvinna*," he moaned and kissed me, grinning. "All for me."

Valen slid his finger into my entrance. Deep, long thrusts dragged me toward a burning precipice. Slowly, he added a second finger, stretching me to the fullest.

I let my head fall back, rough gasps slid from my throat. My legs trembled. "Valen . . ." I couldn't catch a breath. "I need you."

"You have me." Valen widened his fingers inside me until my knees quaked. He tightened his hold on my waist, and bit down on my shoulder. "Always, Elise. You have always owned me."

"I need you inside me." Three hells, I would go mad if I did not feel his body against mine soon.

A deep, growl rumbled from his throat. Valen removed his fingers, glistening with my arousal, and sucked off what was left.

His eyes rolled back in his head for a breath. "I'll never tire of the taste of you." With the same hand he gripped my chin, tugging my face close to his. "On our bed, on your knees, Elise."

A rush of pleasure flooded my core at the mere tone of his demands.

In slow movements, I removed what was left of my dress and back peddled to the bed. Naked, exposed, I turned away from the king.

Valen crowded me from behind and shed his tunic. His bare chest against my spine sent intoxicating trembles up my arms. He snaked his arm around my middle, rubbing his open palm across my smooth skin. A whimper slid from my throat, and I leveraged one knee onto the furs of the bed.

Valen's hands curled around my waist, popping my ass in the air in a tug. How the man could be forceful and gentle was a beautiful conundrum, and I could not get enough.

His fingertips traced every divot of my spine. "You're beautiful, Elise Ferus."

His tongue slicked between my shoulders. I shuddered. There was a delirious need for more the longer he spoke, a need to forget hesitation, any modesty. There was a need to have him inside. Now.

I rocked my hips back, the cleft of my ass rubbing along the stretched length of his shaft under his trousers.

"Why are these *not gone*," I said with a bit of desperation.

Valen cursed and fumbled with the laces on his trousers, stripping them off his legs, until the hot skin of his length finally touched me. His fingers stroked my slit, the sound of my need coating the tips added to my own desperation for more.

My thighs trembled. "Valen . . ."

His finger curled inside me again. Valen leaned over my back until his lips were beside my ear. "What do you want, my love? Want to come on my fingers, my tongue, or do you want all of me? I plan to give you all tell me which goes first."

A choked sob burst from my throat when his thumb circled the swollen apex of my core.

"You. I want you."

"Hmm. I need the particulars. Details, Elise. Speak plainly."

"You bastard."

He chuckled. "Play my games, *Kvinna*, and I swear to you it will be worth it."

My skin was heated the more his hand tormented my slit. Sometimes a second finger, sometimes his thumb. He was a damn villain, always bringing me to the edge, then retreating before I could spill over.

With my face pressed into the bed, my hips up, I widened my thighs, offering more of myself.

"You. I want you inside me. Now."

"Excellent choice." Valen's mouth kissed down my spine. I moaned into the soft furs. He aligned the tip of his length to my entrance. Little by little, my husband slid inside, stretching me. Filling me.

"Gods, Elise," he groaned. His arm wrapped around me again, holding my body to his. One palm slid up and pinched my nipple as his hips rocked. "You are bleeding made for me."

I let out a gasp when he shifted and felt so beautifully deep.

Valen dug his fingernails into my hips, pounding into me. Hells, the angle, the depth, there was nothing like it. With every thrust, Valen tugged on my nipple. He pinched and flicked. Then, slowly worked his hand down my body again until his fingers found my throbbing core.

I cried out, muffled in the furs and mattress. My hips rolled. The wooden posts on the bed slammed against the wall as the king quickened his movements. I was weightless.

"You've always been made for me," Valen grunted through a deep thrust. "From the first night I saw you, I knew you were mine. And this." His hand gently swatted my dripping slit. "Is mine."

My body spasmed. "Valen . . . gods, *yes*!"

Valen drove against me deeper. The bed sounded like it might crack at any moment. My body split into a thousand pieces. A beautiful collision of passion, pleasure, and untamed love.

He pumped his hips once more, and the heat of his release spilled inside. His length twitched, and I felt the slick warmth drip down my inner thighs.

"So good," he gasped, pressing a kiss between my shoulders again. "So damn good, Elise."

I collapsed onto my stomach. Valen slumped over the top of me for a few moments before he slid out and propped his head onto his palm. I rolled onto my shoulder and slung a leg over his hips, grinning.

Valen closed his eyes when I traced the curve of his lips, his jaw, as though memorizing my husband all over again. From the lower pit of my belly, nerves took hold. We'd only settled into our new world. We were adjusting and finding peace. There were so many wonderful new things—like nearness to our neighboring kingdoms. We saw Alvers, a raven, and the mouthy king who came with her, more than we ever had before. We'd already visited Calista and Silas twice since leaving Raven Row.

I think both the fate king and queen found a great deal of solace in their own walls. They didn't make many plans to leave them. For now, we'd visit them.

Life was settling, and it felt like for the first time since I collided with the handsome dowry negotiator outside of that game hall that life was truly calm.

Now, I was going to rock everything all over again.

"I will miss these easy nights," I said, threading my fingers through his hair.

Valen cracked an eye. "Are they going somewhere?"

"Well, I suspect we'll be rather tired again."

He nuzzled the side of my throat. "Because of this." His tricky fingers brushed over one breast again. "We get Liv's nightmares under control, and I plan to love this body frequently. Make up for all those tense turns with battles and such."

I snickered and kissed his temple. "No, I'm afraid even you might be too tired, my love. Well, perhaps not. I am irresistible."

Valen lifted his head. "That you are, but what are you talking about?"

I bit down on my bottom lip and guided his hand over my belly. "Confirmed it with the healer yesterday."

It took a breath or two, but soon Valen's eyes went wide with a bit of stun. "Elise, are you certain?"

I nodded, grinning and clinging to his hand on my stomach.

"Another . . . another child?" Valen's voice grew rough. He tugged me against his chest, legs, arms, his body swallowed me. "Really?"

I nodded, stroking my fingers through his hair. I didn't know if it was Night Folk and Timoran blood, but like Lilianna fought for turns to have her half-fae littles, the same could be said for me and Valen.

It seemed Halvar and Kari were the only fae and mortal pair that could breed without trouble, but after Livia it had seemed like there would only be one child in our household.

Valen kissed me sweetly, resting his head against mine. "I love you, Elise Ferus. You've given me . . . *everything*. My freedom, my home, my life. But your heart, this family you've given me, it is the greatest gift I could ever want."

From the Negotiator to the Blood Wraith, to My King, to my husband, Valen Ferus had been mine. In all his forms, I loved him. The darker pieces, the soft, tender moments such as this. I'd take him all.

There were no threats at our gates. No threats at the gates of others.

For the first time, we could simply . . . live.

EPILOGUE

EASTERN KINGDOM: THE MEMORY THIEF

Kase was convinced there were too many people within our gates. There were a great many people, but there were vows to be had.

What did he expect?

Even Silas and Calista ventured from their comfortable knolls to join us at the new Black Palace. Less dreary than it once was, we'd built gardens where the courtyards once were. Not that they'd survived the shift of worlds. Almost like Calista's and Silas's song had known what horrid memories lived in the remnants of the old masquerade halls.

Now, moonvane stretched from the Northern realms and burst in our lands, connecting us to the Night Folk clans. Lavender toppled over vines, and silky petals of vibrant sea flowers spilled in from the Southern realms. A true show of how united our lands were.

Although, I missed the Howl. The constant flow of sea air was less prominent at the palace. Still there in small bursts of wind that carried from the fort where we'd fought against the sea folk, but I missed looking out on the expanse of the dark sea.

"I hate this tunic." Jonas flopped back on a fur coated chaise, tugging at the high collar of the blue tunic. Sander scratched his neck beside his brother but didn't complain. Merely added a kick to Jonas's shin.

"It's your good tunic, and you'll wear it without complaining," I said, adjusting the black circlet in my braids.

"Damn the hells, I hate this tunic." Kase shoved in from the washroom, tugging at his own collar.

Jonas opened his arms, aghast. "See? Can we just wear something else, Maj? *Please*. Uncle Bard won't care."

"No. Now, tie your boots, and don't try to unravel any braids on any princesses today."

Jonas blew out his lips. "Mira doesn't like braids, so she doesn't mind. And Livia tries to make my hair stand up by rubbing her hands together really fast, then she touches it, and it sticks up. So, I'm just getting her back."

I snorted and shook my head. If we could simply get through these vows without one or more of the heirs of the realms tracking in mud or getting into a squabble the day would be a success.

"Nightrender," I said, tugging on the front laces of his tunic. "Do set a bleeding example for these two heathens."

Kase kissed me, hard and thoroughly, until both boys made retching sounds. He grinned against my lips. "I sort of agree with them today."

"Don't say that," I hissed back. "Jonas will hear you and never stop complaining. I'll take the quiet one and leave him with you all day, Kase Eriksson. I'll do it."

His eyes shadowed for a moment, then he pasted a smile so false anyone would know it was not true and faced his sons. "I love these. They are the finest tunics I think I've ever worn."

Jonas and Sander rolled their eyes.

"Okay, Daj," Jonas said with a sardonic tone. "We know you're just doin' what Maj says."

"As it should be, boy. You better do the same."

"I *do* listen. That's why I'm wearing this stupid thing."

I gently gripped the back of both boys' necks, guiding them out of the chamber. "Let's go. The sooner you sit politely and listen, the sooner I'll let you change your clothes, do we have a deal?'

The twins grinned at each other, then shouted at the same time, "Deal!"

I should've known the deal would soon be forgotten. Already, Livia and Aleksi were plotting with Halvar's son, Aesir, on how to pay the Eastern princes back for placing toads under their seats.

Mira Sekundär was still trying to decide which side to take. She enjoyed a good toad, but Sander had kicked mud on the hem of her yellow skirt.

Kase darkened his eyes when Jonas tried to make another move at Livia's dainty crown, and it worked. For now. Jonas slumped in his chair, frowning as Livia grinned a little smugly, like she'd won the battle, but the war would continue.

Elise and Valen both fought a grin, and pretended to be distracted by tiny baby Rorik, the newest Night Folk prince.

Over a turn since the sea fae had been locked away, since Davorin's head fell, and it felt like peace was no longer a foreign notion. It was real. It existed. We were here.

Niklas and Junie sat beside us as we waited. After the battle, we helped create a new Falkyn nest (below ground) and they'd taken in Von Grym as their own. He lived amongst the Falkyns, learned the art of elixing from Niklas, despite not having mesmer, and knew how to pick a pocket better than us all.

We'd placed totems for Luca and Dagny outside the Falkyn Nest, a way for their boy to always know his mother and father were warriors. They fought for him, for his freedom, from his first breaths.

They died with him as their final thoughts and words.

Ari and Saga sat beside Calista and Silas and kept muttering around the wooden benches with Gunnar, Eryka, and Herja. They laughed at something, but paused when Hagen stepped forward and we were all asked to rise for the couple.

I clasped my hands around Kase's arms. Warm anticipation bled through my veins as Bard stepped onto the blossom coated pathway to Bevan, the old Elixist we considered the foremost Alver in our realms.

Bard's fingers were laced with Tova's, the wide scar over his throat visible, but it was only a reminder of what we'd all survived. Her glistening cat eyes looked nowhere but him.

"Still strange to see Tov in a dress, right?" Raum leaned in from the row behind us.

Kase nodded. I swatted his arm.

Lynx and Fiske were busy taking bets on if their fellow Kryv would stumble on her skirts, Ash kept casting glances at Shelba, the new Lady of the Serpent Court of the South, and Hanna sat beside Laila, finger-speaking how much she adored Tova's gown.

Isak succumbed to the two princes' whines and lifted them up, so they could see over the heads of everyone.

I flashed Tova a wide grin when she passed our front seat. She met my smile, but slugged Kase's arm, cursing at him for trying to trip her up.

Bevan drew them close together, beaming at the crowd, then the new couple. He spoke of the bonds of vows, but the deeper unification that came from two Alver's becoming one. He explained their power would swell, they'd give and take from the other.

A sting burned behind my eyes. I gripped Kase's hand. He glanced at our fingers, offered a gentle smile, then kissed the tops of my knuckles.

"You were worth it all, Nightrender," I whispered. "Every bad memory, every beautiful one, you were worth it for this life we now live."

Kase swallowed. He kissed me quickly, then forced himself to watch the vows of his Kryv and our brother.

Strange to think of all the pieces that brought us here. Those nights in the hayloft where I was certain the skinny boy beside me would always be with me. The wretched turns where he wasn't. Then, to find him as the feared villain of the East—as I told him, I would not take it back.

My heart was always devoted to him. Always.

EPILOGUE

SOUTHERN KINGDOM: THE RAVEN QUEEN

"This is going to be a disaster, sweet menace." Ari crossed his arms over his chest. "I'm telling you. I pride myself on my logic, my ability for reason, but not on this. Not *this*."

I chuckled and pecked his lips. "I think you're being a bit overbearing."

"Overbearing, she says." He scoffed. "Overbearing would be chaining the girl to my wrist and dragging her to this dull council instead of allowing her to attend a masque—a bleeding ball—where stupid, feckless boys will be pawing at her, and don't say they won't be, she's gods-awful lovely and I've been a stupid, feckless boy before."

I kissed Ari a little longer this time. First, for my sheer enjoyment. Second, because it soothed his busy tongue and mind.

When I pulled back, his shoulders relaxed a bit. "Ari, I love you."

"This, I know." He kissed the tip of my nose. "But that is not the point of this discussion, wife. I'm going to box her away. I've officially become that father and it's an awful look on me. I'm not this man. I'm levelheaded—"

"I would challenge that."

"In *most* things," he insisted. "When it comes to this, no. I'm a fiend, and I plan to become so should one sod give her the slightest salacious glance."

Gods, I loved this man. He was utterly enraptured by me, by our daughter, and he proved it every sunrise, and every sunset. Some might laugh, thinking Ari was merely attempting to be humorous, but in truth, he would start an entire war all over again should someone break his girl's heart.

"She's sixteen, Ari," I said, trying to be reasonable. "It is bound to happen."

"I detest that answer. Tell the others I must skip this turn's festivities out of illness. Mira came down with it too. We'll stay here."

"Maj!" As if summoned, Mira burst into the room. Her dark, wispy curls were a bit wild, and her cheeks were flushed as she spun around holding a gown made of satin and velvet and intricately woven runes of gold in the threads against her body. "It came! What do you think?" She didn't wait for my answer and faced Ari. "Daj? Think it's pretty? I love it, but what do you think?"

She swayed side to side, a new kind of thrill on her face.

This turn at the annual Crimson Festival, what we all determined to name the anniversary of the battle's end, the young royals and courtiers had pleaded to attend the ball. They insisted they were old enough to mingle amongst courtiers and warriors without the supervision of their parents. While our children celebrated at the fort of Raven Row, the kings and queens went to Kunglig—what Calista and Silas called their palace.

It was agreed, the littles were not so little any longer.

They were welcome to attend the masque. A masque requested, to our surprise, by Kase and Malin. As if they needed to know joyous masquerades could exist. As if they need to see lightness in the memories of their darkness.

"Daj?" Mira smiled up at him. "What do you think?"

Ari grinned. He cupped her cheek and pressed a kiss to her forehead. "I think you will be the brightest star, Starlight. It looks beautiful."

She faced me.

"Stunning, Mir. I love it."

With a little squeal she turned around, calling over her shoulder, "I can't wait to show Livie!"

Once we were alone, I slipped my arms around Ari's waist from behind. "You know what I think?"

He covered my hands on his flat stomach with his own. "I am always, *always* game to know what you think."

"I think." I kissed the place between his shoulders. "You, Ari Sekundär, are a wonderful father."

Ari lifted one of my palms to his mouth and kissed the center. "I wouldn't be so certain."

"Why is that?"

He turned into me. "I'm going to demand all the prints and plans of that damn fort, so I know where to strategically place every bleeding blood fae watcher. In fact, when we arrive to the Row, Bo will be placed on Mira. He'll track her every move."

I wanted to groan. I thought to tell him he was insufferable. Instead, I laughed, and cupped the back of his head, kissing him deeply.

Ari let out a sigh, his tongue brushed mine as he took possession of the kiss and demanded more of me. My back struck the wall. Ari dug his fingers in my hair. He kissed me until our lips grew raw and swollen. He kissed me until I was on the verge of arriving late to the fort to spend a bit of time tangled in my husband's arms and legs.

When he pulled back, Ari dragged his fingertips across my cheek. "You are my perfect menace, Saga."

"You are the most beautiful bastard," I whispered.

Turns since our battles ended, turns since fate gave us a new path, a new chance to live the life we'd dreamed of, and I had reveled in every moment. Every busy word, every deep, pensive thought. I took all of Ari and held it close to my heart.

No, our life was not simple and quiet as we'd once dreamed. I was not an ambassador's wife. I was a queen; he was my king. We ruled a realm instead of living humbly in a small longhouse somewhere in the fae isles, and yet, I would not change any of it.

I was certain none of the royals would ever change the paths that brought us here. We'd lost much, but we loved fiercely, and we knew by now, there was nothing we would not do to defend those we loved.

We were friends.

We were family.

We were free.

At long last, through blood and pain and tears, the Broken Kingdoms have reached . . .

The End.

DEAR WICKED DARLINGS

Dear Wicked Darlings,

I suppose I ought to thank you. You see, it turns out you altered my fate, a bit like Wraith and our wild little Storyteller.

Seems there were wretched, rather ominous plans for my death in this final battle. It would've been heroic, no doubt. Me, leaping in front of some innocent, maybe one of the little royals. Maybe I would've rescued a fated queen, or even the surly face of the Nightrender. Gods, that would've been glorious. Can you imagine, Kase Eriksson living his days knowing one day he'd need to keep my horn full in the Otherworld for my beautiful sacrifice?

Alas, I still live, and it's been revealed that it is because of you that I did not die. Your desire to know mine and Junie's stunning love story has kept air in my lungs.

So, I thank you. From the bottom of my thieving heart,

thank you. I look forward to meeting you again in the tale of a smuggler and a lie taster. It is, after all, my favorite tale.

All my love,
Niklas Tjuv

SNEAK PEEK
THE EVER KING

There are paths of fate to be written. Want to know what Livia Ferus said to the boy king in the prison cell? Get a glimpse of the Broken Kingdoms spin-off, The Ever King, below.

The ending needed to be altered.

The girl spent the whole of the afternoon crossing out lines with her raven feather quill, then adding new, better words to read to the boy in the dark. A tale of a serpent who befriended a songbird. A tale where they lived happily ever after, for in the girl's version, the snake never devoured the bird.

Long after the moon found its highest perch in the night sky, the girl slipped from the loft in the battle fort near the shore. Crouched low, she used the tall snake grass as a shield until she found her way to the old stone tower. The top had caved in, and it wasn't much of a tower anymore, but the walls were thick as two men standing side by side.

Along the foundation, iron bars covered a few openings. In her head, the girl counted six barred windows before she crouched at the final cell.

"Bloodsinger," she whispered. Since the end of the battle, she'd practiced the breathy pitch to be loud enough the boy inside would hear, but the guards stomping along the borders would think it nothing more than the hiss of a forest creature.

Five breaths, ten, then red eyes like a stormy sunset appeared from the shadows.

He was a frightening boy. A few turns older than her, but he'd fought in the war. He'd raised a sword against her people's warriors. A boy who still had dried blood on his skin.

Her heart squeezed with a strange dread she didn't understand. This was the last night she might see the boy; she needed to make it count.

"Trials come with the sun," the boy said, his voice dry as brittle straw. "Better leave, little princess."

"But I have something for you, and I've got to finish the story." From the pouch slung over her shoulder, the girl took out a small book, bound in tattered leather. Inked over the cover was a black silhouette of a bird and a coiled snake. "Want to hear the end?"

The boy didn't blink for a long pause. Then, slowly, he sat on the damp earth and crossed his legs under his lanky body.

The girl read the final pages marked in her new, palatable ending. The songbird and serpent grew to be friends despite their differences. No lies, no cunning, no tricks. Each word drew her closer to the bars until her head rested against the cold iron and one hand drooped between the gaps, as though reaching for the boy inside.

"They played from sunup to sundown," she read, squinting at her messy writing. "And lived happily ever after."

A smile crossed her features when she closed the bindings and glanced at the boy.

He'd reclined back onto his palms now, legs out, bare ankles crossed. "Is that what we are, Princess? A serpent and a songbird?"

Her smile widened. He understood the whole point. "I think so, and they were still friends. That's why tomorrow at the trials you can, well, you can say we won't fight no more. My folk will let you stay."

No more blood. No more nightmares. The girl couldn't stomach any more blood from hate and war.

When the boy kept quiet, she dug back into her pouch and took out the twine. On the end was a silver charm she'd used her last copper to buy. A silver charm of a swallow in flight.

"Here." She held out the handmade necklace through the bars and let it fall. "I thought it could remind you of the story."

All at once the distance between them was a blessing. Any closer and the boy might see the flush of pink in her cheeks. He might see that her hope in the charm was less about recalling the tale and more about remembering *her*.

With slow movements the boy took hold of the charm. His dirty thumb brushed over the wings. "Tomorrow I'll see the gods or be sent away, Songbird."

Her stomach dipped and something warm, like spilled tea, flooded her insides. Songbird. She liked the name.

"That's what happens when you lose a war." The boy's lips twitched when he placed the twine around his neck. "There's no stopping it."

The race of her heart dimmed. She dropped her chin. Hopeful as she was, the girl wasn't a fool. She knew the only thing saving the boy's neck was that he *was* a boy. Should he be a man, he'd lose his head. He had fought against her people; he hated them.

Like the serpent from the story hated the birds in the trees for their freedom in the skies.

She didn't care. A feeling, deep in her bones, drew her to the boy. She'd hoped he might be drawn to her too.

Hope failed. While he was young, he'd always be marked as an enemy. Banished and forbidden.

She blinked and reached once more into the fur-lined pouch. "I know this is important to your folk. Thought maybe you'd want to see it once more."

The girl cupped the gold talisman, shaped like a thin disk, with care. It was weathered and aged and delicate. A faint hum of strange remnants of magic lived in the gritty edges. If her father ever learned she'd snatched the piece from the lockbox, he'd probably keep her locked in her room for a week.

Overhead, the moonlight gleamed over the strange rune in the center of the coin. The boy in the shadows let out a gasp. She didn't think he'd meant to do it.

For the first time since she'd started reading to him, the boy climbed up the stone wall and curled his hands around the bars. The red in his eyes deepened like blood. His smile was different. Wide enough she could see the slight point to his side tooth, almost like fangs of a wolf, only not as long.

This smile sent a shiver up her arms.

"Will you do something for me, Songbird?"

"What?"

The boy nodded at the disk. "That was a gift from my father. Watch over it for me, will you? I'll come back to get it one day, and you can tell me more stories. Promise?"

The girl ignored the wave of gooseflesh up her arms and whispered, "Promise."

When the sound of heavy boots scraped over the dirt nearby, the girl gave one final look at the boy in the darkness. He held up the silver bird charm and grinned that wolfish grin once more before she sprinted into the grass.

The speed of her pulse ached as she hurried back to the longhouse. Her gaze was locked on the disk in her hands; she never saw the root bursting from the soil. The thick arch snagged hold of her toe and sprawled the girl face down in the soil.

She coughed and scrambled back to her knees. When she looked down, her insides twisted up like knotted ropes.

"Oh, no."

The disk she'd promised to protect mere moments before had fallen beneath her body. Now the shimmer of gold lay in three jagged pieces in the soil. Tears blurred her vision as she gathered the pieces, sobbing promises to the night that she'd fix it, she'd repair what was broken.

Perhaps it was the despair that kept her from noticing the strange rune, once marked on the surface of the disk, now branded the smooth skin below the crook of her elbow.

In time, the more she learned of the viciousness of the sea fae who attacked her people, the more the girl looked back on that night like a shameful secret. She made up tales about the scar on her arm, a clumsy stumble down the cobbled steps in the gardens. She'd forget the boy's promise to come for her.

The girl would start to think of him as everyone else—the enemy.

If only the girl had kept away from those cells that night, perhaps she would not have unraveled her entire world.

Acknowledgments

I'm not crying, you are. No, really I'm sobbing. The Broken Kingdoms, a series that has consumed my thoughts and imagination for four years is at an end.

I will never be able to thank my readers enough for loving these worlds. What a ride it has been. Thank you, from the bottom of my heart, thank you.

I am so grateful for my family for putting up with my early morning rock-Viking music, and late night writing sessions to build these characters. Derek, and kiddos, I love you so much. Across the skies and seas, you all have my heart.

Thank you to Sara Sorensen for catching all my plot holes. You have to find those plot holes across worlds now, and you will always have my gratitude for thinking of things literally no one else would ever think about. Thank you to Megan Mitchell for your skill at finding typos missed even after I've read the book no less than a thousand times. Thank you to my other editor, Jennifer Murgia. Trust me, without you all these books would be rough.

Thank you the Wicked Darlings, you brighten my days with your theories and questions and Gifs, IYKYK.

Thank you to my father in heaven for leading me on this journey. It has been life-changing. Here's to more wickedly romantic tales.

LJ

WANT MORE?

Enjoy a bonus scene from the Broken Kingdoms by scanning the QR code below.

WELCOME TO THE EVER KING

Keep reading in the expanded world of the Broken Kingdoms by diving into the passionate, dark world of the Ever Kingdom. Scan the QR code below and keep reading.